D1264081

Turning Back

JaHUSS

Edited by RJ Locksley
Cover Design by JA Huss
Cover Photo: Sara Eirew

Mistakes are measured in wasted time
Falling to your knees, asking for another chance
Longing's just an aching mind
Giving in to circumstance

The future is closer than your past
And loving you is not a crime
So if you don't want to turn back
We can handle the aftermath.

~Quin Foster

CHAPTER ONE

QUIN

Once upon a time, a long time ago, I was happy.

Two days out of seven were perfect.

But three hundred sixty-five days have passed and all the good times are gone.

One year. Today is the one-year anniversary of Rochelle's exit from the game.

The buzzer near the door of my condo blares. It's Smith. I don't need to answer it. Showing up every Monday morning has been his way of keeping track of me all year. The buzzer is just a courtesy anyway. He has a key.

At first Smith and Chella both came over. It was nice, actually. I really enjoyed them. And they were just worried about me after I stopped talking to Bric and never went back to Turning Point.

I didn't mean to end things with Bric. I mean... I did mean to end the *game* with him, but not the friendship. He's been a part of my life for so fucking long I really never considered just cutting him out completely. It just shook out that way. One day of no Bric turned into one week, turned into one month. And if things keep going, it will turn into forever.

We pretended things were OK for a few months. He even pretended like he was looking for Rochelle. But he never fooled me. Bric is never going to find Rochelle and

I'm not either. If she hates me so much that leaving like that was her only option, well… that's that.

I quit going to Turning Point. I still have a membership—because canceling my membership would involve making a decision, and I'd just rather ignore the whole thing. And then I quit talking to Bric. Stopped taking his calls. Stopped showing up for things. Stopped everything to do with him.

Smith and Chella took it upon themselves to check in on me. Like I'm on suicide watch or an old uncle who needs to be reminded to eat.

They came over together on Monday mornings at first. They'd bring coffee and some food. Pastries or McDonald's. Whatever. But about a month into that schedule the three of us were sitting on my couch, just talking and enjoying the fantastic view I have from the top-floor of the SkyClub Building, watching the weather and having a chat.

And then… my hand wandered to Chella's leg. It wasn't conscious. It wasn't. It was just… we were all sitting pretty close together. Chella in between Smith and me. And it felt so… familiar.

It was habit, I think. Pretty sure, anyway. An unconscious gesture. I wanted a little human interaction, I guess.

Everything stopped when I did that. Smith went silent. Chella, who was in the middle of telling me some silly story I have no recollection about now, went silent.

I withdrew my hand immediately. Gave Smith a sorry shrug. We all sighed. Because it was such a natural move.

I am drawn to them.

Not Chella. Not Smith.

But them.

Us.

And I think Smith knew how easy it would've been for the three of us to slip into something in that moment. It would've been so simple to just morph back into a plural arrangement. I know he likes it. I know she likes it. And I do too. I still do. You can't play that kind of game for more than a decade and not *like* it.

But Chella was the one to end all those thoughts. She leaned over and kissed me on the cheek, stood up, and said, "I gotta get to work early today. Wanna do lunch tomorrow, Quin?"

And I said, "Sure. Sounds fun."

She walked out and left Smith and me there. I knew he wasn't going to say anything, and he didn't. We talked about... I don't know. I don't remember. Stocks, maybe. The weather. Something benign.

So that's how it started. Every Monday morning Smith still comes by with coffee and something to eat. He just comes alone now. And every Tuesday I have lunch with Chella. Alone.

It's funny, I think. That Smith doesn't trust me to be with Chella around *him*, but he does trust me to be with her *alone*.

It's not her I want. It's certainly not him. But another... us. I could go for another round of us.

I'm not dressed right now. Just wearing pajama pants, standing in front of the amazing fourteen-foot-high windows that start at the floor and go all the way up to the ceiling, letting the heat from a vent under my feet warm me from the bottom up.

I go to work most Mondays but I don't show up until noon. It takes me that long to get over the ache. I don't get it. They say time heals all things and I have known that to be true in a lot of ways in my thirty-five years of life. But it's not true this time.

It's getting worse, if you ask me.

I do go to work on time on Tuesdays. Show up at nine, go to lunch with Chella at one. Go home at six.

And the rest of the week I'm fine. It's just Mondays and Tuesdays that threaten to kill me. I go out with Robert, my senior account manager down at Foster Consulting, on Friday nights after work. Just drinks at whatever local club is popular. I check out the women. Might flirt with one. But I don't take them home. I don't do anything with them because every woman I meet is immediately compared to Rochelle.

They have short hair. It's too dark. They're too serious. Not tall enough. Too tall. Too thin. Too thick. Not shapely. Wrong clothes. Bad conversation. Etc. Etc. Etc.

On Saturdays, I work out in the building gym. Three or four hours at least.

On Sundays I run. Coors Field has a running club. You join and they let you into the stadium Sunday mornings at five AM to run the steps.

And then it starts all over again.

Monday with Smith.

Tuesday with Chella.

Get through the week at work.

Friday night drinks with Robert.

Saturdays at the gym.

Run the steps on Sunday.

And pretty soon a year goes by. One year since the woman I loved left me with no explanation. One year since I was happy.

Like I said. Once upon a time, a long time ago.

I am existing and nothing more.

My front door beeps when Smith enters his key, and then he pushes the door open.

I don't even bother turning away from the window.

"What's up, asshole?" Smith says, dropping a bag on the floor as he enters. "You going to work today?"

I listen as he rummages through whatever take-out bag he brought with him and appreciate the scent of coffee.

"You know what today is?" I ask, still staring out at the weather. It's gonna rain today. Last year it was snowing. But it doesn't usually snow so much in late November, so this year we're back to normal with the rain.

"Yeah." Smith sighs, banging a drawer closed in the open kitchen. "I know. But you're going to work today, right?"

I should go to work. What the fuck good would it do me to stay home? "I have a meeting this afternoon. So probably."

Smith walks up to me holding a paper coffee cup. I take it, mumble, "Thanks," and sip the hot liquid.

"I got you the best breakfast burrito from one of the new trucks down near Cheeseman Park," Smith says. "You gotta taste this shit."

"Thanks," I say again, meaning it. I walk over to the kitchen island and grab the one that says 'Quin' on the silver-foil wrapper. Open it up. Take the mandatory bite.

"So listen," Smith says.

But that's when I notice the rat peeking its head out of Smith's... gym bag? Sitting on the floor near the couch. "What the fuck is that?"

"What? Oh, the dog."

"That's not a dog. It's a rat."

5

"Right," he says, shaking his head. "So you know Chella said I could get a dog, remember? Last year she gave me that gift and part of it was a puppy?"

"Yeah, but..." I point to the rat—which is sitting inside Smith's gym bag. Since when does he come here with a gym bag? "That's not a puppy, Smith."

It's small enough to be a puppy. Tiny little thing, for sure. Rat-sized, hence my confusion. And the fur on the top of its head is gathered together with a pink bow.

It stares at me and says, "Arf."

Really. The rat-dog says, *Arf.*

"So we go to the shelter last week because she's dying for me to get a fucking puppy, right?"

"Yeah," I say, more interested than I have a right to be.

"She's practically pissed off that I haven't done this already and Christmas is coming... I didn't like her present... blah, blah, blah. So we go to the shelter and look around. And I see this amazing husky puppy, right?"

"Right," I say, taking another bite of my burrito, wondering how he gets to this rat-thing when he starts out with a husky.

"Like this dog talks, Quin. Like this little husky puppy is chatting me up with all this woo-woo howling and shit."

"OK," I say, sipping my coffee.

"But then..." Smith sighs. "I hear Chella cooing a few cages down. And I melt, man. I just can't say no. She gets the people to let her hold the puppy. And she's talking to it like they've been friends forever. And... well, I just gave in, man. I couldn't walk out of there without that puppy. So here we are. Precious is gonna hang out with me at the gym every day. They say dogs are good for troubled kids and old people, right?"

6

I shake my head at him. "What the fuck are you talking about? What gym? What troubled kids and old people?"

"Dude," Smith says, as he takes a bite of his burrito. I wait for him to swallow his food as I continue to stare at the dog. "Don't you ever listen to me? I've been talking about the youth project for six months. Why do I come here if you're just gonna dwell on the past and be a moping asshole?"

Has he mentioned something about a gym? I have no clue. I know he never mentioned old people. The troubled kids... I'm not sure. That's a maybe.

"I told you that I decided not to do the whole donation thing anymore. It's stupid not to spend my own money, right?"

"Yeah." I snort. "I always thought that was stupid. But whatever. I supported you and your dumb rules."

"I know," Smith says, sipping his coffee. "I really do appreciate that, man. For real. But I decided it was time to invest in my own projects, you know? So I bought five gyms."

"Gyms?" I'm confused. "What kind of charity is a gym?"

"For kids. In bad neighborhoods," he explains. "I told you all this months ago."

"Maybe in passing," I say, defensive.

"Anyway." He sighs. "I have five gyms and five days of the week to fill. You know Chella quit the gallery and started her own bakery business?"

"Bakery?" What the fuck is happening?

"If you say you didn't know about that, I'll punch you," Smith says. "Hard. Like... in the eye."

"No, no," I lie. "I remember now. Just forgot, that's all."

"Yeah, well, Chella graduated pastry school last month. Pastry chef," Smith says, shaking his head, eyes shining with pride. "That was always her dream."

It was? How did I not know this?

"And we've been working on her new business and my gyms. And this is opening week for me, bro. I've got a full-on boxing ring in three of them. You know, so the little deviants can kick the shit out of each other and call it sportsmanship."

I shake my head at him and laugh. "That's so wrong."

"I mean it affectionately," he says, waving a hand at me. "Three of them are boxing gyms and two of them are just regular gyms. And it's free, right? Like kids in these neighborhoods need a place to go hang out. Stay off the street. Eat and stuff. So I'm gonna take care of all that from now on."

"Well, aren't you Mr. Philanthropist."

"You know it," he says, shooting me with his finger. "Anyway, I'm gonna spend my time at each one, one day a week. And I'm bringing Precious along to make me more approachable."

I laugh at the thought of Smith trying to be approachable. "Aren't the little deviants supposed to be in school at this time of day?"

"You can't rush progress, Quin. Of course I *want* them in school, but I never went to school. So I figure I'd hire some tutors and run some GED classes during the day. Get them all up to speed on that in between kicking the shit out of each other. Chella wants to do scholarships too. For the ones who show interest and commitment. So you know, I'm changing the world one kid at a time."

I stare at him, amazed at how much being with Chella has changed him for the better. Smith has always been generous with his fortune. I would never say a bad word about him to anyone other than Bric or Chella. Or Rochelle. And that's just friendship talking, you know? I'm allowed to be annoyed with him sometimes because we're friends and we care about each other.

But it's nice to see him like this. All settled with a woman and excited about his plans. He used to just let Bric handle all his charity work. Now he's invested.

What a difference a year makes.

"Why are you looking at me like that?" Smith asks.

I was the happy one last year and he was the broody asshole.

"What?" he prods. "Why are you staring at me?"

"You're just so damn… satisfied."

"Hell, yeah, I'm satisfied. My life has never been more on track than it is right now. And," he says, lowering his voice and looking around like someone might hear us. Which is stupid. We're in my condo. "We might be getting pregnant soon."

"Shit," I say, running my fingers through my messy bed hair. "Really?"

"I'm not getting any younger, Quin. My biological clock is ticking like a goddamned time bomb. If I want five kids, we need to start pronto."

I try to picture Smith Baldwin with five kids and can't get past the image of him changing diapers. "Chella wants five kids?" I ask, trying to decide if she's into spending the rest of her thirties barefoot and pregnant.

Smith almost spits out his burrito when he laughs. "She thinks I'm nuts. But she'll come around. I have a plan that will change her mind." He taps his head with his foil-covered food. "And it all starts with that dog." He points

9

to Precious, who is still sitting demurely inside his gym bag, her pink-ribbon-adorned head the only thing visible.

"Yeah," I say, just staring at the dog. "Well, I'm happy for you guys. Really. It's amazing what you've done this past year."

"Which is what we need to talk about," Smith says, setting his food and coffee down. "You need to stop, man. You need to let her go. Rochelle is gone, Quin. She's never coming back. She's moved on. Lives a whole other life now."

"You don't know that," I say. "We never found her. Not even Bric found her. And I know he's been looking. He leaves me messages once a month to update me."

"Which is nice of him, by the way. Since you refuse to talk to him or answer his calls."

I sigh. "It's not like I made a conscious decision."

"I know, you say this every time I bring it up. But conscious or not, you fucked up, Quin. He's a good guy. He didn't realize she'd take him so literally, you know?"

"My problem is… he should've known that. She depended on him for advice. That was always his role in the game. The girls have problems, they go to Bric. He talks to them in that stupid reasonable voice of his, and gives them good advice. He told her—"

"He gave her the options, Quin. That's it. He never told her to get an abortion. He's a man. He thinks like a man. He had no idea she'd walk out like that."

I huff out a long breath of air. We've been over this a million times. I get it. Bric made a mistake. Probably an innocent mistake. But it had a very dramatic effect on my life. I can't let it go.

"You need to let it go," Smith says, like he's reading my mind. "It's time, Quin. One year has passed. If she wanted to contact us, she would've done it by now."

"I know," I say, some of the sadness creeping back in. One year is a long time. Enough time to get past something that hurt and try to patch things up. But she's still gone. And no one can find her. She wants to be gone. She wants to stay gone. Otherwise she'd leave a trail. She wouldn't be so careful about not opening credit cards or whatever people refuse to do when trying to hide themselves. She'd be in the open. And she's not.

"And you need to make things right with Bric. He's unhappy too, you know. Both of you are so fucking pathetic right now, I'm about to lose my mind. Just go over there and talk to him."

"Not today," I say. And I say it firmly. With enough conviction that Smith doesn't press. Not today of all days. I can't do it.

"Not today," Smith agrees. "Fine. But soon. You'd both be much happier if you'd fix this part, at least. So Rochelle's gone. I get it. But Bric is still here. I'm still here. Chella is still here. You're OK, Quin. I promise. You are."

I think about that for a few seconds.

Smith waits, then says, "Well, I gotta go. So much to do today. Make sure you go to work this afternoon. And Chella says she wants to have lunch at the Club tomorrow."

"No," I say. "Fuck that."

"Fine with me," Smith says, shrugging as he walks over to his gym bag and hikes it over his shoulder. He pets the dog, who pants excitedly at his attention. "But she told me to tell you she'd be in the White Room waiting for you tomorrow at one. So if you want to stand her up, be my guest. Just don't expect her to show up for lunch the week after."

He walks out without another word and leaves me to my thoughts.

If Chella wants to pull this either-or shit, she can. But I don't like ultimatums. I might not be as rigid as Smith or as dominating as Bric, but I know how to hold a fucking grudge.

I won't be showing up at the Club tomorrow.

No way. Fuck that.

CHAPTER TWO

The curtains in the top-floor apartment of Turning Point Club are closed, but sheer. So just enough light filters through from the rainy day outside to make the atmosphere seem gloomy and dramatic.

It's not a good sign.

I could change the mood, flick on a light or open those curtains, but is the light really the problem?

The girl's hands are cuffed to a chain above her head that attaches to the ceiling. It clinks as she moves, her head turning this way or that as Jordan moves about, getting things ready. She's blindfolded, so she doesn't know I'm here. And she has noise-canceling headphones on, so she can't hear anything but the music and the words Jordan whispers into the mic wrapping down his jaw as he works.

I take my tie off and unbutton my shirt, waiting for my cue.

My phone buzzes in my pocket, but I ignore it and it goes to voicemail after a few seconds.

"Ready?" Jordan asks, holding out the chain harness for me.

I take it, letting the silver links pool into my palm. "Yup." I sigh.

"What? Are you bored?" he asks.

13

"Kinda," I say, surprising myself. "She's not gonna like this."

"You don't know," Jordan says, equally exasperated. "I talked about it with her last night. She said yes... so..."

I shrug. I'm not into this girl. Which is weird for me. I'm into anyone. As long as they go along and do as they're told, I'm generally good. Very easy to please. But this one... she's only been here for a week and I can already tell. She won't last. It's a waste of time.

"I'm going to place the clamps on your nipples now, Sandy. Don't move."

Sandy whimpers and, predictably, moves when I reach up with the first clamp and touch the peak of her nipple.

"Don't. Move." Jordan is not the most patient of men. So it comes out rough. But the girl stills as I attach the clamp. There's a long moment where she doesn't quite know how to react and I almost hold my breath, waiting for the freakout.

She sucks air in through her teeth as the pain eases and then relaxes.

That's my cue for the next clamp. This time I make sure she reacts so she'll pull on the chain and get the punishment twice.

She twists—winces, moans, and then whimpers.

I look at Jordan as he whispers encouraging things into her headphones. This whole headphones thing was a lot more fun when Smith and I did it with Chella. A *lot* more fun.

Am I even hard? I look down at my cock and find it halfway there.

Jordan catches me looking and cuts the mic. "What is your fucking problem today?"

My phone buzzes again. I ignore it. "I just want a fucking pre-lunch blow job, you know?"

"Then get on with it," Jordan snaps. "Jesus Christ."

'Get on with it' refers to the two other clamps, also attached to the harness. I kneel down and smack the inside of Sandy's thigh as Jordan tells her to open her legs wider. My finger slips inside her pussy and finds her... dry.

I shake my head. "She's not even wet." Could this afternoon get any more disappointing?

"Just do the clamps," Jordan says.

I ease the lips of her pussy open and bring the metal clamp up, ready to attach it to the folds of her labia, opening the clamp and slipping it over each side of her sensitive skin.

She freaks out. "No," she yells. "Forget it. Nope. I'm not doing this! I'm done. Unhook me. Take this fucking blindfold off! I'm done! Safe word," she screams. "I'm using my safe word."

I stand up and look at Jordan. "'Safe word' is her safe word?"

Jordan rubs his forehead with a fingertip, like he's got a headache.

I take the nipple clamps off, which makes Sandy writhe. "Hold still," I growl. But she can't hear me, so I snatch the headphones and pull the blindfold down her face and say it again. "Would you hold still, please?"

"I don't like this anymore," Sandy says, on the verge of tears. "I'm out." She glances down at my nowhere-near-hard cock and sobs. "Let me go. I'm going home. I'm taking my shit and I'm—"

"We don't care," I say, just to shut her up. "Go. You know the rules. You can fucking leave any time you want."

"Unhook my hands—"

But Jordan is a step ahead of her and her hands come free from the chain. They drop in front of her and she almost has a panic attack when she realizes she's still cuffed.

"Just relax," Jordan says as he frees her hands from the cuffs.

"You two are a bunch of fucking freaks," Sandy spits, once her hands are free. She goes over to the closet and starts getting dressed.

My phone buzzes in my pocket again.

I take it out and say, "Yes."

"Bric," Margaret, the White Room manager, says on the other end of the phone. "Chella is here to see you about the Tea Room."

"Shit," I say. "I forgot. I'll be right down." I end the call and look at Jordan. "Game over," I say, shrugging.

We're used to this now. We've started a few games since the whole thing blew up last year with Quin. But none of them last. They go a few weeks. One went a few months. But most of them are like Sandy. Women who think they want this, but don't.

None of them were anything close to Chella. Hell, Rochelle was a VIP player compared to the last few.

Sometimes I wish Chella and Smith hadn't fallen in love. She would've been so fucking perfect as a permanent part of my game.

I sigh as I tuck my dick away and walk out. Sandy is still going on and on about what deviants Jordan and I are, but when I leave the apartment and close the door behind me, she is forgotten.

I get into the elevator, punch the button for two, and then button my shirt and tuck it in. By the time the elevator opens I'm mostly put back together—forgot my tie and jacket, but fuck it—and I exit and walk to the top of the stairs that overlook the lobby.

It's busy today. Everyone is having lunch. And it's Cyber Monday, so everyone is still loud and happy, half on holiday.

I walk down the stairs, saying polite hellos to people as I make my way into the White Room, and then head to the back table where I know Chella will be waiting. She stands when she sees me so we can hold hands and do cheek kisses.

Yeah. Sandy is no Chella.

"Hey," I say, backing away after our greeting and taking a seat across from her. "Sorry I'm late. I forgot."

"No biggie," Chella says. "I've kept myself busy." She's got her laptop open with pictures of the pastries we're going to offer for afternoon tea. I bought the building next door and we've been renovating for the past four months getting it ready for opening day next week. It's just an extension of the White Room. A place for wives and mistresses, mostly. So they can feel included in the Club, even though they're not included.

Chella hates it when I say that, but whatever. It's true. Turning Point is about men.

"So this is what we're looking at right now. I've got…"

She goes on and on about the different tea services we'll be offering. I don't care either way. I'm sure Chella knows what she's doing. I just stare at her as she talks, and smile, imagining how much she'd have liked those pussy clamps if she was still playing the game with me.

"And Quin is coming by tomorrow for lunch."

"Wait." I have to snap back to attention. "What?"

"Quin," Chella says slowly. "He's meeting me here for lunch tomorrow."

"He's coming here?" I ask, pointing a finger down at the table.

"Yup," Chella says, smiling.

"How did you manage that?" I ask, suspicious. Quin has not talked to me in a very long time. I haven't even seen that asshole in almost six months. And that last time was a mistake. He and I ended up at a party down at Stonewall Entertainment in the Tech Center. Apparently, Smith and Mac Stonewall are friends in the philanthropy business and it was something he wanted me to attend with him.

Anyway, it didn't end well. Quin is apparently a very skilled grudge-holder. He didn't even see me. Someone told him I was there and he left. I caught a glimpse of him as he was leaving the building and that was that.

"I had Smith deliver the invitation this morning."

"And he agreed?" I ask, doubt written all over my face.

"Sort of. But I know he'll show. Because he won't stand me up for Tuesday lunch. He'll show."

"Well, I wouldn't get your hopes up, Chella. Really. He doesn't give in easy."

"So do you have any news at all?" Chella asks, changing the subject.

"Nope," I say, taking a sip of my water so I can buy myself some time. "You know I'd call if I did."

"Well, I'm getting impatient, Bric. I know I told you I'd let you handle it, but I'm not sure you're as invested as you should be."

"I don't like where this is going," I say, narrowing my eyes at her.

"Rochelle has been missing for one year today. One year, Bric. You're a bazillionaire. We have all this money at our disposal and we can't seem to locate one woman? How is that possible?"

"I'm not a law-breaker, Chella. I told you this. I do it all on the up and up. And my guy says he can't find her. She doesn't want to be found."

"Well, I'm not adverse to breaking a few laws when it's necessary and it's necessary. Quin needs to get over this shit. And while I understand that you're not especially interested in revisiting that one particular conversation you had with Rochelle, it's not fair that you're not trying hard enough to find her. We don't even know if she's alive."

Yeah. Then there's that. The little fact that I didn't tell anyone that Rochelle called me last summer and asked me to tell Quin she was sorry. It wasn't like I meant to keep it a secret, but I was on my way out of town for the summer. I was traveling. And when I got back things were so busy with getting the Club back up and running... I just forgot.

It's too late to say anything now. *Oh, by the way, Rochelle called me last June and told me to tell you she's sorry. And she didn't get an abortion. She had the damn baby because I heard it crying on the other end of the phone.*

Nope. Not gonna say that. I have kept the dark side of Elias Bricman tucked neatly away my whole life. I'm not gonna fuck things up now by being honest.

It's in my best interest for Rochelle to stay gone forever at this point.

"I hired someone," Chella says, bringing me back to the present.

"For what?" I ask, not following.

19

"To find Rochelle."

"No," I say forcefully.

"Listen to me, Elias Bricman." Chella slaps her hand down on the table hard enough to make the silverware jump. "I want Rochelle found. I want to see her again. We were pretty good friends and I want her back. So I'm taking things into my own hands. I know a guy."

"What guy?" Jesus Christ. This is not good.

"He's former FBI. But he's in private security and investigations now. He can get info other people can't. And it's almost legal."

I give her the stink eye at that comment.

"Practically legal," she assures me. "He has connections in the Bureau. He can find things most people can't."

"I'm pretty sure you need a warrant for that kind of stuff. I'm not gonna be involved."

"Fine with me," she says sweetly. "But it's a risk if I do it. Smith will be at risk—"

"Chella," I growl.

"Elias," she counters. "Just meet with the guy, OK? Please."

We both turn to look at Margaret when she approaches the table. "Mr. Bricman," she says. "Darrel Jameson is here for your meeting."

"Who?" I ask, peeking around her to see a tall guy, late thirties, maybe. Dark suit and sunglasses. I roll my eyes and then look at Chella.

She smiles and stands, reaching for Mr. Jameson, just like she did to me. "Thanks so much for taking this case, Darrel. I so, so, so appreciate it."

"My pleasure, Chella. You know I'd do anything for you."

Chella kisses him on the cheek and then gathers her computer. "You guys have fun," she says, stuffing her things into her tote bag. "I'll see you tomorrow for lunch, Elias?"

I nod, resigned to her tricks, and then pan my hand at the chair Chella just vacated. "Have a seat, Mr. Jameson."

"Thanks, Mr. Bricman." He takes a phone out of his suit coat pocket and tabs the screen. "Rochelle Bastille, age twenty-eight—"

Twenty-eight. How did that happen? We met her when she was twenty-four. I always think of her as so young in my head.

"Presently living in Pagosa Springs—"

"Wait," I interrupt. "Presently? You mean you found her?"

Jameson stares at me for a moment. "Of course I found her. Chella asked me to, told me to report to you. Did you... not want her found?"

"Of course I did." I laugh. Uneasily. "Yes, of course. But I've been looking—"

"So Chella tells me." He gives me a look that says, *Liar.* "Chella's great, by the way. I love her to death. She was my very first assignment in the Bureau when she left home at eighteen. Well"—Jameson chuckles—"she ran away a few times when she was seventeen. But I was always there with her. Always watching to make sure she was OK." He shakes his head in a way that says he found her rebellion cute. Something to appreciate about her.

Which makes me warm to him. A little.

"Pagosa Springs?" I ask.

"It's a five-hour drive southwest of here. Near the Four Corners. Just east of Durango. Ever been there?"

"No," I say. "Never even heard of it."

"Still kinda small-towny. Hard to find places like that in Colorado anymore. But they have a hot springs resort there and Miss Bastille has been living at the resort since last..." Jameson checks his phone. "Last November. One year."

"A resort?" I ask.

"Mmm-hmm. Fancy one too. Her and her daughter are renting a pretty nice suite. Five thousand dollars a month. Not doing badly at all."

"Daughter?" I feel sick.

Another glance down at the phone from Jameson. "Adley Bastille. Age six months. Do you want the address? And here's my bill."

"Did you tell Chella any of this?" I ask, panicked.

"No. Didn't have a chance. She gave me Miss Bastille's name last night and told me to meet her here so she could introduce me to you."

"Well, don't tell her yet," I say, picking up the invoice. I flick my fingers in the air for Margaret, who comes immediately, and give her the piece of paper. "Give me the address, Mr. Jameson. And then Margaret will pay you for your time."

"Sure thing," he says, pulling out a business card and writing it down. "That's the resort," he says, tapping the card. "Her suite and phone number are on the back."

And just like that, my world has changed.

"Don't tell Chella," I remind him as he walks off.

"No problem," he calls back over his shoulder.

I get out my phone and tap the private contact for Lisa, my travel agent. She picks up the phone on the first ring. "What can I do for you, Elias?"

"I need a jet. Centennial to Pagosa Springs. Do they have an airport there? Somewhere close, if not."

"One moment. Let me check." I listen to the tapping of her computer keys for a few seconds. "They do have a small airfield in Pagosa Springs. When do you want to leave?"

"Now," I say.

"Well," Lisa says, "I can get you on a private charter in about two hours. But you'll have to stay overnight. The airport closes at sunset. Which is at four thirty-six today."

"Fine. And book me a suite at"—I look down at the card—"Mineral Springs Resort for one night. I need to be back here first thing in the morning."

"And a regular room for the pilot at the resort as well?" Lisa asks.

"Sure. Whatever."

"OK, got it. You need to be at Centennial Airport in an hour to check in."

"I'm leaving now."

I end the call and take a deep breath.

A daughter. We have a daughter with Rochelle.

How the fuck will I ever explain this to Quin?

CHAPTER THREE

ROCHELLE

Mommy and Me just... isn't for me. I kinda knew this on day one when I walked into what amounted to the rural Colorado version of the Stepford Wives.

Pagosa Springs is about as picturesque as it gets. It's up there with any of the postcard places you see in movies and travel brochures if you're into mountains, rivers, and national forests.

I like those things, which is why I chose this place. And I like small towns, so I like that too. But I guess I didn't realize that almost everyone here is on permanent vacation.

Kinda like me, now that I think it through.

Permanent vacation because they are so damn rich, these women have nothing better to do than pretend they live in rural America as they sip mimosas at the club every Monday afternoon and let their nannies socialize their babies.

Anyway... I'm here starting a new life. These women in the Mommy and Me group at the country club (complimentary membership for all long-term residents of the Mineral Springs Resort) are here because this town is boring.

Well... that's kinda why I'm here too.

I'm not what you'd call a city girl by any means. I'm not. I like moccasins and gauzy shirts. Hell, my whole apartment back in Denver was decorated in what the guys liked to call modern-day Bohemian. And I chose to live in Denver because while it's a city, it's a city alone. There are no other big cities anywhere close to it. Colorado only has three cities to begin with and Pagosa Springs is not one of them. Not even close.

So even though whitewater rafting down the San Juan is something I'd totally dig, and even though I could really get behind an off-grid week-long camping trip up in the Weminuche Wilderness, and even though I'd love to be looking forward to an entire winter of snowboarding up at Wolf Creek, I can't do any of those things with a baby.

And I wouldn't want to go alone, anyway.

I sigh as Sheryl, my only sorta-friend here in town, sips her mimosa and flamboyantly waves her hands around as she describes something funny her baby did with the nanny yesterday.

We do not have a nanny, so Adley is sitting in my lap, sticking my hair in her mouth, completely content to watch the Stepford Wives get liquored up and giggle like teenagers.

There are a few full-time local moms here at the meeting too. But they sit off in another area. It's high school all over again. I'd prefer their company by miles, but I'm not really local. And I'm not sure I'm permanent.

I'm probably not coming back next week because all the remaining Stepford Wives are going to their third houses for the snow season in a few days. Apparently Wolf Creek is just not classy enough so they simply must ski Aspen and Vail.

I can't wait for them to leave. I feel like I've gotten too close to Sheryl and if I took off now, she'd ask questions. Although she has never once asked me why I'm staying in the long-term housing at the resort, I'm pretty sure she thinks I'm a battered wife on the run, and if I disappeared she'd probably file a missing person's report.

It's kinda touching, really. That she'd care. But the cops looking into my past is the last thing I need.

So I'm biding my time until they all disappear and then Adley and I are outta here. I think we'll spend the winter in Jackson Hole. That's a nice out-of-the-way place. And winters are crazy fun with all the snow people. Quin took me there for a weekend once and we had a blast.

Adley starts to get fussy and I check the weather outside to see if it's time to go yet. But this place does have one thing going for it. The amazing hot springs in the center of town. My resort has a huge one and I take Adley there every day so we can soak. There's one pool that's not too hot. There's a little inlet from the river that lets cold water rush in, so it's almost tepid. Perfect for a baby.

But it was raining this morning. And there was lightning. Can't go in when there's lightning. Right now it's misty outside. But I think the thunderstorms have passed.

I stand up and start gathering my things.

"Oh, are you leaving already?" Sheryl asks.

Already? Jesus. I've been here for three hours. If I don't get out now I might scream.

"Adley needs a nap," I say in my sweet voice. It's a cross between naive and innocent on the outside, but on the inside it is cynical and world-weary. I smile at that thought and Sheryl thinks I'm being friendly.

"You can put her down in the nap room."

I could. If I was that kind of mother. But I'm not. And she's not really tired yet. I'm pretty sure she's anxious for her dip in the tepid springs.

"I'm tired too," I say. "I got no sleep last night." Adley is a champion sleeper. She never wakes up and I'm probably the most well-rested new-mom-without-a-nanny they've ever seen. But I exhale just the right amount of sigh and hike the diaper bag over my shoulder. "So I'm gonna lie down with her. See you guys next week."

"Oh, we're leaving!" Suddenly there is a big production about how they will never see me again and I get stuck there for twenty more minutes just trying to say goodbye.

By the time we actually do make it back to the suite, we really are tired.

I tell myself we'll just sit for a minute and watch *People's Court* before tackling the bathing suits and heading out. But one minute turns into ten, turns into an hour, and pretty soon we're all cuddled up in the giant king-sized bed, fast asleep.

I wake to the soft, sweet coos of Adley. When I open my eyes and look down at her, she's smiling at me. "Hey, pumpkin," I say. "You ready for a swim? Should we eat first? I bet you're hungry?"

More smiles.

I take that as a yes to all of the above and get busy changing her diaper, putting on her suit. Then I dress her up in a pair of baby sweats and a tiny pink hoodie that says, *Pagosa Springs, Refreshingly Authentic.* The town motto. Most of our wardrobe has been purchased at the tourist shops on Lewis Street. I know Jackson Hole is not much bigger than Pagosa, but at least it will be different. I see a whole new set of tourist clothes in our future.

I velcro a bib under her chubby baby chin and take her over to a chair to feed her a bottle. We're just starting to transition into baby food and she's not cooperating very well. I'm one of those go-with-the-flow moms, so I'm not gonna push. One new food a week is about all I'm up to. Then I make a little note in the journal I'm keeping on her baby days. If she likes it. If she has any kind of allergic reaction. Nothing so far. But we've only tried peas (she hates those), peaches and sweet potatoes (her favorite).

I love feeding her bottles and it will all be over too soon for me, so I'm content with the slow progress we're making.

I settle in the chair near the window with her in my arms. It's got a great view of the mother spring here at the resort. Talk about pretty. My life could be a lot worse, so I like to spend my feeding time with Adley being thankful for what I have and not dwell on all the things I lost.

We did the breastfeeding thing. Tried to, anyway. Didn't work, which led to a—thankfully brief—few weeks of depression when Adley was just a few weeks old. But holding the bottle for her is almost as good.

"Go with the flow, huh, baby?" I coo down at her wide blue eyes as she stares up at me.

A loud knock at my suite door makes both of us jump and Adley's face changes from total contentment to a scrunched-up look of shock.

"Shhh, shhh, shhh," I whisper as I stand up and cross the main room to the door, and pull it open.

Elias Bricman is standing there, knuckles poised to knock again.

"What the fuck?" I say, before I remember I'm holding Adley.

Bric looks at me... looks at Adley... and then looks at me again. "Well, you did good, brat. She's adorable."

Brat. It makes me want to growl at him. I always hated him calling me that. "What the heck are you doing here?"

"Heck?" He laughs, then nods. "Oh, I get it. Kids and shit, right?"

"Bric—"

"I just found out where you were." He stands there stoic, like this explains everything.

"And?" I'm so beyond stunned. Not to mention annoyed. "What happened to the no-follow rule?" I worried about Quin looking for me at first. But after a few months I tried my best to put that part of my life behind me. And Bric? Never in a million years did I expect *him* to show up.

"Look." He sighs, looking around. My suite has a porch, so it's outside. And I share this porch with three other suites. This makes Bric nervous. "Can I come inside?"

"No," I say. "No. We were just leaving."

"Going where?" he asks. "Somewhere where I can't come? Or can I come with? I really need to talk to you about..." He looks down at Adley again. "This... situation."

"We don't have a situation, Bric. And we don't have anything to talk about, either."

Bric leans both hands on either side of the doorjamb like he's gonna take control of this situation right now. Fucking bulldozer. He's always been like that. Elias Bricman needs to get his way or he morphs into an asshole on the spot.

"So..." he says. "Who's her father?"

"Really?" I ask in my most cynical voice. I even raise one eyebrow.

"I think I deserve to know this, Rochelle. You can't just get pregnant and walk away from the father."

30

I snort as I adjust Adley's bottle so she can continue eating. "What makes you think you're the father?"

He shrugs. "Quin would say the same thing if he was here."

I look Elias Bricman dead in the eyes. "What makes you think *he's* the father?"

The look on his face almost makes me laugh. Almost. I hold it in so he figures I'm serious. Asshole.

"Can. I. Come. In." He says each word in little staccato clips. It's not a question. Not the way he says it. It comes out as—*I'm coming in.*

He pushes past me and then, yup. He's in all right. I close the door and whirl around. "What do you want?"

"Who's her father?" he asks again.

"How the heck would I know?" I laugh. "Could be you, I guess. Could be Quin. Could be someone else." I say it to piss him off. And it works. Because he's got that look on his face. The one that says, *Be careful.*

"Are you fucking with me right now?" he says, on the verge of angry. "There are only two possibilities. Smith already told us he stopped seeing you months before you left."

"You think you know me, Elias? You've never known me. At least Quin tried. You never tried. You got what you wanted. I got what I wanted. End of game." I smirk at him and enjoy his confusion. It's not often I get the best of Bric. So I soak it up.

"So you played the game for almost three years and then suddenly remembered you were only there to get a fertilized egg out of it and left?"

"I already said I don't know who the father is. How would I possibly know that without a DNA test? Did I swab your cheek, Elias? Did I get a blood sample from Quin? Why are you *here?*"

31

He calms down after that. I can see it in his expression. I know him pretty well. Three years is a long time. Enough time to understand body language and facial expressions. Enough to be wary of his dark side. "Are you angry with me?" he asks.

"I'm not anything with you, Bric. I'm just... I've just moved on. OK? I'm different now. My whole life is different. And I really don't know why you're here. After a year, you show up now?"

"One year exactly," he says. "It's been one year to the day." I say nothing so he stares at me for a moment and then looks around at my suite, trying to get a grip on the situation.

"Well..." I chuckle as I watch him. "I'm not going back, if that's why you're here. And I'm not falling for all your bullshit. I have a lawyer, in case you think I'm still that same little *brat* you met four years ago. I'm ready for this day. One hundred percent ready. So you—"

"Why not?" he asks, still looking around at all the baby stuff. He picks up a soft teething toy I just bought for Adley since she's due for that little milestone, and then sets it back down on the foyer table where he found it.

"Why not what?" I ask, walking Adley back into the living room area. She's got her eyes locked on his face. I haven't ever had a man over here so I guess he's just... interesting.

"You don't miss us?" Bric asks, still looking around.

"I'm different now. I just told you that. I'm not playing your game anymore."

"Give me a break, Rochelle," he huffs. "The game is over."

"Exactly. I ended it. And I won. So if you're here to ask me to come back to Denver, save your breath. I'm not coming."

"How do you afford this place?" he asks. "My investigator says you pay five thousand a month for this suite. It's a lot of money to live at a resort."

"Are you serious?" I laugh. I'm not surprised he knows how much I pay for the suite, but I am a little shocked he thinks I'm broke. "You paid my bills for three years, Bricman. Gave me a place to live, bought me food, clothes, gifts. And you guys put thirty thousand dollars in my bank account every month. How else would I be paying for the suite?"

"So you never spent it? You saved it all up?"

"Why do you care?"

"I'm just trying to understand how you're living this lifestyle. Do you have another..." He stops mid-sentence. Like he can't continue.

"Do I have another... what?"

"Another... arrangement?"

I laugh so loud, Adley startles in my arms. "Sorry, baby," I say. "But Elias Bricman is on drugs."

"So no... quad?" he prods.

"What the hell is wrong with you?" I pan one hand down my completely disheveled outfit of leggings and t-shirt, lack of makeup, and fucked-up slept-on ponytail hair. "Do I look like I'm playing another sexual fantasy game here? I'm a new fucking mother, Elias." I wince at my f-word. I'm really trying not to swear in front of the baby.

Bric runs his fingers through his hair like he's frustrated. "I'm just trying to understand. You left everything we gave you behind."

"Because I didn't need it." I'm rolling my eyes at his stupidity. Did he really think I was spending thirty grand a month while I lived with them? On what? It just shows me how goddamned clueless he is.

"So you left it all behind to get rid of us? All of it? Put us away and just forget it ever happened?" He stops and scratches the shadow creeping down his jaw. He's one of those guys who needs to shave every day. Something I always enjoyed about him when we spent our nights together. "So you saved your money and you pay for all this yourself?"

That little question mark at the end is almost cute. He's so… un-Bricman-like right now. He came here thinking I had a sugar daddy. I almost laugh at his insecurity. "I have a lot saved still. I bought a nice Lexus. And I put most of it in a trust fund for Adley. But I do get that payment every month, so I'm not strapped."

"What payment?" His eyes narrow.

"The ten grand that gets deposited into my account every month. I assumed it was from you. No?"

"No," he says. "Maybe it was Smith? Maybe you're his new project."

"Ha." I laugh. "Good one. It's probably Quin then. And even though I don't feel like I owe you for it, I do… appreciate it."

It has helped. I had more than a million dollars saved when I left them and I only spent a hundred grand on the car. Which was stupid, but I justified it because I wanted to drive places instead of flying. I don't fly.

"So he's been paying you." He says it more to himself than me. "And you've been accepting it."

"I figured it was child support."

Bric points a finger at me. "Right. Because this child belongs to *us*."

"To *me*," I clarify. "I will fuck you over six ways till Sunday if you came here to pull some custody bullshit on me, Bricman. I'm not even messing around right now."

He holds his hands up, palms facing me. "Back up, sister. I'm not here for the kid. Come on. Get real. I just..." He sighs. Walks over to a chair and sits. Leans back and closes his eyes as he massages his temples. "You have no idea what your little stunt did to Quin." He opens his eyes. "No idea."

I shrug. "It hurt me too. When you said abortion—"

"I never told you to get a fucking abortion." He looks at Adley and lowers his voice. "I never said that, Rochelle. I just said you had a few options."

I shrug again. "I heard what you *weren't* saying. I know you better than you think. I know what goes on inside that head of yours. I've seen it, Bric. Experienced it first-hand. And I already knew Quin wasn't into me like that. So I did what I had to do."

"You left Chella in your bed? That's what you *had* to do?" he says, voice rising again.

"Oh, so it worked, huh?" I smile at that. "How'd that go?"

Bric sighs. "She's practically engaged to Smith now."

"What?" I laugh. "What the hell?"

"I know, right?" I get a small familiar smile from Elias Bricman. The friendly one. The real one. One I hardly ever saw when we were together. He only brings it out for special occasions and I was never special enough. "They hit it off. In fact, we all liked her. She played well. But it didn't last. She quit and went with Smith."

"Well, damn. I never saw that coming."

"But Quin—"

"Bric. I can't. It was hard for me too. It hurt so bad when I left. But I did leave. And I had a good reason."

"What was your reason? Because he'd be into the whole baby thing if he knew."

35

"He doesn't *know?*" I'm shocked. *But he put money in my account every month.*

Bric shakes his head. "I never told him. He thinks you had the abortion. I never told him you called me last summer."

"Sorry about that," I say, looking away. I walk over to the couch next to the chair and take a seat. "I had just given birth and my hormones were all out of whack. Plus I felt like a total failure because I couldn't get the hang of the breastfeeding thing. I was really looking forward to that. But I shouldn't have called."

"We would've been there for you, ya know. Even me, Rochelle. Even Smith. He's the one who went looking for you first. He couldn't stand to see Quin so unhappy and confused."

"Hmm. I never saw that coming either. The Smith looking for me part. Not Quin. I knew Quin would be hurt but... he hurt me too, Bric. You have no idea how bad." We sit there in silence for a minute. Adley is playing with my hair as she drinks her bottle, wrapping long strands of it around and around in her tiny fist. "If Quin didn't know... then why was he sending me money all year?"

Bric shrugs. "He loves you. He probably wanted to make sure you had what you needed."

"He doesn't *love* me." I roll my eyes.

"Shit, Rochelle. He's a fucking mess. He won't even talk to me these days. He's so mad about how it ended."

"You're... not playing the game anymore?" I almost can't believe it. Elias Bricman is nothing but a game. I can't even imagine this man living a normal life. Not just the sexual stuff he's into. But everything. His whole life is wrapped up in controlling people.

"Not with him," Bric says. "Not with Smith either."

"Then who?"

"That new guy. Jordan Wells? Did you ever meet him?"

I shake my head. "But just one guy?" That's not like him either. He likes to keep things off balance. Anything less than plural is just not dynamic enough to satiate his dark appetite.

"I'm not really here to talk about that game, Rochelle. I'm here to beg you for a favor."

"I'm not going back. I told you that. In fact, you're lucky you came today. I'm about to move again."

"Where?"

I shrug. "Dunno yet."

He exhales loudly like he's really frustrated now. "I really think I need to know."

"You don't deserve to know where I'm going." My own frustration is building. Where does he get off? How in the world does he figure I owe him something?

"Not where you're *going*," he snaps. "If I'm the *father*." His head is downcast, but he looks up through a wave of hair. It's longer than I remember. Not long. But shoulder-length. And some of it falls over his face until he runs his fingers through it, putting it back in place.

"Why?" I ask. "It's not like you ever wanted kids."

"Didn't want them. That's right. But if I have one, Rochelle, that's different. I'd need to know that. We really do need a DNA test."

I shake my head. "No."

"Why?"

"I don't want to know."

"Well, we do."

"Quin doesn't even know about her. So he can't want that."

"I'm gonna tell him tonight when I leave here, and once I do, he'll come looking and he'll *demand* a DNA test."

"Is that a threat?" So many things in that statement make me uncomfortable.

"No," he says. *"No,"* more emphatically. "That's not why I'm here. I just... need to know. And I need to make things right with Quin. So I have to tell him."

We have another long silence as Bric picks up a toy from the floor. A red plastic block. He turns it in his hand like he's never seen anything like it before.

"You said you came to beg for a favor. Was that your favor? The DNA test? Because if so, it's not happening. I get why you'd want to know, I do." I look at him with an earnest expression. "I even sympathize about your situation with Quin. But I cannot get involved with you guys again. It was..." I stop and try to pull myself together. I'd forgotten about the feelings. All those desperate moments last year. All the crying and craziness. I know it was just the hormones, but it was real while it was happening.

"It was what?" Bric prods, ever the psychoanalyst.

I let out a long breath of air. "It was hard. I didn't want to walk away, Bric. I wanted what every pregnant woman wants."

"The happily ever after?" he asks, shooting me another small, but genuine, smile.

I shrug. "I guess you could call it that. But right after I found out I was pregnant, after I told you—like the next day, I think—Quin and I were at your last garden party on the Club roof and we were dancing. It was such a great night. I told him I loved him and he looked at me, Bric... he looked at me like I was a stranger."

"So you left."

38

I nod. "I left. I knew he... I knew I was important to him, right? But the minute I admitted that I loved him, I saw the fear in his face."

"What fear?" Bric asks.

"That the game would end. I knew right then that ending the game was the thing he feared most. Not me, Bric. He wasn't going to miss our couple relationship. But us. Me and you and him. That's what he wanted. That's *always* been what he wanted."

They both want that. I thought Smith did too, so that doesn't fit into my assessment of them. Why play this game over and over again? But I don't know Smith that well. I do know Bric. And Quin is just like him, minus the dark Machiavellian side.

Bric picks up a blue block and stacks it on top of the red one on the arm of the chair. He watches Adley for a few seconds. Another smile creeps out. So many real smiles from Elias Bricman today. "She looks just like you."

My gaze falls down to my absolutely beautiful daughter. "I think so too. She's got my blonde hair. And I still have a baby picture of me." I nod to the photo frame on the mantle of the fireplace. It's a cheap frame. Something I bought at the local drugstore after I got Adley's first pictures taken last month when I made a rare trip to the Durango mall. It's me and her, side by side. And we could be the same baby, that's how much alike we look.

Well, except for the eyes. Adley has bright blue eyes and mine are hazel. But that might change.

Bric stands, walks over to the fireplace, and picks up the frame. "Jesus."

He stares at the image for so long I start to feel weird. "That was the favor then? The DNA test?"

"No," Bric answers, still gazing down at the photo. "That was just to piss you off." He smiles, looks over at me from under that curl of hair again. "Because I know you. I know how to push all your buttons, Rochelle."

Right. Bric is all about manipulation. "Then *why* are you here?"

He places the frame back where he got it. Gently. With reverence, almost. "We could play a new game," he says. And then, ignoring the confused look on my face—"A game called Make Quin Happy Again. Give him what he thinks he wants."

I shake my head and huff out something that isn't a laugh. I know Bric cares about Quin. They are like brothers. But he's not here for Quin. He's here for himself. Everything Bric does is for himself.

"Because I think you're right," Bric says. "He likes the us. The three of us, you know. But I think he wants you, Rochelle. And he'd want this baby if he knew about her. I came here because I thought I could bring you home with me. Chella is making us have lunch together tomorrow at the Club. I know Quin doesn't want to see me. Can't even fucking look at me." He winces at his swear word, but doesn't apologize. "So even though when I got on the jet this afternoon I was coming here to beg you to stay away... I had another thought along the way. A small idea crept in. A little fantasy, you know? That I'd show up with you and the baby tomorrow like a... like..."

"Like a gift," I say, filling in the missing word. He nods. Slowly. I say, "I thought you were playing a new game with that other guy?"

He huffs out an exasperated laugh. "It's so fucked up, Rochelle. It's never gonna work. And I miss you too."

We stare at each other for a few moments. I've talked to Bric lots of times. He's an easy guy to confide in. But

I've never talked to him about our relationship. And he's never offered me up anything more than the casual, *You look nice tonight*, remarks. Or, *I like your hair that way.* They always felt so… mandatory. He was always nice to me. Always generous with his money. And careful during sex. But he never looked at me the way he's looking at me now. It makes my heart flutter a little. "You miss me," I whisper. "With you and Quin?"

He nods again. Even slower than the last time. "I have been talking myself into thinking you leaving was the best thing to ever happen to me. But it was a lie. Just like you're trying to lie to yourself right now. What we had was good, Rochelle. Better than good, really. It was pretty fucking great."

I look down at Adley, wondering how I went from hating the fact he was here to… reconsidering all my choices.

He's good, I tell myself. He's always been good at playing on people's emotions.

"Don't you get lonely? Do you have boyfriends?" he asks.

"No," I say. But I'm only referring to the boyfriend part. I get very lonely. I just hide it better than I used to.

He comes over to the couch and sits down next to me. Very close, so our legs are touching. "Can I hold her?"

I almost snort. "You want to hold her?"

Another slow nod of affirmation. "I can't stand it." He laughs. "I need to touch her. She's so fucking pretty."

"Have you ever held a baby before?" I ask, not sure what to make of this unexpected turn of events. Hell, so many turns in this one conversation, I'm getting dizzy.

"I played Santa last year at Christmas."

"You did not." I laugh.

41

"I swear to God. Smith was busy with Chella so I stepped in. I'm that kind of guy, Rochelle. I step in." He holds his arms out, like this is a done deal. And I'm a little off my game right now, not sure what the next move is, but handing him Adley can't be a wrong move, no matter what, right? So I gently slip her into his waiting arms and watch his expression change from badass Bric to melty Elias in the same moment.

"We could make him happy again, brat."

This time when he calls me brat I don't feel defensive. It feels... like affection.

"He'd be my friend again. You'd be my lover. We'd be what we were, Rochelle." He looks up from the baby and stares at me. "But we'd be better."

A new take on an old twist. My head is whirling with ideas, and possibilities, and... maybe even regrets. Did I bow out too soon? Did I not give them enough credit? Did I misinterpret every signal they ever sent me? "I have a car here, remember?" I say, almost whispering.

"We'll have someone bring it to Denver. We'll get you your own place if you want. It might be weird if you stayed with one of us. Quin won't want you at my place and vice versa. It would be much better, Rochelle. I promise. We won't play that game anymore. We'll start something brand new."

"Something... real?" I ask, almost afraid to hope.

He gives me that slow nod one more time. "Something very real. I've missed you. And I know you think I was never invested—and that's fair. I probably wasn't. But I am now, Rochelle. I am. We could start again. Pick up where we left off, but with new rules."

"What rules?" I ask, my heart sinking at the thought of all those fucking rules. I can't do that again. It was way too confusing. The best thing that ever happened was

Smith distancing himself from our game and letting Quin and Bric do whatever they wanted.

Bric shrugs. "Make them up as we go, you know? I don't know what this might turn into, but I'd do just about anything to get another shot at it."

"Do you love me?" I ask, confused.

"Yes," he says, no slow nod this time. Nothing but commitment. "I love you in my own way." He shrugs. "We all loved you, Rochelle. We just didn't pay much attention to that feeling until we realized you were gone."

"We're not supposed to turn back," I say.

"Fuck that," he says softly. "We make our own rules. There's nothing wrong with admitting you made a mistake and then correcting it, right?"

I let out a long breath. "I don't want to get hurt. What if Quin—"

"He won't," Bric says quickly. "He loves you. He really does. He's fucking miserable, Rochelle. If I bring you back to him..." He trails off, shaking his head.

"I'd be your gift to him?"

"Yes," he says, smiling down at Adley. "And her too." He looks up at me again. "I have a jet waiting. We can't leave until morning but one night alone won't hurt, right?"

Jesus Christ. I'm instantly horny. "But it's Monday."

He laughs so loud, Adley starts crying. I take her, laughing with him, because my immediate reaction was to morph back into the game. Then shush her until she's settled again.

"Well?" Bric finally asks, his fingertips playing with my hair. "What do you think? Should we break all the rules tonight and start something brand new tomorrow?"

I look up and bite my lip. Some of this feels wrong. The one night alone with Bric, for sure. Because I've

43

never wanted him. Not alone. It's Quin I dreamed about at night. It's Quin I really love. It's Quin I wanted a million different ways for the rest of my life, and couldn't have.

But I *am* lonely. I have been so lonely for so long I forgot what it feels like to have someone. Someone you know. Someone you love, because I do love Bric. Not the way I love Quin. But I do love him. He's someone I trusted, even though I knew better. And now he's here, asking me to reconsider.

It feels... wrong, but right. Because Bric and I are not going to be a couple. We're going to be a ménage with Quin again. A kind of family.

It's not how I imagined it when I left. Not what I wanted back then. But that's because I didn't think Bric would be interested in a real family. I thought he'd kick me out and they'd all walk away.

But this... *this* is what Quin wanted, right? The three of us forever?

Just imagining myself with both of them again. God. It *was* good. All the fun Quin and I had. The way he made me feel so cherished when he came over every week and made love to me. All the crazy shit Bric likes to do in private. The way he was careful with me even though he wanted to do so much more.

All the... *sharing*.

We'd stopped that for a while because Bric was always looking for more submission. But the times we did share... it was amazing. I loved the way it felt to wake up between them both in the morning.

Why did I leave? Was it the hormones? Was I just mentally unstable?

"OK," I finally say. "It's been so long I could use a night of rule-breaking."

Maybe he's right. It could be good again. It could be so much better. Maybe some part of him has changed? Maybe he's not the selfish, narcissistic player I thought he was? Maybe my time away has made him reconsider the dark part he hides inside that head of his?

I get a big Bric smile for my answer. "Good." And then he leans in and kisses me. One hand touches my face with honest affection, while the other drops to Adley's soft tufts of blonde hair. "Good," he says into my mouth.

It's like I never left. Like we didn't have a year apart. I didn't have a baby. And all three hundred and sixty-five days between then and now never happened.

It's like a second chance.

"Do you want to spank me?" I tease. And then I immediately feel stupid. *What is wrong with me?*

You're lonely, Rochelle. And sad. You're just really good at hiding it.

"I really do," he says, pulling back from the kiss. "After we put the baby to bed."

We?

We?

For some reason that gives me a little panic attack. Did I just agree to share my child with them too?

But Bric stands up and offers me his hand. "Come on. I hear this dinky town has an amazing hot spring. Let's go have some family fun."

It's just one night without rules. I can handle one night, right? I'm a professional game-player. I did this for three years.

But if Bric came to get me, that makes him number one. And we all know why I shouldn't fuck number one.

I'll get attached.

And where will that leave Quin when I see him tomorrow?

Elias Bricman thrives on control. If I let him control me again, nothing will have changed. He'll be the same guy, with the same motivations, as he was when I left last year.

I don't want what we had last year. I need more than that.

"I change my mind," I say.

Bric squints his eyes at me, frowning. "Which part?" he asks.

"All of it."

CHAPTER FOUR

At nine AM on Tuesday morning I was one hundred percent sure I wasn't showing up for lunch with Chella at the Club. By nine-thirty I was at a solid eighty-five percent.

You can see where this is headed.

I show up at Turning Point ten minutes early.

Margaret, Bric's White Room manager, is gushing over me like a mother because I've been MIA for so long. She takes my coat and straightens my tie, asking me a million questions that both annoy me and make me feel special at the same time.

"I'm fine, Margaret," I say, brushing her hands away from the lapels of my suit. "Stop it."

"Sorry. I've just missed you." Margaret stares up at me, hands clasped together in front of her, like I'm giving her a proud moment and she needs to soak it up. "Mr. Bricman and Mr. Baldwin are up in Mr. Baldwin's bar." Margaret shakes her head. "Both of you... back on the same day."

"I'm here for lunch with Chella," I say. "In the White Room."

"Oh, she called a little while ago and said she'd be late. That's why Mr. Baldwin is here, I suppose. And you know how he is about his privacy. Plus he brought a dog."

Margaret *tsks* her tongue. "Mr. Bricman was not happy about that. So lunch will be up in the Baldwin Bar."

I turn around and look up, and sure enough, there's Smith holding that little rat with the pink bow. He waves one of her paws at me, smiling.

I'm not sure I'll ever get used to the dog-dad version of Smith.

I can't see Bric from down here, but I guess I'm stuck seeing the whole thing through. I climb the stairs up to the second floor asking myself why I'm really mad at Bric. I believe him when he says he just gave Rochelle her options. So OK, he didn't actually tell her to have an abortion. But the part where he keeps that little conversation to himself, even after she left and he knew I was devastated—well, I'm having more trouble with that.

He kept things from me. It's on the verge of lying. Not quite, but very close. It was total betrayal. I don't like lies. And I hate the feeling of betrayal even more. What we were doing was based on trust. And loyalty. He broke his oath with me.

Maybe he did mean to tell me about his conversation with Rochelle. But I don't think so. I think he deliberately didn't tell me she was pregnant because he didn't want me to leave the game.

This, I decide, is the root of my problem.

Bric is selfish. Sure, he plays Mr. Philanthropist at Smith's instructions. He looks generous and benevolent on the outside. Always in control, always ready with a big ol' check to hand out just when people need it. But it's not his money and it's not his goal.

He's like a paper-doll version of Smith. The mask Smith refuses to wear.

And I understand now—completely understand—that the reason he didn't tell me about Rochelle being pregnant was because he didn't want to make a change in his life. His life.

Fuck her life and the problems she was facing. Fuck my life and the epiphany I was slowly realizing. If I knew about Rochelle's pregnancy we'd both leave the game. And what would happen to Bric then?

Really, what would happen to him if he didn't have Smith and me around? Keep him in check. That's why we make such a good team. Smith and I keep him in check. The Club keeps him in check.

I'm not surprised that he's selfish. I've always known that. So that's not why I stopped hanging out here or stopped talking to him. I made the unconscious decision to distance myself from Elias Bricman a while back when I realized he was a *dick*.

I'm probably a dick at times. Smith is a dick almost all the time—except with Chella. But Bric—Bric is a dick because he doesn't care. I think Smith cares about people. Why would he give all that money away if he didn't? And I care about people. I'm not usually a dick. I had a few moments with Chella when she first showed up, but I think I was justified.

I'm the nice guy in this group. I like to make the girls happy, and not just sexually. I like to make them happy in *life*.

Smith played the game because he was into the concept of sharing. He wanted things, but they had to be offered. It made sense when *he* said it.

But Bric likes to make them bend to his will, even when they don't want to. He likes this game because he can do

49

all that dark shit he hides up in that head of his and call it *playing.*

When I get to the top of the stairs I turn right and head up the second, shorter set of stairs that lead into the private bar. Smith is in his usual seat, smiling down at his dumb dog. Bric is also sitting in his usual seat, across from Smith, but not on the balcony side of the table.

"Wassup," Smith says, shaking a dog paw at me.

"Where's Chella?" I ask, taking a seat next to Smith instead of my usual, on the other side of Bric. Bric looks at me. Gives me a slight nod of his head. Then snaps his fingers for the bartender to bring me a drink.

"She texted me twenty minutes ago and told me to come here. She's running late," Smith says.

Smith is wearing... sweats. At the Club. I almost can't take this guy. I've only ever seen him wear sweats to bed. And this hoodie? I had no idea Smith Baldwin owned a hoodie. "What the fuck are you wearing?" I ask.

"I was at the gym down in Five Points," Smith says. "I came right over." He looks at his watch. "I can't stay long because I'm boxing with some thugs in an hour."

"They're gonna kick your ass," Bric mumbles down into his glass of whiskey.

"Probably," Smith says. "But it'll be fun." He smiles into his drink as he takes a sip.

The bartender comes with my glass, offers me a smile and says, "Nice to see you, Mr. Foster."

"Thanks," I say, taking the drink. It's a good whiskey. Better than the shit I drink with Robert on Friday nights.

"So what've you been up to?" Bric asks. I assume he's talking to me, even though he's still staring down at his glass.

"Same old shit," I say. There's an awkward silence after that, which I do not feel the need to fill. Hey, if these assholes want me here, they can provide the entertainment.

The three of us are shifting in our seats, unaccustomed to the new relationship we find ourselves in—or lack of one—when Chella comes running up the stairs.

She stops a few feet from the table, huffing. Like she ran across town to get here. She says nothing. Just stares at me. Her face is flushed and her heavy breathing makes her chest quickly rise and fall underneath her cream-colored silk blouse.

"What?" Smith asks. "What's going on?"

She doesn't look at Smith. She stares straight at me. And then she bursts into tears.

Smith and I both get up at the same time. We're surrounding her a second later, Smith holding on to her shoulders, asking her over and over again. "What's happening, Chella? What's wrong? Why are you crying?"

I don't say anything, and I don't touch her. Just hover like a third wheel. *Not allowed to touch her, Quin.* But I want to. And when she reaches for me instead of Smith, I let it happen. I pull her in and let her hug me tight.

"Chella?" I ask. "What's going on?"

Smith is there too, the three of us pressed together tightly. It hurts. God, it hurts. I've missed her. I've missed him too, if I'm being honest. But mostly I've missed... this.

The us.

"I don't know how to tell you this," Chella says, leaning her head on my shoulder. "I have no idea how to tell you this."

"Tell me what?" I ask.

51

"Just say it," Smith urges. "Tell me what the fuck is happening."

"Rochelle is back," Chella says.

"Back *where?*" Smith growls. He goes from soft and caring to angry in the same moment.

"Here," Chella says, still looking at me. "She called me. She called me, Quin. And even though I promised her I'd never say anything to you guys, the promise I made to you last year is way more important to me. I didn't want to be the one who found her. I didn't want to be the one who had to tell you anything."

"Where is she?" Bric says. I'd almost forgotten about him. He didn't rush over to Chella when she started to cry. And he's not pressed up against her like Smith and I are.

Chella pulls away and I feel a sense of loss. God, if only Smith hadn't fallen in love with her. We could still be playing the game. Maybe I'm not as into it as Bric, but I played it for more than a decade because I liked it. And I do miss it.

She turns to Smith and says, "She called me like thirty minutes ago and said she was passing through town. Did I want to have dinner tonight?"

"What'd you say?" I ask. But her words—*passing through town*—they stab me.

"I said yes, of course." She takes a moment to wipe the tears off her cheeks and dab a fingertip at her eye makeup.

"Did she say anything else?" I ask, unsure how much I want to know.

Chella nods. "She said not to tell you guys."

"Which guys?" I ask. "All of us? Or just me?"

Chella's face crumples, so I get that answer even though she never answers.

I walk back over to the table and take a seat. They all wait to see if I'll say anything, but I don't. I just sit there and drink my whiskey.

Passing through town.

Don't tell Quin.

Got it.

"I have her room number," Chella says, coming over to sit next to me in Smith's chair. "She's at the Four Seasons."

"The Four Seasons." I laugh. "Of course she is. The fucking Four Seasons." I raise my glass and yell, "One more for me, bartender. Because the girl I loved got pregnant, had an abortion, left town without telling me, and then decides to come back a year later, except she's just *passing through*. And she's staying at the motherfucking Four Seasons Hotel. That's just fan-fucking-tastic."

"Quin," Chella says in a soft voice. "I have to tell you something else."

"There's more?" I chuckle, watching the bartender refill my glass. "Hit me, Chella. Might as well just plunge that knife in a little deeper."

"She didn't have an abortion."

I choke on that whiskey. Almost spit it out. "What?" I croak, trying not to cough.

"There was a baby crying in the background. So I asked her about it. And she just... she just said she had a baby. Six months old. And did I want to come over while she was in town?"

"Right," I whisper. "Do you want to meet my new baby, Chella? And don't tell Quin I'm just passing through town."

I stand up but Smith has my arm. "Nope," he says. "You're not going over there alone."

53

"I'm not going over there at all, you dumbass." I laugh. "Fuck her. Just fuck her."

Bric is standing in front of me, like a goddamned wall. "Then where are you going?"

"Back to work," I say, pushing him aside.

"No, Quin," Chella says, tugging on my arm. "No. She's here and we're gonna have this out once and for all. If she's only here one night, then this is your only chance to put it behind you."

"Put it behind me?" I ask. "She had my baby, Chella. She got pregnant, took off in the middle of the night. Never bothered to call. And she had my *baby*."

"You don't know it's yours," Bric says.

I glare at him in disgust. "It's *mine*."

Bric puts his hands up, conceding to my anger. "Whatever."

"We're going," Smith says. His no-nonsense voice doesn't quite have the same power when he's wearing sweats, not the way it does when he's in a five-thousand-dollar suit. But it comes close. "We're going over there. All four of us. And we're getting to the bottom of this bullshit. Fuck her. She did this to us, OK? She fucked with us. I for one—I'm getting an answer. And the rest of you are coming with me."

Smith hands the dog off to Chella, who hugs her tightly to her chest, and then he picks up his gym bag. "Meet us in the Four Seasons' lobby. Come on, Chella." He grabs her hand and tugs her down the stairs, leaving me alone with Bric.

I look at him, my eyes narrowed and angry.

"What do you want to do?" he asks.

"Did you know about this?" I ask.

54

"No," he says, defensive. "How the fuck would I know about this?"

I don't believe him. I can't put my finger on why, but I don't believe him.

"I swear, Quin. I had no idea she was in town. But now that she's here you should go talk to her. Say what you have to say. Set things right."

"Set things right?" I ask. "In what way do you see me setting things right? I didn't do anything. I didn't leave her. I didn't run away. I didn't tell her to get an abortion. I didn't do anything wrong."

"I didn't tell her to get an abortion, either," Bric growls. "And now that you know she kept the baby, don't you want to see her?"

"How do you know the baby's a *her*?" I ask.

"Not the baby, asshole," Bric says. "Her, as in Rochelle."

Do I want to see Rochelle?

I can honestly say that up until this revelation, that answer was yes. So many yeses. No hesitation, no qualms, no conditions. Yes.

I thought I'd feel relief when Rochelle was found. We did look for her but Bric never had any luck. And every time he called with a report I'd have a little flutter of hope in my heart that he'd say he knew where she was. I'd imagine how I'd go to her. How we'd reunite and all the bad things would disappear. All the sadness and anger and confusion.

But now that this moment is real… I'm so fucking pissed off.

And she had my baby.

I missed it. I missed the pregnancy. Her belly getting big. The heartbeat. That picture thing the doctor takes that people post all over social media. The birth. What did she name it? What does it look like?

I missed everything. She took it all away from me and I don't think I can ever forgive her for that.

"Quin." Bric interrupts my thoughts. "Come on. You need to do this."

"No," I say, the anger melting away. "No. I'm not going."

I turn to leave but Bric has my arm again. "You're going, Quin. This shit is over now. You and Smith are my best friends and Rochelle tore us apart."

"Exactly. So now it's over, Bric. I'm done. I don't even care what you did or didn't do. We can be friends again."

"We can't," he says. "It's not the same. You know it's not. You're still pissed off at me about this shit and if we just go over there like Smith says, and have it out with her, it will be better. I know it."

I just look at him, trying to figure out his angle. He always has an angle. "Why do you care?"

"Why?" He laughs. "Why? I'm playing the fucking game with Jordan Wells, Quin. He's just not my type."

I laugh. I can't help myself.

Bric laughs too. "I'm totally fucking serious. I can't, man. I can't have sex with that guy two on one. He's an asshole. It's nothing like it was with you and Smith. And OK, Smith is out. Fine. But if you were still in… It'd be a whole lot better than me and Jordan Wells."

I stop laughing but I'm still smiling, trying to picture Bric and Jordan trying to play with some random girl. I miss it, so there's this little part of me that's jealous. But mostly I find it comical.

"And the girls, man. Jesus Christ. We've been through three of them. This last one…" Bric rolls his eyes and lets out a long exhale. "Rochelle was so much better than these girls. Chella was great too, you know?"

I nod. "She really was. I kinda wish Chella and Smith were still playing. I think I'd have handled all this shit better if we were still in that relationship."

"I think so too," Bric says. "But you and me, man. We're still good at this, you know? We could be friends again. Find a new girl."

"With Jordan?" I ask, one eyebrow raised.

Bric shrugs. "I don't care. He was always good enough down in the Club, you know?"

True. We have fucked girls with Jordan plenty of times. I don't really like him, but Bric is right. He's good enough when we're the ones in control. The game was never meant to be played with just two guys. I imagine that makes everything off balance. You really need that third guy to keep the feelings away.

And even then...

"Or just the two of us," Bric offers, his voice low, like he's uncertain how I'd feel about it. "We could come up with a new game. Change things around a little."

"Maybe," I admit, sighing. "I do miss that, you know."

"I do too," Bric says. "But we can't go forward until we deal with the past. Let's just go over there, meet up with Smith, go up, and confront her. You say everything you want to say. Then we'll leave."

"And the baby?" I ask. "What do I do about the baby?"

Bric shrugs. "I dunno, man. You just gotta see what happens, I guess."

I take my own car over to the Four Seasons. It's only about eight blocks away from the Club, so not nearly enough time to process what's happening. I pull into the valet, hand over my keys, and spy Bric, Chella, and Smith standing near the sleek, modern stairs, through the window of the lobby.

Chella walks towards me as I enter, holding the little rat called Precious. "Quin, are you sure you're up to this? Don't let them pressure you into anything you're not ready for."

"Come on," I say. "I'm fine. I'm pissed off, but otherwise fine."

"Just give her the benefit of the doubt, OK?"

"Why should I? What she did—"

"What she did," Chella interrupts me, "was done in desperation."

"How was she desperate? Huh? Explain that to me, please. Because I don't get it."

"She was pregnant, Quin. It's a weird time for some women. I know you don't understand that, but some don't handle it well. They do crazy things. Overreact and become sad. I can't explain it, because obviously, I've never been pregnant. But I was with her, remember? We were friends that whole time she was getting ready to leave. I told you she was sad. I told you something big was happening to her. So just... just be patient and be quiet."

I sneer down at Chella.

"Just listen to her."

"What if she has nothing to say?" I ask. "What if she blows us off and just says, 'Fuck you guys?'"

"Then..." Chella shrugs. "Then walk out and don't look back."

"The *baby*, Chella."

"Shit," she says, biting her lip. "I forgot about that."

"I might want to walk out on Rochelle, but not the baby."

"It could be Bric's," Chella says, a little hint of hope in her voice. We both know Bric isn't into kids. He might be happy if Rochelle walked away with his kid.

"It's not," I say.

"You don't know."

"Sometimes you know, and this is one of those times. I just *know*."

"Well, let's take one step at a time, OK?"

"Ready?" Smith says, walking up to us. Bric looks nervous, which surprises me. But Smith looks... angry.

Why is he pissed off?

"Ready," I say, sighing.

We walk towards the elevator and wait until the doors open. The ride up to the twenty-first floor seems to take forever, but then when the doors open, it's all going too fast as we walk down the hall. She's at the very end. A suite, from the looks of the door.

Smith knocks, no hesitation. I hear a baby fussing inside and look over at Bric. He still looks very nervous. Chella grabs my hand just as the lock disengages and the door swings in.

Rochelle. My beautiful, beautiful Rochelle. She doesn't look anything like the girl I lost. She looks... so much better.

"I should've known," she says, no hello or greeting.

"I'm sorry," Chella says, letting go of my hand and stepping forward. "He needed to know. We'll leave if you want, but I think you owe them a conversation."

"Fine," Rochelle says, waving her hand for us to enter. "I probably do deserve this."

Deserve this. That's all she has to say? Just, *Fine, I deserve this?*

Chella enters first, then Smith, then Bric and I'm last. I hesitate for a second, but then the heavy door begins to swing closed and Bric stops it, last second, pulling it open for me again. "Come on," he says. "Give it five minutes. Then you can leave."

I enter into a hallway—master bedroom off to the right, large bathroom right in front of me with one of those huge soaking tubs—and then go left and follow Chella into the living room. There's a couch, three chairs, a small office table, and, once I get fully into the suite, a dining room off to the left that seats one, two, three... eight. Eight fucking people. Sweeping mountain and city views from the two windows that flank the corner fireplace draw my attention back to what's happening.

I wonder who's paying for this? This room has got to cost two thousand a night, easy.

"Might as well sit down," Rochelle says, picking up the baby from a seat sitting on the floor.

God, they are so beautiful.

Smith takes a seat in a chair, propping a foot on his knee and leaning back like he's making himself comfortable. Chella sits in the chair closest to him, Bric takes the couch and I... I just stare at them.

Not them. Rochelle and the baby.

Rochelle is wearing light-colored jeans, a pale-blue t-shirt that says *Pagosa Springs* in faded white letters, and nothing on her feet. Her hair is even longer than the last time I saw her, and it was halfway down her back then. It's golden in the light that pours into the room from the windows. Her stunning blue-green hazel eyes are trained on me, waiting to see what I'll say.

I say nothing. Just take my gaze to the baby in her arms. A girl. She's wearing a pink and white dress with eyelet lace trim. Downy tufts of blonde hair end in soft curls right at the top of her shoulders. She has a red plastic block in her mouth and she looks like she's about to cry.

"Adley," Rochelle says, still staring at me.

"Adley," I repeat back. "How old is she?"

"Six months."

I nod and look over at Smith. *Help me out, man,* my look says. Because I have no idea what to do.

Chella starts. "We just want to—"

"We want to know *what the fuck*, Rochelle," Smith finishes for her.

"Don't say fuck in front of the baby," Bric says.

We all turn to look at him. Since when does he have baby rules?

"I'm just saying," Bric explains. "Let's try to keep this... professional."

"Professional?" I ask.

Everyone turns to look at me. I don't like the attention and Smith realizes this, because he picks right back up where he left off.

"You have a lot of actions to account for," he says.

"Maybe," Rochelle says. Calmly. She takes a seat in another chair, opposite Smith and just a few feet to my right, holding Adley tightly to her chest like she needs the comfort. Adley. What a pretty name. Something I'd agree to. "Maybe not. We did have an agreement, right? The contract said—"

"I don't give one flying fuck what that contract said," Smith spits, stabbing the wooden arm of the chair with his finger. He's really pissed off. I don't think Chella has ever seen him this way, because she looks at him, aghast, with a hand over her heart. "What you did was bullshit."

"Can we stop with the swearing?" Bric interrupts again.

"Fuck off, Bric," Smith counters. "You're not gonna take her side now. Not after what she did to Quin. Fuck that contract, you know? He loved you, Rochelle. And you knew he loved you. And even Bric cared."

"You never did though, right?"

"Right," he says, matter-of-factly. "Your decision to leave didn't hurt me one bit. But the way you treated them"—Smith hikes a thumb in the direction of Bric and me—"that did hurt me, Rochelle. So I'm gonna be as pissed off as I want right now."

"Look," Rochelle says, huffing out some air. "I don't have to explain myself."

"I paid you ten thousand dollars a month, you sneaky bitch," Smith says. "So you goddamned will explain yourself."

"What?" Bric and I both say at the same time.

"That's right," Smith says, not taking his eyes off Rochelle. "I kept paying my part. And you know why I kept paying my part, Rochelle?" He spits out her name like it tastes bad.

Rochelle stays silent.

"I paid you to stay gone."

"What the fuck is happening?" I ask. "You paid her to leave?" I ask Smith.

"Not to leave, dumbass. To stay away. But now that she's back, and she took my money, now she fucking owes me. I have questions for you, Rochelle Bastille. I paid you over three hundred thousand dollars for these answers. And you're gonna give them to me right the fuck now."

A part of me wants to stop Smith's angry outburst, but most of me doesn't. I have so many questions too. *Where did you go? Why did you leave? Whose baby is that? What day was she born? Is she healthy? How long are you staying?* "And my first question is…" Smith continues. "Why the fuck are you here?"

Rochelle says nothing. She's not afraid of Smith. I've heard them have small arguments before. Nothing this dramatic. But she's not a pushover for him like she is for Bric.

Chella stands up, takes a deep breath, and says, "Maybe we should go."

Smith continues, undeterred. "And once we get past that little formality, I want you to tell Quin just what the fuck happened last year. And then I want to know when the fuck you're leaving Denver. Because we don't want you here."

"I plan on telling you all those things," Rochelle sneers back at Smith.

"Liar. Such a little fucking liar. You were trying to use that fucking contract to get out of it, so don't—"

"Smith," Chella says in an uncharacteristically loud voice. "We're leaving. This has nothing to do with us. This is between Bric, Rochelle, and Quin. So let's go." She stands up, holding the dog in one hand while simultaneously pulling on Smith's arm.

Smith waits a full second, staring at Rochelle. Then he looks at Chella and gives in to her request.

I expect him to get the last word on his way out, because that's just the kind of guy Smith is, but he drops it and they leave quietly.

Rochelle huffs out a breath of air that makes the baby's hair fly up. "Well, he hasn't changed."

"He actually has," I say, feeling the need to defend my friend. "A lot."

Rochelle looks at Bric and shakes her head. "What can I say other than sorry, right?" She switches to me. "I'm sorry."

"Whose baby?" I ask.

"I don't know. If I knew do you really think I would've left without saying something? It could be either of you."

"No one else?" Bric asks.

"What the fuck, Bric?" I say.

"I'm just asking to make sure," he continues, his eyes squarely on Rochelle's face.

"There's no one else," Rochelle says, looking at me. "I didn't think you'd be interested."

I rub a hand down my face and laugh.

"I didn't think you loved me," Rochelle continues. "I told you I loved you and you said nothing that night."

"That's no excuse," I say, turning my back to her. "No excuse for what you did. You told Chella to get in your bed, pretend to be you—" I almost want to fucking choke her right now, that's how angry thinking about that night makes me.

I take a deep, deep breath instead.

"I'm sorry," Rochelle says again. "I'm sorry. I didn't mean to hurt you—"

"You didn't mean to hurt me?" I laugh so loud the baby cries.

Rochelle morphs into some version of herself I have no knowledge of. She shushes the baby, walks to the small counter where the hotel-room-sized refrigerator is, takes out a bottle, and then sticks it inside some contraption as she rocks the baby on her hip.

I look over at Bric, who is watching everything she does with a look of fascination. "What's that thing?" he asks.

I kinda want to know too, but wasn't gonna ask.

"A bottle warmer," Rochelle says, turning to face us. "You came at a bad time. She needs to eat and then nap. We were on the road since early this morning. So we're both tired."

"Where did you come from?" I ask.

Rochelle pulls on her t-shirt. "Here."

Pagosa Springs. "Where are you going?" I ask, wanting to tick off as many questions as I can before she boots us out. Because we are definitely being booted out of here in a matter of minutes.

"Jackson," she says. "I was gonna go up to Jackson."

"You have a place up there?" Bric asks.

"I'm gonna check into a hotel for a while."

"Good luck with that," I say. "There's no rooms in Jackson the week after Thanksgiving. So unless you booked ahead, you're fucked."

"Swearing," Bric says, tired of repeating himself.

I roll my eyes, which makes Rochelle smile. "I'll be OK."

"One night then?" I ask. "You came here for one night to what? Fuck with us again?"

"I called Chella, not you."

"Yeah, I heard. Passing through. Don't tell Quin."

The little bottle warmer thing dings and the baby must know that means food, because she suddenly gets very fussy. Rochelle turns away, juggling the baby and the bottle for a few seconds, until she gets everything straight, and then walks over to the couch and plops down with the baby in her lap.

Tiny hands eagerly clasp around the bottle and bring it to her mouth. Seconds later there is the sound of sucking. I want to touch her. Both of them. I want to walk over to that couch, sit my ass down, and be with them. But I won't. I refuse to give in that easily.

"We should go," Bric says. "It was nice, I guess, Rochelle. But you do what you have to do."

"Do what you have to do?" I say, shaking my head in disbelief. "No. Nope. I want a DNA test. I want that right now, before you leave town, Rochelle. I want a fucking DNA test."

When I look at Bric he's got a weird smug look on his face. But I ignore it and pull out my phone, doing a search for paternity testing in Denver. "Here's one." I press the contact number and let it ring though.

"You're doing this now?" Bric asks.

"She's passing though," I say. "If not now, when?"

"Rochelle," Bric says, swiping my phone from me and ending the call.

"What the fuck, asshole?" He opens his mouth and I cut him off. "If you bitch at me one more time about swearing in front of a baby who can't even talk yet, I'll punch you in the eye."

Bric looks back to Rochelle. "You don't have a room booked, right?"

She shakes her head.

"Then you're not in a hurry. Passing through can mean a lot of things. It can mean one night. It can mean one week. It can mean one month."

"Not really in any hurry," she says.

"So just... hang out for a little bit. Let's talk about this stuff. Take more time with it. You're at least staying one night. You already have the room. So we'll go, let you have time with the baby. Get settled. And we'll come back tomorrow."

They both look at me like I'm the one in charge here.

"OK," she finally says. "I can stay a few days. Try to work this out."

"Good," Bric says. "Perfect. You happy?" he asks, looking at me.

No. No, I'm not happy at all. I'm fucking pissed off.

But Bric moves on and says, "You?" He looks at Rochelle. She nods. "Perfect. Then we'll get going and one of us will call you in the morning."

Bric turns towards the door and I follow, snatching my phone from his hand as he passes me. I don't want to look back as I turn the corner towards the short hallway. But I do.

And it hurts. So bad.

God, I want them.

CHAPTER FIVE

BRIC

When I get back to the Club I head straight for my office. I have two messages from Jordan asking if I have anyone in mind from the Club to take the last girl's place.

The Club girls never work out. I knew this once, but had forgotten it. Rochelle was around too long. Important things like that slipped my mind, even though they were hard-won lessons back in the early years.

I text him back. *No. I'm taking a break.*

I don't wait for his response—I know he's in court this afternoon, so he can't answer anyway. So I take out the card the former FBI guy gave me, and call Rochelle's cell phone using the landline.

"Hey," she says in a soft voice, picking up on the first ring.

"That baby sleeping?"

"Almost."

"I think it went well."

"If you say so," she whispers. I hear rustling, then some hushed shushing, like she's trying to walk away from the baby without upsetting her. And then she's back, talking normal. "Smith? What the hell was that?"

"I have no idea," I say truthfully. "I really have no clue why he was so angry."

"And the money? I feel dirty, Bric."

"Don't be dumb. His money's just as good as Quin's."

"But it's the reason why he sent it. *Stay away.* Fuck him. Just fuck him."

"Anyway," I say, changing the subject. "I think Quin's on board."

"With me?"

"No." I laugh.

"Why is that funny?"

"Because you hurt him, Rochelle. I'm pretty sure he came to see you just for the baby. And he thinks it's his. One hundred percent his. So we probably should let him do that DNA test."

"If he's not coming around for me then... he's coming around for you? Are you guys getting someone else?"

She sounds worried. Maybe genuinely worried that this might not work out the way she's planned.

When she told me she didn't want to take part in my plan down in Pagosa Springs yesterday I thought, *OK. Well, I tried.* But then she explained. She didn't want me taking her back, presenting her like a gift, making things right. Starting the game again, just the three of us.

But she had her own plan. It's not much different from mine, except she wanted to show up in Denver herself, call Chella—whom I knew would go straight to Quin—and Quin would show up at her hotel room and have the confrontation. For lack of a better word to call it.

She didn't want me to bring her into the game because that would make me number one. Which makes sense. I'm not her number one, Quin is. He needs to be the guy to make the first move.

I didn't count on Smith being so dead set on going over there with him. Or dragging me along, for that matter. I figured it would be a one-on-one. Just Rochelle and Quin.

I imagined some tears from Rochelle. Quin comforting her. Then some make-up sex.

Bam, we'd set the stage for me to propose a new game. Quin would object, but I know he misses it. And he admitted that to me before we left the Club. So he'd give in.

My life would be back on track. Maybe not the quad I'm used to, but a threesome arrangement is almost as good. It's practically what we had before, right? Smith was never around. It was just me and Quin. But last time I wasn't invited into their relationship much. Every once in a while, but not often.

This time it'll be different.

And if Smith didn't interfere like that, we'd probably be on our way.

But he did. Asshole. And now we're not quite there yet.

Rochelle came here expecting to be let back in. So it would be a big blow if she had to leave town with her tail between her legs. Worse yet, if she tried to stay and was overlooked when it came to Quin's choice in the new game.

"I don't know, Rochelle. We kinda had a talk today and I admitted I'd like him to play along again. Of course, no mention of your name. That was before we left the Club. But he was willing to give it a try. Just me and him and whomever we decide to choose."

"So you might choose someone else?"

"Was I just speaking another language?"

"Don't be an asshole. And ease up on the swearing-in-front-of-the-baby shit. It's not like you to care about things like that. You're only saying that because I said something to you yesterday."

"But you didn't correct Quin or Smith today."

"I didn't have a chance. You started being weird about it."

"Anyway," I say, looping the conversation back around to my point. "I think he'll come around. Listen, I gotta go. Lots of shit to do this time of year."

"Parties?" she says.

"Is that a hint of wistfulness I detect? You better get over it if it is. Because this game won't look anything like the last one."

"Explain," she says.

"When I know more, I will. But I won't know more until Quin and I talk it over. What time does the baby usually nap? In the morning?"

"Around ten—ten-thirty. She wakes up early so she's usually tired around then. Why?"

"You'll see. Kiss that baby for me. I really do gotta go."

I hang up before she can answer back and lean into my chair.

She looked good today. Much better than yesterday even though she was only wearing jeans and a t-shirt. Yesterday she looked lonely. Today she looked... hopeful.

I might be hopeful too. I mean, Jesus Christ. A few days ago, I was upstairs with Jordan losing the game—yet again. And today Rochelle is back. If everything goes well we're gonna be fucking her tomorrow. And then... who knows?

Rochelle isn't my dream girl, but she's good enough. She was only a fair submissive. She likes the spankings and a little bit of bondage. Blindfolding, tying her hands to the bed, and a few minutes with the gag in her mouth are all things we did together.

But Rochelle is never going to crawl across the floor to suck my cock. Or look up at me, crying beautiful silent tears as I fuck her mouth. She'd knee me in the balls if I ever tried to make her call me Master.

I have to laugh just thinking about it.

So, no. She's not really into the kind of kink I like. But that's what the Club is for, right? Rochelle is like the wife and the Club girls are like the mistresses.

Christmas is coming and even though Smith and Chella will be going to most of the parties themselves this year, I still have a few on my calendar. Rochelle is a good date. Someone I can take out in public. She knows what to do. How to act. What to say—and not say.

She's... trained.

It's a little derogatory. I'll admit to that. But it's also true. I invested three years of my life with her and Quin— why throw that away? I never wanted her to leave. Quin never wanted her to leave. Rochelle didn't even want to leave. She was hormonal, she said. Not thinking straight.

So now she just needs a little help to reconsider all her options.

I smile as I kick my feet up on my desk and stare out at the capitol building.

Quin wants her back, he's just playing hard to get. And Smith told me that he thinks Quin misses me while we were waiting for him to show up at the Club for lunch today. I think he does too. We had something good, man. It was good. No thinking, no awkwardness, no jealousy. Not enough to matter, anyway.

So this is my challenge. Make both of them reconsider their options. Get the three of us together alone so they can remember how easy it is.

It will be easy. I can feel it.

We're a little family. We had a small spat, but family is family.

Plus, there's a baby now. Our baby. No matter who that baby's father is, she's still ours. That right there might be enough glue to hold us together.

Hmmm. I think about this for a moment.

Maybe Rochelle is right about not getting a DNA test? I mean, I know why she doesn't want one. She doesn't want to share that baby with us. But it's too late. She's back, the baby is here, and Quin and I know about her.

Rochelle's game is over.

But... I could take Rochelle's side against Quin in this respect. Put that test off so none of us know who the real father is. That way we *have* to be a threesome.

Yes. Little Adley Bastille is our glue.

As long as none of us know who the real father is, we'll be together. I'll have my stability back, Quin will have Rochelle back, and Rochelle will be right back where she belongs.

In *my* game.

A new game.

The three of us together. All day, every day.

My mind is spinning with ideas. Plots and plans to get what I want. What we *all* want. It's not really all about me.

Well. I chuckle, feeling a little smug. It's mostly about me.

CHAPTER SIX

ROCHELLE

Adley is just about asleep when a loud knock at the door startles her heavy eyes open.

"Shhh," I say, swaying her in my arms in front of the window. It's sunny today and the sun makes her sleepy.

The knock comes again and I want to kill whoever is on the other side of that door right now. I walk across the living room and down the small hallway. Opening a hotel room door is never a quiet affair. There's all those serious locking mechanisms and you really have to pull. So by the time I get the door open Adley is awake.

Bric's knuckles are poised to knock again and Quin is standing off to the side.

"You woke her up," I say. "I was just trying to get her to sleep."

"Sorry about that," Bric says, pushing past me to enter the room.

Quin waits for an invitation, so I oblige by waving my hand and saying, "Come in," as I turn away and go back to the window. Adley is having none of it. Bric comes up beside me and whispers, "I told you to be getting out of the shower. And why is she still awake?"

I vaguely recall my phone ringing this morning at six AM. Even more vaguely the one-sided conversation with Bric that came afterward. I have no memory of this shower request.

"The long t-shirt is a nice touch though. Shows off your legs. I'm going to presume you're not wearing underwear?"

"Am I interrupting something?" Quin says behind us.

I look over my shoulder and see him sitting on the white leather couch, hands in front of him, leaning forward with legs slightly open, looking at me like... well, not quite like he used to.

We are a long way from where Bric thought we'd be today.

His suit is dark blue, his tie and pocket square are light gray, and his shirt is crisp white. He didn't shave this morning, so his face has just enough stubble to make him sexy, but not enough to make him unkempt.

His blue eyes track to my legs when I turn. I *am* wearing underwear—stupid Bric. But that's it. "This is what I wear to bed," I reply by way of explanation.

"I didn't say anything," Quin says, almost smiling.

"I know. But you were thinking it."

We sigh together, thinking of all the ways we know each other intimately. And all the ways we are strangers now.

"Is it a bad time, Rochelle?" Quin asks. "We can leave."

"No," Bric says, pressing into me a little. He's warm, and big, and overbearing.

"She needs a nap," I say, still looking at Quin.

"Here," Bric says, reaching for Adley. "I got this."

Quin covers his mouth with his hand to hide a laugh. I'm not amused. "Forget it, Bric. You'll never get her to sleep. She's awake now. And she's probably hungry."

"I can feed her. Where's that bottle warmer thingy?"

"Bottle warmer thing? Since when are you an expert in feeding babies?" Quin asks.

"I looked it up online. Come on, I'll take her so you two can work this out."

"Work what out?" I ask.

"It's just an expression," Bric says. "You people are so literal today." He reaches for Adley like this is a done deal. I hand her over, more out of surprise than anything else, and Elias Bricman—the man who hates children and doesn't even try to hide it—cuddles her and walks off towards the bottle warmer I have set up by the small fridge in the dining room. "Where do you keep the... milk or whatever?"

Quin is looking at me the whole time. Wondering something.

I hope he's not wondering why he's even bothering with me.

The bottles for the day are all filled and ready, neatly lined up inside the fridge. I get one out, put it in the warmer, and press the start button.

"What does your mommy do all day, Adley? Hmmm?" Bric is talking to my daughter like he's known her forever. "Mope?" he asks, looking up at me to smile. He sways a little, like he knows just what to do with a baby. "Pine for Quin and me?" He looks over at Quin for that one. "Does she miss us?" The warmer dings, but before I can grab the bottle, Bric has it in hand. "Just plug it into her mouth, right?" Bric asks, walking off towards the bedroom down the hall. "I got this."

"Who is he?" I ask, watching him disappear.

"I have no idea," Quin says.

When I turn to Quin, he's leaning back into the couch cushions, both his arms spread along the top, one foot propped up on one knee. They always need to be in control. He was off his game a little yesterday but he's got it back now.

"So," Quin says, looking up at me with those piercing blue eyes. "You've got something to say to me?"

"I'm sorry," I say.

"I know, you said that already. That's it?" he asks, looking like he's ready to get the fuck out of here.

I take a deep breath as I cross the living room. I catch a glimpse of myself in the mirror and stop to frown. "Jesus Christ. I look like shit." My hair is a mess. I look like I just crawled out of bed, when really, I've been up for hours. I'm pale, even though I still have a tan from being outside in the hot springs almost every day for months. And there is no way to hide the dark circles under my eyes. I was up all night thinking about how my life just changed. I had just barely fallen asleep when my phone rang this morning. And then Adley wanted to wake up after that.

"Rochelle," Quin says, making me look back at him. "Do you have something to say to me or not?"

I nod my head slowly as I walk over to the couch and kneel down on the cushion, facing him. "I loved you."

"So that's why you left?"

"No," I say. "I left because I got the impression... you... liked the way things were, I guess. You were comfortable."

"And you weren't? You wanted more?"

"I was pregnant, Quin." I'm starting to get angry. "I felt very alone. And you and I both know that if I kept the baby and tried to stay, Bric would have none of it."

We both look towards the hallway. He's talking to the baby in there in a low voice. Not even spying on us.

"Maybe," Quin says. "But"—he waves his hand at the soft words coming from the bedroom—"maybe not."

"Things are like this now because you've had time to think about it. But if I had sprung it on you back then, it would've been different. Everything would've been different. You know as well as I do that Bric was not about to give up his fun for me."

"You didn't need him, Rochelle. You had me."

"I had you with him," I say. "We weren't a couple, we were pretending. We were a trio. And then I went and fucked up and ruined it. So I'm sorry for that too. I didn't want to ruin it. I wanted more with you, but I *was* happy with the way things were."

Quin stares at me for a few seconds. Like he's trying to decide if he accepts that answer. "And you're just as happy now that it's over?" he finally asks.

"I'm... OK." I say. "Happy, yes, in lots of ways. But I miss you. I miss what we had."

"Me and you?" Quin asks. "Or the three of us?"

"Both. I miss all of us. Well," I amend, "I don't miss Smith at all."

Quin smiles a little and looks away. "He's out of the game, anyway."

"So you're still playing? You have a girl?"

"No," Quin says. "I quit the Club a long time ago. Yesterday was actually the first time I talked to Bric in a while. Six months, almost."

"You're mad at him?" I ask.

"Was," Quin says, looking back at me.

God, he's handsome. Quin is the all-American man. Light hair, light eyes. Tall muscular body. And he's even a nice guy. He's got manners and he's educated. Polite and friendly with almost everyone. I don't know much about his family, other than his dad died before we met. He never talked about them to me at all, but I never got the impression he hates them. Which is... unusual, from my perspective.

"But now that you're here..." He sighs. "And you didn't have an abortion—"

"Who told you I had an abortion?"

"Bric. Well, Chella." Quin shakes his head. "It's a long, stupid misunderstanding."

"And you're ready to be friends with him again?"

"Maybe?" Quin says. "In fact, before we came over here yesterday he was asking me if I wanted to find another girl."

"Will you?" I ask. I know this is part of Bric's plan, but it makes my heart beat fast just thinking about them doing... what they do with someone other than me. They're mine. They were mine for three years. Never has another girl stayed for so long. I was the perfect player. They know this.

At least they did. Maybe I just need to remind them?

"I don't know, Rochelle." Quin lets out a long exhale. "I still..." He stops to stare into my eyes. "The baby is so pretty. I'd love to get to know her. We should get a DNA test as soon as possible," he says, totally taking the conversation in the wrong direction. "To avoid any confusion."

"Because if you're not her father—"

"I am her father," Quin says, looking at the hallway. Bric has stopped talking and things are very quiet in the bedroom.

"You don't know that."

"I do. I feel it."

"Then why do you need a DNA test?"

"I don't. But Bric will. So he knows she's mine and not his." He gives me a sidelong glance. "To keep the facts straight."

I nod my head, looking out the window. "So that's all you need to know?"

"I need to know what the fuck is going through your head right now."

"How do I answer that?" I ask. "I love you. That's it. That's all. And you're only here for the baby so..."

He puts his hand on my bare thigh. It sends a tingle of electrifying anticipation through my whole body. "Don't be stupid. That's not the only reason I'm here. I called you hundreds of times. I left message on your voicemail. You never called back."

"I got rid of that phone. I didn't have access."

"I'm just saying, I tried, Rochelle. I really, really wanted you back and I tried my best."

"And now you're not sure, are you?" I can feel tears welling up in my eyes.

"I don't know what to think. I still want you but I certainly don't fucking trust you. You could've left a note. You could've called at some point."

"I did call—" Shit. I forgot that Bric never told him that.

"When?" Quin asks, his voice suddenly edgy and rough.

"Right after Adley was born. I called the Club, but I didn't know what to say, so I just hung up." Not a lie. Just... not completely true, either.

His hand on my thigh slides up to grab my hip. "What do you want?" he asks.

81

I force myself to look at him, no matter how hard I want to look away. A tear falls down my cheek and he swipes it away with a fingertip.

"Come on, Rochelle. Just tell me what you want."

"You." I shrug. "Bric. I want all of it back. I want to stay. I want to redo everything. I want another chance, Quin. I want another chance."

"I heard my name," Bric says, coming back into the living room. "What'd I miss?"

Quin doesn't answer.

Bric walks over to the couch and sits down on the other side of me. "No one wants to fill me in?"

"She wants to play the game with us again," Quin says.

"That's not what I said. I want you guys back. That's what I said."

"What does that even mean?" Quin asks.

"I get it," Bric says, saving me for once. Good God, this was his fucking idea and he goes and leaves me here to sort out all these messy feelings on my own. "A new game, Rochelle?"

"Fuck that." Quin sighs. "I'm not into it."

"You're not into me?" Bric asks. "Or her? Because you just told me yesterday that we were gonna find a new girl. Just the two of us. And now that Rochelle's back"—I look over my shoulder in time to see Bric shrug—"why not just play with *her*?"

"Because it's not a fucking game, Bric. It's a whole lot of feelings." Quin hesitates, then adds, "And the baby. Once we get that DNA test we'll know who the father is and things will be different."

"So why get a test at all?" Bric asks. "Why not just let that shit ride? Do we need a test?" Bric is looking at me.

This is a new position. Last night he said we should give in to the test.

"I mean, look, Rochelle. I'm sure you want to know who your baby's father is and all, but does it matter? If you want to be with both of us?"

I look back at Quin, his eyes squinting down in confusion.

Oh, I get it. If no one knows who the father is, then they're both the father. "As long as it's unknown, there are two equal possibilities."

"We're both the father," Quin says, catching on. "Even if we're not."

"Exactly," Bric says, wrapping one hand around my front to squeeze my breast. Quin is still holding onto my hip bone, like he's afraid to let go. "Why do we care who the father is? If we're gonna be together as a threesome anyway?"

"Are we?" Quin laughs.

"Aren't we?" Bric replies. His hand lets go of my breast, falls down to where my hand is resting on my leg, and cups it in his palm. He leans into my back as he uses my hand to reach across Quin's lap and rub his crotch.

Quin isn't hard, but it only takes a few seconds. I feel him grow bigger under our touch.

"Come on, you guys," Bric says, rubbing Quin using my hand. "This is us, right? We're good at this."

"I don't know if I want to play another fucking game," Quin says.

"Who says it's a game?" Bric replies, making my hand squeeze Quin's growing cock. "It's a ménage à trois. A family of three. Well, four," he corrects. "But the baby belongs to all of us, right? We made her. The three of us. We don't need a test to tell us that."

Bric begins to unbuckle Quin's pants. He leans into my neck and whispers, "Take off his shirt."

I look at Quin, who stares down at Bric's movements, then looks up at me with more lust in his eyes than I can ever remember. I stare into him as I reach for his tie, loosen it, and then slip it over his head and drop it to the floor.

Bric stands up. Quin's gaze tracks him as he tugs on my over-large t-shirt until I lift my arms and he slips it off. I have no bra on, so Quin's eyes immediately go to my breasts. They are fuller than they used to be. Round and perfectly shaped. Quin just stares as Bric begins to undress himself. The jacket, the tie, the shirt—all come off as I unbutton Quin and hold his shirt open to reveal his muscled chest. I place the palm of my hand on his chest, flat against his beating heart, and look up to find Bric hovering over us, ready to move forward.

I have had sex with both of them many times and it's always Bric who makes the first move. But this morning he waits for Quin. There is a moment when I know for sure Quin will put a stop to it. Everything will end, they will leave, I will go on my way to Jackson Hole, and this opportunity will disappear.

But then, like he's reading the fear in my mind by studying my face, Quin says, "Take out my cock."

CHAPTER SEVEN

Rochelle grips the thick girth of my shaft and begins to pump. I know not one good thing will come of this decision to turn back, but I can't stop it now. She's right here in front of me. After all this time, she's back. She's practically on top of me. Her eyes are begging me for more.

And Bric—well, fuck it. He's right. We're a trio. We've always been a trio. It's one hundred percent going back to the way things were.

Is it so bad? To have them both again, just the way I liked it?

Bric is pressing on the top of Rochelle's head, urging her face down. Her hot breath hits the tip of my cock and then...

Fuck.

I lean my head back and close my eyes, one of my hands on top of Bric's to keep her mouth there. Right... *there*.

Goddamn it, that feels good.

Her tongue. It does the most amazing things to me. I make the mistake of opening my eyes and looking down. I look up quickly, catch Bric's satisfied smile. He's almost laughing at me and I don't care. I haven't had sex in so long.

Bric pulls Rochelle's panties down and leaves them around her thighs. He grabs her hips with both hands and lifts her up, so she's on her knees, sideways across my lap. I slap one cheek as he places his face between her legs and licks her.

Rochelle stops what she's doing to my cock, pausing long enough to enjoy that for a second. But then she's back, her mind on me.

I grab her hair into a ponytail as she sucks. So I can see her. Watch her. Her hand twisting up and down my shaft each time she dives down.

Bric still has his pants on, so he pulls his cock out through his zipper and starts stroking himself as he licks her pussy.

Rochelle squeals softly.

"Get on top of Quin," Bric tells her.

Rochelle straddles my legs without comment. We've been here before. All of this is very familiar. So as soon as she does that I reposition myself so I'm leaning against the arm of the couch, my feet slipping right between Bric's legs, so he's straddling my knees.

Now I can see her face as she stares down at me, her hands pressing on my chest as Bric positions himself behind her ass. I reach between my legs, grab my cock, and slip inside her.

She feels like yesterday. Like no time has passed at all. We are not in a hotel room, one year later. We are in the Club apartment. We are in our bed. We are in our old life.

Her long, golden hair falls over her shoulders and sways back and forth. Slowly. As she moves with me inside her.

I hear the crinkle of a condom wrapper and realize Bric's being careful.

Fuck careful. I don't give one flying fuck about careful right now.

His face dips between her legs. I can feel his warm breath on my balls as he licks her. Makes her wet for him. We slap her at the same time. My hand coming down on the side of one thigh, Bric's hand coming down on the other. Everything is so easy. So familiar.

When Bric slips his dick inside her ass it all comes back to me. Why we had this arrangement in the first place. I can feel him and her at the same time. We move together, but opposite.

I fist Rochelle's hair harder and pull her down, all the way on top of my chest, and I kiss her. Her mouth opens and all I hear in my head is *more, more, more.*

"I'm sorry," she whispers as Bric fucks her hard from behind. Our foreheads pressed together. Her small, soft hands on either side of my face as she looks into my eyes.

"Forget it," I whisper back. "We're here now."

I wrap my arms around her middle, holding her close to me. Holding her tight so she's forced to rest her head on my shoulder and just… let Bric do whatever he wants. Rochelle on top of me again. It's all I need for now.

Small moans start coming out of her mouth. But with each thrust they get louder and louder, until Bric reaches forward and wraps a hand around her mouth. He pulls her up off my chest, forcing her to sit astride me, one knee tucked into the sofa cushion, the other hanging off the couch, her foot braced on the floor.

I grab her tits and squeeze, then slip my fingers between her legs and find her clit with my thumb, pressing my hand against the soft skin of her belly.

Her eyes are open and she's sucking in air through her nose because Bric is trying to keep her from screaming as we fill her up, trying to make her come. Her whole body writhes on top of me, her skin slick with sweat, her long hair fisted tightly in Bric's hand.

I watch her face when the release washes over her. She always closes her eyes and just... melts. Bric lets her go in that same instant, so she falls forward, becoming mine again when I hold her tight and keep her close.

I come too. A wave of relief that consumes me. My whole body tenses up. I hold Rochelle close, almost squeezing her. I never want to let her go.

I never want to be hurt again.

Stop it, I tell myself. *Not now. Do not think about all that shit now. Just enjoy it.*

Bric tenses up too. His cock pushing against me inside her. His pulsing equal and opposite to mine.

I look at him as he comes. His eyes are open. Staring right at me. Reminding me of what I've been missing this past year.

A few seconds later he slaps her ass and falls off to the side of the couch, ripping the condom off and throwing it in a small metal trash can nearby.

"You're sitting on my legs, asshole," I say, trying to pull them away and give him room.

"Move then," Bric growls, slumping back against the cushions and closing his eyes.

Rochelle is still on top of me. Neither of us make any move to get up.

We just sit there, waiting. Our heavy breathing the only sound in the room.

"You gotta get the fuck out of this room, Rochelle," Bric says.

"Yeah," I say. "I agree. It's way too much money."

"Money?" Bric says, opening one eye to look at me. "Fuck the money. Can you imagine how many people have had sex on this couch?"

"Gross." Rochelle laughs. "You're such a mood-killer."

"Adley can't live here," Bric says. "I can't even think about her little pudgy knees crawling across these floors. You need to leave today. And next time you want to scream during sex," he continues, pointing a finger at Rochelle—which only I see because she's all melty and relaxed on top of me—"remember who put that little chubby pumpkin to sleep for you."

"Thank you," Rochelle mumbles. Her soft words vibrate against my skin.

"No problem. But for real," Bric says, getting up and slapping Rochelle's ass once more for good measure. "You're leaving here tonight." He starts putting his shirt back on.

I don't move. I might never move.

"I gotta get back to the Club. Quin, pick Rochelle up at six tonight. I'll text you an address. She's staying there from now on."

I have a lot of questions about that last request, but I don't bother. Bric wants to be in control of living arrangements, fine with me.

A few minutes later he's gone and Rochelle and I are still holding each other in the exact same spot. Like we're afraid to move.

"Are you going back to work?" she finally asks.

I play with her hair and sigh. "Yeah. I need to think things through on my own."

"Are you sorry we did this?"

"No," I say. "Are you?"

"No. I just want to make sure you're OK with the arrangement."

"Why wouldn't I be? It's like going back in time, right? Picking up where we left off. I liked how it was."

"I know. That's why I didn't want to ruin it."

"You realize that makes no sense, right? Leaving fucked it all up."

"I'm sorry."

"I'm not trying to make you feel bad. I'm just saying, I liked it then and I like it now. I'm glad you're back. I'm glad we're here. I can't ask for much more than this. But I want more than this. And I'm still angry, Rochelle. You cannot expect me to just give in and let it all go after one fuck. I have to process shit."

She's silent for a little bit. Thinking over my answer. "You're OK with us not getting a DNA test?" she asks, shifting her body so she's slightly off to the side of me, one hand on my stomach, tracing circles over my muscles.

I've got my arm underneath her, still afraid to let go. "Why bother, right?" I say. "Bric's right. She's ours. As long as you're OK with it, I'm OK with it."

"Do you think he's going to make me move back into the Club?"

"Fuck that," I say. "I didn't get the impression that's what he meant, but if it was, fuck that."

"Yeah, I don't want to go back there. We're past that now."

I agree, nodding my head as I continue to play with her hair. We are past that now. "Do you need anything?" I ask. "For today? For Adley? Or yourself?"

"No, I don't think so."

"Were you really going up to Jackson?"

"Yes. I've been down in Pagosa Springs this whole time and I just needed a change. Do you know where Pagosa is?"

"Little dinky river town on the way to Mesa Verde," I say, picturing it on the map. "My parents took me down there to see those cliff dwellings when I was a kid. Kinda cool, but way too far away from everything."

"Yeah, very far away. But holy shit, Quin." Rochelle props herself up on one elbow. "You'd think it was Aspen the way people buy vacation homes down there." She smiles at me, like she's got a lot to say about this subject. "My only friends were a bunch of rich Stepford Wives who all had nannies and thought it was normal to own three houses and only live in them a few months out of the year."

"You should've called me," I say, suddenly sad picturing her down there all alone with the baby.

"I'm sorry," she says again. And then she leans in and kisses me. It's not the same kind of kiss we had during sex. Just a soft one that says so much more. "I'll never do it again," she whispers. "I promise. I will never leave you again."

I really hope she keeps this promise. I made it through this year without her—barely. But now that she's back I can fully appreciate how fucking awful it was.

"I've played that night at the Club garden party back in my head a thousand times, wondering how things might've been different if I had just said what I felt."

"You loved me with Bric, right? That's why you didn't want to say it?"

"Is it wrong?" I ask. "I'm leaning towards yes, but it doesn't *feel* wrong."

She collapses on top of me again with a sigh. "I like it too. I love you a lot more than him. You should know that. Or maybe just in a different way. But I love him too. Do you think that's wrong?"

I shrug. "If I didn't love Bric in some way, I wouldn't share you with him, would I?"

"I guess not." She laughs.

"We'll see how it goes. But if you ever want to stop this again, Rochelle, if you ever want to leave, you just need to tell me and I'll let him know we're done."

"You'll be able to walk away from him?" she asks.

"I did it once already, right? I walked away and did my own thing for a while."

"But were you happy?" she asks.

Was I happy? Fuck, no. I was miserable. But something tells me this is not the right answer. Not yet, anyway. "I'm happy now," I say instead. "And that's all that matters."

CHAPTER EIGHT

ROCHELLE

After Quin leaves I have a sudden wave of loneliness. Adley sleeps past lunchtime and if we were home we'd be getting ready to go out to our special pool in the hot springs.

Home? Why did I just refer to Pagosa as home?

That's not my home. This place isn't my real home either, but it's the closest thing I have. I grew up in Palm Springs. The desert. Mild winters and summers so hot, you really can fry an egg on the sidewalk.

I hated it there. Hated it. And yeah, most of my hate has nothing to do with the city or the weather. But that hate lingers.

My cell phone rings about an hour after Quin leaves. I know who it is, so I pick it up and say, "How can I help you, Mr. Bricman?"

"That went well, right?"

"Better than I could've hoped," I say, trying not to sound disappointed.

"What's wrong?" Bric asks, picking up on my melancholy.

"How long do you think he'll want to do this?" I ask. "The three of us? Forever?"

"Forever?" Bric laughs. I roll my eyes, because I know his view on relationships and forever. "Nah. Why, you're tired of me already?"

"Not you, really. Just… I'd like something normal. Eventually."

"What's normal?"

"Well, Bric, it's definitely not a ménage à trois."

"Says who?"

It's a losing battle with him. He thinks everything that happens in that Club is normal. "Never mind."

"Hey, if I'm a third wheel, just let me know and I'll bail."

"It's not you I'm worried about. It's Quin. We kinda talked and he's into it."

I can almost hear Bric smile on the other end of the phone. "So what's the problem?"

"Nothing, yet. But like you always say, there's no such thing as forever."

"So just enjoy it while it lasts," he says.

"I don't want to lose this new game," I admit.

"Well, you won the last round. Your chances of winning are good, brat."

"Did I win?"

"You're here, aren't you? That's never happened before. In fact, Rochelle, you're a whole bunch of firsts for us. First girl to play for three years. First girl to get what you wanted. First girl to make Smith Baldwin quit early." We both laugh at that. "First to turn back and play again."

"I don't want to play though. I want it to be real. I told you that."

"It's real," he says, frustrated. "What's not real about it?"

Good God. This man. He has no clue.

"I'm serious," he says. "What part of this is tripping you up?"

"He wants me with *you*, Bric."

"So?"

"So what if you leave? Where will I be then?"

"Why would I leave, Rochelle? I'm the guy who never complains. I'm the guy who sticks around. I'm the guy who makes it work, no matter what."

Right. Back to the game he's playing. I should run away right now. Never look back. Because Bric is always playing. He's always got a motivation. And that motivation has nothing to do with me. Or Quin, for that matter. As much as he likes to play up that tight friendship the three of them share, it's just a screen to keep the world from knowing who he really is.

"And you don't want *me*. You want us."

"Right," he says. I'm boring him, I can tell. "Which is why I don't see the problem."

But I do. I see it very clearly. As long as I want them both, we're fine. But the minute I don't want Bric, we're right back to where we started last year when I told Quin I loved him.

"You want me to bail out, Rochelle?"

"No," I say. I don't want him to bail. I need him to keep Quin.

"Good. Because I like that baby."

"What?" I laugh.

"I'm serious," he says. "She's so fucking cute I just want to squeeze her. She had her little fingers all wrapped around my hand while I was feeding her today. God, I can't stand it. We make good babies together."

"I have no idea what to say to that, other than you don't know for sure that you're her father."

"Doesn't matter. I like her. I'm digging that little pumpkin and I'm gonna spoil her rotten."

"That's what I call her," I say, laughing a little. Feeling maybe just a little better.

"She's like a little chubby pumpkin. Did she trick-or-treat this year?"

"She was five months old, Bric. No."

"Good. Next year will be her first time and I'm gonna pick that costume out."

"Whatever."

"Holy fuck, you know what I just realized?"

"What?"

"Christmas is coming up. OK, I gotta go. I have so much shit to do. See you tonight and kiss that pumpkin for me."

He hangs up before I can respond. Again.

What a strange turn of events. Never in a million years would I have pictured Elias Bricman as a doting father.

Maybe he's not so bad after all.

At five-thirty Quin knocks on my hotel-room door with a bellhop and a luggage cart. Ten minutes later we're downstairs packing all my things into Quin's Suburban. I've been telling him about my car since he appeared at the door, but he waves me off and pays the hotel to have it driven over to wherever we're going.

Our destination is a building on Wynkoop Street, near Union Station. I know where we are before Quin even pulls into the garage.

"This is Bric's place, right?"

"Is it?" Quin asks, shutting off the truck and taking a look around.

"He brought me here that first time we met. I was telling him about how much I loved the new lofts near the station and he started bragging about his new place. So he brought me here to show it off."

"I've never even been here. I knew he had a place, but I always pictured him down in Cherry Creek with all the other assholes in this city. He stays at the Club as far as I know."

If it bothers Quin that Bric is bringing me to his home, he doesn't show it. I get the baby and put her in the stroller, and then help Quin with the stuff I'll need right away. The spot we park in is very close to the elevator, right next to Bric's car. Quin punches a button—which acts like a buzzer.

"Buzzing you up," Bric's voice says through an intercom.

The elevator doors open, we load all my stuff inside, and a few seconds later the elevator doors close and we ascend up to the top floor.

I remember that first night pretty clearly. I'd been in town a while, but I'd been living in a hotel room. So when Elias Bricman, all dressed up in his five-thousand-dollar suit, asked me if I wanted to go home with him, I said sure.

We were at a party. A corporate event that I crashed because I knew he'd be there. I knew a lot about Elias Bricman before I met him at that party. I lost track of him at one point, so I went outside and there he was, looking up at the sky, unlit cigar in his mouth.

He turned and looked at me, pointed a finger, and said, "You don't belong here."

For a second I thought that meant he knew I was a crasher. But then I realized he was flirting. Bric is... kinda hard *not* to notice. Tall, dark, and handsome are just the first words that pop into your head when you meet him. The others are sexy-as-fuck, hot-as-fuck, and boy-I'd-like-him-to-fuck-me. His body is big with muscles, but not too bulky. He's well over six feet tall. And his face. Damn, that face. A perfectly-shaped square jaw, full lips that know exactly how to lick a girl between her legs, and the most unusual eyes. Dark, indigo blue. They look brown, almost black if you don't see them up close and in the light. But they're not. They're blue, like ink.

I was wearing a gold velvet dress I bought at a vintage clothing booth at a local antique mall. It was low-cut and in excellent condition, but very unusual. It got me noticed by Elias Bricman that night. And then Quin Foster too. The rest is history. I called it my lucky dress from that day forward. In fact, I think I met Chella wearing that dress as well. That day she bought my book.

The elevator doors open to half a dozen people bustling about. A few are dressed like maids and a few more look like workers. Some guy messing with the TV. Someone over by one of the windows with a drill. And another one talking to Bric off to the left.

Elias Bricman owns the coolest, trendiest loft condo in the whole state, I'm pretty sure of it. As soon as you step out of the elevator you know it's a special place. The design is that unique combination of modern and rustic you only find in the Rocky Mountains. Exposed brick walls and aged metal accents complement the honey-toned wooden ceiling beams that make you think of a very expensive barn. The floors are an ash-colored hardwood that might clash with the beams and the brick, but the metal accents pull it all together.

The main room is huge and long, with two distinct living sections. Right in front of the elevator is an intimate seating area with three chairs that face a tall window framing the city outside. I'm pretty sure Bric puts chairs in front of all his windows for Smith, even if Smith has never been here.

The loft is right in the heart of lower downtown Denver, or LoDo, as it's called by the locals, facing the west. Three blocks from Coors Field, across the street from Union Station, and a five-minute walk to the northern edge of the 16th Street Mall. The view of the mountains is worth a million dollars all by itself.

Off to the left is the main living area. Comfy couches and chairs surround a square glass and metal coffee table in front of the TV and gas fireplace. That whole wall is brick.

Even the pipes snaking down the walls and across the ceilings are decorative. None of those gaudy silver air vents to disrupt the decor. All the metal in this condo was made by an artist, and that includes the hot water pipes.

The dining room and kitchen are across the living room. An amazingly modern take on the crystal chandelier over the long wooden table complements the others hanging in the living area. The kitchen is white and sleek. Quartz countertops, industrial-sized stainless steel appliances, and a huge island big enough to have sex on.

But it's the bedroom that steals the show in this place. Of course it is, right? Bric is a man who knows how to do up a bedroom. It doesn't have doors, per se. They are sliding barn doors that stand twelve feet high and open at least ten feet wide—like he's planning on driving a tractor through them. And they've got alternating panels of aged wood and opaque-smoked glass.

Everything about this place says... *man*. And yet it's done so well a woman can't help but see herself living here.

I might've gasped for air when I saw this condo that very first night.

I might've pictured myself sleeping in that bedroom forever and ever, even if my reason for coming to Denver had nothing to do with forever and ever.

I might've said yes to his weird offer just to see if I could make things happen.

Of course, I ended up in the Club apartment. Which was disappointing, but only a little bit.

Bric is standing in the kitchen talking to some worker and pointing to the cabinets when he notices Quin and me. "Oh, good," he says. "You're here. OK. Everyone out. Thank you for coming on short notice. Send Margaret your invoices and she'll pay you tomorrow."

"What the hell is going on?" Quin absently asks as he pulls open one of the massive fridge doors and grabs a beer.

"Baby-proofing," Bric says, smiling at Adley. "So the pumpkin can't accidentally eat cleaning products and what not."

Quin shoots Bric an annoyed look over his shoulder, then pops the top off his beer with a bottle opener and takes a swig. "Baby-proofing?"

"Yeah, you know?" Bric says, walking over to me, grinning down at Adley. "Kids do weird shit like shake cleanser canisters and then lick the dust up off the floor. You gotta be one step ahead at all times." He reaches down to tickle Adley's chin. "Right, pumpkin?" She squirms in my arms and shoots him a gummy smile.

"What do you think, Adley? Do you like it here?" Then he looks up at me. "You do, right?"

I nod. "You know I love this place."

Quin walks over and sets his beer down on the island. "How come I thought you lived in Cherry Creek?"

"I have a place there," Bric says. "But I don't live there." He almost snorts. "With all those rich assholes? No thanks. I'm fine at the Club. This place rents out on one of those internet sites for a thousand dollars a night. But it's gonna be home base for Rochelle and the pumpkin from now on."

"That's awfully nice of you," I say, looking around. My dream, right? But when I glance at Quin, he's not reacting quite the same way. "Hey," I say to him. "I've never seen your place, Quin."

"No," he says, taking another sip of his beer. "Never have."

"Well, this is your bedroom, Rochelle," Bric says, pointing to my fantasy bedroom. "That one's for Adley." There's a second bedroom down the hall—if you can call it a hall, since it's eight feet wide, wide enough to have a small settee against the wall and not even notice. "I have a crib coming, but it won't be here for a few days. Assholes said they only had the floor model left in the store. And we're not letting our baby sleep in a floor model."

Our baby.

Quin's look quickly turns to annoyance. "You picked out a crib?" He leaves off the words, *Without me.* But we all hear them anyway.

Bric looks a little regretful. "Sorry, man. It was all last-minute, you know?"

"Whatever," Quin says, exhaling loudly.

A buzzer breaks the awkward silence that follows and Bric says, "That's the food," as he walks over to the elevator. "Rochelle, look." I follow him over to the elevator and watch as he points to the security panel. "When someone comes to visit, they buzz from the lobby or garage. There's a camera here, so you can see who it is. And a speaker, so you can ask them what the fuck they want. Then you buzz them up the elevator by pressing in the code. The code is just 1234." He pushes the buzzer and we watch the delivery guy get in the elevator. There's cameras in there too. "I only had two parking spots, but I bribed another tenant out of his this afternoon. The paperwork's not done yet, but it's open for you. It's right next to the one you parked in, Quin. We're all three right by the elevator."

"How many people in this building?" I ask.

"Ten. One condo for each floor. But there's two elevators. One on this side of the building, one on the other. So you only share the elevator with five."

"Cool," I say.

"Where's the outside space?" Quin asks.

"Well," Bric says. "This place doesn't have any."

"Oh, that's too bad," Quin says, his tone slightly sarcastic. "I guess Rochelle will have to bring Adley to my place for outside time."

"There's a park," Bric says, pointing to the window. "Down there by the river. Chella is only a few blocks away."

"Not really," Quin says. "It's not walkable. You have to go all the way around Union Station and then down 20th."

"Well, it's just temporary," Bric says. "And besides, Rochelle has a car. She can go to any park she wants."

Quin shrugs, like he's not crazy about the idea of me living here at all.

"Where do you live, Quin?" I ask, mostly to take his mind off whatever he's dwelling on right now. But also because I've never been there. And I'm interested. "A man's home says a lot about him."

"Down by the convention center," he says, a hint of regret in his answer. Like it's not a great place for parks either.

The elevator doors open and Bric walks off to get the food delivery.

"I'd like to see it," I say. "Whenever you have time."

"Sure," Quin says, looking around at Bric's amazing condo. "But it's nothing like this. So I hope you're not disappointed."

"Do you have outside space?" I ask, hiking Adley up on my hip. She's getting so heavy now. Her tiny baby days are almost over.

This is the right question. Because Quin smiles big. "You're gonna love my terrace. Bigger than this whole condo."

"Really?" I ask, trying to imagine his place. Then why would he think this is better than a Central Business District condo with a two-thousand-square-foot terrace?

"I have my own park." He laughs, feeling better about the arrangements. "Just wait."

"OK," Bric says. "Food's here." He holds up three giant white bags that say "Anna Ameci's South" on them. "I hope you like pasta." And then he looks at me. "I wanna see that pumpkin eat noodles."

"She doesn't eat noodles." I laugh. "She's six months old." But when I look back at Quin he's… thinking again.

What's going on with him?

CHAPTER NINE

BRIC

I set the food down on the table and start pulling out dishes. "Here, Rochelle. I got her a high chair today too. Just scoot that up to the table."

Rochelle hands the baby off to Quin, who takes her awkwardly, and walks over to the high chair looking confused.

"What's wrong with you?" I ask Quin. "You don't like the idea of them staying here?"

"You could've told me you were going baby shopping." He's shifting Adley in his arms, like he has no idea what to do with her. I want to intervene and help him out, but somehow, I think that might make things worse.

"Sorry, man. I didn't think about it. Just had to get shit done, you know?"

"Whatever."

Well, Mr. Foster has a jealousy gene. I never got this vibe off him before, so this is something to note. I know how to work the high chair, so I press the lever, flip the tray down, and then point to the seat. Quin sets Adley inside and I put the tray back up. "I had to look up how to use it too," I tell Quin, so he won't be annoyed at not being able to work the high chair. "But it's easy."

When I met Rochelle, Smith, Quin, and I were between games. We had just gotten rid of a girl who really sucked. She was my idea, so I was looking to make it up to Quin and Smith for the fuck-up. Rochelle kinda reminded me of a girl Quin brought into the game a couple years back. Someone he got along with. Someone he had fun with. Can't even remember her name now. Lacey? Lisa? Lindsey? I'm not sure. She was a stripper down at Old Joe's on Colfax. But she insisted she was only doing that to pay for her first year of college out in Utah. She informed me she had big plans. Was going to be a lawyer one day.

I didn't believe her for a second but it turns out she was telling the truth. She spent the summer with us and then she was out.

Quin didn't get sad over Lacey/Lisa/Lindsey. But he did remark that he'd miss her.

And Rochelle looked a lot like her—if you didn't count the dress. I figured that dress was from a thrift store and it was her only option. But I learned later she's into that kind of stuff. That's her style. If I had known she was one of those throwback flower girls I wouldn't have ever invited her into the game. Smith hates those girls.

I really don't give a fuck about a game girl's style. Or her personality. Or her hopes and dreams, for that matter. It's a fucking game. It's short-term. Temporary. Sex. That's all it is for me. As long as I find a woman attractive and she likes to please, I'm happy.

Hippy style aside, Rochelle is beautiful and she's submissive enough to keep me satisfied. Not a fighter. Not a complainer. Not even close to high-maintenance. I think Chella is probably more high-maintenance than Rochelle.

Most of the time she's easy-going. She's laid back. She's cool.

So I liked her when we were playing these past few years. She never once asked for more. She never once got mad at me for like—anything. And she was always there when she was supposed to be. She did what she was told.

She was... someone there... but never on my mind. Right?

That's about all I ask for in a player.

Be there, but not there, if that makes sense.

So I'm sure Quin picked up on that. I liked her but I never cared if she left. I fucked her on my days then went on with my life.

I was no threat to him and all his *feelings* back then.

But this baby changes everything.

I want her here. Things are different now. We're trying something new. We've never shared a girl outside the game, but if it can be done, it will be done with Rochelle.

I've never wanted kids, but this little pumpkin fascinates me to no end. And maybe it's just because I know I'm not ever going to be her father. Even if I was her real father, I'm not the father type.

But I am the uncle type. The semi-absent father *figure* who shows up with presents and then disappears for days, or weeks, or months. The one you call when you're sixteen and get arrested for smoking pot under a bridge somewhere when you should be in school. The one who would show up in court, pretending to be your father, and never tells your parents. The one who hands over money, no reason necessary. The *fun* one.

I feel the need to be the fun one with Adley. I don't want a kid. That kind of responsibility is not my thing at all. No, I'm not here to take that away from him. But I gotta keep Quin happy in this little arrangement or my surrogate kid might disappear.

"It's good," Rochelle says, shoveling a heaping forkful of pasta into her mouth. She follows that up with a shrimp and then goes for the meatballs.

Quin is oddly silent.

"So hey," I say, pointing my fork at Quin. "I guess we should get the rules out of the way, right?"

When we had our first meeting with Chella about the rules, it was pretty out of the ordinary. She was in control the whole time. *What's my dream? I don't need a dream, I'm just here for the sex.*

Rochelle's rule meeting was more like… OK. OK. OK.

Whatever we said, she was OK with it. You're gonna pay me thirty grand a month to fuck me on alternating days of the week? Sure thing. You want to give me a free place to live, buy my food, and give me gifts? I'm in. You want to dress me up like a socialite and take me to parties? No problem.

When we dished out our rules to Rochelle, she took it like a champ. No touching from Quin unless Bric is there? Kinky fun. Smith can do whatever he wants with me? I can deal. And when I told her no feelings—like none—or we'd kick her to the curb, well, she didn't even blink an eye at me.

She was on board.

Rochelle is as easy-going as they come.

This rule meeting is not going to be like that at all. I've been thinking it over ever since I left her place down in Pagosa Springs.

I need her to balk. I need her to resist. I need her to be uncomfortable. That is the only way Quin will think this is real. He wants to punish her. He might not admit that to us, or even himself. But that's what he wants. I know him. *I got this, Quin.*

"What rules?" Rochelle asks. "I thought this was—"

"Yeah, what rules?" Quin eyes me suspiciously.

I already know what Rochelle thinks about my rules. We discussed them earlier and I told her what to think. We're back together so she can snag Quin. Get him back. Make him commit to her. And I'm only here as the buffer.

And I know what Quin thinks too. I told him as well. Planted all the little ideas in his head. We're good together. We have fun. Rochelle is the perfect player. Things can go back to the way they were.

We will be happy again. My manipulative personality will make sure this game goes to plan. But there's a very fine line with these two. My happiness depends on both of them thinking they need me.

Here's the problem with that. I don't think Quin really needs much convincing to fall hopelessly back in love with Rochelle all by himself. And I don't think Rochelle needs me to keep Quin interested.

I need *them* way more than they need *me.*

Usually, I'm happy no matter what. Last year I was happy with Rochelle just as much as I was without her. But I like fucking girls with Quin, OK? I like it. He's the best player ever. Smith sucks at it. And he's out for good now, anyway. And Jordan, Jesus. If Smith sucks, then Jordan is absolutely awful. It will take me years to turn Jordan into Quin. *Years.*

I don't want to wait years for happiness. Why should I when I have these two right here, right now?

So I only have two choices. Keep Quin and Rochelle for myself and have a good time by manipulating them into thinking they need me. Or let them go be happy together and be left with an endless string of stupid games that never last and end badly.

This is a no-brainer.

Quin is too afraid to have a one-on-one relationship with Rochelle because he doesn't trust her, plus he only thinks in plural relationships right now. And Rochelle is too afraid to cut me loose because she thinks Quin won't stay if I go.

So why not use them both at the same time?

And I get to spoil that baby and never have any real responsibilities.

I almost laugh at my genius.

"I was thinking every other day," I say, answering them both at the same time. "You know. Mondays with Quin. Tuesdays with me. Etc. Etc. Etc."

"What about Sunday?" Rochelle asks, slurping up a noodle so loudly, Adley looks over at her mother and squeals.

"Do whatever you want on Sunday, just like always."

"Not quite like always," Quin says. "I wasn't technically allowed to see her on Sundays."

"You want to see her on Sundays?" I ask him. "Go ahead. I've got plans. So I won't be around."

Quin thinks about this. It's just my opening bid. I know exactly what he'll say next.

"I don't think we need rules," Quin replies.

"Me either," Rochelle says, placing a noodle on the tray in front of Adley.

I watch to see what she does. God, I can't stand the anticipation as her little fingers fumble for it. She fists it, breaks it in half, then makes another grab. A few jerky movements later she's got it up to her mouth.

"Ha!" I say. "I knew she'd like noodles."

"No rules," Quin says. "I can come here any time I want."

I shrug. "What do you think about that, Rochelle? No rules? Not much of a game, is it?"

She shrugs, unsure how to play this out. If she says she's into the game, Quin might take that to mean he's allowed to play along forever. Happily refusing to admit he's got a fear of commitment. Or... whatever the fuck his problem is. Honestly, Quin is a catch. He's a good boyfriend. He's always been a good Number Two. And he was Number Three a few times, and he was good at that too. It's being Number One that freaks him out.

He's absolutely Number One in this game. He just doesn't realize it yet.

But if Rochelle says she's not into the game, then why am I here?

Hmmm. What a dilemma. Poor Rochelle.

"How about we all just live here?" Rochelle finally offers.

"Here?" I say, trying to hide my amusement. "Like... just live together like a family? OK," I say. "I'm fine with that. If you guys don't mind that I'm at the Club every night doing Club things."

Rochelle squints her eyes at me. "Fucking other girls? Down in the basement?"

"See, this is why we might need rules, Rochelle. I own a sex club. I have to be down there most weekends. And if I'm down there, I'm gonna be *down* there, if you know what I mean."

"I don't care if you go down there," Quin says.

"Are you going down there?" Rochelle asks him.

Quin shrugs. "I might. I'm not really a member anymore, though."

"Ah, shut the fuck up, Quin," I say. "You're still a member."

Rochelle is well on her way to pissed off right now, but I don't care.

"Well, maybe I'll have a few extracurricular activities going on too," she says. "How about this for rules? Quin gets Monday and Tuesday, like always. You get Wednesday and Thursday, like always. And I get Friday through Sunday to myself."

"Sounds good to me," I say.

Quin isn't so sure. "What will you do on the weekends?"

She shrugs. "Whatever I want."

"Do you want to get paid?" I ask her.

"No." She scowls at me. "I don't need your money."

"Then why are you here?" Quin asks.

Ah ha! I almost don't stop the laugh.

"I was invited to play a game," she says.

"Then you have to get paid," Quin counters. "That's rule number one. We pay you to do what we want."

"Fine," Rochelle says, twirling pasta onto her fork. "Pay me then. Ten thousand a month, each."

"OK," I say. "I guess we've got all that settled. It's Wednesday, so it's my night. But look, Rochelle, I wasn't expecting this to be the rule. I really thought you'd go for the every other day thing. So I made plans for tonight."

"What plans?" she asks.

"Club things. You know I gotta be there most of the time. When people come in they expect to see me at the bar. Plus, Jordan already texted me like six times today asking about the next girl."

"The next—"

"I told him no, Rochelle," I say, cutting her off. Is she pretending right now? Or is this real jealousy? I'm not sure. She's a good fucking actress. "But I should go take care of it anyway."

"Oh," she says, putting her fork down. "Are you leaving?" she asks Quin.

"I guess I have to," he says. "Not my night."

I throw my napkin down and stand up. "Fuck it. We always get a free night, right?"

"Do we?" Quin asks, confused.

"Yeah, you know. The break-in-the-new-rules night. So how about you just stay with Rochelle and the baby tonight. Help her out and shit. Come by the Club tomorrow," I say to Rochelle, leaning in to kiss her.

It was just gonna be a small kiss. A peck, really. But she opens her mouth for me and we linger. I get a little hard, actually.

When I pull back, she's staring up into my eyes. "Come by?"

"Yeah," I say, my voice softer than it should be. "Both of you." I nod to Quin. "We'll have dinner and stuff. Together."

"I think that should be a rule," Quin says. "Meals together. At least once a day. So this doesn't get weird. We need to stay in touch. Be together. Alternating days can lead to... isolation."

Rochelle's face softens at his rule. Like he just said he loves her. "Yeah, OK. I'd like that."

I'm trying to figure out if this is a good idea or not, but before I can, Rochelle says, "Let's have breakfast tomorrow. Like we used to."

And damn... if that doesn't sound like a good idea after all. We've had some pretty kinky breakfasts in the back of the White Room in our day. "Breakfast," I say. "Sounds perfect."

And then I do something I probably shouldn't. I lean down and kiss her again. And this time my hand is on her leg. Sliding up to her pussy. She moans into my mouth a little, forcing me to make a decision.

Stay and fuck her?

Or get out quick.

I pull away. "See you tomorrow then."

The whole way back to the Club I have doubts. Is this really a good idea? I do like Rochelle. I certainly love fucking her.

The threesome was fun this afternoon, for sure. I love it. I can't wait to do it again. But Rochelle and I used to have a lot of fun on our nights out alone. I liked dressing her up, fucking her in the car, and going to parties. And I have a few parties coming up that will require a date.

I'm going to need her at those parties. And then we will go home together. Be alone together. End our night with dirty sex and it will all be very, very familiar again.

I'd forgotten about that. And that goodbye kiss back there... it just reminded me.

How the hell did I forget how much I enjoyed her?

Hmmm. I really need to make sure Quin is around most of the time. Or come up with excuses why I can't go over there on my nights.

I can't fall in love with Rochelle. That's ridiculous. That can't ever happen. She belongs with Quin.

Doesn't she?

I pull up to the valet at Turning Point and hand my car over. When I get inside Jordan is already at the Black Room bar, so I make my way over there and hold up a finger to the bartender to ask for a drink.

"Where have you been?" Jordan asks.

"Busy with Quin and Rochelle."

"So she's really back, huh? I heard."

"From who?" I ask. I never told him anything.

"Bumped into Smith at that little European cafe down the road. He was scoping it out for Chella. You guys are opening a tea room next door?" He nods his head in the direction of the new tea room.

"Yeah. What did he say?" I cannot even begin to imagine Smith chatting with Jordan about Rochelle.

"I told him our game was over. Started talking about a new girl I had in mind. And he said you weren't gonna play. You and Quin were back with Rochelle."

"Hmm," I say, taking my snifter of brandy from the bartender. Smith is on to me. That sneaky motherfucker might even be planning something I don't know about.

"Is that such a good idea?" Jordan asks.

"Why do you say that?"

"You know. Quin, man. He's all in love with her and shit. You just complicate things, right?"

I shrug. "Maybe we like things complicated?"

"Yeah?" Jordan laughs. "Well, if that's true, then why are you out? Why not kick the complications up a little? We could still have a game on the side."

"What do you have in mind?" I ask, knowing I should put a stop to this right now. But that kiss back there with Rochelle. Damn, it felt fucking... good. I'm kinda horny.

"Her?" Jordan says, nodding his head to a woman sitting in a booth. She's staring at us, looking very fucking uncomfortable.

"You brought her here for a night? Or?"

"Or?" Jordan says. "Your call."

The young woman is pretty. Oval face. Long dark hair flowing over her breasts. Slim body. Very slim, in fact. Kind of willowy.

"She's a ballerina," Jordan says. "New. Just got hired on over at Mountain Ballet for the spring season."

"Really?" I ask, unable to take my eyes off her now.

"She's got a very intriguing view of what rough sex means."

"Is that so?"

"Yeah," Jordan says, almost sighing. "She likes to be dom, but I said, no thanks."

"She a top?" I ask. "Fuck that. How old is she? Like twenty-three? She has no clue what it means to be a dom."

"I know, right?" Jordan laughs. "But I'm thinking we can put her back in her place." He gives me a sidelong glance. "If we try hard enough."

"Sounds like a helluva fight."

"Right?" Jordan is smiling so big, I have to chuckle.

"Well, if you can get her to submit for you, let me know. I like them highly trained."

"Your call," Jordan says, walking away. "But if I do get her to submit, then I won't need you, will I?"

I watch him as he slides into the booth next to her, his hands all over her body. She stiffens and slaps his face, making everyone in the bar look over at them for a moment.

Goddamn.

I wonder what her name is?

Rochelle who? I laugh, taking a sip of my brandy.

"Mr. Bricman?" Margaret says in an apologetic tone. "I'm sorry to bother you tonight. But you've been gone all afternoon and the Christmas tree people say they need to set things up early this year. They're overbooked."

"Early?" I ask. "Fuck that."

"I know you hate Christmas, but they say they have no choice. The Club takes two days to decorate and—"

"Wait," I say, remembering the little pumpkin back at the loft. "Yeah, OK. Tell them OK."

"Really?" Margaret asks, stunned at my reversal.

"Yeah. Rochelle came back. She's got a kid now, did you know that?"

"No," Margaret says, her face all scrunched up. "Is it—"

"We don't know who the father is," I say, reading her mind. "Either me or Quin. But she's damn cute, Margaret. So let's get this Christmas shit started. I can't wait to see her on Smith's lap at the party. I'm gonna need a million pictures of that."

Jordan can have that wannabe-dom girl who thinks she knows what kinky sex is.

I'm in a new game now.

CHAPTER TEN

"I guess it's just us," Rochelle says after Bric leaves.

We eat for a few minutes in silence. I watch the baby play with her noodles. God, I'm a lucky guy. She's so beautiful. Both of them. They are so damn beautiful.

But... things feel... different.

"Are you going to stay the night?" Rochelle asks. Probably just trying to fill in the awkward silence.

I think about this for a while, trying to figure out what's happening.

"Quin?" she asks again.

"You know when you're in a relationship and your boyfriend goes out with his buddies for a night of drunken debauchery?"

Rochelle just looks at me from across the table. Blinks. "Um... OK."

"And you're kinda pissed off about it, but what can you do, right? Be *that* girl?"

"Yeah."

"No woman wants to be *that* woman, right? She wants to be cool about this. She wants to trust her man. She wants to know he'll come home to her when he's done with his friends and fuck her. Tell her she's the only one he loves."

"Where are you going with this?" Rochelle asks.

I ignore that. "But it's like midnight, right? And he's still out. So you text, *Hey, how's it going? Having a good time?* Of course he's having a good time. That's why he's still out with his buddies."

Rochelle squints her eyes at me.

"He doesn't answer. He's drinking with the guys. No one answers a text when they're out with the guys."

"That's not true. You always answered me."

I hold up a finger. "Stay with me here, OK? So he doesn't answer and you get mad, right? It's three AM now and the bars are closed. Where the fuck is he? And then you think, holy shit, he got in a car accident. He's in a ditch. He's at the hospital. He's dead. And then you start looking up the phone numbers for hospitals. And you consider calling to see if there was an accident. You're imagining this whole life without him and you're so fucking sad you just want to cry."

Now she knows where this is going.

"But then, at four-thirty he stumbles through the door and flops on the couch. Passes out and shit. No hello. No sorry for making you worry. No nothing. He's just too drunk to care. How do you feel then? Still sad?"

"Quin—"

"No," I say, cutting her off. "No. You just need to listen for a second. I'm not trying to be a dick here, OK? I'm not. I just need you to know how I feel right now."

"I'm sorry."

"I know," I say. "You already said that and I don't need to hear it again. But I feel like *that* girl. I imagined all the worst-case scenarios. I had you dead and buried. At one point I even thought you might've killed yourself. That I might have *caused you* to kill yourself."

"Quin—"

120

"No. Just fucking *listen* to me, goddammit." I stop talking and wait for her to decide. I don't want to talk over her. I just want her to hear me.

"OK," she finally says. "I'm listening."

"A whole year," I say. "I felt like that girl for a whole year." She opens her mouth—then closes it. She was probably going to say sorry again. I know she's sorry. Rochelle is not a mean person. There is not a mean bone in her body. She's good. She's sweet. She's loving and caring. But she did something really fucking shitty to me. And she needs to understand this. "And that whole time I prayed to God you'd reappear. Or Bric would find you and bring you home. Or you'd call, for fuck's sake. Call me. Tell me you were alive. But you never did. And then you came back and all I felt in that first moment was relief, right? She's alive. She's safe. She's OK. I will see her again. I will talk to her again. I will get another chance."

She sighs, puts her fork down and looks at her plate.

"I'm not trying to make you feel bad. I'm not. And I don't need another apology. I have already accepted the one you gave me. It's done. I'm over it."

"Obviously you're not over it."

"I'm over *that*, Rochelle. I'm over the part where I missed you."

This stuns her. She stares at me with the most hurt expression I've ever seen. It kills me. That look on her face kills me inside.

"I see why you left. I understand why you left. I don't blame you for leaving. I get it, you were pregnant and Chella says girls get weird when they're pregnant. So fine. You got weird, you got better, you came back. OK. The boyfriend is home from his drunken night out with the guys and he's ready to pass out. But you want an explanation, right? Even if it's just one sentence."

"I was in Pagosa Springs."

"Obviously I know that. That's not what I want."

"Then what do you want?" she asks.

"I don't fucking know," I say. "I don't fucking know, Rochelle. All I know is that I'm mad. I'm so fucking pissed off."

"Then why are you here?" she asks.

"Why?" I ask, smiling through my heartbreak. "*Why?* Because I fucking loved you, that's why."

"You did love me? Or you still do love me?"

I shrug. "That's the part I don't know about."

"So I'll ask again. Why are you here? Why get involved?"

"Because Bric asked me to."

"So you're here for Bric?" She laughs.

I really want to call her a stupid fucking bitch right now. I really want to yell and cuss her out. And tell her she's all kinds of bad things just to make her feel what I'm feeling. But I keep my mouth shut. It's nothing but a way to make me feel better at her expense and that will make everything worse.

"I'm just fucking mad," I finally answer. "You just stumbled into the house at four-thirty, drunk. And the only thing on your mind is passing out. You can't help that. You're drunk. You're not in control. You just need to sleep it off. But I want to say things mad people say. Except it's pointless. It's not going to help because you're drunk. You won't hear me. And even if you did, you wouldn't remember when you wake up later. So I'm not going to say them."

"I'll just have to guess then?"

"At least you'll know what it feels like."

We both let out a long breath of frustration. When I look over at the baby, she's staring at me, big blue eyes looking up at me like, *Who the fuck is this guy?* "She doesn't even know me, Rochelle."

"She doesn't know Bric either."

"Bric isn't her father."

"How do you know that?"

"I just know."

Rochelle is silent after that. Probably coming up with all kinds of comebacks. I don't know for sure, but I feel it. Adley is *my* daughter. Mine.

"I missed everything, you know. So I'm mad about you leaving, I'm mad about you never calling me, and I'm mad that I missed the birth of my daughter. I'm just fucking mad, OK?"

"So leave, then. If you're so mad, then just leave."

"God, you just don't get it. I don't want to *leave*. I never want to let you out of my fucking sight."

"You make no sense."

"I know," I admit. "I know I make no sense. And the answer to your question is yes. I'm staying the night. I might stay every night and say fuck the rules. I'm gonna sleep with you in that fucking bed. Or wherever you plan on sleeping. In the second bedroom or on the couch. I'm gonna be there. Because I have lost all sense of... *trust*, Rochelle. I have become *that* girl. I want you to stay with me forever. I don't want you to ever go out and get drunk with the guys again. I don't ever want to text you at midnight desperate to know where you are. I don't ever want to be sitting up at three AM wondering if I should call hospitals to see if you're alive. I never want to let you out of my sight because I'm afraid, Rochelle. I'm afraid if

I leave you, you'll leave me too. And then you'll disappear again. You'll walk out and find another new life. Only this time, you won't bother coming back in a year."

Rochelle frowns. "I don't know what you want from me."

"That makes two of us," I say. "I don't know what I want from you either. I just know I have no trust. And it makes me mad. And so fucking sad. Because last year I had so much faith in who *we were*. What we were to each other. And so I'm mad that I lost that. I guess that's all I'm trying to say. I'm mad that I lost you. And I'm sad that I'm now being forced to consider the possibility that we will never be that way again. That we might be over."

She starts to cry. A stream of silent tears fall down her cheeks.

"I don't want us to be over, Rochelle. I don't. But it's not really something we have control over, is it? Because I'm working off fear right now." I stop and look at her, surprised at how easy this is to articulate out loud. "It's all based on fear."

I take a deep breath and let it out, waiting to see what she says to all that. I wouldn't blame her if she told me to leave. And even though I told her I was staying, I would. I'd leave. And I might not ever come back.

Adley begins to fuss. She's sliding down in her chair a little, looking very uncomfortable. There's a noodle stuck to her face and her jerky fists are trying to swipe at it, with no luck.

Rochelle's chair scrapes across the wood floors as she pushes back from the table. She sighs, wiping her tears off her cheeks with both hands, then starts messing with Adley's high chair. "I need to give her a bath. We're out of sorts right now with all the changes."

"OK," I say, almost afraid to move. Afraid I'll spook her even more than I just did. She talks softly to Adley as she picks her up and then disappears into the master bedroom, pulling the massive barn doors closed to shut me out.

"Good going, Quin," I mumble. "Way to go."

I've pictured our reunion in my head a million times over the past year, but none of those fantasies ever included me being pissed off and her being... indifferent. I know she said sorry. I know she's here and that's really all that matters. But things feel... off. Like why? Why did she come back? Did she plan on staying gone for one year? Is her return just another move in the game?

The door buzzer goes off, so I push back from the table and walk over to the elevator. On screen is a guy, looking up at the camera. I press and hold the speaker button. "Yes?"

"I'm from the Four Seasons," he says. "I was told to drop a car off here."

"Right. I'll be down in a moment."

When I get down there I take Rochelle's keys from him. "Thanks. Did you change the oil?"

"Yes, sir."

"And wash it?"

"Yes, sir. It's parked down a few spaces. Didn't know where you wanted it."

"No problem," I say, pulling out two twenties from my wallet and handing it over. "Thanks a lot, I appreciate it."

He nods and gets in a waiting car. They disappear and leave me there, holding Rochelle's keys.

I click the key fob and a white SUV a few spaces down beeps to life. She owns a Lexus. A nice fucking Lexus. I wonder who it's registered to?

I walk over to it, get in the driver's side, and start it up. Then I reach over and pull open the glove box to find her registration. Rochelle Bastille.

Not even trying to hide.

So how come it was so hard to find her?

I slam the glove box closed—because I don't want to think about that answer—and back out so I can pull into her new parking space next to my Suburban.

The back of her car is stuffed with a baby seat and all kinds of things. Nice designer luggage, something that looks like a folded-up baby crib, and a super-sized pack of diapers.

Might as well bring it all upstairs for her.

I spend the next ten minutes stacking all her worldly belongings next to the elevator, then punch the code Bric gave us to call it. A few minutes later, I'm back upstairs unloading.

I don't know where she wants any of this stuff, so I go over to the bedroom, slide the doors open, and peek inside. "Can I come in?" I ask.

No answer.

So I push the doors open a little more and slip inside. The bathroom door is open a crack, but it's silent in there except for a few cooing noises from the baby.

I push the door open and Adley is lying back on her mother's breasts in the bath with one foot in her mouth. She smiles at me.

"Hey, baby."

"I'm not sleeping," Rochelle mumbles. "We're just relaxing. We did this every afternoon in the hot springs. She likes it. Hell, I like it. I like it so much, I almost wish I was back in Pagosa sitting in my hot spring."

I dwell on that for a minute. Because it plays right into my fears, right? She could leave again. She could leave and never come back.

But then Adley starts talking in that babble language babies have and I lose my train of thought. She is so fucking pretty. Both of them. So beautiful. I take out my phone and snap a pic.

"What are you doing?" she asks, hearing my shutter click.

"Your car came. I had them change the oil since you just drove hundreds of miles. And they washed it."

She opens her eyes. "That was sweet of you."

I shrug. "That's me, right? The nice guy." *The one who always gets fucked*, I don't add. "I brought all your stuff upstairs too. Didn't know where you wanted it, so it's just stacked by the elevator."

"Thank you," she says, still staring at me.

I shrug and lean against the vanity, crossing my arms. "So she likes the water?" I ask, hating the new awkwardness of our... relationship. If that's what this is.

Rochelle smiles down at Adley, who is still sucking on a toe. "She loves it. She can swim. I taught her by accident. She always wears a floaty swimsuit in the hot springs. You know those ones that act as a life jacket?"

I have no clue what she's talking about, but I nod yes anyway.

"And one day about a month ago, her diaper leaked just before we were going to soak. Well, she likes her soak, so I took her in a regular swimsuit. And holy shizz, she could swim!" Rochelle laughs. "I looked it up later and some people say that all babies know how to swim. I think it's bullshit, hence the floaty swimsuit. But Adley can. Of course, I'd been coaching her for weeks by that time. I'd hold her up and she'd kick her legs. Or I'd hold her around her waist and she'd paddle her arms like a dog. She got lots of water in her mouth, and she hated it, so she started holding her breath."

I picture it in my head as she talks, imagining them down there in picture-perfect Pagosa Springs, living a nice, quiet, peaceful life in a resort town. Soaking in the hot springs. Making a new routine. Playing their own game with their own rules.

It hurts.

"And that day I let her go—just for a second. Just to see if she learned anything. And she kicked and paddled away. I snatched her up immediately. It scared the hell out of me. And then I took her home and decided never again. But it was cool. I taught her something, you know? I barely had to try and I taught her something."

I want to be a dick about this right now. So bad. But I decide it's a horrible idea. I can't win. I can't be mad, even though I'm so fucking pissed off. Being mad won't make anything better. It will, in fact, make everything worse. My little analogy about the drunk boyfriend has already started to fuck things up and we just got back together. If I want to stay here with her—them, including Bric—I need to find a way to get past the anger. So I say, "Sounds amazing," instead of, *So glad you got all that alone time with her and I was left with nothing.*

"I wanted to call you," she says, looking down at Adley instead of me.

"When?"

"That day. Every day. I wanted to tell you everything."

"So why didn't you?"

She shrugs and stands up in the tub, holding Adley close to her breasts. "Will you get a towel so I can wrap her up?"

I grab a towel from a row of shelves filled with them, and then walk forward, holding it out. Rochelle pushes Adley at me and says, "Take her for a second, will you? I don't like stepping out of the tub with her in my arms. I have a little floaty seat I usually set her in, but obviously I don't have it right now."

I take a deep breath and take squirming Adley. She balks, twists, and there's a moment when I just know I'll drop her.

I don't. But it's not a seamless transition, and Adley begins to cry.

Rochelle steps out, grabs a white robe off a chair, and wraps herself up.

I can't take my eyes off her, but she's not looking at me. She's paying no attention to me at all. She only has eyes for very fussy Adley.

I hand her over when Rochelle reaches out, kinda relieved. I have no clue what to do with a baby. I'm an only child so I never had nieces or nephews. None of my friends have kids. And Smith's rat dog does not count, regardless of what he thinks.

Fucking Smith. What was all that bullshit back at the hotel? It's like he's got a personal grudge against Rochelle. And while it's flattering that he's kinda protective of me, that he paid her money this whole year just so he could ambush her into an explanation if she ever came back, it's also... very weird.

Bric and Smith have been my best friends for so long, I sometimes take it for granted that we all want the same things. But I'm wrong. We don't. And Smith's quick exit from the game once Chella came along just proves it.

"Can you grab the diaper bag?" Rochelle asks, walking past me and into the bedroom.

"Sure," I say. How hard can that be? But when I go back out to where Rochelle's stuff is, I can't decide which one it is. They all look like suitcases to me.

"It's this one," Rochelle says, picking up something she brought with her when we first got here. I thought it was her purse.

Nope. It's a diaper bag.

I suck at this new game.

"Hey, Quin?" Rochelle asks a few minutes later.

"Yeah?" I say back.

"Can you put that little porta-crib in the second bedroom for me?"

"Sure." Porta-crib. It's gotta be this massive folded thing, right? I feel confident it is, so I pick it up and take it into the second bedroom. Rochelle is busy doing a million things, it seems. She talks to Adley in a soft voice the whole time, like she's trying to convince her to be happy.

Adley is not convinced.

I flip the crib open and have a moment of satisfaction. "See. I can adult."

I look over my shoulder to see if Rochelle heard me. She didn't.

"Does she always sleep in a separate room?" I ask.

"Yes," Rochelle answers. "God, I made the mistake of sleeping with her when she was little and it took me weeks to get her to go to bed in the crib. I won't do that again."

"Did you have a two-bedroom hotel room?" I ask, trying to imagine how much that costs. I don't know why

I'm so focused on her lifestyle while she was gone. But it's sorta irritating that she was living like a princess this whole time and I was so damn miserable.

"No." She laughs, coming into the room with a bottle.

They are both dressed now. Rochelle is wearing shorts and a t-shirt that is way too big for her. It says "Mineral Springs Resort" on the front. Adley is wearing a pink one-piece thing that looks like underwear, and says, "The coolest people are from Pagosa Springs, Colorado." It's like everything they own came from a tourist shop.

"But I had her crib set up away from the bed," Rochelle continues. "So she knew I wasn't right there the whole time."

"Oh." I watch her get in the bed with Adley and give her the bottle. Adley takes it eagerly, her tiny hands wrapping around the bottle like she won't let it get away. Her eyes get heavy and begin to close immediately.

So do Rochelle's.

I back out of the room and go watch some TV. I guess that's all she needed from me. Why did I say I'd stay the night? I should just leave. Go home. Forget about it for a while.

But I don't. I just stare mindlessly at the TV. Because Rochelle owes me. She owes me that last fuck she skipped out on.

She's gonna make this up to me. Whether she knows it or not. One last time. I'm gonna fuck her alone one last time to wipe the past away.

Because starting tomorrow, the only time I'll touch her is with Bric.

New game. New rules. New life.

I'm almost asleep and I'm all caught up on sports news when Rochelle finally comes out of the second bedroom. She looks at me, then closes the giant barn doors as quietly as she can.

"I was almost sure you'd be gone when I came out."

"I told you, I'm not leaving." I take my feet off the couch to give her room and she gets the hint and sits down, pulling her knees up and tucking the giant t-shirt over her legs.

She rests her hand on my knee. Tentatively. When I don't object she eases her head down on top of my thigh and lets out a long, tired breath. "I'm glad I'm back."

"Me too," I say. I am. I'm happy she's back. I don't even want to think about all the days she was missing.

"I missed you a—"

"Take off your shirt," I say.

She squints her eyes at me, then grabs the bottom of her shirt and lifts it over her head, tossing it on the floor.

I stare at her breasts. They were always spectacular but now they are even more tantalizing. "Play with them," I say. "I want to see you play with them."

She cups them, her small hands squeezing. Then she pinches her nipples, both at the same time, and closes her eyes. "I want you to touch me," she says. "I want it more than anything."

I ignore her request and say, "Turn around. Face that way." I point to the other end of the couch. "And put your pussy in the air for me."

She bites her lip and draws in a deep breath, probably surprised by my directness. I was always the nice guy. The considerate lover. I had my rough moments with her. And Bric and I are always rougher with her together than I am alone.

But why should I care? Why should I be considerate when she's not?

"Do it," I say. "Or I'm going to sleep."

That look on her face might be confusion. But I don't think so. I think I'm making her angry. Good. Now she knows how I feel tonight.

She huffs out the breath she was holding and turns around, crawling forward a little until her ass is right up in my face.

"You want me to touch you, Rochelle?"

She looks over her shoulder at me. Her breasts are hanging down, almost begging me to play with them. "Yes," she whispers. "Touch me."

I slap her ass hard as I stand up. She looks over her shoulder again. "What are you doing?"

I say nothing as I undo my tie and pull it through the collar of my shirt. I take my suit coat off next, walking over to a chair and hanging it up so it won't be wrinkled in the morning. When I come back I'm already unbuttoning my shirt. She watches my fingers very carefully. I slip the shirt off and place it over the jacket.

My pants are unbuttoned when I walk back over to her. She watches me take them off and fold them up. I stand over by the chair as I drop my boxer briefs and fist my cock so she can see I'm hard for her.

I can't deny my desire. I fell in love with her for a reason. And that reason has a lot to do with what she looks like naked.

"Touch me," she says.

"Lie down," I answer. "Flat. With your legs straight."

"Quin—"

"Do it," I say.

She huffs out another breath. Like I'm frustrating her. Good. Now she knows how I feel tonight.

She lies down, her face turned to one side so she can see me, and straightens out her legs. They are long and tanned from lots of time in the sun down south. Her whole body is golden, just like her hair. It spills over her shoulders and back like a waterfall.

I walk towards her, place a hand on her outer thigh and put one knee on the couch next to her hip. Then I force my other knee between her body and the cushion, so I'm sitting on the back of her knees.

"Yes," she moans.

I play with her ass. My hands are all over her ass. Rubbing it. Letting my fingers slip between her legs just a little bit. Just enough to tease her with what's to come. I bend over her body, letting my chest press against her back, and lower my lips to her neck. I slip a hand underneath her so I can squeeze her breast.

Her whole body trembles from the sensation of my lips.

"Did you miss me?" I ask.

"Yes," she says. "Every night, Quin. I missed you."

"I missed you too. One year is too long."

"I know. But I promise, I won't ever leave again. You can trust me, Quin. I promise I won't do it again."

I say nothing. Just enjoy the heat our bodies create together.

Her outside leg falls and one foot drops to the floor. It's kinda cramped on the couch so I don't make a big deal about it. Instead I dip the hand on her breast and slip it down her belly until I'm playing with the wetness between her legs.

She moans. "I like that," she whispers, pressing her ass up into my cock.

I bet she does.

My dick presses between her ass cheeks and she opens her legs—just a little since I've got her boxed in with my body—and I slip inside easily.

"Yes," she moans. "Fuck me."

Oh, I fully plan on it. One more hard thrust and I'm all the way in. She gasps from my forcefulness, her back arching, but I sit up a little and press my palm right between her shoulder blades, pinning her beneath me.

Her pussy clamps down on my dick, her muscles tightening around my shaft.

I slap her ass cheek so hard, she squeals as I watch it turn red.

"You're a fucking whore, aren't you Rochelle?"

"Yes," she says, raising her ass up again, practically begging for more.

I give her what she thinks she wants. I start slow, just like that other time. I start slow and then gradually fuck her a little harder.

She begins to moan, so I grab her by the hair and force her up, holding her against my chest, and just pound her from behind. Pure fucking. My other hand wraps around her throat and I squeeze. Not a lot, but enough.

She goes wild. Gasping for air, trying to fuck me back by pushing her ass towards me, even though I'm the only one in control tonight.

"You like it when Bric and I fuck you together, don't you, Rochelle?"

"Yes," she says. "Yes."

"You like the way he slaps you around, don't you?"

"Yes," she moans again. "Fuck me, Quin. Fuck me harder."

"You want us to fuck you at the same time, don't you?" I say, my breath coming out long and hard. "You want both our cocks inside you at the same time, don't you?"

"Yes," she moans. "Yes."

I look down and watch myself fuck her. The way my dick slips and out of her pussy. I pull her hair harder. I squeeze her throat tighter.

She starts gasping for air, so I stop that and cup my whole hand around her mouth to keep her screams inside, and force her head back so she has to look me in the eyes.

So she has to see me.

I thrust inside her, hard. Then harder and harder until we come together. Her whole body shaking and trembling as she reaches climax. Her hot breath on the palm of my hand, gasping for more air. And then she goes limp as her come coats my dick.

I let her go and her body falls forward on the couch. I fall on top of her too, and we lie like that. Together. Skin to skin, as we try to catch our breath and calm our racing hearts.

I am so fucking tired.

I get off her and stand up, fisting my cock as I reach for her t-shirt on the floor and clean myself off. She rolls over on her back and watches me, and when I'm done I throw it on top of her belly.

"Did you like it?" I ask.

She nods, looking a tiny bit worried. This is not how things usually go when we have sex.

"Good," I say. "Because that's how I fucked Chella that night you told her to sneak into our bed and pretend to be you. Now you know what you missed."

CHAPTER ELEVEN

ROCHELLE

"So then what happened?" Bric asks.

We're sitting at our booth in the White Room. Before I left, I'd sit in the middle of the bench, Quin would sit across from me in a chair, and Bric would sit to my left.

Bric is still to my left, Quin isn't here yet—if he's coming at all—and Adley is in her baby seat on my right.

Everything is familiar—but off.

"Then he went to bed."

"What'd you do?"

"I sat there on the couch for a while trying to figure out what happened."

"What did you come up with?" Bric is looking very intently at me. Like everything I'm saying is critically important.

"He hate-fucked me, that's what I came up with, Bric!"

"Rochelle," Bric says, throwing me one of those *Don't overreact* looks.

"I'm serious. There's no other explanation for it. He hate-fucked me. Revenge fuck. Whatever you want to call it. That's what happened last night." I sigh and try not to feel depressed and sad. "And then this morning I got out of bed to go check on Adley when she woke up, and when I came back, he was gone."

"Gone?" Bric asks. "Where'd he go?"

"Just left," I say. "I texted him. Asked if he'd be here for breakfast. And he never texted back."

"He's just mad," Bric says.

"I know." I huff. "He told me that last night too. He spelled it out very clearly. He was worried about me. Sad about my leaving. But then when I came back—"

"Now he's just angry."

"Right."

"It's a pretty typical reaction," Bric says.

"I realize that. Which is why I'm not going to make a big deal about this. But I don't know if this is going to work, Bric. He might not want me. He might just want to hurt me. Exactly the way I hurt him."

"No," Bric says, like I'm being ridiculous.

"I'm not being ridiculous," I say. "Maybe he's not out to hurt me. But he's doing something, Bric. He's playing a game, but I'm pretty sure we're not all playing the *same* game."

"He's mad, Rochelle. You have to expect that. He's gonna come around."

"What does that mean? Come around? Do you really think he's gonna fall back in love with me the way he was? Because I don't. I think he's here for *us*. Me, you, and him together. And that's all."

Bric rubs his hand across his scratchy jaw as he thinks this over, so I check on Adley. She fell asleep in the car on the way over here and hasn't woken up yet. Bric is still thinking.

"I don't want an *us*, Bric."

He looks me in the eye and says. "I do. But I get it. And I'm fine with you and Quin getting your little happy ending. But I'm telling you, Rochelle, he's just trying to protect himself right now and the best way to let him work that out and ensure you two get back together is to have an *us*."

"He said he doesn't trust me."

"He has a good reason," Bric counters.

"I know that," I say, starting to get angry. "I understand that. But the whole point of us doing this... game... or whatever it is, was so that you can help me figure this out. I want him, Bric. You're supposed to help me."

But as soon as the words come out of my mouth I realize how stupid that is. I trust no one and I have very good reasons for that. I've learned over the course of my life that people are selfish. People are out for themselves. People are liars. I have a lot of experience in being lied to.

Elias Bricman definitely fits all those assumptions I have about people. And then some.

Adley starts whining. Our conversation probably woke her. So I reach over, unsnap her safety belt, and pull her into my lap.

"Hey, pumpkin," Bric says.

Adley buries her head into my sweater and rubs her eyes.

"I'm having all the Christmas decorations put up early," Bric says, reaching over to tickle Adley's chin. She squirms in my arms and then giggles through a mouthful of bubbly spit.

I can't help but smile at that.

"Are you hungry, Adley?" Bric asks, picking up a section of mandarin orange from my plate. He offers it to Adley, who makes grabby fists and stuffs it right up to her mouth and begins to suck. I will have to write that down in her baby book. She's never had oranges before.

"Christmas is coming early, huh?" I ask. "That's a first."

"Well," Bric says, leaning back in the booth. "First year I'm a father."

I throw him a look of caution. "You don't know you're the father. You might not want to think that way."

Bric shrugs. "We're never gonna know, so might as well think that way."

That's very confusing for me, but I don't have time to think about it, because Quin walks up to the table and scoots into the booth next to Adley's seat.

Not across from me.

I asked Quin once why he always sat in the chair and never sat next to me in the booth. He told me, "Because I like to look at you." So apparently even that has changed.

I frown and concentrate on Adley.

"What's up?" Quin says, looking over his shoulder for the waitress. She comes up, pen and pad ready, and Quin says, "Coffee and cornflakes." Which kinda makes me happy again, because Quin and cornflakes go together like bread and butter.

At least that's still the same.

Quin moves Adley's seat, placing it on the empty chair, and then scoots in closer to me. Puts his arm around me. Leans in and kisses me.

I kiss him back. But just when I start to get in to it, he pulls away.

I look at Bric. Bric is smiling. Like this is a good sign.

This is not a good sign. He didn't mean that kiss. He's not sitting across from me. He walked out on me this morning without saying goodbye.

Everything is wrong.

"Hi, Adley," Quin says.

Adley has turned her head now to face Quin. She's got her tangerine slice smeared all over her face.

"Do you like that?" Quin asks in a low voice as he touches her pudgy fist.

Adley turns her head away, smearing my sweater with tangerine juice, and goes back to staring at Bric.

Quin sits back in the booth, and when I look over at him, he's frowning. "What's wrong?" I ask.

"I don't think she likes me."

"She doesn't even know you, Quin," Bric says. "It's been two days."

"She seems to like you well enough," Quin says, picking up the coffee the waitress just set down and sipping it. "And you hate kids."

"Other people's kids," Bric corrects. "Why would I hate my own kid?"

Quin says nothing. But I can read his mind. *She's not yours. She's mine.*

"So what are you guys gonna do tonight?" Quin asks. "Big plans?"

I stare down at Adley's head. It's my night with Bric.

"I was wondering if you'd like to join in," Bric says.

I look up at him, then over to Quin.

Quin shrugs. "I guess. I have a late meeting today, so I'll probably just show up after dinner."

When I glance over at Bric he's got a smug look on his face that says, *Leave everything to me.*

But show up after dinner? To me, that means, *I'll show up to fuck.*

"We can have dinner together," I say, testing out my theory. "We'll wait for you."

"Nah," Quin says. "I'll get dinner at work and then come by around eight."

Eight. Yup. Just for the fuck.

The waitress brings Quin's bowl of cornflakes and a small pitcher of milk, so I spend the next several minutes watching him eat as Bric talks to Adley. Quin misses none of that interaction. His eyes are on Bric and Adley the whole time.

He never once glances at me.

At one point, Adley holds her arms out for Bric, like she wants him to pick her up. And to my surprise, he obliges her, taking her from my lap and placing her in his, as he makes faces and talks about all the different kinds of untouched fruit on my plate.

Quin pushes his cereal away and places his hand on my leg. I look over at him, startled that he's actually touching me. He slides his hand up my thigh and then presses his fingers against my pussy, stroking me through my jeans as he leans in and kisses me on the mouth.

His lips are cool and sweet and taste like milk. "Have a nice day," he says, still kissing me. And then—again—just when I begin to kiss him back, he pulls away and slips out of the bench, opening his wallet and throwing down a twenty-dollar bill. "See you guys tonight."

Bric and I both watch him walk away.

"Did you see that?" I ask, after we sit there in silence for a few seconds.

"Yeah. I think it went well."

"Are you kidding me?" I ask.

"What?"

"That didn't go well," I say. "That was a disaster. He didn't sit across from me, he sat next to me. He kissed me, but pulled away the second I tried to kiss him back. And he's not coming to dinner tonight, he's coming at eight. All he wants is the threesome, Bric."

"You're reading way too much into this, Rochelle."

"Am I?" I snort. "I know him, Bric. I know him very well. And that was a very bad start to this new relationship."

Bric thinks about this for a second as I take the mushed-up tangerine slice from Adley's hand, grab a wet nap from my diaper bag, and start cleaning her up. She fusses and balks, trying to bury herself into Bric's suit coat.

"You're going to regret holding her," I say, "when you figure out you've got sticky juice on your lapels."

He grins and looks down, where, yes—there is a dark spot on his lapel. "Might just be drool. But hey, there's worse things than smelling like a tangerine baby all day."

"Who are you?" I laugh. "And what have you done with Elias Bricman, hater of children and Christmas?"

He shrugs. "Like I said. I only hate other people's kids. And I'm looking forward to Adley's first Christmas. I've already started thinking about gifts."

"She doesn't need gifts," I say. What she needs is two parents. And by that, I'm not referring to Bric and me.

But that's definitely how this is starting out. And I'm beginning to think Elias Bricman has no idea who Quin is anymore. He's changed. Something about him has changed.

I'm the reason he changed.

"This isn't going to work," I say.

"Just stop it, Rochelle. Give it more than one day, all right? He just needs a little time. And don't worry. We both know he's into the threesome stuff. So we'll just enjoy that until he comes around."

"I guess," I say, to placate him. But I don't think he's right. I think we might be starting something very

145

dangerous. Something that could rip Quin and I apart for good.

"Anyway." Bric sighs. Like he knows what I'm thinking. Probably does. We've been friends for a long time. "What are you guys doing today?"

I shrug and take out a bottle of water from my diaper bag. "I dunno. It's weird being back here after so much time away. Maybe I'll drop by the gallery and see Chella?" I pick up a slice of tangerine and squeeze it into the water to flavor it.

"She doesn't work there anymore," Bric says.

"Oh," I say. Of course she doesn't. Why should anything stay the same?

"But I'm sure she's probably next door."

"Why would she be next door?" I ask, reaching for Adley, who is busy patting Bric's cheeks with the flat of her hands. I cannot believe Elias Bricman is into babies. What were the chances of that happening? Adley fusses when I take her back, but she eagerly accepts the bottle of tangerine water and settles into her seat. I buckle her up and tuck a strand of hair away from her closing eyes.

"We're opening up a tea room. Turns out, Chella's dream was to be a pastry chef. And she came up with this tea room idea. You know," he says, waving a hand in the air. "For the Club women. But open to the public."

"Oh. Well, that's sorta cool. I never pictured Chella as a baker."

"It sorta makes sense to me," Bric says. "In a weird way."

"All that school. A PhD and everything. Just to make pastries."

"Sometimes," Bric says, sliding out of the booth. "Sometimes the road to satisfaction is long and twisted,

146

Rochelle. Who cares what she does with her education? I'm sure whatever she got out of that degree is helping her now. Even if it's in some small way not easily identified."

I watch him as he gets out his wallet and pays for breakfast. It always intrigued me how he pays for things here. Even his drinks at the bar. He always pays his way. "What time are you coming over?" I ask. And then I wonder if I sound needy.

I sorta feel needy.

"Since Quin isn't coming until later, you wanna to go out to dinner?"

I look down at Adley and shake my head. "I like to stay in, to be honest. She's still on new baby schedule."

"OK," Bric says. "I'll bring something with me then. Have fun with Chella."

I watch him walk off, pointing at people sitting at other tables as he makes his way to the front. He stops five or six times before he finally makes his way to the front podium and whispers something to Margaret. They both look at me, then Margaret nods, as Bric disappears to start work.

Margaret comes towards me, pushing my stroller. "He said you were ready to go," she says, stopping at the table. "And to bring you the stroller."

"Thanks," I say, scooting out of the booth with Adley's car seat. Margaret holds the stroller as I snap it in, then adjust Adley's blankets.

"Chella is next door," she says. "Bric says you were looking for her."

"Oh, yeah, thanks. Is it literally right next door?"

"We have a connecting door," Margaret says. "Would you like to go through that way?"

"Sure." I follow her as she leads me into a short hallway, then through a revolving door—a smaller twin of the one in front of Turning Point Club—until we finally come to the tea room. "Thanks, Margaret," I say. She smiles and disappears.

I bet she is so confused about why I'm back.

Hell, I'm starting to be confused about why I'm back.

"Hey," Chella calls from across the room. She breaks away from another woman and starts walking towards me. When she's close enough, she takes both my hands and we do cheek kisses. This is something I have always loved about Chella. She is money. Sophisticated, smart, and wise to the ways of socializing.

It's a life not many can relate to. But I can. Three years with Bric has taught me a lot about that kind of stuff.

Chella is so put together today. She's always wearing tailored suits that show off her long legs. And her hair is always pulled back into some sort of fashionable bun or braid.

Today she's wearing cream-colored leggings with a pale pink fringe cape, and light suede over-the-knee boots. Her long dark hair is pulled back, except for a few curly tendrils that frame her face.

She looks like a fashion model.

I look down at my outfit. I'm wearing an old pair of denim jeans with more frayed holes than I can count, a blue Pagosa Spring t-shirt, shearling winter boots that have seen better days, and an old army jacket that is three sizes too big.

The only thing that saves me from looking homeless is the thousand-dollar stroller I'm pushing and the Prada tote I'm using as a diaper bag.

"What are you doing here?" she asks.

"I was having breakfast with the guys and Bric told me you're not at the gallery anymore."

"No." She laughs, wrapping my hands around her arm and pulling me to a table in the back where there are no workers. "I quit about six months ago, after I talked Bric and Smith into this tea room idea."

"I heard. Pastry chef? I had no idea, Chella. None."

"Well," she says, beckoning me to take a seat. I do, and she does the same, sitting across from me. "You know how you think about doing things, when you're little and stuff, but it's so impractical?"

I laugh. "You mean like… playing guitar at street fairs and poetry bars?"

"Yes," Chella says with a big smile. "I guess you know all about that. Well, to be honest, I was kinda jealous of you for that."

"Me?" I ask, pointing to my chest and laughing. "How could you ever be jealous of me?"

"You always had your dream. And you just went for it. So one day Smith and I were just sitting around the house and I was watching some bake-off show on TV. And I said, 'I could do that.' And he said, 'So do that.'"

I look around at the tea room. It's not done yet. There are a dozen people here working on things. But I can tell it's going to be fabulous. It's got Chella written all over it. Everything is very rustic, yet modern. Not how you'd picture an old-fashioned tea room in movies and books and stuff. Her style. Her taste. Her dream. "And you did it."

"Yeah, Bric has been great about it. He gave me the space and just said go for it."

Bric seems to be great at everything these days.

"Do you see Quin much?" I ask.

"Oh, all the time," Chella says. "We meet for lunch every Tuesday. We were meeting at the Club this past Tuesday when you called. That's why everyone came over to your hotel. We were already together."

"Oh," I say, almost wistfully.

And it's in that moment that I realize—I have missed this life. These people. Even Chella, who was also part of my world back then. But separate. She's probably the closest friend I've had in like... ever. Which is sad because we only knew each other for six months before I disappeared.

"He called me this morning," Chella says.

"He did?" I ask. "When? He slept at my new place last night. But then he disappeared early."

"I know," Chella says. "He told me."

"What did he say? Did he talk about me?"

Chella frowns and nods. "He said you had a fight."

"We didn't fight," I say, more defensively than I should. "He was just... mad at me."

"I know. He told me that too."

"What exactly did he tell you?" I'm kinda pissed off that Quin is shutting me out and sharing everything with Chella now. I was that girl last year. I was Chella. And now... I have no idea who I am anymore. I can't even say, *Well, you're Adley's mother*. Because Bric and Quin are here too and it's almost like they are taking some of that identity away from me. Before I came back I was all she had. Now she has two fathers. I feel... left behind.

"He just said he was confused. I mean, look, Rochelle, you did disappear. And have a baby, which might be his. And you never called."

I did call. Yeah, it was six months later, but I *did* call. And I can't even tell him that because stupid Bric kept it a secret. And I can't out Bric and cause trouble between him and Quin, because let's face it—Bric is the only one in my corner at the moment.

I realize Chella is still talking. "And he asked if Smith and I wanted to go to dinner with him tonight."

"Hmm," I say, instantly angry. That jerk. "Bric and I invited him to eat with us tonight, but he said he was working."

"Oh," Chella says. "I didn't realize it was a secret. Well"—she waves her hand—"Smith won't go to dinner. So it will just be Quin and me. Smith doesn't like to have the three of us together too much. He thinks Quin wants..." She blushes. Shakes her head.

"Quin wants... what?" I prod.

"You *know*. Smith thinks Quin misses me."

"You?" I ask. What the fuck is happening?

"Not me. Us, I guess." She blushes again. "You know. The whole quad thing. But without Bric. Tuesday was the first time they talked in... hell, months."

I feel like I'm having a stroke. Like I'm hearing her words and they make no sense.

"It's weird too," Chella continues. "Quin's never like that when it's just him and I together. He doesn't want *me*, Rochelle. It's like he wants..."

"The us," I say, filling in the blank.

"Yeah." She nods. "I think he misses that. The us."

So there you go. That's where I'm at.

The us.

I can have Bric, or Bric and Quin, but not Quin alone.

These are the new rules, I guess.

It's just another game to them.

That's all it's ever been—a game.

"I have something for you," Chella says, bringing me out of my horrible realization. "If you let me drop you off at home, I can swing by my house and get it on the way."

"Sure," I say. I wait patiently as she does a little business, then we get in her car and drive over to the Little Raven house. Adley fell asleep in her seat, so I wait in her car. A few minutes later she comes back with a box I know very well.

"Here," Chella says, handing it to me as she gets back in the car. "I can't keep it. Not after reading what Quin wrote to you in there."

I take the lid off the box and unwrap the book. It feels heavy in my hands. It feels right. Perfect. I open it up and read the inscription.

Dear Rochelle,

Mistakes are measured in wasted time
Falling to your knees, asking for another chance
Longing's just an aching mind
Giving in to circumstance
The future is closer than your past
And loving you is not a crime
So if you don't want to turn back
We can handle the aftermath.

Love,
Quin

The book is filled with inscriptions, but not all of them are from Quin. It's like this book has been passed around between lovers for decades. And each time it changed hands, the person giving it away wrote something about their longing.

Quin wrote in this book a lot over the time we spent together. Every now and then he'd see it in my closet, or on my shelf, or my bedside table because I was reading it. But I've never seen this poem before.

"Thank you," I say as Chella smiles at me. But God, my heart hurts for him. He must have written this while I was gone. I hold it to my chest and sigh.

"I know it means a lot to you, so I need to give it back. And don't try to pay me for it. I don't need the money."

"Thank you so much," I repeat. "I just wanted to sell it. It was a way to start the process of leaving, you know? And you're right. Those words Quin wrote to me..." I close my eyes. Feeling heavy with dissatisfaction. "I knew there was no way out of the game if I didn't leave. And if I kept these words, held on to them, well, I'd never have the nerve to leave him behind. It made me feel desperate back then. Desperate to cling to what little we had. And selling this book gave me strength. Getting rid of it got rid of my longing, you know? Or so I thought." I sigh, looking down at my book. "It's not gone though, Chella. My longing is as strong as ever. It scares me," I say. "I don't trust people easily. I trust you because you don't need anything from me. But—

"But you think Bric and Quin need you for the game."

"Yes," I say. I take a deep breath and let it out. "I'm gonna get hurt. I'm falling for it again, Chella, and it's not good."

"Hey," she says, placing a hand on my arm. "It's going to work out, Rochelle. I know it is."

But I'm not so sure about that. Bric isn't the man I thought he was. He can't be that selfish asshole and be so sweet to my daughter at the same time. Unless he's only doing it because he thinks she's really his?

And Quin isn't making any move to leave the game.

I'm not winning this time. Because I want to trust them. I want them to be real and I know they're not.

I'm so off my game. The rules have changed and no one bothered to tell me.

I'm an amateur. All my moves are clumsy, all my motivations jumbled.

I learned a long time ago that you can't trust people. I have lived with too many lies and disappointments to count. I have learned the ways of the world through the lens of dishonesty. Deceit. Cheating and backstabbing. I have wounds from those lessons. I have deep scars.

I'm gonna lose, I realize. I'm gonna lose this game. Because I desperately want to trust these men and I know it's a bad idea. I want them to heal me, but they have long claws and sharp teeth.

Bric is trying to claim my heart by going through my daughter. And it's working. I like him so much more now than I ever did before.

And Quin has always had my heart. But now I don't have his.

No. There is no win in my future.

CHAPTER TWELVE

BRIC

"Is everything OK?" I ask Rochelle as we eat dinner. I stopped by this new restaurant a block away from the Club and picked up the most amazing sea bass tacos. Plus a little side of candied sweet potatoes that they whipped up special for the pumpkin. Almost none of it made it to her mouth because she's got it all over her chubby face and fingers.

"Fine," Rochelle says. She ate her food, so I'm going to assume that was an honest answer. When she goes off her food, that's when I know to worry. That was, after all, the only weird thing I noticed about her behavior right before she took off last year. "But he's late."

"Only five minutes," I say, glancing down at my watch.

"He used to be early. And whenever we had breakfast in the White Room booth, he used to sit across from me. He told me he liked it better than sitting next to me because he wanted to stare at my face."

Hmmm. Is she overreacting? I'm not sure. "Well, look, Rochelle, you need to give the guy some time. He's processing."

She sighs and gets up. Disappears into Adley's bedroom and comes back with a little pink washcloth to clean her messy face.

Adley balks. Squirms. And when Rochelle is persistent, she cries.

"You're a good mother, Rochelle."

She stops cleaning up Adley to smile at me. "Thanks."

"I mean it too. You did good. And all by yourself. Don't let this thing with Quin derail you. Don't let it upset you or rob you of all the great things happening in your life right now."

"I know," she says, releasing Adley from the chair and picking her up. "You've been pretty great." I shrug, going for a sheepish response. Rochelle doesn't fall for it. Sheepish isn't a word anyone would use to describe me. "We both know you're going out of your way to help me right now. I'm just not sure what you're getting out of this, Elias."

"I'm getting you."

"Typical, *typical* answer," she says.

"And the pumpkin." I smile big at the new addition to my typical response. "I like her. A lot." I get a sad smile from Rochelle. And I know her well enough to read her mind. So I add something else to the new addition. "But don't worry. If you and Quin work out and want me to back away, I will."

Rochelle stares at me for a moment, unsure if she should take that promise at face value.

Even I'm not sure she should take that promise at face value. So I don't make another addendum.

"I'm gonna give her a bath and get her ready for bed. Be done in thirty."

"Sure," I say, standing up. "I'll be here."

I gather up all the dinner trash and hit the elevator button to take it down to the dumpster in the garage. When the doors open, I practically slam into Quin.

"Shit," he laughs. "You almost knocked me down." He's still wearing his work suit, but he's holding dry-cleaning bags.

"So you showed," I say, some of Rochelle's irritation rubbing off on me.

"Why wouldn't I come?" Quin asks.

"Rochelle told me what you did last night."

"What'd I do?"

"You're kidding, right?"

"No," he says. "I'm not. What did she tell you?"

"Revenge fuck? Hate fuck? Those are two ways she described what happened last night."

"What the hell are you talking about?"

"She said you fucked her and then told her that's exactly how you fucked Chella when she ambushed us."

"So? Did I miss the memo where everyone is supposed to lie and spare Rochelle's feelings?"

"Are you gonna be a dick about this? She said you left this morning without saying goodbye."

"I needed to go home and change, Bric." And then he shakes his dry-cleaning. "Which is why I brought a fucking suit this time."

Oh. Yeah, that kinda makes sense.

"And she was with the baby. I thought she went back to sleep."

Hmm. All this adds up. "She said you didn't sit across from her today at breakfast."

Quin laughs. "Why the fuck would I sit across from her when I can sit *next* to her? What the hell is going on?" he asks. "Why is she back if all she's gonna do is complain about everything I do?"

"I don't think she's complaining, Quin. She feels like you're not invested in her."

157

"I'm here," he says. "With a suit to wear to work tomorrow because we're gonna sleep together tonight. What the fuck do you guys want from me? A goddamned contract? Am I the game, Bric?"

"Of course not," I say, walking over to the compactor door and throwing the bag of trash in.

"Hey," he says as I come back. "If you don't want me here, just let me know. We can get that DNA test out of the way and just take it from there."

"Quin," I say, softening my stance. "We discussed this. We're not getting the test. She's ours."

"She's mine," Quin says. "Just so you understand that. But I'm willing to share."

For a second I'm not sure if he's talking about the baby or Rochelle. Or both. I'm actually speechless.

"Are we going upstairs or what?" he finally adds.

I punch the keypad to call the elevator and when the doors open, we both step in. "Did you eat with Chella?" I ask, trying to find a way to break the awkwardness.

"Yeah. How'd you know?"

"Chella told Rochelle. They hung out today."

Quin shrugs off getting caught in that lie. "We met my mother for dinner."

"Your *mother?*" Jesus Christ, I feel like I'm talking to a stranger.

"Yeah, we have dinner with her about once a month."

"Really?" I ask dryly. I try to picture how Quin introduced Chella to his mother. *Hey, Mom, this is my friend, Marcella Walcott. Why, yes, she is the senator's daughter.* Or does he say, *Hey, this is Chella, Smith Baldwin's girlfriend?* Maybe he says, *Hey, Mom, this is the girl Bric and Smith and I all fucked together last year?* What? What does he say?

I know his mom pretty well. Kitty Foster is every kid's mom. I bet when Quin was living at home they had the hang-out house. The place where you just went. Probably didn't even have to knock. Just let yourself in, grab one of those homemade cookies off the kitchen counter, and head to the garage, or the basement. Wherever.

But I cannot, for the life of me, picture Kitty Foster knowing what her son does with me and Smith.

The doors open and Quin steps out, walking purposefully down the hallway to the coat closet. He hangs his suit in there and then goes to the fridge and grabs a beer. After that he settles on one of the couches and flips the TV on with the remote. Broncos are playing. Two minutes into his visit and he acts like he's lived here for years.

"You're here," Rochelle says.

Both Quin and I turn to look at her in the hallway. She's all wet still and wearing the white bathrobe. Adley is bundled up in a baby towel that has a hood to cover her little wet ringlets of hair.

"I'm here," Quin says. "I don't know why you guys are all paranoid about me. Is there something going on I should know about?"

Rochelle squints her eyes at me. "What do you mean?"

"I didn't hate-fuck you last night, Rochelle. I was just telling you how I feel."

"Thanks a lot, Bric." Rochelle takes the baby into the other bedroom and slides the barn doors closed to shut us out.

"Why is this suddenly so hard?" I ask. "We never used to fight."

Quin takes a long sip of his beer. "I've been asking myself the same thing, Bric. All damn day."

"I can hear you," Rochelle yells from the bedroom.

I sigh and take a seat on the couch opposite Quin.

"Don't worry," Quin calls back. "In about an hour it will all be sorted."

Will it? I wonder.

"Fucking cures everything," Quin mumbles as he takes another sip.

"Does it?" I ask out loud.

"Always used to," Quin says. "So it better. Or things are very fucking wrong with this arrangement." He whispers this so Rochelle can't hear.

Yeah, I decide. Then I guess it better. Because I just got them back. And I'm not ready to make new arrangements and start all over again.

We watch the end of the football game and Quin is up throwing his beer in the recycle bin when Rochelle finally tiptoes out of the bedroom and slides the doors closed behind her.

"She's asleep?" Quin asks. She stops in the hallway to look at him. I can *see* the longing on her face. She's wearing it like a dress right now. It's almost painful to watch her.

She just nods.

Quin walks over to her with his hand outstretched. "Good. Then come with me." He leads her into the master bedroom and shoots me a look over his shoulder. "You coming, or what?"

Something is very different about Quin these days. And I can't figure out if it's because we've grown apart these past few months or if he's playing me.

"Yeah," I say, standing up to follow him into the bedroom. I decide it's the former. He's never been a great player, right? Mediocre at best. I mean, he *is* the one who fell in love and fucked it all up. So maybe he's just trying harder than usual. We just need to find our groove again, that's all.

Quin takes off his tie and throws it on the floor, his fingers already unbuttoning his shirt. He and Rochelle stare at each other for a second, but then she unties the belt of her robe and lets it slide over her shoulders.

Her body is so fucking hot. She's all curvy now from having the baby. And her tits are huge. Her nipples large and round. So different than they were before.

I walk up behind her and start playing with them, studying Quin's face as he watches us. He walks forward, taking his shirt off and dropping it on a chair as he passes. His hands cover mine and we play with her tits together.

"See," he says, leaning down to whisper in her mouth. "All better now. Last night is over. Let it go, Rochelle. Just be here with us and let it go."

"I want to," she says. "But I need you to know—"

"Shhh," Quin says, silencing her lips with a kiss. "No talking. You need to behave or I'll have Bric bend you over and spank your pussy."

His threat to Rochelle excites me. I've never played too hard with her. Never did much more than introductory bondage. But I'm totally up for making changes. "Feel free to mouth off, Rochelle."

She laughs and reaches up, slipping her hand around the back of my neck to draw me closer. Her head tilts and I start kissing her neck. Quin's hands are still on mine, both of us vying for the privilege of playing with her tits. Quin continues kissing her lips, but he reaches for my suit coat, pulling it down my shoulders. I let it slip to the floor and back off one step so I can loosen my tie.

Quin grins at me, even as he kisses Rochelle.

This part, at least, feels *very* familiar.

161

"Tie her up," Quin says.

I squint my eyes at him for a second.

"Tier her up," he repeats. "I want her tied to that bar." He nods his head up towards the ceiling at the metal pipe bars I have hanging in various places over the bed, indicating the one that runs lengthwise from the foot of the bed to the head. "You have rope here?"

"Well," I say, looking around. "Sure." The baby wasn't the only thing I prepared for when I got the loft ready for us.

"Tell him what you want, Rochelle," Quin says. He's grasping her face between his thumb and fingers, holding her tight as he makes her look in my direction. "Tell him."

I think I'm a little startled at this new development. "Rochelle?"

She looks at Quin, then me… and nods. "OK."

"You know what he's doing?" I ask her.

She nods.

"What am I doing?" Quin coos in her ear as he resumes playing with her tits.

"Punishing me," she says.

He chuckles. And then he gets dead serious and says, "Fuck, yes, I'm punishing you. But it's your choice, Rochelle. So if you're not into it, just say so."

"And don't blame you tomorrow if it all goes to shit?" she asks.

I have to hand it to her for not cowering.

"If you think multiple orgasms is 'going to shit,' well. So be it." Quin waits for her answer. He wants to hurt her right now. And he's going to use me to do it because he's not into the punishment stuff—and I am.

I let go of Rochelle and walk over to one of the bedside tables. Inside is a coil of soft rope, some lube, a blindfold, handcuffs, and a few other essentials.

I get the rope, slip the lube in my pocket, and close the drawer, uncoiling the rope as I walk back over to them. "How do you want her?" I ask.

"Hanging. Heels high."

"Jesus, Quin," I say.

He shrugs at me. "She can say no." He turns to look at Rochelle. "Do you wanna say no?"

"I'll let you know when to stop," she says. Defiance is written all over her face. He's challenging her to tell him no. She's challenging him to keep going.

Quin grins. "Good. Then let's begin."

Well, this is about to get interesting.

Stepping closer to Rochelle, I grab the two ends of the rope together, then slide it through my fingertips until I find the center point. "Have I ever tied you this way?"

"Once or twice," Rochelle says. She looks at Quin. "But never to a bar above my head. And never on tiptoes."

Quin just smiles.

"Make a fist and put your wrists together," I say. She obeys and I begin looping the rope, tying it off with a square knot. I hand the other end to Quin's outstretched hand. He reaches up to the bar positioned over the end of the bed, loops the rope around it, pulls—so Rochelle has to go up on her toes—and then ties it tightly to the metal pipe.

Rochelle lets out a small squeal and when I check her, there's fear in her eyes.

God, I love it.

And she knows it. She knows how much I enjoy the bondage.

"You deserve this," I tell her. "Don't you?"

She nods her head and says, "Yes."

"You were very, very bad when you left last year, weren't you?"

"Yes," she says again. Her eyes leave mine for a moment to look for Quin.

He's sitting on the end of the bed, his pants open, fisting his cock. "Keep going," Quin says.

I place my hands on Rochelle's hips and turn her. She swivels on her toes, until she's facing the bed. And Quin.

I want him to see her reactions.

I want her to see his too.

"How many spankings do you deserve, Rochelle?" I ask her.

"As many as pleases you," she replies.

I almost laugh. Where the hell did she learn that answer?

But Quin clears his throat, telling me to stay professional.

Fine. He wants her punished, I'll punish her until he's had enough.

I move up behind her, pressing my chest into her back, then reach around to grab her tits. I pinch her nipples hard. And if she wasn't almost suspended, she'd arch her back in pain.

She tries it, but the movement only makes her go off balance and pivot into my hold.

Quin reaches between her legs and begins to stroke her pussy. I look down and watch his fingers slip in and out between her legs. It only takes a few strokes before they are shiny with her wet desire.

Her shoulders relax. Her head falls forward a little.

All good signs. She's enjoying it. And he doesn't really want to hurt her. He just wants to make his point.

I caress her ass, my fingers slipping between her legs from behind.

This time she moans.

I reach further between her legs until I bump up against Quin's knuckles. His fingers are deep inside her pussy. I gather some of the wetness and slip back to her asshole, pressing against her puckered skin.

She stiffens when I press harder, so I reach into my pocket for the lube and make her slick enough to take the pressure when my fingers resume.

I close my eyes and enjoy the moment as Quin and I finger her from opposite ends.

Her breathing kicks up. Just soft and heavy at first. But as our playing gets harder—rougher—she begins to moan.

"You like that, don't you?" Quin asks. "You like both of us inside you at the same time."

"Yes," Rochelle murmurs, her body twisting as we play with her. And for a second, I think she might actually come.

But Quin moves, positioning himself directly in front of her, slightly sitting on the end of the high bed. "Put your knees on the bed," he says, holding her hips so she can obey.

She straddles his legs, one knee on each side of his thighs. The relief on her wrists has to be immense, so I wonder what Quin is up to since I know he really *does* want to punish her. He wraps his arms around her waist and holds her close to his chest. Rochelle's head rests on Quin's shoulder, her arms ring around his neck in a hug—

as much as she can manage with her wrists still tied to the bar.

Oh, that's an amateur mistake. I practically grin at Quin when our eyes meet.

When he nods I smack her ass so hard, my hand stings.

Rochelle yells in surprise, but Quin is there, holding his hand tightly over her mouth. "Shhh," he says. "You have to take it quietly."

I smack her again and this time she huffs into Quin's hand, then starts to breathe heavy through her nose. Her chest is rising and falling, like she can't get enough air and needs to take deep breaths.

Quin removes his hand, lets her inhale, then replaces it, just as I strike her a third time.

Her ass is already bright red. Hell, my hand is stinging. But Quin's other hand is still between her legs, stroking her. Making it better. I slap her once more and this time her whole body writhes.

But I know just how to ease her back down. I rub the heat radiating out from her ass cheeks as Quin kisses her. Fisting her hair. He hooks an arm around her waist and pulls her towards him, making her ass stick out and beg me to keep going.

I smack her three times in quick succession, until she's straining on the rope, trying to get away. Trying to get closer to Quin and farther from me.

Her wrists are already red and scratched, so I reach up with both hands and quickly untie her, setting her free.

Quin leans back on the bed, just as Rochelle collapses on top of his chest. I lift her hips up, find Quin's hard cock, wrap my hand around it, and slip it up to her wet opening. She eases down on top of him, burying his dick inside her pussy.

Fuck. All three of us moan.

Quin grabs the hair on either side of her face and pulls her into him. They kiss like they've never tasted lips before. Sloppy and wet. Tongues searching and probing.

I smack Rochelle again, and this time she sobs. "I'm sorry," she says. But Quin holds her tighter, uninterested in her apology. He just claims her mouth in the kiss and stifles her crying.

Her ass is so red and hot. She will be sore when she sits down tomorrow. My own dick is hard just thinking about it. I might have to drop by for lunch just to see how she handles it.

When I look at Quin to see if we're done, he pulls away from the kiss and says, "You have five more, Rochelle. Five more and I'll forgive you. We can start fresh. Do you want to stop? Or keep going?"

"Keep going," she whimpers.

Quin smiles and says, "Use your belt," as he looks me in the eye.

I open my mouth to protest, but then stop.

She *will* let me do it. And he *does* want it. Needs it, probably. And if Quin said this is it, then this is it. He will forgive her and we can start over.

And don't we all want that?

I unbuckle my belt. Rochelle looks over her shoulder, eyes on my hands as I pull it through my belt loops. The sound of leather passing across fabric echoes up into the high ceilings.

I fold the belt in half, holding onto the buckle, and then I bring it down on her skin, smacking the same place I did before.

She cries and begins to count. Quin kisses her, holding her head so she has to look him in the eyes.

When we get to five, it's over.

Quin unties her wrists, massages the red scratches, and pulls her fully into his lap, his arms around her tight, his cock still inside her. She hugs him back, burying her face into his neck as I drop the belt and massage her ass cheek.

The last five spankings were cathartic. I didn't hit her hard and she knows it. Quin knows it too.

But he got his point across. She owed him this if she ever wanted a real second chance. He needed her to feel some of his pain, and she needed him to know she was willing.

They kiss. Softly now. Tentative, like the trust we just built between us. I push my pants down, letting my cock spring free, and step forward, pressing it into Rochelle's back as I place a hand on Quin's head. I lean down and kiss Rochelle's neck. Then her jaw, then her lips.

We both kiss her lips.

She kisses us back and it *finally* feels right.

That's all the invitation I need. I push down on her back, right between her shoulder blades, pinning her to Quin's chest. Her ass is in the air like an invitation. Still wet from the lube I rubbed into her before the spankings. She starts to move on top of Quin, fucking him just the way he likes it. Her tits hanging down in his face. His mouth reaching for her large, round nipples he squeezes them. I reach between Rochelle's legs and cup Quin's balls.

"Fuck, yeah," he moans. "Get inside her now, Bric."

I press a finger against her ass, find her semi-relaxed, and then shove my cock through her tight muscles.

Quin's hand is over her mouth before she can yell. Cupping it tightly once again, so she's blowing air through her nose.

I push on, feeling the motion of Quin, just millimeters of soft, thin skin separating us.

He feels so fucking good. After all these months as strangers, he feels so fucking good.

Rochelle is squealing from behind Quin's hand and I know this first one won't take long. She's close.

Hell, I'm close too.

I watch Quin's face as we fuck her hard. Him thrusting up from below, his balls slapping up against mine. Me pounding her from behind, my hands digging into her hips like I never want to let go.

Quin releases his hand from her mouth and Rochelle moans out her climax. Quin's body stiffens underneath us. He stops, his cock buried deep inside her. And then the pulsing of his cock sends a thrill through my whole body as he comes inside her.

I slide out of her ass, pull her hair so hard, bending her neck back until she's looking me in the eyes, and then I come all over her red-hot ass.

I let go of her hair and she falls back into Quin as I collapse off to the side of them. One hand reaching for theirs. I find Rochelle's first. Then Quin grabs hold of us.

That's it. It's over. The past is over and we can start again.

CHAPTER THIRTEEN

"Fuck," I mumble, my heart hammering inside my chest. "That was pretty damn fun."

"Yes." Bric laughs. He pulls Rochelle closer and for a second I'm reluctant to give her up. "Don't be stingy, asshole," Bric says. So I let her go. Halfway.

"Are you going to leave now?" Rochelle asks.

My eyes are closed so it takes me a second to realize she's talking to me. "What?" I ask, opening one eye to peek at her.

"Are you going to leave?"

I stare at her for a moment. Then look at Bric. He's got his eyes closed too. The hand I'm not holding grabs one of her thighs, hiking it over his leg. He opens one eye to look at me in the ensuing silence.

"Why the fuck would I leave?" I ask. "I just got my revenge. I'm happy now."

Bric laughs.

Rochelle frowns. "So that *was* a hate fuck last night?"

I shrug. "I needed more from you, I guess."

"You're a dick."

"You pissed me off," I say, then open both eyes to look at her. "Really. Fucking. Pissed me off, Rochelle."

"I was allowed to leave. It was in the rules."

"Fuck the rules," I say, pushing her off me and sitting up.

"Come on, you guys," Bric mumbles. "Not now."

"No," I say. "I'm gonna have my say and then I'm gonna let it go. I fucking hated your guts when I saw you in that hotel room. One year, Rochelle. No note, no phone call, no mention of a baby until Chella told me you kept it. You just walked away like I meant nothing. And you think you can just turn back, show up, and things would what? Go back to normal?"

"You guys," Bric interrupts.

"I just wanted to set things right," Rochelle says.

"And we did," Bric says, sitting up and bringing Rochelle with him. "We sorted it out, right?" Bric looks at me, shaking his head a little, as if to say, *Not now.*

But why not now? If we don't do this now, we'll just do it later. Tomorrow, or next month, or next year—if we're together that long. It has to be said, so why not now?

"What you did, Rochelle, was a total cunt move."

"I said I was sorry."

"And I told you, I accept your apology. But an apology can't erase what you put me through. It can't erase one year of helplessness, and sadness, and wondering where the fuck you were. What the fuck you were doing, and why the fuck you left. Why *did* you leave?" She opens her mouth to speak, but I interrupt her. "And don't say because I didn't love you. Fuck you if you think I didn't love you."

"Because you're invested in the game, Quin. You wanted me and Bric. Not just me."

"If that's not what you want," I say, "then why the fuck are you here?"

She stumbles for words. "I... You... We..."

"Jesus Christ," Bric says, standing up and walking into the bathroom. "Just let it go, Quin." He starts the shower and then comes back out. "We're here because we want to be here, OK?"

"So you don't care that she's basically saying she wants me alone, and not us?" I ask.

"Do you care?" Bric asks.

"Dude," I say. "If I wanted her to myself, I'd *have her* to myself."

"I can't believe you just said that. Admitted it," Rochelle says.

"Why not?" I ask.

"Well, I, for one," Bric says, "am flattered."

"Shut up," Rochelle growls at him. "And thanks for those spankings by the way."

Bric shrugs. "You deserved them."

"And," I say, "if you didn't want them, it's your responsibility to say no."

Rochelle huffs out some air. "So you're ganging up on me now?" She's talking to Bric. "Taking his side?"

"I'm not taking his side," Bric says. But we both know he's taking my side. He's not into the couple relationships. He's not going to be with Rochelle as a couple. Even if he was Adley's father—and he's *not*—he would not settle down with her, for fuck's sake. "But this is what we have right now, Rochelle. The three of us. Is that something you're interested in? Or not?"

"I am," Rochelle says, looking at me. "I'm into the three of us, Quin. But you and I have something different."

"Had," I stress. "We *had* something different. And you know what? If you had stayed, if you had just stuck around a little longer, I would've left the game for you."

173

"But you won't now?"

"I don't even *know you*, Rochelle."

"What?" she asks. "How could you say that?"

"I know nothing about you. Not one thing outside our limited time together. You blew my fucking mind when you walked out. Made it explode in confusion. I had no idea you'd do something like that to me. Never in a million years did I imagine you'd hurt me that way." I point to Bric. "Him I know. I know his body, his mouth, his fucking cock. But beyond that, I know his mind. I know the depth of his loyalty. I know his past, what he wants from the future. I know he's got my back. I trust him."

Rochelle draws in a deep breath and lets it out very slowly. "Well..." she says. "I'm glad you *think* you know him so well."

"What's that supposed to mean?" I ask.

She shrugs and gets up off the bed to join Bric in the bathroom doorway. "I'm taking a shower."

Bric and I stare at each other for a second. "Come on," he says. "Just let it go. You had your say, you had your revenge fucks. Two," Bric says, holding up two fingers. "You got it twice. You paid her back and made your point. Now just settle down and let it go." He walks towards me, puts a hand on my shoulder. "We have a good thing here, Quin," he cautions me. "We got her back, we got each other back, and we've got that adorable pumpkin baby. Don't fuck it up with *hate*."

I sigh, not wanting to give in, but unable to help myself.

"Right?" Bric says. "Come on. Let's just take a shower and go to bed."

"I think we need rules," I say.

"What?" Bric is annoyed now.

"More rules. The rules kept things straight, you know?"

"Quin, we broke all the rules with Rochelle. It's too late. We're off the rules. We can try, if you're gonna insist. But look, we made rules last week and we're already off the rules."

"Well, we need guidance, then."

Bric laughs. "OK. Thriples therapy here we come. Get real." He bumps me as he walks towards the bathroom. "In a week you'll be past this," he says over his shoulder. "In a week we'll be settled back into our regular routines. I promise. Just give it a week."

I don't think a week will fix what's wrong with us.

A few moments pass. Me just standing in the middle of the bedroom. Rochelle and Bric talking in low voices in the bathroom. They are in the shower together. I can tell by the sound of the water.

I'm glad you think you know him so well.

They have a secret. That's what she meant by that statement. She and Bric have a secret.

I let out a long breath of air and rub my hands down my face.

What could it be?

"Quin," Bric yells from the shower. "Come on."

It's got something to do with her leaving. Or the baby. Or her coming back. Or all of the above.

"Quin," Bric shouts again. "Get in here now."

It's true. What I said. I don't know her very well. I didn't think about it much before she left. She was just... Rochelle. Our player. The best player we ever had. Did I ever wonder where she came from? Did I ever wonder why it was so easy for her to slip into the life we offered her? And stay for *three fucking years*?

"Asshole!" Bric yells.

175

"I'm coming," I say, slipping my pants down and kicking them away. I kick the doubts away too. Does it matter if they have a secret?

Not really. I know she doesn't want Bric. She wants me. But beyond that, I know Bric doesn't want her without me.

So does it matter if they have a secret?

I walk into the bathroom and decide it doesn't. Not yet anyway.

I open the glass shower door and slip inside. There's a double shower head—one on each side of the shimmering lavender glass-tiled walls. Plus a rain shower overhead. Plenty of room for three people.

It's kinda odd. I know people have fancy showers like this. Hell, my bathroom is fancy too. I have a rain shower and a regular shower head. But there's plenty of space in here for two large men and one slight woman.

Almost as if Bric designed it this way on purpose.

"Here," Bric says, holding a shampoo bottle. "Hold out your hand." I do, and he squirts some shampoo into my palm. "Wash her hair."

Rochelle is standing under one of the side showers. She glares at me through a curtain of water.

"Turn around," I say, making a swirling motion with my finger.

Rochelle steps out of the water, wiping her eyes as she turns her back to me. I gather up her long, blonde hair and begin to wash it.

"See," Bric says. "That's nice, right?"

It's kinda funny that Bric has to babysit this relationship. The one who never gives a fuck. The guy with absolutely no nurturing gene in his DNA.

"Do you know where I grew up, Rochelle?" Bric asks.

"No," she says softly.

"Do you want to know?"

She peeks over her shoulder, finds me looking at her, then averts her eyes to Bric. "Of course," she says in her soft Rochelle voice. "I'd love to know."

"Great Falls, Montana. Well"—he laughs—"not in town. I grew up on a fifteen-thousand-acre cattle ranch about an hour west of there."

"You're a cowboy?" She says it seriously. But then she laughs with him. "That's ridiculous."

"Right?" Bric says. "But it's true."

"Why did you leave?" she asks. I'm still lathering her hair. I'm sure it's clean by now, but I like it. I like being this intimate with her so much, it almost hurts.

"Why does anybody leave home?" Bric asks.

"I dunno," Rochelle says.

I wonder where her home is?

"To get away," she adds after thinking about it a second.

"To get away." He nods. "I like Montana. There's a lot to like about that place. The mountains, the rivers, the sunsets. I liked it."

"But not enough to stay," Rochelle says.

"Nope. I just had to get away. To a bigger place. I got accepted to a private high school in Denver so when I graduated, I just stayed for college. And when I graduated college, I just stayed forever."

"How did you get the Club?" she asks.

I don't know why I find the telling of this story so fascinating—I know it. All of it. But I'm quiet as I continue to wash Rochelle's hair. Just listening, waiting for the best part. The way we met Smith. Those early days when things were simpler. When all we thought about was ourselves. Each other. And how we came up with the idea for the game. And later, how we came up with all the rules.

It was hard at first. Not to feel jealous of each other. Even Smith had trouble in the beginning, and that's saying something. He and Bric both did. They expected me to be jealous, but I never was. I don't mind sharing. I like it.

Women are hard to please. That's something I learned early. It's hard to fuck it up with three men to give them what they need. At least, that's what we thought. I almost laugh at the memories. We made a lot of mistakes in the beginning, but by the time Rochelle showed up, we were experts. The whole thing just ran. Like a complicated, but well-calibrated, piece of technology.

"I met Smith when I was a freshman at DU. He was on campus. Illegally, on campus. You know Smith never went to school, right?"

"I read that somewhere," Rochelle says.

"But he used to crash classes all the time. Just show up on the first day like he went to school there. I saw him in economics freshman year. And I totally thought he was a student. He took the tests and everything."

"Why?" Rochelle laughs.

We've never talked about this with her. Hell, anyone. Why not? Why didn't we ever tell Rochelle personal things about ourselves?

"I guess he just wanted to get a feel for it. I dunno. I never asked him. He was so fucking weird. He got caught too. Right after the first exam. The professor was like, 'Mr. Baldwin, you're not a student here. Get out of my classroom.'"

Bric and I both laugh. "I wasn't there," I say. "I was two years behind Bric in school. We went to the same high

178

school, so I was still a junior when all this was going down."

"Which is a good thing in retrospect," Bric says. "Because if you were there, I'd never have bothered with him."

"Were you guys friends already?" Rochelle asks, looking over her shoulder at me.

We both nod.

"Were you playing a game together back then?"

"Sorta," Bric says. "We double-teamed a girl in high school."

"God, that was a disaster." I laugh.

"You little perverts," Rochelle says.

Bric shrugs. "It was hot as fuck. No guy is going to turn that shit down. And it was Quin's idea. Blame him."

"It was a joke," I explain when Rochelle looks over her shoulder at me again. "I was fucking around and that chick said yes. You don't say no to that."

"So how does Smith come into the picture?" she asks.

"I saw him the next semester," Bric says. "Trying to take differential equations. That class was smaller. A lot smaller. So I was just waiting for it this time. He got busted the second week. And when I walked out of that class, he was outside the building. He stopped me and asked if he could have my hoodie because he was cold."

"Your hoodie?" Rochelle laughs.

"You have no idea," I say. "That was just the first strange request we got from Smith that year."

"So you became friends with him?"

"I wouldn't even call it friends," Bric says. "He was so fucking odd. He didn't have a home. He was only eighteen. So basically, he lived on the streets. But every now and then he'd show up on campus dressed in this five-thousand-dollar suit, you know?"

"Like he does now," she says.

"Right. So I couldn't figure it out. I was fascinated, if I'm being honest."

"We invited him to a party," I say. "And he was almost normal when he arrived. At least he was dressed normal. Jeans, t-shirt, boots and flannel, you know? Classic grunge. He must've gotten some cool kid to donate to his cause that day." Bric busts out laughing at the memory. "So the three of us were just hanging out. Drinking beer and getting high and shit. And this girl comes up and points to each of us. One at a time. And then she says, 'Follow me.'"

"We fucked her upstairs in someone's bedroom. All three of us," Bric says.

"And you weren't virgins?" Rochelle laughs. "Because I'm picturing the three of you like a bunch of virgin nerds who get the offer of a lifetime."

"Nah," Bric laughs. "Quin and I had double-teamed for a while by then. I think she knew that."

"For sure knew that," I add.

"We dated her on and off, the three of us, all through college. Smith's parents died when he was eighteen and he became this über-rich multi-billionaire. That's when he went on his I-refuse-to-own-anything kick. He semi-lived with me in the dorms that second year of college. Then, when Quin graduated and we had enough money saved, we got a place together. That girl was around a bunch. But we had others. And then I went to med school, Quin started his business, and Smith donated money for the building we'd later turn into the Club."

"So you guys have been doing this a very long time?"

"Very long time," Bric says. "You know… since we were teenagers, Rochelle. Our whole adult lives."

"And it's not something you can easily see yourselves leaving behind?" she asks, her voice smaller now.

"Not easily. No," Bric says.

"Oh," Rochelle says. She peeks over her shoulder at me. "I think it's clean." Meaning her hair, which I am still shampooing.

I nod and step aside so she can stand under the water on the opposite side of Bric.

"But we're trying, Rochelle."

I look at Bric. *Are we?* But I don't say it.

"We like you. Obviously," Bric says. Rochelle stares at him as she rinses her hair under the water. "So just give it a chance. Let's settle into whatever this is. And don't make any decisions without talking it through this time. Do you think you can do that?"

She nods, then drops her head and puts her hands over her face.

"Hey," I say, stepping towards her. "Don't."

She wraps her arms around my waist and presses her face into my chest. I look at Bric, who shrugs as he grabs the bottle of conditioner and squeezes some into the palm of his hand.

"I didn't want to hurt you. I swear," Rochelle says.

"It's OK," Bric says, picking up Rochelle's hair and massaging in the conditioner. "That's over now. We're here. Let's just stay here for a while."

I grab the soap and start washing her shoulders. It does feel different now. Sharing that story was good for us somehow. It brings us closer. She knows something now. Something real. Sees us as people, not players. I almost feel guilty for making Bric punish her tonight.

181

Almost. But not quite. It helped me, I think. Get over her betrayal. And she stayed for it. That was the apology I needed, I guess. I just wanted her to feel something. Sorry doesn't tell me much. Letting Bric spank her tells me more. Watching her cry... well, I wasn't going for that, but I won't lie and say it's not meaningful.

The three of us rinse off and step out of the shower. We take turns drying each other off. This isn't something we normally did before. We didn't spend the night together much. Not the three of us, anyway. Bric would usually leave. Or if it was Bric's night, I'd leave.

But none of us are leaving now.

We all climb into bed, Rochelle between Bric and me. Arms find their places. I have one above my head, the other across Rochelle's belly. She's facing Bric, so he has one hand on her cheek, the other on her hip. Our legs tangle together. Rochelle pressing the soles of her feet against my shins, Bric's knee between her legs.

And then there is one long collective sigh as things calm down and we settle.

This, I decide. This is what I've been waiting for.

The settling.

The bed moves, waking me up. The sliding barn doors are open and Rochelle is just slipping through them, tying a white robe around her naked body. Bric is gone. I get up, pull on yesterday's pants, and follow Rochelle.

She's in the baby's room with Bric. He's holding Adley, who is sniffling back tears. He hands her over to Rochelle, who smiles at me when she slips past, on her way to the kitchen.

"What time did you get up?" I ask Bric.

"About an hour ago. I heard Adley waking up. But Rochelle was still out, so I came in here to see what the problem was."

"What was the problem?" I ask.

"Diaper." He makes a face.

"You changed a diaper?" I ask.

"Yeah. I did OK. You ever change a diaper, Quin?"

"No," I say. "I wouldn't even know how to start that process."

"I looked it up online, just to make sure I had it right. But I did OK."

We laugh and follow Rochelle into the kitchen. She's getting a bottle ready for hungry Adley. When that's done, she takes her over to the living room and slumps down on the couch.

"I gotta go," Bric says. "I need a suit and I didn't bring anything over. But I will."

"When?" Rochelle asks. "Tonight?"

"No," Bric says over his shoulder. He's heading back to the bedroom. Probably to find his clothes. "I have the Club this weekend, Rochelle. You know that."

Rochelle makes a face. "What about you?" she asks me.

"I won't be by either. You said you wanted weekends to yourself, right? Well, this is the weekend."

She frowns, clearly unhappy with that answer. "Are you still punishing me?"

"No," I say. I might be. "But I have a different life now. I have plans this weekend."

"So Sunday night?"

I kinda feel bad, so I shrug instead of saying no. "We'll see."

"You have plans at midnight on Sundays now too?"

"No. But I do have plans on Monday morning with Smith. It's something we just... do now. And I like it. So I'm just not sure yet."

"OK, then." She takes her attention back to Adley. "Last night was good, but I guess we're back to real life."

Bric comes out of the bedroom, tying his tie, his wrinkled suit coat over one arm. "I'm gonna be late," he says, leaning down to kiss Rochelle. "Come by for breakfast. Or lunch, if you want. Dinner. Whatever you want, Rochelle."

She nods, but he's already on his way to the elevator.

"Catch you later," I say.

The elevator must be waiting on our floor, because it opens as soon as Bric calls it. He disappears inside, saying, "Yup."

"When do you have work?" Rochelle asks.

"Now." I laugh. "I have a nine o'clock conference call."

"What are you doing tonight?"

"Drinks with Robert. You remember Robert?"

"Sure."

"We go out on Friday nights."

"Oh," she says. Clearly she was not expecting to be alone this weekend. But she asked for it. I guess I am still punishing her. "So breakfast in a couple hours?" she asks.

"Can't."

"Lunch?" She's really annoyed with me now.

"Sorry. I'm just really busy today."

She sighs.

I grab my suit out of the coat closet and take it back into the bedroom.

Rochelle follows a little while later. I'm standing in front of the bathroom mirror, shaving with a new disposable razor and shaving cream I found in one of the drawers. She cocks her hip against the door, Adley resting her head on her shoulder, looking at me with wide eyes.

"She doesn't have your eyes," I say, rinsing off my razor.

"Nope."

"Or your lips."

"Nope." Rochelle sighs.

"But she does look like you."

"I think so too. Everyone thinks so."

"Have your parents met her?"

Rochelle shakes her head. "Nope."

"Is that all you have to say?"

"I'm estranged from my family."

"Why?" I ask.

"Because..." She pauses to inhale. And probably think through her answer. "They hurt me."

I just stare at her for a moment. "Like... physically beat you?"

"No, not like that."

"Like the way you hurt me?"

She huffs loudly, like my question pisses her off. "No, not like that either."

"Are you going to tell me about it?"

"Maybe one day."

"But not today?"

"Not today."

"OK," I say, grabbing a hand towel and wiping my face. "Another time."

I place my hands on her shoulders as I scoot her out of my way so I can get dressed. She lets me, moving aside amicably, and then watches me as I strip and start getting ready for work.

"It's just a long story," she adds, like we're still having this conversation.

"I said fine, Rochelle."

"You never asked before."

"I figured it was something you wanted to put behind you."

"It is. So why are you asking now?"

"Because we have a kid together now. And like it or not, we're in this forever." I nod my head towards Adley as I sit on the bed and start putting my shoes on.

"You don't know that she's yours," Rochelle says.

"She's mine," I say, standing up and grabbing my suit coat. Rochelle rolls her eyes. But when I walk over to kiss her, she kisses me back. "She's mine," I repeat, whispering the words into her mouth. I place a hand on Adley's blonde head of fluff. "Be good, Adley."

She's mine. There is no doubt in my mind that kid is mine. I'd like a DNA test, but it can wait until the whole threesome thing wears off with Bric. He won't want a real relationship. Hell, his mind is already on the weekend at the Club.

I give Bric a month before he gets tired of Rochelle's objections with the Club. She won't put up with it. Not this time. Not with the baby involved.

Bric might not want rules, but Rochelle will.

She'll get tired of his half-assed commitment. He'll get tired of her expectations and questions. And then Rochelle and I will have a real talk about what's going to happen going forward.

CHAPTER FOURTEEN

ROCHELLE

We're in this forever. Not, *We're in this together.* Which is how that saying usually goes.

I sit quietly in the small sitting area in front of the elevator, just staring out the window. Wynkoop Street is busy at night. And during the day as well, I guess. But not in the same way. I can't see the street unless I stand right up next to the window and look down. So from my chair I can just see the mountains peeking over the not-so-tall buildings.

Adley is sitting on the floor playing with some brightly-colored plastic blocks that she likes to taste instead of stack, perfectly content to explore her new world on her own terms. She's very easy-going as far as babies go. Easily satisfied, easily entertained, and a champion sleeper. This probably means she'll be a wild teenager and I will be forced to reflect back on my own wild teenage days, consoling myself with stupid mom-isms like, *Just wait until you're a mother.* Or, *Paybacks are a bitch, sister.*

The buzz of the elevator startles me out of my introspective thoughts and I look quickly over at the security panel. Someone is in the elevator coming up. I don't stand to greet him, not even when the doors open and he steps into the loft.

"Well," Smith says, wearing his trademark dark suit. "This place is quite nice."

"What do you want?" I ask, annoyed. Why does he bother with me? I never understood it.

"It's my day, right? Fridays? They still belong to me?"

I stare at him, open-mouthed. "Are you joking?"

"I am the one who kept paying. I still have a stake."

"You want me to fuck you—"

"No," he says, a disgusted look on his face. "Hell, no."

"Then what are you talking about?"

"It is still my day, Rochelle."

"The game is over, Smith."

"You came back, *Rochelle*. I might need a refund."

We stare at each other for several long moments. His eyes narrowed in... I don't know. Hate, probably. He has always hated me. I could feel his hate even before he started ignoring me. He was never interested in anything. Bric is also like that with me. At least he was. But Bric's indifference is based on selfishness and ego. Smith's indifference is based on... dislike. I'm a bad taste in his mouth. A foul smell or that grossed-out feeling you get when you're walking barefoot in the dark and step on something... squishy.

Disgust.

"How did you get up here with no code?"

"I have the code. I just told you, it's my fucking day."

"So Bric gave you the code? He knows you're here?"

"Quin gave me the code."

I turn away and find the mountains on the other side of the window again. *What the hell is going on?* "Well," I ask, "what do you want to do?"

I catch a shrug from the corner of my eye. "Talk, I guess."

Whatever.

"Adley," Smith says, getting down on his hands and knees and crawling over to my daughter. "What are you doing?"

She smiles at him. Like he's a nice person. And then she waves a red plastic block in the air before putting it back in her mouth.

"She's very cute, Rochelle," Smith says.

"Thank you," I mumble.

"So you really don't know who the father is?" he asks.

I don't even bother answering that stupid question. "What did you want to talk about?" I ask, trying to find a polite way to move this along so he'll get the hell out.

Smith chuckles as he gathers up all Adley's colored blocks and starts stacking them. Adley watches him intently. Her eyes follow each move from the time he picks up a block, until the time he stacks it. She never loses focus. "It's not me who needs to talk."

"OK," I say. "What do you want to know?" I have found it's far easier to give Smith Baldwin what he wants than it is to fight with him. Giving in makes him go away.

"I want to know," Smith says, placing the last block on top of the swaying tower, "who that guy was you were arguing with on the corner of Fifteenth and Champa the day before you disappeared. Because I was stuck at a red light that day and I saw you."

I stop breathing.

"And as a follow-up," Smith says, standing up and then sitting back down in the chair, "I want to know if that guy is the reason you don't want a DNA test."

I inhale and then let it out with a chuckle. "Get the fuck out."

He ignores my order. Just absently rubs a palm across his scratchy jaw. "I know what you are, Rochelle. I might not know anything about your past, but I saw enough of you while we were together to form an opinion. You're an opportunist. You got yourself invited into the game. You played until you got what you needed. And then you left to go get something else. So why are you here?"

My stomach tightens up. I feel sick for exactly three seconds as I internalize his characterization of me. "I know what you are too. And we're not so different."

"Is that so? Do you think we're equals, Rochelle?"

"Well." I laugh. "We're both playing the same game, Smith. So I'd have to say yes. We are equals."

He thinks about this for a little while.

"Do you know why I decided to give my money away?" he finally asks.

"I have no clue. And I don't really care. I'm not here for anyone's money. Certainly not yours. I'm happy to pay back what you gave me. In fact, I insist on it. I will have that money—"

"Because rich people are weird, you know?" He looks at me with one eyebrow raised, like that question was not rhetorical and he's expecting me to agree.

"Oh, you guys are weird all right. Bric and his game. Quin and his revenge. I get the picture, thanks."

"We grow up segregated from the real world. In my case, it was the good kind of segregation. Up in Aspen—"

"Yeah, because Aspen is not a microcosm of rich assholes. Not at all."

"—in the fresh air. All that nature shit people are into up there. The hiking, the kayaking, the skiing. Whatever. It's a good life for a boy. But you, Rochelle. You didn't get Aspen, did you?"

I say nothing. He has no idea what he's talking about and he's certainly not going to be the first person in Denver who gets to hear my story. No way.

"Anyway," he says, waving a hand in the air. "It took me a long time to figure you out. But I did figure you out. Can you guess when I figured you out, Rochelle?"

"Hmmm," I say, putting a finger to my lips like I'm pretending to think. "When you stopped coming by the apartment on Fridays?"

So what if he sees through me? I don't care. I don't have to care about his opinion. I'm not even here for him.

"Yes," he says, pointing his finger at me. "That's exactly when I figured you out." He opens his mouth like he's going to say more. But then reconsiders and stays silent. But as the moments tick off, his face changes. His whole expression, really.

Anger, I realize. He's silent right now because he's angry.

"What do you want?" I ask.

His jaw is clenching. And those eyes… they are filled with hate. He hates me. I have never understood that, but it's always been there. What the fuck did I ever do to him? Nothing. I've done nothing to him. I don't deserve this asshole's scrutiny.

"I want you to listen, Rochelle Bastille. And I want you to listen good. I don't know what the fuck you're up to. I don't know why you came back. But I will give you two million dollars, right now, in cash, if you pack that adorable baby up and get the fuck out of my town."

"No," I say firmly. "No. I'm not leaving. I'm here for Quin."

"And Bric?"

"I'm not the one who wants the game, Smith. They are. They want it. I want Quin. I came back for Quin. I'm not leaving until we at least have a conversation about it. And he's not ready for that yet so I'm going to stay and wait it out. So you can take that money and shove it up your ass. I don't need your fucking money."

He smiles at that. Lets out a breath of air... like he's... relieved. "So you're just gonna what, Rochelle?" Smith's voice is lower now. Not as agitated. Maybe even sympathetic. That stupid offer might've just been another one of those fucked-up tests he's so fond of. *Let's dangle money in front of desperate Rochelle and see if she takes it.* Pathetic. "You're just gonna let Quin pretend that child is his?"

I am so beyond exasperated. "This is not my fault," I say, huffing out some air. "I keep telling him she might not be, OK?" I look at Smith and study his reaction. What is he thinking right now? Why is he here? "I do. I swear. But he won't even consider it. He just says, 'She's mine,' every time I bring it up."

"I could end this any time I want. Just remember that, Rochelle," he threatens again. "Quin trusts me. I can change his mind about you any time I want. I can make him love you again. I can also make him hate you. But you know what?"

I can barely meet his eyes as he waits for my attention. "What?" I whisper.

"I'm gonna let it ride for a little bit. To see what happens. But if you fuck anything up with me and my friends, I will ruin you."

He gets up, kneels down in front of Adley, who smiles at him—again, the tiny traitor—and says, "See you later, Adley," in a very sweet voice. His words come with this huge smile he must reserve for everyone else but me. I can only assume this is the side he shows Chella, and that's why she likes him.

He walks back to the elevator, presses the button, and then straightens his tie in a small mirror hanging above it, like he didn't just offer me two million dollars to break his best friend's heart.

He looks at me. My eyes meet his in the mirror. "I hope you don't think this is me giving up. Because that would be a serious mistake."

I'm just about to reply, but the elevator doors open, he steps in, and then smiles at me as they close and take him away.

When we lived in Pagosa Springs, Adley and I spent our Saturdays lounging in the hot springs along the river on the resort property. There was little traffic noise from the main street and the rushing of the San Juan River drowned out the playful voices of families there for a weekend away.

It's something I miss right now.

Our condo in LoDo is a place for young people. Mostly people interested in partying and not new mothers interested in... well, mothering. But I'd like some new clothes and Adley could use something too—shirts that don't say Pagosa Springs on them—even though right now I'd really like to get in my car and drive us five hours south to our little tepid pool. So we brave the streets.

The 16th Street Mall intersects my new home on Wynkoop Street, but it's blocks and blocks away from the trendy shops, so Adley and I take the mall bus down to the more populated section to get breakfast and spend money.

Saturday mornings are busy, it seems. I feel like my life in Denver was a lifetime ago. I feel like a stranger. An interloper. Adley is agitated. Not cranky. Yet. But it's clear we are on the same page about the traffic, noise, and bustle of city life.

I'm having doubts right now. Lots and lots of doubts.

Things with Quin are not going the way I imagined. I had pictured a warm welcome. Which, I admit, was pretty naive on my part. I left him with no explanation. But I was, in my defense, upset. Hormonally upset. Everything that seemed so rational at the time just appears thoughtless and crazy right now.

And all I keep thinking about is Smith's visit last night. Will he really try and mess things up with Quin?

Yes, I decide. That's something he'd enjoy.

After I get a muffin at Starbucks, Adley and I claim a window table and stare out at the gray day as we absently eat. She is chewing on one of those baby cookies, the kind that come in a box in the baby aisle and have no taste whatsoever. I tried one. I try all her baby food. The organic peaches are my favorite. But her gums are sore from the threat of teeth and she gnaws on it until her mouth is lined with mush and I'm lost in thought as I drink my coffee and wonder how I can make things better.

I called Chella to invite her to come with us, but she's working today. Something about her tea shop having a soft opening next weekend and problems with a pastry recipe.

OK, I sigh. I get it. I left and everyone else moved on. I've been alone for a year, I can manage a few more weeks as they try to figure out how I fit into their new lives.

Eventually I drag myself up out of the chair and we head out into the cold windy day to shop. I used to enjoy shopping, but that was then. Back when shopping meant thrift stores and whole afternoons wandering the long aisles of antique stores.

Now, it's a chore. But I manage to find me some nice things in shops where they will box everything up with pretty bows and have them delivered to you. And I find some cute clothes for Adley too, but I take those pretty bags with me onto the bus as we finally make our way home in the late afternoon.

But when I get to the lobby on the ground floor of the loft building, and call the elevator by punching in my code, it doesn't come. I can hear people inside. Loud people. Laughing people. So I know it's working. But someone must be moving in, because I also hear a lot of swearing, and grunting, and banging.

So I unlatch Adley's baby seat, fold the stroller, and lug everything up the stairs. Someone peeks out on the fourth floor, a man about my age, who sees me struggling and says, "Need some help?"

Normally I'd say no. But… "Yes, thank you," I say through my heavy breathing. "Someone has the elevator for moving, I guess."

He takes the stroller and the packages, which leaves me with just Adley's carrier, and we trudge up the stairs to my loft. That's when I realize, with blushing cheeks, that the person who is hogging the elevator is me.

Well, not me.

But Bric.

CHAPTER FIFTEEN

The alarm beeps as the door leading to the stairs opens and Rochelle appears with a man.

"What's going on?" she asks.

I could ask her the same thing. "The furniture came in," I say, eyeing the man. "What's going on with you?" It comes out... challenging. Which surprises me. Almost... jealous. Even more surprising.

"Oh." Rochelle laughs and turns towards the guy. "Thank you."

"No problem," the guy says, and then disappears back into the stairwell.

"I was coming..." She stops, then starts again. "I went shopping. Got some new clothes." She holds up some pretty bags as her proof.

Was she going to say, *I was coming home?* And then felt conflicted on whether or not this place was home?

"The shops are going to deliver the rest of my stuff on Monday. This is just Adley's things. What furniture?" she asks.

I look over my shoulder at the team of people—all busy inside Adley's bedroom. "The crib, remember? There was just the floor model left. Well, it came in yesterday afternoon so I hired people to pick it up and put it together. So she can stop sleeping in that travel thing."

Rochelle leaves all her things in the front sitting area and brings Adley's baby carrier over to the couches and sets it on the coffee table so she can unbuckle her. "She likes the travel thing, Bric. You shouldn't overspend on a crib."

"How do you know I overspent?" I ask, sitting on the couch across from her. "You haven't even seen it yet."

Rochelle is making a silly face at smiling Adley, but she pauses to shoot me a look. "Because I know you well, Elias Bricman. Subtle isn't in your DNA."

I consider this. She does know me. I know her. We know each other. Three years—even three years of two-days-a-week game playing—is a long time in the relationship world. If Rochelle was an illegal immigrant looking for a green-card marriage, we could pass that investigation thing they do. That one where they ask you your partner's favorite color and stuff. Their favorite movie. Do they cry at weddings? Do they like burgers with onions?

Purple. *The Blues Brothers.* Yes. And no.

In fact, I might know more about Rochelle Bastille than any other woman on this planet, including my mother and Marcella Walcott.

"You like antique stores and old things that smell weird," I say.

Rochelle bursts out laughing as she slips a pink sock off Adley's foot. "What?"

"I know what you like," I say. "Velvet and lace. Especially if the lace has that little yellowing edge to it. And long flowing skirts that someone found in their grandma's closet after she passed away and decided to donate to the unfortunate. You really shouldn't take clothes from the unfortunate, Rochelle."

Adley is laughing at her mommy, who is laughing at me. I stand up and walk around the large square coffee table and sit down next to them, reaching for Adley at the same time.

She comes to me happily, her wide blue eyes staring up into my dark ones. "I read somewhere that all babies have blue eyes," I say.

"I don't think that's true. Not entirely, anyway. But I asked her doctor if she thinks her eyes will change color. She said she didn't know."

"Whose eyes will you have, baby?" I ask Adley. I hold her up in front of me like a prize. Trying to see her future. Wondering if she has anything of me inside her. She sticks her chubby little foot in my mouth in response.

"Well, you like five-thousand-dollar suits, Mr. Bricman. And that's an excessive use of money if ever there was one. You could feed an entire village in India for that kind of money."

"Not true," I say, setting Adley down on my knee. "Smith and I actually support an entire village in India and that shit is expensive."

Rochelle chuckles as she leans back into the couch arm, resting her feet right up next to my leg. "I forgot, you're a habitual do-gooder. Never mind. Wear your damn suits if you want. Now tell me—what's really going on in that bedroom?"

I look over at the bedroom. There's a lot going on in there. But right now, I'm distracted by this woman and her baby. The surprise I planned is not even in the top ten things on my mind. Plus, Rochelle has kicked off her shoes and is pressing her socked toes into my thigh. I look over at her with... well, a *look*.

She smiles and shakes her head at me. As if to say, *Sorry, you horny man. I have a tired baby and you have half a dozen workers in our house.*

Our house. Is this our house?

"Jesus Christ," Rochelle says. "What are you thinking so hard about? You have smoke coming out your ears."

Adley laughs and slaps my face with her little fist.

"I know a lot about you," I say.

"Do you?" Rochelle says. And when I look at her, her face has gone serious.

"I think so," I say.

"Aside from where I like to shop—and I'd just like to say I spent a fortune on brand-new clothes down on the mall this afternoon, so your assessment is no longer valid—what do you know?"

"I know you like holidays. You even put up an Easter tree one year and decorated with pastel pictures you cut out of vintage magazines."

"Yeah." She sighs. "I'd forgotten about that."

"And I know you're kind. You don't like to argue. And you will avoid a fight at all costs."

"Does that make me meek?" she asks.

"Meek?" I laugh. "No. It makes you sweet."

"Aww. Elias has a soft side."

I shrug. "I'm glad you're back."

"Holy shit, you're like—serious right now, aren't you?"

I nod and look at Adley. "Yeah," I say. "I am. I didn't realize how much I missed you until this week."

"Do you love me, Elias?"

"Yes," I say. "I love you, Rochelle. Probably not the same way that Quin loves you, but in my Bricman way, I do."

200

"*Loved* me, you mean. You heard what he said the other night. Doesn't even *know* me."

"Well, he knows all the things about you that I do. So you have to internalize it in a different context. He doesn't trust you because you hurt him when you left."

"But I didn't hurt you, did I?"

I shake my head and lean back into the cushions. Adley leans over towards Rochelle and I hand her back. She crawls her way up her mom's chest and rests her head on her breast, closing her eyes as Rochelle pets her hair and kisses her cheek.

"Nah," I say. "I wasn't hurt. I was... a little relieved. Secretly happy."

"God." Rochelle huffs. "Way to make a girl feel special."

I'm not sure if that's a real scoff or just a fake one. Probably something in between.

"I knew you liked Quin better," I say. "And Chella... well. Chella was a whole bunch of new fun, you know?"

"Is that what Quin thought of her? A whole bunch of fun?"

"No. He was mad at first. Smith and I kinda tricked him into it just to get his mind off you."

"And it worked?" Rochelle asks.

I nod. "Yeah. It worked. They're like... best friends now."

"I'm getting that."

"Are you jealous?" I ask, giving her a sideways glance.

"Maybe a little."

"Well, don't be. Chella is in love with Smith. If Quin was ever invited into that little arrangement, he'd say yes in a second. But he won't be. Ever. Smith doesn't give two shits that they spend so much time together alone. But he knows better than to be with Chella and Quin at the same time."

"Because Quin wants the game," Rochelle says in a mocking voice. "I don't know if this is going to work, Bric. He wants the game with us too, but the problem is still the same. He doesn't want me all to himself."

"It's only been a few days, Rochelle. Give the guy some time."

"He says he's not coming over tomorrow night. Says he's got breakfast with Smith on Monday morning. He chose Smith over me. God, I want to die of humiliation."

"Like I said, give it time."

Just as that last word leaves my mouth, the woman in charge walks up to us. "Excuse me, Elias. Sorry to interrupt, but we're finished. All the linens and clothes have been laundered and put away. Everything is perfect. Would you like to inspect it?"

I stand up and shake her hand. "Not necessary, Abbey. I trust you. And thanks a bunch for coming over on a Saturday." I lean in and kiss her cheek, then walk her and the other men to the elevator. They are lugging out trash and large cardboard boxes.

When I get back to Rochelle, she's got her eyes closed. "Perfect, huh?"

"My command is law around these parts," I say.

"Do I get to see it now?" she asks, not bothering to look at me.

"For sure."

Adley is fast asleep in her arms, so Rochelle maneuvers her body carefully, holding the baby to her chest as we walk slowly down the hallway.

"Oh, Bric," Rochelle says as we step in front of the wide doors. "It's gorgeous." She walks in, looking around with surprise and happiness.

And even though I really, *really* like the dark side down in the basement of the Club, this kind of stuff feels just as good.

"That crib." Rochelle sighs. "It's beautiful. How did you find something to match the decor in this loft?"

"It's a limited-edition piece by the same artist who did the metalwork." And she's right. The crib perfectly matches the old reclaimed wood look of the loft ceiling beams. And the metal bars are a sleek pewter color that look a little industrial, but work with the rest of the theme.

"This color," Rochelle says, walking up to the deep purple velvet drapes and feeling the fabric between her fingers. "God, I love it."

"Much nicer than the thrift-store version you had hanging in your old apartment."

"Yeah." She laughs softly, so not to wake Adley. "I'll admit it. They are stunning. I love the yellow accents. The bedding. Oh, my God. Who knew you had an eye for design?" She goes over to the crib, peeks in, and then places Adley inside. I walk over and watch, fascinated with the idea that she will sleep in here tonight. Now. She's sleeping in something I gave her.

"Oh, that's all Abbey," I say. "She has a design studio that specializes in children's rooms."

"Is she a Club member?"

"Well... her husband is. Women can't be members, you know that."

Rochelle scowls at me, but only for a second. I wait for the inevitable next question. *Did you ever fuck her?* And my truthful answer would be yes, dozens of times. Just last weekend, in fact. But thankfully Rochelle never asks.

"Look, she loves it." Adley never wakes up as Rochelle covers her with a light blanket.

"Either that or all that shopping tired her out."

"No," Rochelle says, turning to put her arms around me. I hug her back and enjoy the thanks. "She loves it. I can tell."

"How long does she usually sleep?" I ask, trying not to sound like a sex-craved pig.

"Long enough to get your reward, Mr. Bricman." Rochelle pushes off me, grabs my tie, and then crooks her finger in a come-with-me gesture as she leads me out of the room.

I close the sliding barn doors as quietly as I possibly can, and then pick Rochelle up, throw her over my shoulder, and carry her to our bedroom. This time I slide the doors closed with less care, and then I throw her down on the bed.

"I've missed you too, Elias," Rochelle says, already unbuttoning her jeans.

I slide my tie over my head, fingers flying down the buttons of my shirt, and whip it off. Rochelle has her pants off and is crawling over to the edge of the mattress, her long, blonde hair dragging across the white linen duvet cover.

I stand still and let her deal with my belt. The buckle clinks as it falls aside, and her small, nimble fingertips open the button of my slacks and unzip my fly. She reaches in and presses her palm flat against my growing cock, then steps off the bed and sinks to her knees in front of me.

Those wide hazel eyes are trained on mine. She has been properly schooled in all the ways Elias Bricman loves to be sucked over the last few years, and I can't wait.

Her mouth opens, just a little. Just enough to taunt me as I watch her lick her lips. Her hands are sliding up and down my shaft, pumping me with an experienced rhythm. She is a woman who knows me. Every sexual thing that turns me on is inside her head. All she has to do is reach in there, pluck it from her memory, and take it out.

"Fuck," I moan. She took them out.

Her tongue swirls along my tip, tasting me. Teasing me. And then her lips open and her warm, wet mouth covers my head. I close my eyes and reach for her hair. Bunch it up in my fists, like it's a length of rope and I need it to hold me steady.

I don't need to push her down on my dick. She swallows me eagerly. But I push anyway, reaching down with my hand to cup my balls. And then I push those up into her chin as she takes me all the way down her throat.

I hold her there, choking and gasping, until she presses both hands on my thighs and pushes me back. She looks up at me, sucking in air. Eyes trained on mine. Drool running down her chin.

She grabs the drool in her palm and slaps it around my cock, pumping me in long up-and-down twisting strokes. And then she leans forward, presses her mouth to the tip of my cock, and kisses it, spitting out more lubrication at the same time.

That is a move I have dreamed about dozens of times over the past year. Dozens of times. She is the only woman who kisses my cock that way.

I pick her up, twirl her around, and then bounce her on the mattress so her head is hanging over the edge.

"Ready?" I ask her.

"So ready," she says.

I ease forward towards her wide-open mouth. I can't see her eyes, and that's the only thing I hate about fucking her throat this way. But I can almost see her goddamned tonsils. So, good enough.

Her tongue flattens against my shaft as I enter her mouth. Her lips seal against my skin. I hold her face with both hands and... I fuck her. I fuck her until she is gagging on her own spit. I fuck her until her hands are pressing so hard against my thighs, I can't ignore her plea for release.

I come down her throat as she gags, then swallows. Once, twice. Three times her throat muscles caress my cock.

When I'm done, I pull out, grab her legs, spin her around, and sink my face down into her pussy.

She writhes beneath me. Her back arches and bends. Her whole body contorts as I lick and suck her until she, too, has no choice but to let go.

She comes in my mouth. Her orgasm is wave after wave of spasms and creamy liquid. And once I have it all, once I'm drunk and intoxicated on her climax, I crawl up her body, my cock slipping between her legs.

And then we truly begin to fuck.

CHAPTER SIXTEEN

Friday night, everything's cool. I do the usual club and drinks thing with Robert. He goes home with some girl he's never met before and will probably never see again. I pretend like this is fun and go home alone.

There's about ten minutes at the end of my day where I wish things were different.

Saturday, I start wondering where she is and what's she's doing.

Thinking about Rochelle has been forbidden for the past year, so it's weird to allow myself this luxury. Before last week thinking about Rochelle was something to avoid. It would inevitably lead to that familiar dull ache in my chest that would turn into sadness and despair if I let it fester too long.

But now she's back. I have her back. I still can't believe how quick life changes. So I do think about her. And Adley. What did they have for breakfast? What did they do all day?

I hardly ever see Smith and Chella on the weekends and I've gotten used to no Club and no Bric, even though that Club was my life for more than a decade.

I don't call him. I don't call her, either. And I get through Saturday by going into the office and working on a proposal for a new client who came in last week. And then I hit the gym for a few hours and go home with take-out Chinese.

But by Sunday morning, I'm hopeless. The entire time I run steps over at Coors Field, they're on my mind. Adley and her big blue eyes and little chubby face. Rochelle and her curvier new sexy body. How much she's changed. Her hair is longer, her tits bigger, her hips wider. And by the time eight AM rolls around I'm sweaty as fuck, my legs are aching, and I've imagined a million ways this can go wrong and only one way this can go right.

When I get home I shower, make a protein shake, and wish it was summer so I could go outside and sit on the terrace. It's not snowing today but it's gray and dim. I need a little sunshine in my life.

By noon I'm regretting my decision to stay home tonight. What the hell was I thinking? I almost call Bric to see what he's up to, but decide that's probably a bad idea. He'll be at the Club. He's always at the Club. Nothing about that guy's schedule ever changes. He is the definition of habit.

By six PM I'm counting the hours until Smith shows up in the morning.

What a sad life it is when a Monday morning coffee visit from Smith Baldwin is the highlight of my weekend.

It's been like this for a while now, though. I've been like this for a while now.

How long should I punish her? How long do I refuse to let her in? How long do I have to torture myself in order to trust her again?

I almost want to call her up. See if her weekend has been spent the same way. Has she been sitting around feeling sad? Has she been thinking about me too?

Are we in fucking high school or what?

By nine, I'm sitting on my couch staring at the clock over the fireplace. It's modern and artsy. A chrome thing with a second hand. Which I watch, relentlessly, as it sweeps around the center point, counting off minutes.

Minutes that turn into hours of me sitting here alone in the silence. No lights on except the ones pouring in through the two-story walls of glass from outside.

At ten minutes to midnight, I give in.

Did I ever think I wouldn't?

I drive over to LoDo, which is still pretty busy for this late on a Sunday, and park in my designated spot between Rochelle's Lexus and Bric's BMW.

I have to think about that for a second. Take a moment to wonder how I feel about him being here on my night. Reevaluate how I imagined she spent the weekend.

Was he here the whole time? Did they just spend two days together? Alone?

I'm just about to start the engine and leave when I make myself be rational.

Bric will stay with her. He doesn't want her for himself, but he does want her. So he will stay. And he's not a thinker, like me. He doesn't dwell on shit. He gives in to his wants and needs and just goes for it.

So if this bothers me, I'll need to be the one who takes care of it. Who sets things straight. He never will.

I get out of the car, close the door, and call for the elevator with my code. The doors open immediately, then close after I step in, and eight seconds later I'm in the loft.

It's quiet and dark, except for soft light flowing out of Adley's room down the long, wide hallway. Her barn doors are open just enough to let the glow escape.

The doors to the master bedroom are closed.

They're in bed together.

I glance at the kitchen as I walk by and see the remnants of dinner.

They ate together.

I walk towards the master, but a soft rustling makes me turn towards Adley's room. I slide the doors open just enough to slip inside and take it all in.

I guess that crib came. And a whole bunch of other stuff. Adley's room has been transformed into an elegant nursery. The deep purple and light yellow color scheme reminds me of Rochelle's apartment above the Club. The velvet curtains and tulle canopy over her crib add rich textures against the pale walls. There are baskets filled with toys and stuffed animals. An open closet made out of that artistic piping Bric has lining the walls along the ceiling shows me dozens and dozens of baby outfits hanging on small, appropriately-sized wooden hangers. A wooden dresser along the exposed brick wall, which obviously matches the crib, has a small crescent moon-shaped lamp, which is where the glow of light emanates from. And a rocker, upholstered in light yellow fabric, sits in the corner, next to a changing table.

His new princess, I guess.

Princesses, I correct myself.

I sink into the rocker with a sigh, not one bit surprised that Elias Bricman is making the most of this situation. Making the most of my absence. Not that he's trying to crowd me out. I don't believe that at all. But Bric is not only a man of habit, he's an opportunist, and I left the goal wide open for him to score.

"Hey," Rochelle says in a soft voice.

I turn my head to look at her. One hip cocked against the wooden frame, head tilted. She's wearing a light-colored silk robe. Maybe yellow, maybe cream, maybe white. It's hard to tell in the low light. Her long, golden hair flows over her shoulders, one pale breast almost visible, the sleek fabric slipping.

"Hey," I say back.

"You said you weren't coming."

"I changed my mind."

"Are you mad?" she asks.

"No." I shake my head. "No, I'm not mad."

Rochelle walks over to me, her bare feet padding softly across the wide-planked wooden floors, and straddles my legs, settling in my lap. She wraps her arms around my neck and places her head on my shoulder. She's completely naked under that robe. I can smell her sex when she opens her legs.

"How do you guys not get jealous?" she asks.

I shrug and place both of my hands on her hips, enjoying the weight of her body in my lap. "It's Bric. He doesn't want to take things from me, he wants to share them with me."

"Do you love him?"

"Yes," I say.

"Do you love me?"

We already talked about this the other day. And I lied to her. I mean, there's still a part of me that feels like I was duped. That she tricked me into believing she was this person, and then she was someone else. Someone who would pick up and leave without a note. Someone who would walk out.

"Yes," I answer.

"Are you going to leave now that you know he's here?"

"I knew he was here before I came upstairs. I saw his car in the garage."

"He's moved in, Quin. He brought his clothes over this morning."

"OK," I say.

"You should bring your clothes over too."

"Is that what you want?" I ask. "Both of us. Full-time?"

"He's not full-time." She laughs, but softly, so as not to wake Adley. "He'll be at the Club every day. And most nights, too. Every weekend for sure."

"He obviously wasn't there this weekend," I say.

"No, but the nursery furniture came in. So he rearranged his schedule to see to that."

"It's nice," I say. "Lovely, really." It's not what I would choose for our daughter. But I don't say that.

"It is," Rochelle admits with a sigh. She sits up straight and places her hands on either side of my face. Leans in and kisses me.

I kiss her back.

"I want you," she says. "And if you want him, I want him too." She pauses to stare down at me. I can just barely make out the swirls of blue and green in her eyes. "Do you want him?"

I think about this for a second. When was the last time I had a couple relationship? Have I ever had a couple relationship? Sure, Rochelle and I pretended. We were together as a couple two days and nights a week. Sometimes we'd even cheat and I'd come over on Saturday night, after I knew Smith's time was over, and we'd get in the Suburban and drive up to the mountains. Spend all day Sunday together when it was supposed to be her day alone. Two days turned into three every once in a while. That's how we spent the summer boating before she left. That's how we took that trip up to Jackson Hole.

But when was the last time I wasn't sharing with Bric and Smith? Aside from a one-night stand, which I have never been into on any kind of regular basis.

Never, I decide. I've never been in a real relationship before.

"I need him, Rochelle."

"I see," she says.

We're silent for a little while. I can hear Adley's soft breaths from across the room. "Do you like the nursery?" I ask her.

She nods, but stays quiet.

"It's nice. It was nice of Bric to do this."

"Do you want to come to bed?" she asks.

I glance down at my watch. It's a little past one in the morning. I'll have to leave very early to be back at my condo before Smith shows up.

Rochelle doesn't wait for my answer. She gets up off my lap, her pale breasts fully visible now, since the silky tie around her waist has slipped, and holds out her hand.

I take it and she pulls me to my feet. Leads me out of the nursery and into the master bedroom.

The city lights filter through the sheer curtains covering the window. Bric is sprawled out on his stomach across the king-sized bed, arms and legs all over the place.

He makes me smile.

Rochelle drops her robe to the floor, where it becomes a puddle of gold, or cream, or white. She takes my hands and places them on her breasts, helping me caress her softly. When she lets go, she begins to undress me. Slips my coat off. Drapes it over a chair. Lifts my t-shirt up, her fingertips grazing the hard planes of my stomach. I reach behind my neck and pull it all the way off, since she will never be able to reach that high. She unbuttons my jeans, unzips my fly. Slides my pants down my legs. I step out as she reaches for my boxer briefs, her hand against my cock as it thickens from her pressure.

She gets me naked and leads me to the bed, crawls in first. I follow, slipping under the covers with her and Bric.

He groans and turns on his side. Exhausted.

I pull Rochelle in close, my hands slipping between her legs. I find her wet and that's the only signal I need. My fingers play with her as she begins to breathe harder. We kiss as I slide my body on top of hers. Pressing my chest against her breasts, moving my hips until my cock finds her entrance.

I slip inside her and move slowly, lifting my chest up slightly, so I can stare down at her face.

Bric is there. Awake. Leaning in to kiss her face as I watch. His hand sliding in between Rochelle and me. Pressing on her flat stomach, pressing on mine too. He plays with her clit as I continue to move. Her eyes are closed in ecstasy when I leaned down and kiss her. Kiss him. Kiss them both.

She moans into us, her hands reaching for Bric, who kneels on the bed, his hard cock aimed at her mouth. She opens and the tip of his head disappears. I watch as he places both his hands on her head and urges to take him deeper.

But it's a nice, soft fuck. Not usually how we do things as a group.

And when I look up at him, he smiles.

He's got me, that smile says. He wins.

I don't care who wins. I just want to enjoy them. I lean down and kiss Rochelle. She pulls back from Bric's cock just enough to slip her tongue inside my mouth. I reach under, holding on to her waist as I flip us over. Bric is there, positioned behind her. Ready to join in.

But instead of taking her in the ass, like I expect, he eats her out from above while I continue to fuck her from below.

Rochelle begins to moan.

I begin to moan. Bric's tongue lapping against my shaft. His hot breath and hard chin bringing me to the brink.

I pull out before I come, because I want to be on top. Bric and I trade places. He places her on top of him, so she's looking at me when his fingers press against her ass, before positioning himself. I watch as he enters her. Then I grab Rochelle's knees to open them wide as I straddle one of Bric's legs, my balls dragging along his thigh, and press my cock against her pussy.

When I'm inside her—we—when we're inside her—I just... float away.

There is no dirty talk. There is no hard grunting or screaming. There is no "Yeah, baby," or "Fuck me harder."

It's just us.

I come inside her, the muscles of her pussy clamping down on my cock as she comes too. Bric pushes us off him, kneels on the bed next to Rochelle, and comes in her throat.

After that we're tangled again. Like we used to be. How we *should* be. Arms and legs crossing. Hands here and there. Mouths kissing.

And we all go still.

Smith walks through my condo door just like usual. He drops the gym bag to the floor and two rat heads peek out at me from the partially open zipper.

"What the fuck is that?" I laugh. "You got another rat dog?" Two of the little things now. Both with pink bows atop their heads.

"Chella and I are thinking about having twins," Smith says. "So we're practicing."

"You don't get to *decide* if you're having twins, dumbass," I say, looking in the bag he brought for my pastry. It's a cherry sugar dumpling. Why do I work out every weekend when Smith just brings me this crap every Monday? I take a bite and ask, "Where the hell did you get this? My mom used to make sugar dumplings just like this when I was a kid."

Smith points a finger at me. "Chella bet me ten dollars you'd recognize it."

"Wait," I say. "My mother made this?"

"No, Chella made it. But your mom gave her the recipe. They've gone partners in the pastry recipe business, it seems."

I almost choke. "My mom is a pastry partner?"

"Can you believe how fast things can change in a week?" Smith asks, taking the lid off his cup of coffee to gulp it. "You and Bric are back together, Rochelle came home, Chella and I have twins. Life is good."

"Hmm," I say. "Why are you so upbeat? The last time I saw you, you were talking some major shit to Rochelle for coming home."

He gives me a sidelong glance. "I'm just looking out for you, man. And we chatted on Friday. I'm happy with her responses."

"What did she tell you?" I ask, going for my own coffee.

"She told me…" He stops, like he's thinking back on it. "We just came to an understanding. Let's just leave it at that."

My phone buzzes on the counter. I pick it up and read the text from Bric. *Come to the Club for breakfast. I need a favor.*

"So how's things?" Smith asks, nodding at my phone.

"We're working it out."

"Hey, men of habit," he says. "The both of you."

I have often wondered how invested Smith was in the game before he and Chella got together for real. I mean, I cannot see Bric leaving it behind. Ever. I can see myself leaving, but it's such a trade-off for me, it's not going to be easy. So whatever, maybe we're both men of habit, just like Smith says.

But Smith didn't second-guess his decision when Chella walked out. He left with her. Cold turkey. One day we're a quad, the next day they're a couple. No turning back for him.

I craved it all year. And the past six months, when I wasn't talking to Bric, it was… a longing. Some deep part of me that was missing.

Today, I feel whole again. Like things are back in place. Like life is good, and this is the first day of the rest of my life. And all the other clichés that run through your head when you get exactly what you always wanted.

217

"You'll get over it though," Smith says, picking up his twin rats and slumping down on my couch. "One day you'll wake up and be like, 'I'd like Rochelle all to myself.'"

"Well, that's not going to happen," I say. "Because Rochelle and Adley are a package deal. And we don't know who the father is."

"So as long as you don't know, you're both the father, is that how this works?"

"Why not?" I say. "That's how everything works. You don't know what you don't know."

"Or you just stick your head in the sand and hope it goes away."

"What the fuck?" I laugh.

"You need a DNA test, Quin."

"Why? We're doing good for now. If we know, that'll spoil it."

"That'll set things straight, not spoil it. Once you know you can decide how to move forward."

"We already have. Me, and Bric, and Rochelle, and Adley."

"You think this game will last forever?" he says.

"It's not a game when no one's playing, Smith."

"Well," he says, kicking his feet up on my glass coffee table. "I hate to break it to you, but everyone's still playing."

"You don't know what you're talking about."

"I know more than you think," he says. "And I'm not trying to be a dick, but I'm serious. You need that DNA test. You need to know who the father is. And beyond that, Adley needs to know too."

"She's six months old."

"I know, but kids grow up, Quin. And secrets tend to stay secrets. Don't fall for it."

"It's not a trick," I say, starting to get pissed off.

"Fine," he says, slapping his hands on his knees and standing up. "I've gotta go beat the shit out of some thugs at the gym. Little bastards kicked my ass last week. But I'm ready now." He tucks his little rats back into the gym bag and hikes it over his shoulder. "You're gonna show up on Saturday for the opening, right?"

"What opening?" I ask.

"Oh, Chella didn't tell you? I guess she was gonna do that tomorrow at lunch. The Tea Room is having a soft opening on Saturday to nail things down before the grand opening next week. Chella told her about the baby. But don't worry, I'm running interference for you, bro. I'm gonna make sure—"

"My mother?" I ask, cutting him off. "She knows about the baby?"

"See," Smith says. "This is why you need that test. That cute mother of yours is going to fall in love, Quin. And if that baby isn't yours, it will break her heart."

I think about this for a minute and decide he's probably right.

"And yours," Smith adds as he opens the front door. "You need to get that info soon, Quin. Because Bric is falling in love with that kid too."

CHAPTER SEVENTEEN

ROCHELLE

I knew three things when I found Elias Bricman four years ago.

One. He was hot.

Two. He was half-owner of Turning Point Club.

Three. He liked to play games.

If I had to make a list of three things I know about Bric now, none of those things even come close to mattering.

I didn't even know who Quin was until Bric took me to dinner at the Club the day after we met. He was sitting up in Smith's bar—both of them were—when Bric brought me upstairs for a chat. That's what he called it. A chat. That chat ended up being an offer to play the game. Which was the whole reason I was there.

I'd heard about this game they played from a girl named Lindsey up in Salt Lake. I was just passing through Utah on my way to Colorado, but my car broke down and I ended up staying for a few months, trying to get the money together to fix it. Lindsey was just a roommate I had at the time. She was a law student at the University of Utah. And since I was on a very tight budget, I was looking on campus for temporary housing, and got a room in her house for fifty dollars a week. She liked me, she said. And when she found out I was heading towards Denver, she got chatty. It turned out that Lindsey had played a game in Denver with three men. She told me all about it. Told me about the money, the sex, and, of course, the Club.

So Bric was my goal when I came to town. And there I was, twenty-four years old, sitting in a private sex club in Denver, talking to three men about sharing.

Not cheating. Sharing.

It was such an interesting idea for me. And Lindsey made it out to be a pretty sweet deal.

Looking back, I decide it was a sweet deal. Still is.

Bric can be summed up in three words. Self-absorbed, self-obsessed, and self-serving. They almost mean the same thing, but Bric is so egomaniacal, he deserves all three, even if it's just for poetic reasons.

Add in a dark Machiavellian psyche that likes to twist people's perception, and you get one messed-up man.

But most people don't see that side. I'm not even sure Quin and Smith see that side. If they do, they just go along with it. But I see it. I have always seen it. You have to be a certain kind of person to make an offer like that.

I think he's so likable because you see him coming a mile away. He's like a bulldozer with a blinking neon sign that says, *me, me, me*. And he's set his life up in such a way that he never has to hide that from anyone.

Or maybe people are just pretending? He's rich, powerful, handsome—and isn't that all you need to be liked in this world? It's only what's on the outside that counts in society.

There are no women in his life except for the game players and the wives the members of his club share with him downstairs.

And the game players are managed using Quin. He's the one who keeps them together. I realize that now. Bric is too selfish. Smith was never invested enough. But

Quin... everything about Quin is the real deal. If he's in, he's all in.

When I saw Quin at the first meeting he was sitting across from Smith looking like the perfect contradiction. That same night I was inside that top-floor apartment making myself at home.

One week into the little Taking Turns game and I was falling for Quin Foster. For *them*, really. Not Smith. Never, ever. But Quin is like a kinky perfect gentleman. He opens doors, he likes to buy me gifts, he's never late, and he's fun. We hit it off immediately and even though the rules of the game were challenging, we got around them. Eventually we ignored them, but that was much later. We played by most of the rules for more than a year. Hell, even Smith played along for a while.

But Bric was another matter altogether. Yes, he was the first of them I was with. But I didn't fall for Bric until this past weekend. Four years after we met, he showed me something real. And I can't even say I was waiting for it, because I wasn't. I wasn't looking for any kind of gesture from him. And never in a million years did I ever imagine that Elias Bricman cared enough to try for a second chance at a first impression.

The car pulls up in front of Turning Point and a valet rushes up to my door to open it. I'd forgotten how nice it was to have a driver take me places, but I still have to take a moment to unlatch Adley's car seat, and he waits patiently.

"Good morning, miss. Are you having breakfast with—" But another valet is there, whispering in his ear.

"Ooohhh," he says, smiling. "Come this way, Ms. Bastille. Mr. Bricman and Mr. Foster are waiting for you."

I wrapped my arms and legs around Quin so tight this morning to try to make him stand up Smith for their stupid Monday morning breakfast date, he had to pry me off him. I lost, obviously. But we laughed, so it was worth it.

An hour later Bric woke me with the sound of the shower going. He said I could go into the Club with him, but who the hell wants to get up at six AM if they don't have to?

Of course, Adley woke up two minutes after he left, so joke's on me.

But the clothes from my Saturday shopping spree were delivered promptly at eight-thirty, so I'm glad I stuck to my lazy schedule. Because I look fantastic right now.

I'm wearing a cream-colored, oversized, cable-knit sweater dress that hits me at the knee, cream-colored knee-high socks, and some brown leather chunky-heel, below-the-knee boots. None of which were purchased at a thrift store or in the t-shirt department of a Pagosa Springs tourist trap. I even have a matching cable-knit scarf that is so long, it hangs down to my hips after it's wrapped.

Adley is trying to show me up, because we match in color and knitted textures—except she's got on a sweater coat, tights, and little furry booties—and she's cuter than me by miles.

Mondays are always busy in the White Room. These damn rich people can't wait to get back to work, and what better way to start your week than Monday morning bacon with your business bros?

Quin and Bric are both at the table—laughing at something—as I walk up, lugging Adley in her seat. Bric gets up to take her, and she smiles brightly at him as he wedges the carrier into the booth.

I lean down and kiss Quin, who is looking me over like he might throw me down on the table and fuck me right here.

"I approve," he says, finally finding my eyes.

"Thank you." I curtsey, holding my sweater dress out with fancy fingertips. "And you'll be happy to know, Mr. Bricman, everything was purchased new."

"Love it," Bric says. "And love the pumpkin's outfit too." He doesn't look at me. My little girl really is showing me up in the eyes of Elias Bricman.

The waiter comes and I order a plain pancake for Adley, and a bacon and cheese omelet for me.

"I'm glad you got new clothes," Bric says, still making stupid faces at Adley so she'll giggle. "Because you and Quin are going out on a date tomorrow night."

"We are?" I ask, looking at Quin.

"He's got an ulterior motive," Quin says. "Needs you to be his date for a party on Thursday night, so he's going to babysit and we get to have a nice dinner. Or... dancing. Or anything you want."

"Babysit, huh?" I eye Bric cautiously. "I'm not sure you're ready to be promoted to babysitter, Mr. Bricman. You just became babysitter assistant four days ago."

"Five," Bric counters. "And I got this. I have like seventy-five nieces and nephews."

"You do not." Quin laughs.

"Why do you think I hate kids? My family reunion is like three hundred people."

225

"I don't know," I say, picturing him alone with my daughter.

"It's fine, Rochelle. I swear to God, I know what I'm doing. And anyway, the hospital is only three blocks from the loft."

"That's not a good selling point!" I laugh.

"I tell you what. I promise to call if there's any problem. But I'm picturing a nice quiet evening in front of the TV and then a nice warm bath before I put her to bed in that fabulous nursery. We'll be fine."

I look at Quin for his opinion. He shrugs. "He's not as stupid as he looks. Med school, remember?"

I actually did forget about that. It's weird how much my thoughts about Bric have changed in the past week. He is capable. He's highly educated, he's calm, he's caring. He's considerate. It's stupid to assume he can't take care of Adley simply because he's a man.

"Fine." I sigh. "You're right." I wrap my hands around Quin's arm and lean into him. "And anyway, it will be really great to go out with a grown-up." I lean up and kiss him. "Especially when I get you all to myself for one whole evening."

CHAPTER EIGHTEEN

BRIC

Monday night is like the last year never happened.

Rochelle never walked out. Quin never got hurt. I never gave a baby called Adley the nickname 'pumpkin.'

One week ago, I thought Jordan Wells was my new partner, Quin was never going to talk to me again, and I was happy—or, at the very least, relieved—that Rochelle had pulled off such an amazing disappearing act.

I don't even recognize that life when the elevator doors open and I step into the loft. Music is playing. Not loud, but just loud enough. I instinctively know that Adley is asleep just by the atmosphere. The smell of good food lingers in the air, the lights are dim, and I can hear the soft sounds of Rochelle and Quin talking in the kitchen.

I'm late getting home because of work, but I'm so ready to be here with them.

I slip out of my coat, throw it on a chair, and loosen my tie as I turn towards their low voices. They are happy voices. Content. The way they used to be. There was never any tension in our relationship with Rochelle before she got pregnant. Looking back, I can see that I missed the change from easy, to strained, to unbearable after she confided in me and asked for advice. I won't make that mistake again.

They are drinking wine. Rochelle always did like wine. I see the bottle—something French and expensive—on the counter, and just... enjoy them for these few moments before they see me.

I spy on them. Like a voyeur.

Quin is leaning against the countertop. Rochelle's legs are pressed up against his, so their hips touch. He has one hand on her waist, she has one hand on his forearm. They both hold wine glasses as they talk, and smile, and look into each other's eyes, like they are the only thing that matters.

It's erotic, I think. The position they're in.

It's easy again. Like it used to be before.

One week and we are caught in her web. She is a spider wrapping us up in silk. We are the food that feeds her.

I'd lost sight of that last year when Chella appeared in her bed. It all happened so fast. Smith was there to persuade me that things had gone on too long. Remind me of the game and hint that we needed a new player.

And I went along because that's what I do. I like *same* and I'm not afraid to admit it. I liked *same* with Rochelle more than I ever cared to admit.

She was—is—the perfect player in the game of Elias Bricman. She knows all the rules, all the shortcuts, all the perils, all the ways to win and lose, and win again. And I never had to teach her these things. She never asked questions like Chella did. She never questioned anything at all. She just played to the best of her ability and along the way we discovered she's a fucking gold-medal Olympic athlete in this game. She is breaking record after record. First to stay so long. First to walk out. First to come back. First to have our baby. First to make me want...

It's the last one that's starting to bother me a little. Just a little. Just a tiny bit.

I won't admit to it. If I admit to it, things will not be easy anymore. Things will be strained and then things might become unbearable. She's not walking out, I know this. I feel this. No, she's here, and she's here to stay.

But Quin and I are another matter.

His trust might not be back but he's forgiven her. He's OK with the setup so far. He's OK with the share. But it's tenuous. Like one wrong move could set him back.

I refuse to be that one wrong move.

"Hey," I say, stopping to lean against the quartz island. "Did I miss dinner?"

They both look at me, smile bigger, and some of the uneasiness melts away.

"I saved you a plate," Rochelle says, breaking contact with Quin to motion to the microwave. I can just barely make out a plate through the mesh pattern of the door.

"I'll eat later," I say, so I don't become the reason this moment breaks. Food can come later. I'm not hungry for food right now.

Quin sets down his wine glass, grabs a cut-crystal rocks glass on the counter next to him, and uses a pair of silver tongs to drop in three ice cubes with a series of clinks. The bottle of brandy is expensive, just like the wine, and it's sitting on the counter, waiting for me. He pours, offers the glass to me, and I walk over and take it from him, our fingers touching—just slightly—in the process.

He's been waiting for me.

No. Correction.

He's ready for me.

"Busy day?" Quin asks, sipping from his glass.

I take a long drink of brandy, almost finish it, and exhale. "Not busy enough to make me forget where I was coming home to tonight."

Rochelle pulls me into them like I belong there. Rises up on her toes and kisses me on the mouth. Our tongues tangle together, the sweetness of her wine mixing with the citrus of my brandy.

Quin joins in. No hesitation.

I have missed his mouth, I realize. I have missed these moments. And Chella just wasn't the same. Chella was new and inexperienced. A novice in the game of Bric and Quin. Rochelle is a professional. The three of us together are the definition of team.

The music is perfect. Ray LaMontagne, *Be Here Now*. So very, *very* Rochelle.

She smiles at us, her hands on the waist of our pants. Like an expert, wise to the ways of unbuckling the belts of two men at the same time, she unbuckles us. Unbuttons us. Unzips us. Her hands slip inside and pull us out. Thick, and long, and hard. We kiss again. It's slow, but the kind of slow that precedes something hard and fast.

It's a kind of savoring, I realize.

Rochelle drops to her knees. Her mouth is eager. Hungry. I am so close to Quin, our arms press against each other. Still, Rochelle has us draw closer, his chest pressing against mine as she opens her mouth and the tips of our cocks slip inside and disappear.

I have to close my eyes when his hand rests on my hip. His fingers gripping into my skin, pulling me close, so we change position slightly. I know what he wants, but this standing position isn't the way he'll get it. Three people fucking at the same time requires careful maneuvering.

Stop thinking, Elias. Just enjoy.

Quin settles for less than perfect and places his hand over Rochelle's. They fist my cock together. I join in, my hand over hers, on him. This is how we connect when Rochelle is on her knees in front of us.

Quin's other hand is in Rochelle's hair, holding tightly. I imagine how that pulls on her scalp, and groan.

We've done this dozens of times and each experience is better than the last. This time is no different. This is the best it's ever been. This is the pinnacle of perfection of what we have.

We let Rochelle have her way for a little longer, but I can tell that Quin is as eager as me to move things along to the next wave of pleasure. He grabs her arm, signaling for her to stand. And we begin to undress her. I work on her pants. Unbuttoning, unzipping, then a forceful tug. She helps me from there, maneuvering her jeans over her hips until they fall to the floor.

She and I both start undressing me as Quin unbuttons her blouse, opens it up, and then pulls her bra down so the underwire will push her tits up. He sucks on her nipple as my shirt comes off. Fingers slip between her legs, making her moan as my pants drop to the floor and I step out, kicking them aside.

Then it's Quin's turn. She takes off his t-shirt as I wrap my hand around his shaft and slowly pump it up and down. Quin closes his eyes. He's missed me just as much as I've missed him, I can tell.

I make her kneel again, push her head towards his cock, and she opens. I guide her as she sucks. Encourage her to take him deeper. I glance up at Quin and find him staring at me.

We smile.

Rochelle yanks his pants down his legs and then he too has kicked aside the rest of his clothes.

Rochelle rises to her feet and we stand there naked for a few moments. All three of us picturing what comes next. We don't need to talk. Explanations and instructions aren't necessary. Rochelle backs away until she bumps up against the kitchen island. She places both of her hands on the edge, palms down, and lifts herself up so she's sitting on it.

I walk towards her, place both of my hands on her knees, and open her legs. Her pussy is pink and wet. Ready for us. I lean in and lick her. Swipe my tongue across her folds and then tickle her clit.

Quin pushes her backwards and she obeys without comment or protest. When her skin comes in contact with the cold, hard quartz, she bucks a little, arching her back. But Quin is there, fingers between her legs, joining my tongue, as we make it all better. He leans down to kiss her lips as I watch, staring across her flat belly. His other hand is squeezing her breast. I reach up, both hands sliding across her abdomen at once, still licking her pussy and making it wetter, to squeeze her breasts too.

I want to do so many, many things to Rochelle right now. But we are constrained by the kitchen island she's lying on. I know Quin is thinking the same thing. He wants to lift her up, carry her to the bed, or the floor, or the couch—or wherever—so we can fuck her right.

But he waits. We wait.

We worship her just a little longer.

I make a bet with myself as I lift her knees up towards her chest. Open her legs wider so I can lick her deeper. I think he'll take her to the bed.

But he doesn't. When he pulls Rochelle up to a sitting position, signaling me to back away, he slides in between her legs and picks her up. She instinctively wraps her limbs all around him. Her legs around his waist. Her arms around his neck. And he carries her to the couch. He sets her down on the floor and spins her around, pressing her chest down on the arm of the couch.

This is one of our favorite ways to fuck her, and she knows just what to do when I sit down on the couch. Her hand is on my dick, her body leaning over into my lap as she takes me in her mouth and begins to suck.

The real show for me is Quin. Who presses his hard, erect cock against her ass, both hands on her hips. I watch his face. I wait for it. That look. The way he closes his eyes when he first enters her.

When he opens them again, he's staring at me.

We smile.

This is why we play the game, and Rochelle is the only girl we've ever had who never has to be told what to do. Never has to think twice. Never has to second-guess herself.

We are a team of professionals.

I place a hand on Rochelle's back, stroking her softly as Quin fucks her slowly. He pushes in hard and deep, then withdraws in increments. Slow. Too slow for Rochelle. She wants more now. We all want more now. But Quin will deny us until he's ready. He enjoys his time inside her. Savors it, just like we savored that preliminary kiss.

When I know I'm getting close, I grab Rochelle by the upper arm and tug on her. She responds just the way she should. Climbing onto my lap, straddling my thighs. Quin's dick slips out of her, slick and shiny from her wet pussy.

I feel that wetness a second later when she grabs my cock in her hand, guides me to her entrance, and lowers herself.

When I look at Quin, he's watching me the same way I did him.

We smile.

Quin repositions himself as I tug Rochelle down to my chest and wrap my arms around her, holding her tightly against me. I love the way her breasts press against my skin. I love the way her hair tickles my shoulders. I love the way she pants her hot breath into the sensitive skin just under my ear.

Quin starts with a finger in her ass. He pumps her and I feel it. I can feel his fingertips against my shaft as she moves her hips over mine in small circles. I want to tell him to stop fucking around and just shove his cock inside her ass, but I don't. I'm patient. The best part of all this is the expectations.

But then the waiting is over—too soon, almost. And the tip of Quin's cock is pressing against her ass. There is no smacking of her cheeks. No dirty words to turn her on more. We like it that way too, and we'll do it that way next time, for sure. But this time, words aren't necessary. There is no need to pull her hair, or slap her face, or choke her neck—even though she will beg us to do all those things next time.

This time we don't fuck her. We love her.

It seems to last forever and then it's over too quick.

I come inside her, wondering if she is on birth control, and not caring one bit.

Quin waits until I'm done, then kneels on the couch, urging her to suck him, and then he comes in her mouth.

She swallows, her pussy clamping down on my dick as she comes too, my semen mixing with her climax, leaking out, dripping down my shaft and over my balls.

We are a hot, sweaty mess of perfection as Quin leans into us. Our bodies tangled up the way they were always meant to be. Arms and legs wrapped around each other as we kiss her, and each other.

In this round of the game, we are, once again, all three winners.

CHAPTER NINETEEN

ROCHELLE

I dress in front of the full-length mirror as Adley plays in the new walker Bric bought. Her little socked toes do their best to maneuver the thing, but the hardwood floors are clean and slick. There is a maid, I guess. A team of them who come with the loft. Bric says they're on salary because he was renting this place out by the night before we moved in together. And he feels bad taking the contract away from them, so they will come twice a week from now on. The floors are spotless.

Bric should be here in a little bit to babysit. Quin said he got stuck doing a conference call at the last minute so won't be home until seven or so. But I don't care what time he gets here. I have a whole night of Quin to myself.

I love being with Bric and last night's lovemaking was exceptional, even for us. But I came home for Quin. I haven't lost sight of that goal. Not one bit.

Quin sent the dress I'm wearing. This is something both he and Bric have done many times in the past. Especially Bric, who likes to control what I wear to the parties he takes me to. Quin less so, only a few times. But we've been apart for a year, so he probably has a fancy restaurant in mind and doesn't want me showing up for our date underdressed, and in order to avoid an awkward moment at the beginning of the night, he has provided me with his wish.

I am happy to oblige.

The dress is red and long. It has a strapless sweetheart neckline and it's made of the most luxurious silk my fingertips have ever had the pleasure of caressing. It came with a thin diamond belt to heighten awareness of my waist. I am sure the diamonds are real, as these men do not do fake anything, but they cannot possibly be real.

They're real.

I had forgotten how much my men like to buy jewelry.

It also came with a platinum choker, diamond earrings set in white gold, and a white gold cuff bracelet.

And the black shoes have red soles.

He also provided me with a black cashmere evening coat with the most beautiful red silk-covered buttons, because it's snowing again.

Even though it's Tuesday and we are going nowhere special, I'm ridiculously excited about our date.

The elevator dings and I catch Adley turning her head to see who is here. She's made her way into the hallway, but I can see her smile in profile as Bric walks up to her and drops to his knees to have a chat.

"What are you doing, pumpkin?"

She giggles.

"We have a date tonight," Bric coos, lifting her out of the walker. "Your mom thinks I set her up with Quin to make her happy, but I didn't. I just wanted you all to myself so I can tell you a bedtime story using fake voices and no one will hear me."

I shake my head at him, laughing. "I have no idea who you are right now."

Bric whistles low as he looks me over. "Wow. That's some dress."

"Zip me, will you? Quin won't be here for another twenty minutes and I want to be ready."

He sets Adley back into her walker and her socked feet get busy trying to move again. She gets some purchase and follows him into the bedroom.

I turn my back to him as he walks up behind me, lifts my hair carefully aside, making it drape over my shoulder, and then leans into my neck for a warm kiss. One hand is on my breast, the other flat against my stomach.

I melt backwards, enjoying his touches.

"I'm jealous," he whispers into the shell of my ear.

"You are not," I say back, my heart picking up a faster beat. "Elias Bricman doesn't do jealous."

"But if he did, he'd be jealous now. You look beautiful. I will have to rethink my choice for tomorrow night. There's no way I'm letting Quin make you prettier than I will."

"Men." I chuckle.

He backs off, slightly, and reaches for the zipper low down on my back. His fingers touch my bare skin for just a moment, and I sigh.

It's dangerous to love him so much. I know it's a different kind of love than what I feel for Quin. It's more like lust. But still, it's dangerous.

A part of me is wondering if we'll ever leave this game. A part of me is wondering if I want to. A part of me is terrified about those parts of me.

I am here for Quin. I came back for Quin. I want Quin.

And yet I want this too.

I have become Elias, I think. Addicted to the game. Addicted to the familiarity of the three of us. Addicted to the way they make me feel when we make love together.

I'd forgotten that while I was gone. The last year or so of the time I was playing, Bric was emotionally absent. Content to visit me on his days and nights. Content to take me out to parties and events. Content to let Quin have me in a special way. To claim me, to own me, to love me just for me.

But now he seems... invested. I think it's because of Adley, to be honest. I think he's bonded with her. Correction, I know he has. Adley has changed the dynamic in ways I hadn't thought of when I decided to come home. She has changed the way Quin thinks about me, for sure. Adley was the reason he was so angry with me those first few days. Missing out on my pregnancy and her birth was a blow he won't easily forget. Forgive, yes. Maybe. But forget? Sex is not enough to make him forget.

And now Adley is the reason Bric is invested, I'm sure of it.

What does that mean for the long-term plan? I admit, Quin doesn't seem to be thinking about me as his sole partner. He is invested too, but in a different way. He's invested in the *us*. Even more so than he was last year when I left.

Am I setting myself up for failure? Am I pushing the possibility of me and Quin away, and replacing it with the surety of me, and Quin, and Bric?

Bric finishes the zip, gathers up my hair, and places it down my back just the way he found it.

He's so tender. I wonder if anybody else in the world knows just how tender Elias Bricman can be?

I don't know first-hand how he likes to fuck women down in the basement of the Club. But I have an idea. He's warned me before. I have asked him for certain things during sex. I have moaned out phrases like, "Choke me" and "Fuck me harder" and "Slap my ass". And sometimes I wanted it harder than he delivered, and would beg for more.

He would always put me back in my place with a firm, "No, Rochelle. You don't understand how much farther I can go." One time he even confessed that he was dangerous. We weren't fucking at the time. Just talking. And I said I liked being choked. And I do. I don't want to be suffocated, for fuck's sake. But I crave his unpredictable dominance when I'm about to come.

So I said that. And he replied, "I will hurt you. I will enjoy hurting you. I am dangerous. So don't ask me to do that in the middle of things, Rochelle. Don't ever ask me to do that when we're wild."

I believed him. And I never asked again. There was a dark look in his eyes. A raw blaze of rage that scared me a little. But it went away and I forgot about it. Until now.

I won't ask. I believe there are a lot of things locked deep inside Elias Bricman's head. And I know for certain that no woman he's ever fucked down in that Club has ever had the pleasure of him zipping up her dress and whispering his quiet jealousy in her ear.

I am special.

CHAPTER TWENTY

I catch them in a quiet moment. I came up the stairs, the elevator being used or broken. But either way, I was impatient to get home so I took the stairs, and I catch them.

Adley is wandering down the hallway in a baby walker, a bright red plastic block in her mouth, drool running down her chin. I stoop to look her in the eyes—those blue, blue eyes—and she smiles at me. I'm just about to pick her up and hold her close, really feel the connection, when I hear whispers coming from the bedroom.

"Be right back," I whisper down to Adley. When I get to the door Rochelle is standing in front of a massive framed, full-length mirror propped against the wall. Bric is standing behind her, almost possessively, as he adjusts her hair. I think he was just zipping up her dress. He leans down into her neck and whispers something I don't catch. Rochelle laughs, closing her eyes like she's enjoying the moment.

They are beautiful people.

"That dress," I say, walking into the bedroom. "I almost want to rip it off you."

"Do it," Bric growls.

It comes out way too serious to be a joke, and both Rochelle and I laugh. "Do not touch this dress until after dinner, Mr. Foster. I like it way too much to take it off now."

I come up next to them, put my arm around Rochelle's waist, and pull her close to me. Bric reciprocates, his arm sliding past mine, and pulls us both close to him.

We stare at each other in the mirror.

We are beautiful people.

I reach into my coat pocket and pull out my phone. "Hold still a sec," I say, bringing up the camera. There is no flash and no shutter click as I take the picture. But we all feel the way the moment was just captured.

"We make a nice… thriple." Rochelle chuckles. "That's a real word, by the way. I saw it on a Showtime series last year."

"They have a thriple on Showtime?" Bric asks.

"Mmm-hmm," Rochelle says. "But it's not nearly as hot as the one in this room."

"Stay home and let me fuck you," Bric moans.

"Later," I say. "We need this night."

He knows it's true. I have a lot of things to say to Rochelle and I need to do that away from Adley and away from Bric. Away from this house. This family, I guess. It's something between us, and only us.

"Are you ready?" I ask Rochelle. Bric backs away, shaking his head like it's a damn shame. It probably is. But we'll be back, and he knows that.

He leaves Rochelle and I alone and a few seconds later we hear Adley squeal as Bric greets her in the hallway.

"Should I be nervous?" Rochelle asks me in the mirror.

I turn, get her coat off the bed, and then hold it open so she can slip her arms inside.

I lean into her ear, the same way Bric was just a few moments ago, and whisper, "No."

This settles her.

She knows I have something to say, but she also knows I won't lie to her. Would never lie to her. So she trusts me.

That's all I'm hoping for at the end of this night. Just a little more trust. On my part, not hers.

We need this night.

I take one more look at us in the mirror, decide this requires another picture, and pull my phone out again. I want to look at both those pictures right now. Compare them. Weigh the merits and pitfalls of each scenario in my head. But it's premature and we have a night planned anyway, so instead I say, "Ready?"

Bric is sitting on the couch holding Adley in his arms. She's slapping his cheeks as he makes funny faces. "She's got bottles in the fridge, Bric," Rochelle says, slipping into mom mode. "She should only want one, but we might be late. Feed her, give her a bath, and then put her down in about an hour. There's a jar of baby food on the counter if you want to give that a try." She laughs, picturing it, I think. "But it's not necessary. She likes the bottle at night. Call me if you have any questions."

"I got this," Bric says through lips being pinched together by Adley's little fingers. "Go away now. We're having fun without you already."

Rochelle lets out a long sigh as I call for the elevator. Whatever was holding it up a few minutes ago has passed, because it comes immediately. We step in and watch the doors close.

Bric and Adley disappear.

"This is the first time, isn't it?" I ask.

Rochelle nods. "First time leaving her behind. I have a little pain in my heart, Quin. Hold my hand."

I smile, but take her hand. When the doors open, I lead her to the Suburban and open her door. It's not classy, and she practically has to climb into it, it's so high off the ground, but it's me. It's us. We've done so many fun things with this fucking truck.

I go around to my side, get in, and start it up. Rochelle is biting her finger, like leaving Adley behind really is causing her pain.

"Are you OK?" I ask.

"Yes," she says. "I'm not worried about Bric. It just… it feels weird leaving her behind. She's been my little sidekick for six months, you know?"

"We're coming back, Rochelle. We can even come back early if you like. But I do have something special planned for after dinner."

"What?" she asks.

"It's a surprise."

"Give me a hint," she begs.

There is a recognizable brightness in her hazel eyes. Something that has been mostly missing since she came back. Something I've missed as well.

So I give in. "Well," I say, backing the 'Burban out of the parking space. "You've never been to my house. Bric brought you here back when you first met. But I never took you home. I've always regretted that."

"We're going to your house?" she asks, a quiver of excitement in her voice.

"After," I say, as if this explains everything.

I have taken Rochelle out to many nice restaurants since we started… dating. All over the city. In fact, it was something we did for fun. We'd scour the *Westword*, looking for new restaurants, and we even had a list ready to go on the refrigerator, held up by a vintage Pepsi magnet she found in an antique store once. If we ever got bored, we'd just look at the list and choose one that had not been marked off yet.

Tonight's pick was all on me. I don't have that list anymore. She left it stuck to the fridge when she disappeared last year and I took nothing out of that apartment, even though Bric told me I should. So the list is gone. That whole life is gone, I realize. Everything we're doing now is new.

I like that. A lot. I like that it's a do-over, of sorts. A way to look at what went wrong and fix it. Make things better.

I think it's going well. It was hard for the first few days, but after I went up there Sunday night and found Bric has filled in for me, I felt better knowing he was there. He picks up my slack. He smooths over my wrinkles. He compensates for my shortcomings. And he set up this date. He said it was for a selfish reason. He wants to take Rochelle to a party on Thursday night and to make it fair, he gave us a night out alone.

But it was not selfish. It was very generous. I like that about Bric. And Smith too. Even though most people don't see him as selfless, Smith is the definition of the word. He's a giver. And Bric is his partner in crime in that endeavor.

We end up at Sallie's. It sounds like a diner, but it's not. It's a very fancy Italian restaurant down in Englewood. An unassuming place down on South Broadway. A good twenty-minute drive at this time of night, but Rochelle talks excitedly the whole time. She tells me about her day. Something I've missed a lot over the past year.

"We took a walk to see if Chella's neighborhood really wasn't walking-accessible the way you said it was," she says.

"So is it?" I ask, getting off the freeway and turning left. It's snowing, which I think is good luck.

"You know, it's so close, but so far. That stupid train station takes up the whole north side of the block. So we had to walk all the way around and…"

Long story short, I was correct. In order to get over to Little Raven Street from Wynkoop, you have to go out of your way. They got as far as Coors Field and turned back.

I want to be magnanimous and say, *You can just drive over there. She has guest parking.* But I take the win and say, "I'm never wrong."

She agrees with a sigh, just as I pull into Sallie's parking lot and find a space.

The only thing you can see inside Sallie's are small orbs of light from the crystal chandeliers. The place is made of dark tinted glass. During the day, it's just another building made of glass, but at night it's inviting and mysterious. The way houses are at night when you drive by and get a glimpse of someone else's life through a lit-up window.

As soon as we walk in, the host, dressed up in black and white, invites us to sit in the elegant, but comfy couches and offers up champagne. They do this even if your table is ready. It's called greeting time. If it's not too busy, and it's not tonight, the champagne comes within two minutes and three minutes later, the waiter will appear to escort your party to the table. Just enough time to take a sip and enjoy the atmosphere properly without feeling rushed.

This is exactly how it happens tonight.

We sit and settle, looking over the slim piece of fine paper with tonight's menu on it.

Once we decide, and order, Rochelle picks up her champagne and asks, "What was your day like?"

It has been so fucking long since anyone asked me this question. Not even Chella has asked me this question. Sure, she asked about me. *What did you do all day? Did anything interesting happen? How are you feeling, Quin?*

But only Rochelle says it precisely this way.

"My day was filled with thoughts of you."

She smiles. Blushes, even. Because that was always my opening answer. It's like old times. Good times. Predictable times. When we knew where we stood and how things would play out.

I don't think we know either of those things right now. But it doesn't matter. We're starting over.

I tell her. It's nothing interesting, just work stuff. But she responds with interest and drills me when she thinks I'm leaving out details.

There is no lull in our conversation. She has always been a talker with me. She tells me all sorts of things. Asks me all kinds of questions. We eat, still talking, and finish, never running out of things to say.

Bric texts us a picture of sleeping Adley and we admire her. Talk about things that only new parents can relate to.

Even when we get back in to the truck and drive towards downtown, we talk.

It's just little things. Unimportant things, but things that intimate people find fascinating about their partner. There are no life-altering revelations. No excuses for past behavior. Nothing that might upset the order of the evening.

When I pull up to the valet of my building Rochelle looks up with wide eyes. "You live in the SkyClub?"

"I do," I say, just as the valets appear, opening our doors. I hand off the keys, tip the kid, and meet Rochelle on the other side of the truck.

We walk through the lobby and get on the higher-floor elevator using my access card.

"This is pretty fancy, Quin," Rochelle says.

We both watch the digital numbers ping off as we ascend to the penthouse, and when the doors open, I wave her forward into the condo.

"Wow," she says, automatically walking towards the fourteen-foot, floor-to-ceiling windows. I have never had a visitor up here, aside from my mother—and she doesn't count—but I imagine this is everyone's first reaction. It was mine, for sure. "Holy... I love this."

I walk over to her and take off her coat. I drape it over a dining room chair and then take mine off as well. "This isn't the surprise, but since it's your first time here and all, I'll give you the tour." I turn us around so we're facing the great room and pan my hands. "Voilà." Rochelle giggles. Because a tour isn't really necessary. It's just a giant room with fourteen-foot ceilings that holds the ultra-modern kitchen, the dining room space, and the living room. I have ten pieces of furniture in this massive room, and four of those pieces are barstools pushed up against the kitchen island. "It really needs a woman's touch," I joke.

Rochelle hangs on my arm and laughs. "Well, I love it."

"The bedroom is next."

"Is that where my surprise is?" she asks, as we walk down the hallway.

"Just wait."

The guest bedroom has the same wow factor. Or lack of it. The windows and the view of the buildings outside are the only thing worth noting. I have nothing in there at all. No guests stay here.

The master bedroom does have a bed, since I do—did—sleep here. And a long dresser where I empty my pockets every night. Other than that, there's not much else to say about it. Elias Bricman, I am not. But again, the windows are the only thing people see. The view is the only thing they care about. Especially at night.

Tonight, though. There is one extra thing in my bedroom. A gift on the bed with Rochelle's name on it.

"What is this?" she asks, picking up the box and shaking it.

"I missed last Christmas. I wish I could say this is what I had planned on giving you, but I'd be lying. I had a trip planned."

She pouts her lip.

"I was going to take you somewhere far. Not a place we can drive to in twelve hours." Which was our limit since we never had more than three days in a row together.

"Where?" she asks, putting down the box and turning to face me. "Where would I have been last Christmas if I had stayed put?"

I shrug. "It was going to be your choice. Wherever you wanted. I was going to ask you if you wanted to leave the game with me."

She pouts again.

"I was going to make you put your finger on a globe and choose a place. Two weeks alone. Fourteen days in a row. No Bric, no Smith, no Club, no rules."

"And I fucked it all up."

251

It's my turn to shrug. "It's in the past now. And anyway, I didn't bring you here to make you feel bad. I brought you here to make you feel better. Open the present and I'll show you."

She walks over to the bed and sits down. Places the white box in her lap and pulls on the red ribbon. Lifts the lid. Opens up the tissue paper. Pulls out...

"A bathing suit?" She gives me a weird look. "Are we going on vacation tonight?"

I nod, smiling. "Yup. Right here, right now, I'm taking you somewhere else." I place both hands on her shoulders and turn her gently around so she's got her back to me. I unclasp the thin diamond belt at her waist and place it on the dresser. She pulls her hair aside, revealing the back of her neck to me, and I remove the choker. She takes off the earrings as I unzip her dress and let it fall over her hips and puddle at the floor.

Her panties follow and she stands there naked. Little goosebumps rise up her arms and she shivers.

Her shoes come off and she is three inches shorter.

I reach for the white bikini and turn Rochelle so she's facing me. "Put your hand right here," I say, motioning to my shoulder as I kneel down.

She smiles, blushes. But obeys. Her warm hand presses down on my shoulder and then she steps into the bikini bottoms and I pull them up.

"I'd take you outside naked, but... the city, right? People and their telescopes. This is not the tallest building in Denver."

"I'm OK with this," she says, chewing her lip.

It's a nervous habit. Tells me lots of things right now. She's turned on. She's happy. She's exited, but unsure of what's happening.

I lean in and kiss her, wiping all that away. I play with her breasts and twist her nipple. Just a little. Just a tiny bit.

When I pull away she's breathing harder.

"Turn around," I say, twirling my finger in the air.

She obeys.

I pick up the bikini top and drape it over her front, tying the strings together around her neck. I reach around to play with her breasts one more time. Kiss her neck. Breathe words into her ear. "I think this will be better than last year's trip would have been."

"I think so too," she whispers back.

I let go, allow her to adjust the top, and then tie the strings together behind her back. She turns to face me. Unsure of herself.

Rochelle Bastille has no reason to be unsure of herself in front of me. She is perfect.

"Take off my clothes," I say.

She steps forward one pace, and unknots my tie, pulling it through my collar with a slick sound that turns me on so bad, I'm ready to bend her over and say fuck the romance.

But I behave because she's slipping my suit coat down my shoulders, then pulling my crisp white shirt out of my pants. She starts unbuttoning it from the bottom and works her way up. Her hands make a small flutter of air that drives me crazy and makes me hard.

She slips that down my arms, lays it on the bed, and unbuckles my belt. Just like I stopped to play with her, she stops to play with me too. Her hand cups my hard dick through my pants. She leans in, kisses me exactly the way I kissed her.

She squeezes me, caresses my balls, and then unbuttons, unzips, and pulls me out.

When she looks up at me for permission—or maybe just a warning of what she's about to do—I shake my head. "Not yet," I say. "Take them off."

She pushes my pants down, taking my boxer briefs with them, and I step out, kick off my shoes and pull off my socks. They end up in the pile with the rest of our clothes.

Now I'm the one facing her for consideration.

She sighs. Places her hands on my chest. Sighs again.

I reach over to the dresser, open up a drawer, and take out my swim trunks. I don't let her dress me, but I do let her watch closely as I pull them up, tuck my dick away, and then take her hand.

"Come on," I say. "It's this way."

We walk to the glass terrace door together. I open it up, and we step out in to the snow, barefoot.

"Holy shit, it's cold," Rochelle says, crossing her arms in front of her chest and rubbing her upper arms.

"It won't be for long," I say, leading her towards the left. My condo is a corner SkyBox and has a wraparound terrace. The terrace is much bigger than the actual condo. There's only a few inches of snow on the ground, but the bottoms of my feet are burning by the time we round the corner and the pool comes into view.

The blue water shimmers from the gold underwater lights.

"Holy shit, Quin," she says, a laugh in her voice.

I have to admit, it's magical right now. The water is hot. Not the hot tub, the entire fucking pool. It's taken me three days to get it to this temperature, but it's worth whatever that cost will be at the end of the month. Because the snow has piled up around the edges. Steam is coming up off the water, creating a mist. And the city lights are a dancing reflection of gold, and red, and blue on the water's rolling surface.

"You said you missed the hot springs. And, well, I'll be honest here, Rochelle, I don't want you getting any ideas. If you need a hot spring to settle down, I'll make one for you."

She turns to face me. Her feet have to be frozen. Mine are. But she doesn't seem to care. She just looks up at me, frowning. "I love you," she says.

I give her a lopsided smile which reflects my conflicted feelings about hearing those words again. Especially on a rooftop terrace surrounded by magical lights. I don't hesitate this time. "I love you too. And I'm sorry I didn't say it back. I wanted to, Rochelle. I already knew I was in love with you, but I didn't think I was enough."

She swallows hard and then we both realize our feet really are freezing. So I take her hand, lead her down towards the steps, and we sink into the faux hot springs together.

She glides across the water and then turns around. The serious mood is tempered with the new sensations of the hot water mixed with the cold air. "This is better than the springs. I couldn't go in the hot ones. Adley is too young for that kind of temperature. So this is way, way better than anything I had while I was away."

I am relieved. And happy that my plan worked.

I swim towards her, a laziness in my movements. "Tell me all about your days away. Tell me about your pregnancy. The birth. What was it like? Were you scared? Did you want to call me?"

She treads water for a few seconds, like she's wondering how much to share. It can't have been fun. I'm sure Adley's birth was a happy moment, but all the

255

unhappy conditions she found herself in probably ruined it.

I feel one hundred percent responsible for that. Even though I wasn't the one who left, I'm the one who made her leave. I wasn't enough for her back then. I failed. Miserably. And I caused an entire year of pain, for both of us, because I refused to give her what she needed. Three easy words. Three true words. For the past week, I have asked myself how much different life would be if I had just said those three short words.

For a few moments, I wonder if she'll say anything, ever again. I wonder if she has finally realized what a fuck-up I am. If she'll walk out of this pool, put her clothes back on, and then walk out of my life. For good, this time.

But she doesn't do any of that. She takes a deep breath and the words pour out of her like a waterfall. Like a dam bursting. Like she has so much to say and I'm the only one who could possibly listen.

We sit on the steps, mostly submerged to keep the cold at bay. We hold hands as she talks. She ends up in my lap, just our heads peeking out of the pretend hot springs. She tells me about her time in Pagosa Springs. The people she met, the resort. The tourist trap shopping. Which makes me smiles because that is so... *her*. So something she would do. No one else would do that. Just Rochelle.

She says her birth was easy. She was only in labor four hours. She almost had Adley in the waiting room. They had to rush her to delivery and before she knew it, it was over.

She cried for three weeks. But only when Adley was sleeping. And it was hormonal, she insists. It faded away and then she felt like it never was.

I tell her about my year too. The blank year. A year of emptiness and regret. I don't bring up Chella. She's already figured out that I like Chella. Not love her like I do Rochelle, but we are friends. I leave all that out because it doesn't matter anymore. Rochelle is back, we are together, and this time it will be different. I will not fail.

I talk about work, mostly. The projects I've started. New clients and stuff. Business has been good.

But I have more to say than that. This is why I wanted her to myself tonight. "I failed you," I say.

"You didn't," she insists. But it's a lie and we both know it.

"I failed you because I didn't believe in me, Rochelle. I didn't think I was enough for you."

"Why would you say that? You're all I want, Quin. I can't even express in words how much I want you. All to myself. I like Bric. Love him, probably. But I came back for you."

"You did?" I ask. "I thought you were just passing through?"

"I was," she says quickly. "But secretly, I stopped for you, Quin." She takes a moment to smile at me. It feels real. So real. "I didn't need to stop in Denver. I didn't need to call Chella and tell her I was in town. I could've kept driving and stopped in Fort Collins for the night. It's only an hour away. But I did stop. I knew I had to see you and I knew Chella would not be able to keep my secret."

"Hmm." I think about that for a second. "I'm very glad you stopped. Because I can't imagine life without you again. Or Adley. I really can't, Rochelle. And I just wanted one night alone with you to explain this. I'm sorry I didn't forgive you right away. It felt necessary at the time, but now I just feel bad. So I'm sorry for that."

"I'm not sorry," she says. "You made me feel what you felt. I needed that. I needed to know how deeply I hurt you so I'll never do it again." Rochelle places both her hands on my cheeks and stares into my soul. She closes her eyes and kisses me. I kiss her back. It's a romantic kiss. One that says so much more than words. "I love you," she whispers. "I want you, and only you. But if you want Bric, then I want Bric too."

I wonder how much I should tell her. If I tell her why I play the game, then she'll know what a fuck-up I am. She'll see through me. She'll see everything.

I don't think we're ready for that yet. Soon, but not yet. She's holding her past close too, so I let it slip away and just smile at her.

"I want you both," I say. "For now. Just for now."

There is silence. Or as much silence as possible, considering we're in the middle of the city.

"I'll keep the hot spring open all winter if you promise to come here with me, and only me, at least once a week."

"Deal," she says, smiling. "One day a week we can be alone. Try it out, right? See if it's what we want?"

I nod. "I'd like that, Rochelle. I really would."

"Then I'm happy with where we're at right now. I'm fine with Bric. And Adley loves him."

"Yes." I sigh. "She does."

"She loves you too," Rochelle says, leaning in to kiss me again. "And you're going to be the perfect father."

I doubt that. But I don't say anything because we've got something good going here. It's a great night and all I want is to take her inside and love her. Have her all to myself for just a little bit longer.

We run inside, Rochelle squealing like a happy child, as the heat from the pool dissipates from our bodies in a matter of seconds. We drip water all over the living room floor as I hastily untie her bikini top and she tugs on my trunks. I flick a light on the wall and a fire whooshes into existence in the fireplace. I lead her over to the rug in front of it and lay her down.

Open her legs.

Eat her pussy.

Her hands tug on my hair.

She begs for more. She wants me inside her. She wants me on top of her.

But she ends up on top of me. Sitting up on my hips, rocking back and forth as she closes her eyes, her half-wet hair swinging back and forth, dragging across my chest. And we come together in all the ways. We climax, and meld, and become a couple again.

It's perfect.

And it scares the shit out of me.

When we get back to the condo it's after two in the morning. There is one light on in the sitting area and one light on in the kitchen, but it's only an under-counter light, so it's just a low glow. The rest of the house is dark and silent.

"What's this?" Rochelle laughs, picking up a folded piece of paper propped up on the kitchen island. It says, *Watch me.* Underneath it is a tablet.

We take it to the couch and sink into the cushions, so close together, she's almost in my lap.

Rochelle wakes the tablet and a still shot of a video comes up. It's Bric and Adley, both smiling.

She presses the play button.

"Say hi to Mommy and Quin," Bric says to the camera. He's holding up one of Adley's chubby hands, making her wave. "We wanted to show you what we did tonight."

There is a ten-minute video chronicling their night together. Bric and Adley eating dinner. He's got a piece of pizza in one hand, Adley cradled in his arm with the other. She's drinking her bottle.

Then it's bath time. She's splashing in the super-deep tub in the master bedroom as Bric laughs and plays some kind of game with a rubber duck and a red block. He's even using imaginative-play voices. Dumbass.

Then it's story time. Which is interrupted by stinky diaper time. And even though Bric complains to the camera the whole time he deals with that unexpected detour, he handles it like a pro.

The last shot is of Adley sleeping in her new crib. Bric whispers, "She loves me," into the camera. And then I hear him mumble, "I can't wait for Christmas," as he turns the camera off.

"That's so adorable," Rochelle says, kicking her feet up on the couch and laying her head in my lap. I play with her hair. We still smell like the pool, our night still fresh in my mind as she drifts off muttering, "I don't think I really know Elias Bricman. I don't think I know him at all."

We get sleepy but we're too tired to move. Finally, I pick her up, carry her in to the bedroom, undress us both, and we crawl in next to Bric. He only wakes up long enough to hike a possessive leg over Rochelle's hip and pull her close to his chest.

I let him have her now. I had her all night and while I might be a failure at a lot of things when it comes to relationships, I do know how to share. So I share.

260

CHAPTER TWENTY-ONE

BRIC

"What?" I ask, looking up at Chella, then glancing down at the invoices again. "Why are you staring at me like that?"

"You're in a good mood," she says.

We're sitting in the new tea room going over final details. The soft opening is this weekend. Chella has invited twenty-five people, but I don't think it's enough to do a proper assessment before the real opening next week.

"Did you get laid last night?"

"What?" I laugh. "Nope. Not even close. I spent the whole evening alone with Adley while Quin and Rochelle went on a date."

"So that's why you're like this today."

When I look up at her again, she's got a crooked smile on her face. A knowing smile. "Like what today?"

"You're glowing, Bric."

I let out an actual guffaw at that. People turn to stare at us.

"You lost your baby virginity. Oh," Chella says, placing her hand over her heart. "They grow up so fast." She pretends to be overwhelmed with emotion, dabbing at fake tears in her eyes.

"Ha ha," I say. "It was fun. She loves me, Chella. Like digs me, man. She laughs at all my jokes. She never whines when I change her diaper. She lets me play blocks with her and she enjoyed my version of *The Princess and the Pea* at bedtime. God, I wish I had known more about decorating nurseries before I bought all that stuff. I think I might need to redecorate. Don't you think she needs a princess room?" Chella stares at me, her mouth half-open, like she was about to say something, then forgot what it was. "A Princess and the Pea room?" I clarify.

She still stares.

"What?" I ask.

"You..." she says. "You love kids."

"No," I huff. "I love *my* kid. Other people's kids can fuck off."

"No," Chella counters. "You were a great Santa last year. You rocked it. I think you have the dad gene, Bric."

I scratch my arm with a pen. "What's that?"

"You're a natural father. You have all the instincts."

"Hmmm." I consider this. "Well, I am pretty good at spooning those sweet potatoes into her moving mouth. I almost never get it in her eyeball."

Chella smiles. "I might love you even more right now." She shakes her head, smiling. "Elias Bricman, you will never cease to surprise me."

I shrug. "Just my natural charm, I guess."

"You guess? Well, I'd bet a million dollars—like I'd put up a million of my own dollars—if I could ask ten women from the Club if they think your list of qualifications includes the words 'family man,' if one of them—just one—said yes, I'd give that money to your favorite charity. What do you say?"

"What's your point?" I ask.

"My point is, those words do describe you, Bric. But you're so busy showing the world that you're always in control, they think you're nothing but a selfish asshole."

"Nobody thinks that." I laugh. "I give away billions of dollars a year."

"Your company gives away billions of dollars a year. Elias Bricman gives away nothing."

I think about this for a second. "I make personal donations. I think I probably make a lot—"

"I'm not talking about money, you oaf." She's shaking her head at me again. Like I'm ridiculous. "I'm talking about love."

"I love people. I love you," I say, winking at her.

"And Rochelle," she says.

"Yeah, so?"

"And Adley. And Quin. And Smith."

"There you go. That's five fucking people right off the bat. Plus, I have a huge family. Seven brothers and four sisters. And like a bazillion cousins. I love all of them."

"You come from a family of twelve kids?"

"Didn't I ever tell you that? We could have our own TV show. You know, like those baby people do? The ones who never seem to stop fucking?"

She laughs loudly. It's so nice to see her happy all the time. Smith is good for her. They are good for each other. "No, you never told me that. Where the hell are these people? Here?" Chella looks around like I might be hiding my family in the kitchen.

"Not here, you dingbat. They live up in Montana."

"I... I'm... floored by this. I had no idea."

"Well, the point is, I love lots of people. I grew up on a huge ranch. We have, like, our own town going on up there. It's crazy. Twelve kids total. Abrem, Benjamin,

Candace, Delilah, Elias—me." I laugh, counting us up on my fingers, so I don't forget anyone. "Then Felix, Gaius, Hannah, Isaac, Jason, Keren, and Luc is the baby. And every one of them is married but me. My baby sister, Keren, she already has three kids and she's twenty-four. So—you're wrong."

"Your parents have an ABC theme for naming?" Chella is astounded. This is why I never tell people about myself. It's weird. "And are those all Old Testament names? Are you like... Amish?"

I laugh again. "Jesus Christ, no. My parents were just... happily married, you know? And yeah, they go to church, but town is so far away. It's not a big deal to miss. It's just..." I sigh. There is no easy way to explain my family. "It's just weird."

"I have no words right now. Like seriously, you just floored me. Knocked me down. What the hell happened to you?"

"What do you mean?"

"You own a sex club! Do your parents know that?"

"Do you think they know?" I laugh.

"Don't they come see you? Don't they like... look you up on the internet?"

"Turning Point isn't on the internet. And no, they're happy with my yearly end-of-summer visits. When you have twelve kids you don't pay too close attention, you know?"

"But Smith is on the internet. You're his partner."

I shrug.

"And you hate kids."

"I do hate kids. When I go home, it's torture, man. I'm telling you. I have so many nieces and nephews, I can't count them. They hang all over me. *Uncle Elias, play with me. Uncle Elias, take me somewhere.* Every year there's like two new ones. I can't keep up with it. It's so complicated. I like simple, Chella. This life I have is simple. I am quite capable of love. I hand it out all over the place when I'm home. But when I come back here, to my own space, I like... peace. I want to be left alone."

She takes a few moments to think about all this new information. "Is this why you like to share? It's something you're used to—growing up with all those siblings."

I shrug. "I guess. I never thought about it much."

"You're practically a psychiatrist, Bric. You cannot tell me you've never psychoanalyzed yourself."

"I have, but not about the sharing. The game is fun, that's all. And I can walk away if I want. I can't really walk away from my family, can I? They're always there. There's always drama. Kids are sick, parents are arguing, dishes are everywhere. It's chaos, is what it is."

"So you came down here to Denver to get away from them?"

"Maybe. I dunno. I didn't think of it that way. I just didn't want to get stuck out there on that ranch. It's like sixty degrees below zero with wind chill in the winter, Chella. Have you ever birthed a cow at four AM in the dead of winter in Montana? It's not fun. Not even close. Denver is nice. The climate is pretty mild. I have mountains here. I have everything I had there, except the stress."

"I need to go up there and meet them."

"Never." I laugh. "Ever. That's so not happening. Bric's life and Elias' life shall never meet. You don't cross proton-pack streams, Chella. First rule of Ghostbusters. Bad things will happen."

She ponders this, her eyes on mine, darting back and forth from one to the other. "So you're never getting married?"

"Why do I need to get married? I have Quin, Rochelle, and Adley. That's all I need."

Her mouth is hanging open again.

"What?" I growl.

"But... this is temporary, right? I mean... Rochelle and Quin are... in love, aren't they?"

"Sure," I say. "What's that got to do with anything?"

"Elias Bricman," she scoffs. "You're not that delusional, are you?" She just stares at me.

"What? Rochelle is happy. Quin likes me involved. And plus, Adley is mine."

"You don't know that."

"I feel it." I shrug. "Anyway, didn't you ever take physics?"

"What?" She laughs.

"It's called quantum superposition and it goes like this—and this is one hundred percent true. Look it up. If you have a cat in a box and you don't look inside to see if the cat is alive or dead, like there's no possible way of knowing one way or the other unless you physically *look*, then it's both alive and dead at the same time."

"No..."

"Yes, for real. It's been proven and shit. Reality depends on observation. On knowing things. So if we never know who Adley's father is, then we're both her father. It's science. So she really is my daughter."

"Until she's not, Bric. If you guys do get the test, then you'll know for sure."

"But we're not getting the test. So she is. We've locked her paternity in a box with the cat and none of us want to change that. I think we're happy."

Chella frowns. Takes a moment to think. "You know how you have that rule about the game? When the girl wants to leave you're not allowed to follow?"

"Yeah."

"Well, one of you will want to leave, Bric. Eventually. The world is not made for threesomes. It's made for couples. You're playing a game. It's a very dangerous game because it was designed to end. One day it *will* end. You know that, right?"

I shrug her off and stand up to stretch and glance around, feeling the need to get back to work. "I'll take my chances," I say. And then I turn to walk away, but I stop, remembering why we're here in the first place. "Invite more people to the soft opening. We need a better feel for a packed house." I walk off, then call out over my shoulder. "Tell Smith I said hi."

She's wrong, I think. She's wrong about the new game. It's more than a game. We're more than players. We're *professional* players. We know how to handle it. We've been together for years. Quin is happy, I can tell. And Rochelle loves me. Maybe not the same way she loves Quin, but it's up there. I'm in the running.

It won't end.

I can't end.

I love that baby.

She's mine as long as we don't open that box.

CHAPTER TWENTY-TWO

ROCHELLE

"You're sure you're OK?" I ask Quin.

"Hey," he says. "We're fine. I got this." He's holding Adley in his arms and she's smacking his face with both hands. Each time she does it, he blinks and laughs. She squeals and wiggles.

They are adorable together. Does she look like him? I can't tell. How do people tell? How do people say, *Oh, she has your chin*, or, *Yes, those are your ears?* I don't get it. When I look at her and me in the same photo, I do see it. She does look like me. But Quin and Bric... I just don't know. I can't tell. It makes me sad.

"I have two bottles of milk in the fridge—"

"I know," Quin says. "I heard all the last-minute directions the other night when we left her with Bric. Baby food on the counter if I'm up to it. Bath time, story time, bed time."

"Plus, you've got my video if you need a cheat sheet." Bric comes out of the bedroom adjusting his cufflinks. He's in a tux. This is a formal event at a local historical mansion over on Pennsylvania Street for one of the charity things they do. It's only like three miles away. Bric bought me a long black dress with a white fur cape. I have my hair in a loose updo, and the diamonds around my neck and wrists are heavy.

I have missed going out to fancy places. And the diamonds. Maybe more than I'd like to admit.

"Ready?" Bric asks, holding out my cape so he can drape it around my shoulders. I turn and the soft satin lining settles on my bare skin. It's heavy and I'm glad. Because the dress is strapless and even though it's not snowing tonight, it's cold.

"I'm ready," I say, smiling at him. "You look handsome."

"You look stunning," he replies, leaning into the back of my neck to give me a kiss.

"Go," Quin says. "Have a good time. We'll be here when you get home."

Bric offers me his arm and we walk into the waiting elevator together. Quin is holding up Adley's hand to wave at us, both of them smiling.

He deserves this time alone with her. Bric has had a lot more time with her than Quin. So it's good for them both. But a part of me wants to stay behind. Share this night with Quin and Adley as they get to know each other, and not leave them behind.

Bric gives me the rundown on the party as we drive over to the mansion. I've been here before. Several times. All of them with Bric. In fact, I'm pretty sure I was at this same party the first two years we were together. That was something we did a lot. Go out. Quin and I never went out like this before. We stayed home or went fun places together, just the two of us. Bric was always the party guy.

The party is at a neoclassical mansion built in 1902. I remember this from the first time I was here. The third governor of Colorado built this house after he left office. Tonight, it's lit up and festive when we arrive. More than a hundred people are dressed up in black and white. There is a dinner later, but for now we mingle. I see dozens of people I know. They all come up to me, elated that Bric and I are back together.

I wonder how many of them are Club members? I wonder how many of them know what we do in private?

All the women stare, but I can't tell if they are staring at me or just appreciating the fact that Elias Bricman is hot. One woman in our small-talk party is scowling just a few feet away, so she is obviously looking at me. It doesn't bother me. I'm not embarrassed by our relationship. So we're a thriple. Who cares? I privately think they are all jealous. That woman, for sure. I would be, if I were her. Her husband is handsome, but not attentive. He's busy chatting with the other men about golf as she stands there demurely. He's ignoring her.

Bric is holding my hand, talking to me, even though I'm not even participating in the conversation. He brings me in. Includes me on purpose. Looks at me, not them.

Yes, she's definitely jealous. I lean into Bric and he looks down at me, then brings my hand to his lips and kisses it.

I wonder what these people would think if three of us showed up, instead of two?

I smile, but don't laugh, even though I want to.

Quin would not ignore me either. Both of my hands would be held at the same time. Both mouths would be kissing my knuckles. We'd take turns dancing. I'd sit between them as we ate dinner. They'd bring me festive, bubbly drinks. And delicious canapés. I'd never have a moment to myself.

It would be wonderful, I decide.

"How have you been, Rochelle?" the scowling woman asks. She leaves her husband's side and comes over to stand next to me. "I haven't seen you in forever."

"I know. I've been gone," I say. "I spent the last year at a resort, just being lazy and, you know... having a baby."

"You have a baby?" she asks, surprised and smiling. "Well, that's interesting. The last time I talked to your father, he didn't mention it."

My world stops. Simply ceases. Jesus Christ. I don't show it, but holy fuck, I need to take a sip of my champagne to gather myself. Who is this woman?

"No," I say. Once I swallow the warm fizzing liquid I'm collected again. "I don't speak to him."

"I did know that, I'm sorry. I shouldn't have brought it up. Do you have pictures?" she asks. "Of the baby? I bet Elias is so proud."

"Have we met?" I ask. "I've been introduced to so many of Elias' friends over the years, but I don't recognize you."

She cocks her head at me, like she's wondering if I'm serious. "We have met before. But it wasn't here in Denver. Justin and I just relocated. I was so happy to see you here at the party. Friendly face and all."

Are we friendly? I find that very unlikely.

"You really don't remember me," she says. Not as a question, just a statement of fact.

"No," I say. "I'm sorry. You do look familiar, but I can't place you. Can you refresh my memory?"

"Well, I was..." she looks around, then at her husband. She leans in to me, like she's sharing a secret. "Your father's mistress," she whispers. "I'm almost relieved you don't recognize me, to be honest. It's good to know that one's reputation does not precede her."

"Ohhhhh," I say, nodding my head. Snap. Out of the fantasy life I've been living for the past four years and right back to the real world.

"I'm Justin's mistress now. And you're with Elias?"

"And Quin Foster," I say. I can't let that opportunity pass.

"Mmm-hmmm. I did hear that as well. It doesn't surprise me."

"What doesn't surprise you?" I ask.

"That you enjoy two men at the same time." She laughs. Heartily. "You're a lot like your father."

Uh. I feel sick.

"But you have your mother in you too. I can see that as well."

Does she think this makes it any better? Or did she say that on purpose? *You're just like your parents, Rochelle.* I want to slap her. I want to scream at her. I want to ask her, right here in front of Denver's most powerful people, if she ever thought about me when she was fucking my father. "Do you?" I say, instead. I hate the fact that this woman knows me. Both the old me, and the new me.

"Justin was just invited into the Club," she says, changing the subject. "I'm really looking forward to spending time there. Maybe we'll see each other?" She smiles. A kind of... sick smile.

Yuk. That is disgusting. I cannot imagine any scenario where I would end up in that basement with this woman. Gross.

"I doubt that," I say, still using my fake high-society manners. "I don't belong in the Club. Elias and Quin keep me far away from that life. But I'm sure you'll have fun with all the other..." I want to say tramps, but it's not fair, because they're not tramps. They're just people. People like me and Chella. So I don't. I say, "Partners," instead.

"Why, thank you," she says. But I've offended her because she presses her lips together. "Do you still play music? I know you had that guitar hobby back when you were a child. In fact, I'm the one who talked your father into giving you your first guitar back when you were eleven. I can still picture you that one night he brought me home to your house for a party. You were—"

"Excuse me," Bric says, pressing into me. "Helen, is it? I'm going to steal Rochelle from you. I'm dying to dance with my lover."

I almost laugh. Almost. But the sting of that last statement is enough to quell it.

"Would you like to dance, Rochelle?" he asks politely. As if I would say no.

"Love to," I say. "Can you hold my drink?" I ask the woman. She takes it out of habit, mumbling something about it being her pleasure, but I don't wait and thank her—*can't* wait and thank her, because Bric is pulling me away.

"What the fuck was that?" he asks.

"Apparently," I say, as Bric puts his hand on my waist and we begin to dance, "that was my father's old mistress. How wonderful it was to see her again."

"I bet," Bric says, smiling down at me.

"What a cunt. God."

"You've never mentioned your father before."

"No," I say. "For good reason. He's an asshole."

"And your mother?"

"Stepmother, you mean. Another cunty bitch. My father loves the cunty ones."

"Got it." Bric laughs. "So where's all this animosity come from?"

Really? Tonight, of all nights, in public, he wants to ask me about my old life?

"You don't want to talk about it," he says.

"Got it in one," I say, trying to keep the mood light. But he's serious now, so I try again. "No. Not here, anyway."

"Do you think we'll ever meet them?" he asks.

"Will I ever meet your families?" I counter.

He shrugs. "Not mine. They live far away. But Quin's family is in town."

I picture this meeting in my head. I know his father passed away a few years back. So no worries there. But his mother is still alive.

"Would you like to meet his mother?"

"Have you met her?"

"Of course." Bric laughs. "Kitty and I are old friends."

"Kitty," I say, trying out her name. I wonder what Kitty Foster would think of me? Probably exactly what I thought of that woman back there. Gold. Digging. Slut.

"I haven't seen her much lately, but we bump into each other every once in a while."

"Well." I sigh. "I'm going to pass on that. I can imagine that if I meet Kitty, the two of you would demand to know someone from my family. And I can't think of a single person I'd be happy to introduce you to."

"Not one?" he asks.

"Not even one," I say. I wonder if he's talked to Smith lately. I wonder how much Smith really knows about me? "I don't want to think about my past, Bric. And I certainly don't want to associate with my father's ex-mistresses. I left my life behind for a reason. I don't want her reminding me of that."

Bric leans down to kiss me. "Hey," he whispers into my mouth. "Don't worry about that woman."

"She says that Justin guy is a member of the Club. Just got an invitation."

"I can uninvite him. And I'm going to make that very clear to Justin tomorrow. She'll never talk to you again."

"You'd do that?" I ask. "Give up a member just because I'm uncomfortable?"

"Why not?" he asks. "Do you really think I need another member? The only thing I care about these days is you, and Quin, and Adley. I will do anything to keep us happy. Kicking out a new member doesn't even require a moment of consideration. It's done."

I sigh. Then smile. "Thanks," I say. "But it's really not necessary. I'm fine. I'll probably never see her again. It's not like the Club is my life anymore."

"It's not. You'll never have to go there again. Not even for breakfast. We'll find another place to call our own. Hell, maybe I'll just buy another restaurant down in LoDo. Make it easy for everyone to stay away. The past is the past, right? No need to go backwards."

"I could kiss you right now." I laugh. "Somehow, you always know the right thing to say."

He frowns.

"What?" I ask.

"Except when you came to me last year. To tell me about your pregnancy. I wasn't thinking, Rochelle. I'd like you to know I'd never ask you to have an abortion. I would've stuck by you. Maybe I didn't know it at that moment, but I would've figured it out."

"I know," I say. "It really wasn't you. It was… Quin."

"Have you talked about it yet?"

"A little. But I don't want to bring it up again. He was mad at me. He had a right to be mad at me. And now he's forgiven me, so let's just leave it there."

"Done," he says. "And hey, if you wanna leave the party, I'm all for it."

"No," I say. "Don't be silly. You're here for business. I'm fine."

"Well, shit. I was hoping you'd say yes and then we could fuck in the car before we got home."

I laugh. "Yes, Mr. Bricman. You really do say all the right things." And then I lean up on my tiptoes, until my mouth is right next to his ear, and I whisper, "I promise. After dinner, we can take a quick trip to the car for dessert."

CHAPTER TWENTY-THREE

Adley and I are sitting on a blanket on the floor of her room, playing blocks. She's a good stacker. Great stacker, actually. She got two the first time, then three. Three blocks stacked. She's probably a genius-level stacker.

"Are you hungry yet?" I ask her. She takes the red plastic block out of her mouth to drool and smile at me. I think she's getting teeth. I looked it up on the internet and this is the age when they first start appearing. Bric is a genius as well. That comment about checking for how-to-diaper-a-baby videos was legit. They have everything you can think of on the internet when it comes to babies.

All day at work I was searching. How to make a bottle, what kind of bottle you use (we're already using the good kind—Rochelle is a genius too), what kind of diapers to buy. How many times a day they need changing. I tried changing her as soon as Bric and Rochelle left, just to have one under my belt before the real deal happened.

I'm basically a baby-diapering prodigy because I got it right the very first time. Some dads said they put them on backwards. Some said the diaper fell off because they made it too loose. But me—sailed through that lesson like a champ.

I have no experience with babies at all. None. So I'm pretty proud of myself. "I'm good at this, right, Adley?" I ask her.

She drools and smiles again.

I take that as agreement.

"We're a whole family of geniuses."

I get a giggle for that.

"What do you say? You want a bottle?" I ask. She squeals and knocks our tower of blocks down.

I stand up, pick her up, and hold her close to me. Babies smell good, too. She smells sweet. Like soap. Nice soap. Not guy soap. Baby soap. I looked up soap too. And baby powder. So much shit to know about babies.

"But I'm learning, right?" I take her into the kitchen. I know she likes to be held when she drinks a bottle, so I settle her on my hip as I get the bottle out and put it in Rochelle's little bottle warmer thing. I looked that thing up a couple days ago. No idea what it was. Who knew mothers had these secret appliances that warm bottles?

That's when I spot the baby food. "Ohhh," I say, picking up one with a very colorful label from the counter. "This looks good. Tropical fruit. Do you like tropical fruit, Adley?"

She laughs. Which is another yes in my book.

"I'm dying to try out the spoon. If Bric can do it, I can do it, right?"

She kicks her legs.

"But I think we should do the bottle first. I think that's more important." I read that online too. I'm practically an expert now.

The little warmer thing dings, so I get the bottle out, open the lid, still balancing Adley, and make sure it's not too hot.

Nope. Perfect.

I got this shit *down*.

We go over to the couch and I put on a Nuggets game. They're losing, but I don't care. "I got you, huh, Adley? Who needs basketball?"

I settle her in my lap and as soon as I aim that nipple at her mouth, her little chubby hands grab it. She looks at me as she sucks it down, her little fingers tapping on the bottle.

God. I love this dad stuff. I had no idea babies were so cool.

"I think you have my eyes. Do you think you have my eyes? They're blue, like mine. Nice bright blue. Just like mine."

I have to admit, I have been thinking about her eyes more than I should. I really think she has my eyes. Bric's eyes are dark. Really dark blue. Not like this at all. And I read that babies with fair skin and light hair can change eye color as they get older. But she's six months now. I think these are her eyes and I think they look like mine.

"I'm definitely your real dad," I say.

Then I want to take it back. I shouldn't say that in front of her. She probably doesn't even know what I'm saying, but if we're gonna all be together, she needs to think Bric and I are both her dads. Not one over the other. We might as well just get the DNA test if it matters.

I decide it doesn't matter. I know she's mine. No need to rub it in.

I was with Rochelle way more than Bric was. He didn't even see her every night he was supposed to. I did.

Adley is definitely mine.

If this lasts, who knows? Maybe we'll have another one. Maybe next time we'll be more careful about it. Plan it and shit. I spend the next several minutes thinking about having a whole pack of kids. "We'd need a bigger house," I say.

Adley kicks her feet.

"You'd probably want a pony."

Her little pink lips form a smile around the nipple.

"And a kitten. And we'd need to look for a good school. Hey, you could go to our school. That would be neat." Our kids will go to the school Bric and I went to. Of course, that was middle and high school. We're gonna need to find a pre-school and an elementary school.

So many things to plan for now that Adley is here.

She throws the bottle aside and I lean over and pick it up, offering it to her. She throws it again.

"Done? Cool. Now we get to try baby food." I get up and walk into the kitchen. "But first we gotta wipe that milk off your face."

She shakes her head and squeals when I do that.

Kids.

Man, do I rock this daddy stuff, or what?

I get the spoon and the jar of tropical fruit, and take Adley over to her high chair. I really did need a video to understand this thing. That little hidden latch almost got me. But nope. I find it now, slide the tray down, put her in, and slide it back up.

So fucking good at this.

"OK," I say, popping the lid on the jar of food. "I'm ready, Ads. I'm gonna feed you with a spoon for the first time. Are you ready?"

She spits out some drool, but it's a happy spit. I can tell. Dads know this shit.

I dip the spoon in the jar, scoop up the goop, and head for her mouth. It's wide open. No here-comes-the-airplane trick for me and my kid.

Mouth closes, lips smack, food gone.

"So easy," I say, getting another spoonful. She gobbles it up. She gobbles up about ten spoonfuls, but then she starts kicking and getting cranky.

I think I smell the reason why.

"OK. It's go time. The real deal, Ads. Don't worry, I got this."

I get her up on the changing table, clean her up (like a pro, I might add) and then decide it's a good time for the bath.

"You want bubbles?"

I take her into the bathroom, holding her on my hip—really hoping she doesn't pee on me, since she's naked now—and start the water. Rochelle has this ring thing for Adley to sit in the tub. It's new, I think. But when the water is the right temperature and depth, I set her in and she knows just what to do.

Splash.

Her skin is pink from the warm water. I start thinking about the hot springs and how I'll need to lower the temperature in the pool if we want to take Adley swimming.

I picture her at my house.

Then stop.

My house is so... sterile. And not in a good way. It's clean, yeah. But sterile as in... not homey, like this place. My condo is a place for adults. I'll have to work on that.

"Hey," I say, taking my attention back to Adley. There's bubbles in the tub now and Ads is kicking her feet and laughing.

But she's all flushed. "Is it too hot?" I ask myself, feeling the temperature. Rochelle will kill me if I burn her in the tub.

No. Seems fine.

But damn, her skin is so pink. In fact, I think it's getting pinker as I watch. Red, almost. And right before my eyes, little dots start appearing under her neck.

Like… hives, or something.

"Holy shit," I say, forgetting I'm not supposed to swear around her. "Holy fuck. Holy shit." I grab my phone from my pocket and search 'baby rash.'

Noooooooooo. Insect bites, food allergies, pollen, illness… it's a long list. I was doing so well. I had this shit down!

I pick Adley up from the tub, wrap her in the little baby towel Rochelle keeps in the back of the door, and take her in to her room to get a better look.

Maybe I'm imagining it.

Six more welts have appeared on her stomach,

No. I'm not imagining it. I poisoned her. I fucked something up. She got bit by a black widow spider. This is bad. Oh, my God. She's got welts all over her little body and she's crying!

Diaper, sweat suit. Socks, no shoes.

Pick her up and run for the elevator.

I suck. I suck as a dad. I totally suck.

Rochelle trusted me for one damn night and now I have to call and tell her we're on our way to the hospital.

I am the worst dad ever.

CHAPTER TWENTY-FOUR

BRIC

I give Rochelle props for keeping her cool. When Quin called and said he was taking Adley to the hospital, there was a moment. One long moment where I had enough time to imagine a full-fledged freakout from Rochelle.

But I said—in the calmest doctor voice I could manage—"It's probably an allergic reaction, and nothing more."

And she took a breath, nodded her head at me, and dealt with it rationally.

Of course, people die from allergies every day. But I left that part out.

We were five minutes from the hospital once we got in the car. Closer than Quin was, for sure. So he was only there a few minutes before we arrived and a nurse was already assessing Adley's condition and reassuring Quin.

"Oh, my poor baby," Rochelle says, rushing towards Quin. He's holding Adley in his lap. She's doing that little hiccup-cry kids do when they're done crying, but can't actually stop. She holds her arms out to Rochelle as she gets close and they hug each other.

Rochelle's eyes close in relief.

"So what do you think?" I ask the nurse. "Food allergy?"

"Elias? Is that you?"

I turn to see Dr. Tanya Yates, wife of Terrence Yates, Club member since 1999. "Tanya. Nice to see a familiar face."

"OK," another doctor says, coming up behind Tanya. "Let's bring her back now and just take a look."

Quin and I follow Rochelle and the new doctor towards the double doors to the emergency room, but the nurse puts a hand on my arm and says, "Parents only, please."

"I'm her father," I say.

She looks confused, then points to Quin. "He said he was her father."

"He is," I say. "We're both—"

"Linda," Tanya says, coming up with a firm smile to interrupt the questioning. "Let it go. Go ahead, Elias."

"Thanks," I mutter, and turn to follow them in.

Quin and I stand aside as the doctor and nurse do an assessment. "Well," the doctor says. "I don't think it's going to get any worse. Did you feed her something new tonight? Something she's never had before."

"Oh, shit," Rochelle says, looking over at Quin. "I left a new baby food out on the counter. Did you give her the tropical fruit?"

"Yeah," Quin says. He looks devastated. "I'm so sorry, Rochelle. I didn't know. I mean I did know about food allergies, I looked it up on the internet. So I knew. But I didn't think of it. I just..." He shakes his head. "I just didn't think."

"It's not your fault, Quin," Rochelle says, giving him a sympathetic smile. "I was going to try it out this morning but she didn't seem hungry after she had her bottle. So I saved it for later. I should've put it away. You didn't know.

I told Bric he could feed her the food on the counter so it's not your fault, it's mine."

"It's not anyone's fault, you guys." I say this in my calm rational, doctor voice. "She was going to have this reaction no matter who was feeding her. Could've happened to any of us."

Everything I said is true, of course. But Quin still looks devastated.

"It's kind of unusual to have an allergic reaction to tropical fruit, but mango has been showing up in the past few years."

"Ah," I say, slapping my head. "Shit. I have a mango allergy." I look apologetically at Rochelle. "I should've told you that."

"And you're the... father?" the doctor asks, tilting her head at me in confusion. Tanya is not here to help me this time. I look over at Quin and he just shrugs.

"We're both the father," I say.

"OK," the doctor says, fake good-naturedness in her response. "But one of you is the biological father? Or... she's adopted?"

"She's my daughter and one of them..." Rochelle stops talking, trying to figure out a way to explain things without really... explaining things. "We don't know," Rochelle finally says. "We're not sure. And we're not getting a DNA test."

Quin and I get one raised eyebrow from the doctor, and a disapproving look from the nurse.

"OK," the doctor says again. "Well, it probably is mango then. The reaction isn't severe now, but if she's exposed again, it could get much worse. We can schedule an allergy test if you'd like. Would you like to do that..." She looks down at the paper. "I'm sorry. Are you Mrs.

Foster? This one only listed his last name on the intake form." Apparently, Quin is now called... *this one.*

The rest of the visit with the doctor, and the nurse, once the doctor leaves, is just as awkward.

But we suck it up, get the referral for the allergist, Adley gets some antihistamines, and we are told to bring the baby food jar with us to the appointment.

We can't get out of there fast enough.

"Rochelle?"

Oh, shit. Not now.

"Rochelle, is that you?"

"Lucinda," Rochelle says, smiling for her old therapist.

"I heard you were back. And I heard about the little bundle of cuteness you brought with you." Lucinda takes a moment to smile and coo at Adley. "I've been meaning to stop by the Club and see how you're doing but—"

"I'm not at the Club," Rochelle says, nervously looking over her shoulder at the eavesdropping nurse. "We live over on Wynkoop now. Right across from Union Station."

"Oh, that's nice," Lucinda says... to Quin. Not me, but *Quin.*

"Ah, I live there too," I add, feeling left out.

"Oh," Lucinda says. "Sorry." She laughs. "I'm sorry Elias. I just assumed you were... done. Playing the—"

"We're not playing," Quin says. "We're just... together now."

"I see," Lucinda says. "All three—err, four of you?"

"We gotta go," I say, taking hold of Rochelle's arm. "It was nice seeing you again, Lucinda. Tell Clark we said hi."

I don't wait for an answer, just lead her out. Quin goes ahead of us and says, "I've got the car seat, so... you wanna come with me, Rochelle?"

"Sure," Rochelle says. "Meet you at home?" she says to me.

"Yup, I'm right behind you."

Quin's car—Rochelle's, really, since that's the one with the baby seat in it—is parked in a spot right next to the emergency dropoff. My car is down a ways, so I tuck my hands into my pockets and head the other direction.

"Bric," someone calls my name. "Bric, wait!"

I turn around to find Lucinda following me. *Jesus Christ. Just go away.*

"Do you have a second?" she asks. "Just a second," she says again, coming up to me a little out of breath. "I just wanted to see how everyone's doing. I've been meaning to call. Drop by." She waves her hand in the air and smiles. "How's Rochelle doing?"

"Great," I say. "Just fine."

"And this new... ah... arrangement the three of you have? That's going over well? With Quin?"

"Why would you even ask that? Quin's always been a part of—" I almost say the game. But it's not a game. "Our relationship. It's a relationship now, Lucinda."

"Do you think that's wise?" she says. "Considering... well, you know. The reason she left in the first place?"

"Look, Lucinda, I know it was pretty confusing last year for Rochelle. Quin rejected her and she was pregnant. Her leaving devastated him, but we've worked through it. We've decided to parent Adley all together. We're in a real relationship now. And no, we don't know which of us is the father, OK? Jesus Christ. Why can't people just mind their own business? We're not getting the test. Everything is great. We don't want to know."

"So... you guys are OK with that... other thing?"

"What?"

289

"I'm sorry," she says, shaking her head a little. "I feel like we're not on the same page here. Did Rochelle tell you why she left?"

"We all know why she left, Lucinda. She was pregnant."

"Well, yes. She was pregnant. And yes, it was confusing since she was sleeping with both of you at the time. But... there was another... matter." As soon as she finishes her sentence, Lucinda realizes she's at her limit. She's not allowed to talk about anything Rochelle told her in confidence. She made that very clear to me when I asked her about Rochelle again last fall. So her tone changes. "She didn't mention that, did she?"

"What matter? What the fuck are you talking about?"

"I'm sorry," Lucinda says. "I'm totally out of line here. I'm wasting your time. But please, tell Rochelle to call me." She stresses those words. *Call me.* "I think we need to talk."

She turns around and walks away, leaving me standing out in the cold night, speechless, confused, and, if I'm being honest, upset.

What the hell was that all about?

CHAPTER TWENTY-FIVE

By the time we get home, Adley is exhausted and ready for bed. "She should sleep with us," I say, taking off my coat and grabbing Rochelle's to hang it up.

"Yes," Rochelle agrees, kissing Adley's flushed face. She's still red. And the hives are still there, but not as bad as they were before. The doctor thinks it will go away in a few days as long as she doesn't scratch it. They put some cream on it to prevent that. "I can't even think about leaving her alone in that bedroom."

She walks off towards the bedroom and leaves me behind.

I really fucked this up. I feel terrible. My first night alone with my daughter and it ends with a trip to the hospital. I didn't even get to make a video. I totally had that planned, but I forgot. I didn't get one picture to commemorate our night together, let alone a video. And we did a lot of stuff together before I practically killed her.

Bric didn't forget.

Mango allergy.

I'm not a doctor. I've got no idea how allergies work, but pretty much everyone knows they are hereditary.

This whole time I've been convinced Adley is my daughter. One hundred percent. Hell, I even talked myself into believing she had my eyes.

I slump down into one of the chairs in front of the window, trying to come to terms with this new development.

If it turns out Bric is the father... what will happen to us?

Will Rochelle feel differently about me? Will I feel differently about her? Will we stay together?

I want to say no, no, and yes. But I've been in a lot of plural relationships. I know how precarious they are. The dynamics are fragile. It takes a lot of self-control to avoid jealousy and confusion. And even though I don't want to admit it, most of my clarity this time around was based on the knowledge that Adley is my biological daughter.

The elevator dings and Bric walks into the loft. "Hey," he says, taking off his coat and hanging it up. He walks over to the chair next to mine and takes a seat. "What're you doing?"

"Thinking," I say, curter than I intend.

"About?"

I give him a sidelong sneer. "What do you think?"

He sighs, props a foot on one knee. "Will it change things?"

"Will what change things?" I know what he's talking about, but I want to hear him say it.

"If she's allergic to mango?"

"Because that would mean you're the father?"

"I mean, look, Quin. You and I both know the chances I'm the father are probably small. I have always assumed it was you and I'm still here. So I really fucking hope you're not gonna walk out if it turns out the other way."

"Maybe walking out wasn't what I was thinking?" I don't look at him because that right there, that was fucked up. But I've been thinking it. So might as well just test the waters now.

"What are you saying?"

I turn a little to look him in the eyes. "If you are her father, I don't know how I'll feel about that, Bric."

"So you'd want me to walk away?" He says it evenly. His tone is normal. Polite, like always. "You'd really want me to leave?" But his jaw is clenched. And when I glance down at his hands, they are gripping the chair so tight, his knuckles are white.

"I said I don't know. But I do know I love Rochelle. You know I love Rochelle."

He nods. But he's angry, I can tell. "And you won't love Adley? If she's not yours?"

"Don't be fucking stupid," I snarl. "Of course, I will. You don't turn off love."

"So I'm just supposed to turn it off? And let you have your little fantasy?"

"Look," I say, trying to fix my fuck-up real fast. "I'm not saying any of that, OK? I'm just saying… it will be an adjustment. I'm not sure I'm ready for it."

"Should we not go to the allergist?" Bric asks.

"Don't be an idiot. Of course we need to do that. We already have this knowledge, Bric. We can't just pretend things are the same tonight as they were this afternoon. Everything has changed."

"Nothing has changed, Quin. Nothing. We're still the same. She's ours. Both of them. They're ours. Don't fuck it up, man."

I sigh and look out the window again.

"Come on," he says, standing up. "We don't know anything yet. It might not be mango. And even if it is, she might still be yours. Don't jump to conclusions. Just come to bed."

He waits for me. Gives me several long seconds to think this through. And when I realize he's not gonna let me sit in front of this window feeling disappointed and confused, I stand too.

We go in to the bedroom. Rochelle is in bed with Adley, looking down at our daughter with a mixture of love and concern. Adley's eyes are closed and she's sucking on her lip. Rochelle watches Bric and I strip down to our underwear, and then Bric gets in one side and I get in another.

Somehow, even though I don't want there to be, there's a message in this.

We are on opposite sides now. And maybe it's always been this way? Maybe I just never noticed because I was so sure Adley was mine. That my claim on this relationship was pure and inevitable.

But Bric has changed everything. He was never invested before. He viewed Rochelle as someone to play with. Something temporary. I'm not stupid. I know he saw her as an opportunity. When Rochelle came home he probably thought it was the perfect way to get me back in his life. And it was. Here I am.

I don't think that's why he's here anymore.

I don't think he's here for me. For our friendship.

I think he's here for them.

"So, what do you know about allergies?"

"Yeah, that sucks, man," Smith says. I called him up from work to get a second opinion. I know this is Bric territory, but Bric is the last guy I want to talk to. "Chella told me this morning. Rochelle called her."

"Are you allergic to anything?" I ask.

"No. Why?"

"Because I'm not either. But Bric is. Says he's allergic to mango. And they think..." I stop talking.

"They think? What?" Smith asks.

"I'm gonna be devastated, dude. They think Adley might be allergic to mango too. And that means..."

"Fuck," he says. "Do they know that for sure?"

"No. We have an appointment with the allergist in two weeks. We tried to get in sooner, but they're booked up and they say this isn't urgent. Just don't feed her anything new until we get it sorted. I guess they're gonna prick her with needles and we'll know for sure. God," I say, running my fingers through my hair. "I don't know how to feel about this."

Smith is silent.

"How should I feel about this, Smith?"

"I dunno," he says. "Does it matter? I mean, you guys look happy. Everything is working out the way you want it, right?"

"Yeah, but..."

"But?"

"But that was before, you know. When I was sure she was mine. If she's not mine—I mean, I'm not leaving them over this. If it turns out Bric is the father. But... I think if we know for sure, it will change things."

Silence.

"Are you there?" I ask.

"Yeah, I'm here. Just thinking."

"Well, you got any answers for me?"

"Just..." He sighs. "Just wait it out. See what happens. I mean, I don't think she looks like Bric, you know? She doesn't have his eyes. And she doesn't have Rochelle's eyes, either."

"She does have my eyes, right?"

"Sure," he says. But then there's a bunch of yelling in the background that takes several seconds to die down. It gets silent again and he's back. "I had to go outside. Goddamned gym rats. Think they know what's up. Little fuckers."

"What the hell is going on?"

"Listen, I gotta go. I'm at the gym with the kids, you know? I gotta kick their thug asses today. They got me good again last time, but third time's the charm, right?"

I chuckle picturing Smith boxing with wild teen boys who think they own the world. "Right. I'm gonna laugh my ass off when you come over on Monday with a black eye."

"Don't say that. These kids are serious about kicking my ass. They have this pool going to see which one of them will knock me out first. I'm not as young as I used to be, man. Fucking teenagers."

"All right then. You going to Chella and Bric's tea room party tomorrow?"

He laughs.

"I'll take that as a no."

"Well, I'll probably have to put in some kind of appearance. You know, be supportive and shit. Why are you going?"

"Yeah, Chella hit me up too. Rochelle is going. So... Sure. Why not."

"OK, I gotta go take care of business. These punks are calling me *maricón* now. You know what that means?"

I just laugh.

"Never mind, asshole. Later."

I hang up still smiling. Fucking Smith.

Robert knocks on my office door. "Hey," he says.

"What's up?" I ask, pulling myself out from my personal problems.

"You done for the day?"

"Yeah," I say, looking at the papers on my desk. "Pretty much. Why?"

"You wanna take off early? Hit the bar? I'm done too."

I check the time. It's only two. And I'm about to say, *Yeah, why not,* when I get an idea. A sneaky idea. An innocent, perfect, sweet idea. "Nah," I tell him. "I'm gonna go home early today."

When I get home, Rochelle and Adley are sitting on the couch, half asleep. "What are you doing here?" Rochelle asks. But the question comes with a big, happy smile.

"I missed you," I say, dropping my keys on the kitchen island. I walk over to the couch and sit down carefully. Adley's eyes are heavy and she's almost out. "How's she feeling?"

"She's fine, Quin. I really hope you don't think this is your fault. Like Bric said, it was going to happen, no matter who actually fed her the food. And the rash is almost gone. It's not going to be a big deal."

Her neck is still a little bit red, but Rochelle is right. She's fine.

It's me who's struggling.

"Let me put her in her crib and I'll be right back, OK?"

"Sure," I say. Rochelle gets up, shushing Adley as she walks down the hall to try to keep her asleep.

I don't want to lose them. I don't want to lose Bric either, but I'm willing to give him up for them. I need this to work out in my favor. I really do. Because if it doesn't... if it doesn't, I see a really fucked-up life in my future. A future that validates all the preconceived notions I have about myself. A future that validates the reason I started playing this game with Bric and Smith in the first place.

It might ruin me.

I get up and walk towards Adley's room, listening to Rochelle talking quietly to the baby. She's a good mother. She's the perfect girlfriend too. We have argued more recently than we did in the past, but we had big problems. We talked through them. We got over them. And yes, Bric was a big part of that. I'm gonna be thankful for his help, no matter what.

But they're mine. He has to know that. He has to.

Rochelle walks to the door, slides them closed, and smiles at me. "What are you doing?" she asks, coming forward to press her head into my chest and wrap her arms around my middle.

"Thinking about how much I love you guys. What a great mom you are."

She leans back so she can look up at my face. "You have no idea how much that means to me."

"I can guess," I say, wrapping my arms around her too.

"Now tell me why you really came home early."

She knows me. She gets me. That's the reason I fell in love with her in the first place. And I know her. I get her too. We get each other.

"I wanted some time alone with you," I confess. "Both of you, really. Just the three of us. But I'm not afraid to say, I'm kinda happy Ads is sleeping." I stop hugging her, take her hand and lead her towards the bedroom. "Because I'd be lying if I said I don't want you all to myself. I don't want to share you, Rochelle." I look over my shoulder as we enter the bedroom, then, once she's inside, I slide the doors closed.

"You don't want to share?" she asks. Hesitantly.

And I'm not sure if that means she's hesitant for what that means for Bric. Or if she's happy I have finally been able to admit this to her. To myself.

"No," I say, shaking my head. "I don't feel like sharing anymore." She's wearing a thick cable-knit sweater, which I begin to unbutton.

She blushes like a girl as I do this. And when I slip the sweater down her arms and let it fall to the floor, she lowers her head, like she's embarrassed. She stands there like that. Her bra is pink and made of cotton and not black and made of lace. Something sweet. Something a girl would wear. It feels so much like a beginning, I want to die.

"Undress me," I whisper. "Slowly. So I can enjoy it." *So it feels like it used to*, I don't add. But that's what I mean. We used to have all these moments together. No one else to think about. No one else to interfere.

We wasted our beginning on doubts and fear. We pretended our way through a two-night-a-week relationship. But it's just not enough. None of what we've been doing will ever be enough for me.

She takes off my tie. Tugs my shirt up out of my pants and starts unbuttoning from the top down. When she gets to the last button, her hands slip inside my shirt and she presses her palms against my skin as she slides them around my back. She leans in. Sighs into my bare chest.

"I've been waiting for this for a very long time, Quin Foster."

"I'm sorry," I say, reaching down to tuck a piece of hair behind her ear so I can see part of her face. "I have loved you for so fucking long, Rochelle Bastille. None of that has changed. My feelings for you have not changed. It's how I feel about myself that's changed."

She pulls back and takes off my cufflinks. Sets them on the dresser. Makes my shirt slide down my arms. Unbuckles my belt. Looks up and gives me a shy smile.

Yes, I decide. This is definitely a beginning.

She unbuttons me. Unzips me. I do the same to her. And then we take off the rest of our clothes and face each other.

Naked. Stripped bare. Nothing to hide.

"We're gonna make it," I say.

"I know, Quin."

I lead her over to the bed and sit down. She climbs onto my lap and holds me tight.

We sit there for a little bit. Just enjoying each other. We're not in a rush. There is no hurry. So we take our time. We kiss. We touch. And when we've had enough of that, I lie back on the bed and she straddles my hips. Puts me inside her.

My cock slides in and fills her up. She closes her eyes and moans as she begins to move. Rocking her hips. Pressing into me and leaning forward so she can rub her clit across my lower stomach.

I place her hands on my chest. Flat. One of them over my heart so she knows how much I like this.

I make love to her. Slowly. I burn each moment into my brain. This is us. This is what's real. There's no game. There's no rules. There's no doubts.

We're in love.

CHAPTER TWENTY-SIX

ROCHELLE

Chella's Tea Room is a contradiction in style. On the one hand, it's very opulent and luxurious. Just like the Club next door. But on the other hand, it's old-fashioned and comfortable. The floors are made of perfectly polished rustic wood. Maybe even reclaimed wood. They are distressed and beautiful. Most of the tables are small and square, with four comfy, over-stuffed chairs placed around them. Some tables are rectangles and have couches along the long ends. The fabrics are all different, but all are some variation of yellow and white. There are more than a dozen crystal chandeliers hanging from the ceilings, and each of them is different. They are antiques, I realize. One wall is lined with distressed china cabinets that all hold eclectic sets of white china.

It says lazy, summer afternoons—not dirty, dark nights. If I were to design a tea room in my head, it would look just like this.

The place is packed. I recognize some of the ladies. They are Club wives and Club mistresses whom I've seen over the years. I'm not friends with any of them, and this is very clear when we come in because everyone—I do mean everyone—stops talking to gawk at me.

I take a deep breath and kiss Adley's head. We're dressed up like spring today. She's wearing a tiered pink chiffon dress with long, cream-colored lace sleeves, off-white leggings, and furry pink booties. I'm in a long dress as well. Vintage-looking, just like Adley's. My old style, updated, I realize.

I haven't lost myself. It makes me feel good.

The sun is shining through the tall windows that face the street, making the room the perfect illusion of a lighter season.

Chella comes up to us with her hands outstretched, looking sophisticated and fabulous, as usual. But also approachable and casual. Her wide-legged winter-white trousers are paired with a matching double-breasted jacket with rhinestone buttons that reflect the light from the chandeliers above. It's got a little flare at her waist, making her look powerful and feminine at the same time.

"You made it," she says, kissing my cheek and running her fingers through Adley's silky blonde wavy hair. "And you two look gorgeous."

"Thanks," I say, still looking around with uneasiness. "Everyone is staring at me." And whispering, I don't add. Because that makes me sound paranoid.

"Just jealous, sweetness. That's all. You own the hearts and minds of the two most eligible bachelors in this town."

Yes. I guess I do.

"Come on, I have a special table set up in back for you and the little princess."

I follow Chella through the maze of tables and people. Some are sitting down, but many of them are standing and they make no attempt to hide the fact that they are staring at me as we pass.

We are led to a table near the revolving door that leads to Turning Point. There are already four people sitting at the table, none of whom I recognize.

"Rochelle," Chella says, stopping at the head of the table to smile. "These are my friends from the gallery. Michell and Kathryn."

"Hi," I say, hitching Adley up on my hip. They greet me with pleasant hellos, which makes me feel better. At least I'm not stuck at some table with a bunch of Club women.

"And this is an old friend of mine, Darrel. He used to be my security detail when I was younger."

A man wearing a light gray suit, probably in his late thirties, stands, bows, and then says, "Very nice to finally meet you, Miss Bastille."

Oh. Well, I guess that means they've been talking about me, because Chella never said my last name. No awkwardness there. "Pleasure," I say. "And this is Adley," I say, looking down at her.

"Oh," the other woman says. She's older, maybe fifties? Sixties? "I would recognize her anywhere."

"What?" I laugh nervously.

"This is Kitty Foster," Chella says with a wide smile. "Quin's *mother.*"

Holy fucking shit. You have got to be kidding me. I look at Chella, ready to bolt. But she places a hand on my arm and smiles. Even bigger, if that's possible. "Rochelle, she's been dying to meet you. Apparently, Quin has talked quite a bit about you over the past week."

"This baby!" Kitty Foster says, standing up and coming over to us. She is tall and slim and dressed up for a tea party. "She's adorable! May I hold her?" Kitty already has her arms outstretched, so what I can say?

"Sure." I smile. I'm secretly hoping Adley will get fussy, but nope. Her happy personality shines right through my discomfort.

Adley coos up at Quin's mother. She coos right back at her and takes her seat again.

I take my seat as well, and everyone resumes their conversations. Except Kitty Foster. She's too busy to deal with anyone else. She's dressed up like a... I try my best to give it a name. It's a style I recognize. Very vintage, which is cool. 1920's, I decide. She even has one of those floppy lace hats on her head. Garden party—that's her costume. And it's definitely a costume Something I'd wear. Her dress is pale pink, made of silk chiffon with a pretty lace bodice and a large clasp—maybe rhinestones, but if I know Quin, it's diamonds—at her waist. She and Adley match, I realize.

Isn't that special.

There's a high chair next to me, but it goes unused. Because Kitty has no intention of giving my daughter back until she's forced.

"I am one lucky grandma!" Kitty exclaims.

This is just fucking great. Does she know what kind of relationship Quin and I are in? Did he tell her Adley is his? He was so certain before that allergic reaction to the mango. But now... I think all of us are having serious doubts about that.

"Have you been enjoying your time in Denver again?" the man named Darrel asks.

"What?" I say, still preoccupied with my new... mother-in-law? Maybe? Kinda? Sorta? "Oh, yes. It's nice to be back."

"You know," Kitty says, leaning in my direction, "she looks just like Quin when he was a baby."

"Does she?" I ask. I'm so uncomfortable right now. I have no idea what to say to that.

306

"I bet you'll grow up to be just like him," she squeals at Adley. Adley, to my dismay, is eating it all up. She is cooing, and babbling, and performing for her... grandma... *God help me.* "His father was so proud of him."

"Oh?" I say, paying more attention. I guess this is a good opportunity to get more personal info on Quin. I should enjoy it while I can. Quin has never talked about his family life. I have no real idea who he was before we met. "What was Quin like as a child?"

"Perfect," Kitty says between coos at Adley. "He was a good eater, a good sleeper, and he loved everyone."

"Well, Adley is like that too." I laugh. "She's definitely a people person. So where do you live?" I ask.

"Oh, we still live in the same house Quin grew up in. If you bring this bundle of sweetness over sometime, I will show you his childhood bedroom."

"Oh, Lord," I say, smiling as I imagine that. "I bet I'd learn a lot about him from that."

"Indeed, you would, young lady." Kitty says, with what might be genuine affection for... me. She likes me? Even though I'm in a plural relationship with her son? She cannot know about that. Can she? No, I decide. Absolutely not.

"All his baseball trophies are still lined up on the shelves and his debate awards are all framed on the walls. In fact," she says, turning towards me, taking her attention off Adley for a moment, "it's the exact same bedroom set we bought back when he was eight." She shakes her head, like she can't even begin to imagine where the time went. "Our house hasn't changed much. He's got that fancy place in downtown now, but he came from humble beginnings."

"Really?" I ask. Why have I always thought of Quin as a trust-fund kid?

"Yes. I think he's embarrassed to bring you home and that's why he hasn't."

I highly doubt that's why he's too embarrassed to bring me home. But I don't say anything.

"Our house in North Denver is so small. Just two bedrooms. But that's all we needed. We had each other."

"Hmm," I say.

"And he went to the local public school until junior high when he got that scholarship."

"Scholarship?" I ask.

"Yes," Kitty says, in between kisses to Adley's cheeks. Those make my daughter squeal with delight. "He worked so hard to get that place at the school. And then his whole life changed. He met Bric, and Smith. And just look at him now. So successful and important."

"Yes, he is," I say, absently.

"I'm so proud of him."

"Yes," I say. "Me too. Quin is one of the good ones."

"He is," Kitty says, looking poignantly at me. "I always worried that he'd inherit too much of his father and not enough of me. But it was silly. He is my boy, through and through. He never complained about church, even though I never made him go with me. He was always polite and well-mannered. Helping the older single ladies on the street whenever they needed their lawn mowed. He still does that." Kitty chuckles. "Every summer he mows Mrs. Jolenki's lawn. And never takes a dime from her. Not even when he was a teenager. She pays him in homemade casseroles to this day."

Kitty Foster talks about Quin for long stretches of time. We are served tea and champagne and she is telling me how he ran the church bakery booth for her when he was fourteen. They sold so many pastries, the church got new desks for the office that year.

By the time we're done eating tiny cakes and cookies from the triple-tiered pastry stands, most of the women in the room are well on their way to drunk and I've learned that Quin was an Eagle Scout, sang in the church choir, and spent two weeks every summer building houses for underprivileged families until he was seventeen.

What the hell is happening?

All this time I thought he was like Smith, and Bric, and... me. Wounded. Damaged. Ruined.

But he's not. He's... *normal*.

And if we're not the same... then we're different.

If we're not two fucked-up people just trying to fake their way through a fucked-up life... if we're not in this together, then who are we?

And that's when I see her. The mistress. The woman from the mansion party the other night.

And she's walking straight for me.

CHAPTER TWENTY-SEVEN

BRIC

"Hey," Smith says, walking up to the Black Room bar. He motions to the bartender for a drink. I'm trying my best not to look at Jordan Wells as he fights with that new girl he's got over in one of the window booths. I can't quite figure out if it's real, or they're in some kind of playful sexual spat.

Either way, I'm fucking turned on. She's slapped him twice already. If she ever did that to me, I'd chain her ass to a fucking wall and make her think twice about her domination idea.

"What the fuck are you looking at?" Smith says.

"Nothing." Not my problem. I face the bar again and smile at Smith. "You showed."

"It's Chella's dream. I can't *not* show."

"Well, I'm giving you points anyway. Even if you never make it over there." We laugh.

"You're not over there either," he jokes.

"Fucking women. I have prepared myself for major drama. If these women think the rules don't apply over there"—I shake my head—"I'm gonna have to set them straight. I'll pop my head in eventually. Expectations and all. But tea parties are not my thing."

"Where's Quin?" Smith asks, looking around the bar.

"Not sure. Don't think he's here yet. Kitty's here though. She's probably sitting with Rochelle right now."

"What?" Smith asks, looking over towards the White Room, like he can see through walls or something. "What are they doing?"

"Talking?" I say. "I dunno. Whatever a grandma talks about with her granddaughter's mother, I guess. I have no clue."

"And you're not worried about this?" Smith is giving me an incredulous look.

"Why would I worry?"

"He didn't tell Kitty that the baby was his, did he?"

I shrug. "Who cares?"

"Because it's not his kid, Bric. He can't go telling Kitty that's his kid."

"Why not? It's his mother. I don't see the big deal."

"She's like... everyone's mother. That's not the point. The point is, Kitty knows she's not my real mom, but she likes to mother me, right? And she knows you're not her real son either. But what's one more man to take care of in Kitty's book? She knows Quin is her biological son. She treats him like a son. She doesn't stay up nights wondering how I'm doing. She doesn't want to have lunch with you every month. That's stuff reserved for Quin. And I don't want Kitty thinking that Adley, adorable as she is, is her blood. Because she's not."

"You don't know that," I say. He's starting to get on my nerves.

"I *do* know that."

"Look, the allergy doesn't mean anything concrete. Lots of people have allergies and aren't—"

"I'm not talking about the fucking allergy test, you idiot." Smith is actually seething.

"Dude, what is your problem?"

"Rochelle, that's my problem. I don't want Kitty thinking that's her granddaughter because I figured her out a long time ago. I know something about her you guys don't."

"About who? I'm so fucking confused."

"Rochelle, you idiot. Did we ever ask her about her past?"

I think about it for a second because I'm almost positive we did. "I don't know," I decide. Because I can't quite remember. "It was a long time ago. I'm sure we did."

"We didn't. And did you ever ask yourself why I really stopped associating with her?"

"You don't like her. I think you've made that pretty clear."

"Why don't I like her, Bric?"

"Who knows. You hate everyone."

"Not true. I love a lot of people. I just hate opportunists, Bric."

"Like me," I joke. I take another sip of my drink.

"It's not funny, asshole. I have a pretty good idea what kind of person Rochelle really is and this stupid fucking game the three of you are playing is gonna turn very bad as soon as you pull your heads out of your asses and get that DNA test."

"Why's that?"

Smith and I both turn away from the bar to find Quin right behind us.

"What?" Smith says, playing dumb.

"Why would we regret playing this game if we got the DNA test? I just talked to you about this yesterday and you were all supportive and shit."

"No," Smith says. "I was evasive. And if you didn't have your head up your ass, you'd have recognized that."

"Evasive about what?" Quin asks. He looks as confused as I am.

"About your goddamned girlfriend. You don't know anything about her, Quin. You never ask. Why the fuck do you let her get away with all this shit?"

"Hey," I say, putting my hands up, trying to defuse the situation. "We're not gonna do this again. Not here."

"We've never actually done this," Smith says. "I just keep minding my own business, hoping the two of you will finally come to your senses about this woman. She's playing you assholes, Can't you see that? I looked her up last year. Something you guys never bothered to do. But hey, who am I to interrupt someone's fun, right? So I let that go. But then I fucking saw her last year—"

But my phone buzzes on the bar next to me and interrupts him. "Shit," I say, looking down at the text. "We have a problem at the tea party."

CHAPTER TWENTY-EIGHT

"Saw her where?" I ask. But Bric is on his feet, already walking towards the White Room. Smith goes after him, so I have no choice but to follow. We push our way through the revolving doors just in time to see a woman throw a drink in Rochelle's face. Some of it even lands on my mother. And Adley.

"What the fuck is going on here?" Bric bellows the words out so loud, the whole room lets out a shocked gasp.

The woman, who is so drunk she's swaying, takes her fury to Bric. "This little cheating whore!" she yells. "She's just like her mother. Just like her father. The disgusting deviant side in her comes naturally. She thinks she's so much better than me? Well, let me tell you a little bit about Rochelle Bastille! She's—"

But Bric has his hand over her mouth and is dragging her ass back towards the doors we just came through.

I walk over to Rochelle and take Adley from my mom. "Are you OK? What the hell was that?"

"I'm fine," Rochelle says, wiping champagne off her face. I take my pocket square out of my suit coat and offer it to her. "Thanks," she says, with a frustrated sigh. "And that was my father's ex-mistress throwing a tantrum because Bric threatened to kick her sugar daddy out of the

Club if she didn't keep her trap shut about how she knows me."

"How does she know you?" I ask. Smith's words are still ringing in my head. *You don't know anything about her, Quin. You never ask.* But then some guy in a gray suit starts dabbing my mother's dress with a handkerchief. "And who the fuck are you?" I ask him.

"Sorry," the guy says. He's about Bric's age, I'd guess.

"Quin," Chella says, coming up next to me. "That's Darrel Jameson. He's a former FBI agent. Used to be my security detail back when I was young and wild." She laughs.

"Oh," I say. "Sorry about that. But I'm kinda wound up. My girls just got a drink thrown on them."

"No problem," Jameson says. "It's nice to finally meet you. When Bric hired me to find Rochelle, we didn't have a chance to talk. I got the info so fast." He laughs. "It's almost like he didn't want her found. Anyway, I only reported to him. And it's all working out, I see." He beams a smile over to Rochelle, who looks very confused.

"What?" I have to shake my head a little to catch up with the conversation.

"Quin," Chella says, taking my arm. Adley is smacking me on the face, babbling her little heart out, completely oblivious to the commotion. "I didn't even have a chance to tell you. I introduced him to Bric and the very next day, Rochelle came home on her own. So we never needed him."

"No." Jameson chuckles. "I found her thirty minutes after you gave me her name, Marcella. I came to the Club to tell you that, but you left. So I told Mr. Bricman—" He stops talking. "Ohhhh. Yeah. Oops." He winces. "Mr. Bricman did tell me not to tell you."

"He what?" Chella says.

"What the fuck is happening right now?" I look at Rochelle. "Did Bric find you? Did he tell you to come home? Did you lie to me?"

"Listen," Chella says. "I'm sure this all a misunderstanding. Rochelle came home because she missed you, Quin. Right, Rochelle?"

I look at Rochelle and she's pale. So fucking pale. That's not why she came home. I can tell. I can read her mind.

I look at Smith and he's leaning up against the wall near the revolving doors, his arms crossed, big smug smile on his face. "There's more," he says. "Isn't there, Rochelle?"

"Smith," Chella barks. "Would you shut up! You're not helping."

Rochelle snaps out of her shock and comes up to me, taking Adley right out of my arms. "We need to go clean up. Excuse me."

Everyone, and I do mean everyone in this tea room, watches her walk away. As soon as she disappears into the restroom, the whole place explodes in whispers.

Bric appears behind me. "I'm so sorry, everyone. Please, continue to enjoy your tea. Helen will not be back, so if you're in her party…" He stops, like he's thinking. "Well, just get the fuck out now. I have no tolerance for this kind of bullshit."

He waits, but not a single woman gets up to claim that Helen woman as a friend.

"Good," Bric growls at them. "If any of you think you're going to come in here and start some catty bullshit, you're mistaken. You know the *rules*."

317

Everyone turns away from him, pretending to be interested in their tea and not the complete scene we're making here in the back of the room.

"Well, that was quite a show," I say. "You wanna fucking explain what the hell just happened in here?"

"No," Bric says, combing his fingers through his hair. "We can have that discussion at home."

"I think we should have it now," Smith says, walking over to us.

"Smith," Chella cautions him.

But Smith is not deterred. He's risking Chella's anger because he's got something to say to me. So I put a hand up to stop her. "Just let him talk, Chella."

"Not here," Bric growls at us.

"Here," I say back. And then I look Bric in the eyes. "Now."

"Rochelle has a lot of explaining to do, Quin," Smith says. "Do you really think I'd pay her ten thousand dollars a month to stay away for the fuck of it? Why did Rochelle leave so suddenly, Chella? You told us she took off unexpectedly. Why?"

I look at Chella. "Do you know what he's talking about?"

She shrugs, looking confused. "Rochelle did leave unexpectedly, but—"

"But that's not even the worst of it," Smith says. "The worst of it is..." He stops. Like he's got a lot more to say, but he's not sure if he should say it.

"You might as well keep going," I say.

"I know why she left and it's got nothing to do with you."

I look at Chella again. "What's going on?"

"She doesn't know anything," Smith says. "I didn't tell her. And I wasn't going to tell you either, but I cannot let you continue this farce of a relationship, especially since you're dragging your mother into it. There's a very good chance Adley doesn't belong to either of you," Smith says.

"What?" Bric and I say together.

"She was cheating on you guys," Smith says. "I saw her in a very heated argument with a guy on the street the day before she took off."

"You must really hate me," Rochelle says in a small voice from behind us. She's standing just outside the door of the restroom. "That is some kind of hate, Smith Baldwin." Then she looks at me. "I don't have any idea where he's getting this."

"So I didn't see you with another man the day before you took off?" Smith looks at me and shakes his head. "Don't believe her. Don't believe a single word she says. She comes from a long line of liars. I looked her whole family up that spring I stopped coming by. I always knew you were someone, Rochelle. You had no cares. You had no worries. You had no commitments. I looked your family up. I even made a special trip out to Palm Springs to meet your father once. What a guy. So, yes, Rochelle Bastille, you absolutely do have some idea of what I'm fucking talking about."

Rochelle looks at me, anger washing over her. "I think it's ironic that I'm here, in a place filled with cheaters, being called a cheater. This Club is nothing but cheating. You people are the height of hypocrisy. And if you believe him—well, then I'll happily pretend I never came back. Helen just accused me of being a stupid little slut, just like my mother. And now Smith Baldwin is going to say the same thing? After he used me for years, just like the rest of you?" She shakes her head. "No. I don't think so."

Rochelle lifts up her head, straightens her spine, and walks right past us, disappearing through the revolving doors.

CHAPTER TWENTY-NINE

ROCHELLE

I will not cry. I will not cry. I repeat this over and over in my head as I make my way through the White Room and the lobby and right through the big revolving front doors. I don't even have my car here. I'm fucking at the mercy of the drivers.

I wait.

Thankfully, they keep Bric's car parked right down the block, so it pulls up and the valet opens the door for me. I scoot in, relieved to see that the car seat is still strapped in.

The door closes and I let out a sad sigh. So this is where it all falls apart? I should've known Smith would start more shit after he paid me that visit last week. Asshole.

And now I know the little secret he's been keeping about me. Well, fuck him. Just fuck him.

The door opens again and Kitty Foster is standing there. "Oh, good. Hahaha." It's a nervous, happy laugh. "I was afraid I'd miss you."

"Why, God?" I say out loud as I buckle Adley in her seat. She smells like champagne. That stupid bitch Helen. I cannot believe she threw a drink on me.

"Oh, honey," Kitty says, still nervously laughing as she gets in the car and closes the door. "What's a little public humiliation between friends, right?"

She smells like champagne too. "I'm sorry, Mrs. Foster."

"No, no, no," she says, patting my arm. "It's Kitty. We're family now."

"Didn't you just hear all that? She's not Quin's baby. Smith Baldwin is an asshole."

Kitty looks at me sympathetically. "I don't know what's going on, but Rochelle, I have some idea. These boys..." She looks away. "Well, they like to think I'm naïve and innocent. But I just play along, honey. No mother wants to discuss her son's sexual... preferences, right? Hahaha!" Another nervous laugh. Then she stops the laugh and says, seriously now, "Maybe proclivity is a better word?"

I just look at her, then lean forward to talk to the driver. "Can you take me home, please?"

"Sure, Miss Bastille," he says.

"And button up the divider, huh, Ben?" Kitty says. "Us girls need to talk."

"No problem, Kitty." The glass between us and the driver slides up and we are left alone.

So. She's a regular around here. I don't know why that surprises me, but it does. I have never seen her around the Club. Was her husband a member? Is that why Quin's a member?

Maybe that life he led wasn't as normal as I first thought.

It shouldn't make me feel better, but it does. I cannot believe how fucking all-American Quin Foster is. It makes me... insecure. Why would he want a fucked-up girl like me? Why? When he could have anyone he wants?

But no, that's not right about his father being a member. Not at this Club, at least. This Club belongs to

Smith and Bric. I know that for a fact. And they haven't owned it that long.

But everyone seems to know her. And she knows about Bric and Smith.

"Listen." Kitty leans into me and whispers. "I know what they do here."

I feel even worse knowing she knows.

"And I know who you are. Quin has talked about you a little. But he's not the one who told me about Adley." She takes a moment to look at her. "It was Chella. Quin didn't set this up to ambush you into meeting me, sweetie. I did. I talked Chella into it. So don't be mad at Quin."

"I'm not mad at Quin." I sigh. "I'm not mad at him at all. There is absolutely nothing about Quin to be mad about. He's perfect, in fact. Way too perfect for someone like me. And now that Smith just told him about that fight I had with—" I sigh again. Louder. Longer. "Well, now he's gonna know what a total piece of shit I am."

"Smith is Smith, Rochelle." Kitty's snapped into mother mode. "You know him far better than I do. But even I know how he is. He has some facts right, maybe?"

I nod my head and swallow hard.

"So he knows something you haven't told anyone else?"

"Yes," I say. "What he said was true, but he doesn't know the whole story. He should not have said that. Especially in front of all those people."

"I believe you," she says. "I think he probably knows that as well. You handled that altercation with grace and dignity."

"Thanks," I say. "I really wanted to tell him to fuck off."

We laugh.

323

"But not in a room filled with people."

"I totally understand. But the reason I came in the car with you was to make sure you understand why my son does this."

"This?" I ask.

"Sharing business," Kitty says, waving her hand in the air. "I know about it. I have seen him change over the years. Especially since his father died. You see, this is probably all my fault."

"What?"

Kitty laughs again. "Hahahaha. I can't say for certain how I know. Quin and I don't talk about our sex lives. But it goes back to my relationship with his father."

"You shared men?"

"I wish. Hahaha."

"I'm sorry, what are you saying then?" I'm so confused.

"I'm going to let him tell you. I think he's figured it out. He's been struggling lately. And I know most of that goes back to his relationship with you."

Well, that's just great.

The car pulls up to the loft and stops in front of the lobby doors. The driver gets out. "But don't walk away before he tells you, Rochelle. Even if it takes him a little while to work through it. This is my granddaughter," she says, patting Adley's arm. "I can tell. Grandmothers know these things. But even if she isn't through blood, she is through love. Remember that."

My door opens. I unbuckle Adley's seat and the driver lifts it out for me.

"I'll see you soon, Adley," Kitty calls.

I walk into the building and get into the elevator. When I get upstairs I take Adley out of her seat and just sit in front of the window, wondering how the hell this day went so wrong.

And how am I going to explain myself to Quin?

The elevator dings and opens. Bric walks out. "Hey, Quin's not here yet?"

"Is he coming?" I ask, looking back at the window.

"Of course he's coming," Bric says. "Why wouldn't he come? I told him to meet me here so we can discuss what the hell just happened. Are you still wearing that dress?" he asks, walking over to me. "Go change, Rochelle. Everything is going to be fine."

I don't think anything is going to be fine. But I get up anyway. I have to get Adley out of her clothes too.

"Here," Bric says. "I'll take care of Adley. You take care of yourself."

I don't fight him. I can't. The mistakes are all I can think about. I just hand Adley over and go in to the bedroom. I pull on a pair of jeans and one of my well-worn Pagosa Springs t-shirts.

Bric brings a refreshed Adley into the bedroom, just as I'm finishing up.

"You're quiet," Bric says.

"I just keep hearing Smith's accusation over and over again."

"Yeah, well... I just keep hearing that stupid detective announcing the fact that he's the one who found you. I cannot believe he did that."

"There's just... so many lies," I say. I feel so defeated. I don't even know how to describe it.

"Just stick to the story," Bric says. "Come on, we'll get a drink and wait for Quin—"

"I'm right here," Quin says. He's standing in the hallway. Still. Like he was about to come in the bedroom, but he heard us talking and decided to see what we had to say when he wasn't around.

"Perfect," I mutter, taking Adley from Bric and going out to sit in my window chair again. "That's just perfect."

CHAPTER THIRTY

"Hey," Bric says, running his fingers through his hair. He always does that when he's nervous. It's a tell with him. "What's up?"

"What's up?" I raise an eyebrow at him. Is he fucking serious? "There's so much bullshit going on here, I have no idea where to start."

Bric pushes past me and follows Rochelle over to the window. "I hope you're not gonna start shit. I think we've had enough for one day."

"Me?" I just can't. "None of what's happening has anything to do with me."

"You'd be surprised," Bric says. He walks into the kitchen, grabs two beers from the fridge, and offers me one. When I don't acknowledge him, he shrugs, puts one back, and pops the top of his.

I laugh. He's got some balls. "Is that how you plan on spinning this? Everything is my fault?"

"Of course not," Rochelle calls out from the other end of the loft. "Didn't you hear? Smith Baldwin blames me for everything. According to pretty much everybody, I'm the bad guy today."

I stare at the back of her head. I can see Adley's smiling face. It hurts my heart to look at her. So fucking much.

"I've thought things through on my way over here," I say in a low, calm voice. "I even sat down in the garage for a few minutes, making sure I have it straight. I can deal with Adley being yours," I say to Bric. "I can. It won't be easy, but I'd be OK with it in the end. But I have no idea how I'd feel if she's neither of ours."

Rochelle shakes her head and grunts in disgust.

"We're never going to know," Bric says. "So just stop."

"Yeah," I say, looking back at Bric. "I figured that'd be your response. That's the line you've been feeding me this whole time, right? We're both her father. We're a team. A thriple, Rochelle calls it. How cute. So damn cute. But what I want to know—what I *need* to know—is what's really going on with that investigator guy, Bric. Let's start there."

"It's not a big deal," Bric says.

"No?" I ask. "You lied to me and you don't think that's a big deal?" My voice is still calm. I refuse to have a fight in front of Adley. I will not do it. But I'm gonna have my say. Right now. "Because if that's the case, Bric, I don't know who the hell you are."

"That's not what I meant," he says, walking over to the window to sit in the chair next to Rochelle.

"It's OK," Rochelle says, sniffling. "He doesn't know who I am either, remember?"

Stay calm, I tell myself.

I count to ten, then join them, taking the chair on the other side of Rochelle.

"Is that going to be your angle too?" I ask her. "Blame Quin?"

"You have no idea what's going on."

"So tell me," I say, turning in my chair so I can see her face better. "Tell me, Rochelle. Explain to me again how you ended up in Denver after leaving me behind a year ago? And this time," I say, looking at Bric, "don't leave out the part where Bric finds out where you live the day before, OK? Do me that favor. Don't lie this time."

Bric lets out a long sigh. "Chella did hire that guy."

"And he did find her," I add.

"Yes. He found her right away."

"Yeah, he mentioned that after you left. Said it took nothing at all to pull up all kinds of bank transactions in Pagosa Springs, including," I say, my voice getting louder than I want it to—I look down at Adley, so fucking sorry this has to happen right now—"including," I repeat, softening my tone, "the bill for the resort on her fucking credit card. Were you even looking, Bric? All last year, did you even bother looking? Or was all that a lie too?"

"I looked," he says, narrowing his eyes at me. "But I can't see credit cards, Quin. And I wasn't going to do anything illegal."

"OK," I say. "I'll accept that. I don't exactly believe you, but fine. You looked, never found her, then Chella hired an old friend, who found her immediately. Am I right so far?" Bric glares at me. "Stop me when I get it wrong."

"I called the Club last summer," Rochelle says. "Right after Adley was born. I was upset. Crying. Sorry for leaving like that," she says, looking at me with watery eyes. "And then Adley started crying and I knew Bric was gonna ask a bunch of questions about me keeping the baby, so I hung up. And then Bric came to my suite at the resort," Rochelle says. "The day before I came back. He spent the night."

"You called him?" I ask, looking at Bric. "And you never thought I'd need to know that? When you knew damn well I had no idea she was dead or alive?"

"I was on my way out of town," Bric says. "I was closing the Club for the summer and I had a flight to catch."

"A flight to catch?" I want to laugh, it's so ridiculous. "So you're telling me your summer vacation was more important than letting me know the woman I love was OK? That I had a baby?"

"You don't even know if Adley's yours," Bric says.

"No." I laugh. "I guess I don't. But that doesn't even matter at this point. You stayed the night with Rochelle and Adley?"

"In another room," Bric counters, seething at me.

"Then what happened? How did you two decide to lie? And better yet, why? Why the hell did you even bother? What did you think you were gaining by not telling me the truth?"

"You weren't even talking to me," Bric says.

"He didn't think... we didn't think..." Rochelle falters. Which means she's trying to tell me the truth, but the truth is gonna hurt too much, so she can't say it.

"Just tell me," I say. "For fuck's sake, just tell me what the hell is going on with you two?"

"Bric wanted to play the game with you again." Rochelle says. She looks at me. Her eyes are glassy with the threat of tears. "And I figured the only way to get you back was to play the game with both of you. Because you never wanted me, Quin. You only wanted us."

"So why lie?" I ask. "I don't get it."

"Because if I brought her home, I'd be Number One."

"Oh." I laugh. "That's amazing. You'd be Number One. And you were afraid she'd what? Fall in love with you?"

"Hey," Bric says. "Stranger things have happened."

330

"So let me get this straight. Just so everything is crystal clear. You went down to Pagosa Springs to talk Rochelle into coming back—"

"No," Bric interrupts. "I went down there to tell her to stay away."

"Which is an amazing coincidence," Rochelle sneers. "Because Smith came here last week offering me two million dollars to leave town." She shakes her head and laughs. "And when I said no, he decided to find another way to break us apart."

I can't speak. Everything I thought I knew has just been turned upside down.

"At least Bric changed his mind and wanted to bring me to you as a gift," Rochelle adds.

"A gift?" I look at Bric and put all the pieces together. "You wanted me back in your game, didn't you? That's why you wanted Rochelle here. To lure me back."

"I really don't see the problem," Bric says. "I love her, Quin. And the baby. I really don't understand why you're so pissed off. We're all getting what we want."

I'm seeing red right now. "You selfish motherfucker," I say. I hate swearing in front of Adley. I hate the fact that all of this is taking place in front of my daughter, but I need to make things very clear. Right here. Right now. "He doesn't love you, Rochelle. You know that, right? He's not capable of love. The only thing Elias Bricman is capable of is playing games."

"Fuck you," Bric says.

"Language, Bric. Oh, let me fill in the blanks about the swearing thing too, while I'm at it. You'd already spent the night with Rochelle and Adley before they came back to Denver. So you knew the rule that first day. That's why you were all over people and their swearing, right?"

"You're making a big deal out of nothing, Quin," Bric says.

"You're the one who couldn't commit," Rochelle says. "Bric had no problem committing to this second chance."

"Really?" I laugh. Adley laughs with me. "He doesn't love you, Rochelle. He doesn't love anyone but himself. Elias Bricman is the most self-centered, selfish person I've ever met. He's a master of manipulation. Do you even know why he's not a doctor? After all that school? After all that work? It's because he was playing a fucking game with three medical students during his psychiatry residency." Bric looks like he wants to kill me right now. But I don't care.

"At least I don't walk away," Bric says.

"You're saying that about me?" I ask. "After Rochelle left Chella in her bed that night? Walked out on all of us?"

"I felt like I had no choice," Rochelle says, her voice cracking with emotion.

"Why? Because you didn't know who Adley's father was?"

"Because you were never going to end the game, Quin." She spits my name out with venom. "So I figured it was up to me to do it for you."

"Right. We're back to blame Quin time. I didn't do any of this, you guys. You two did. You two lied to me. You manipulated me. You plotted in secret. God, it's so disgusting, I just don't know where to start. And I don't even have the capacity to think about who Adley belongs to right now. I'm still so stuck on the lies."

"She belongs to me," Rochelle says. "She's mine."

"You mean she did belong to you." I say it even and cold. No emotion at all.

"What's that mean?" Rochelle says, her eyes wide with fear.

"It means," I say, standing up, "I want a DNA test. Both of you need to drop by Lucinda's office any time on Monday. We'll have the results by the end of the week."

And then it's my turn to walk the fuck out.

CHAPTER THIRTY-ONE

ROCHELLE

"They're not coming," I say.

"Just relax, Rochelle," Lucinda says. "It's only five after three. They're only a few minutes behind. Let's talk about something else while we wait. Did you ever explain the reason why you came to Denver in the first place?"

"Jesus," I say, shuffling a squirming Adley in my arms. "I didn't even have a chance, Lucinda. It's not a great time for that, OK? I can't think about anything else but what's happening *right now*."

We did all come by Lucinda's office last Monday. Separately, of course. She took a cheek swab from Adley, who thought it was great fun. I want to roll my eyes right now, but Lucinda is watching me closely and she'd just ask me why I felt the need to roll my eyes. I've been her patient for years. Ever since I came to Denver. She is the only one—aside from Smith, apparently—who knows how that all came about.

Lucinda has a large envelope on her desk and it's taking every ounce of willpower I have not to lunge across her desk, snatch it up, and rip it open.

But no, she says we have to do it all together.

And they agreed. Which surprised me.

I haven't seen either of them since last Saturday after the tea party. Quin walked out and never came back. Bric stayed the night, but I moved out in the morning. I'm back

335

at the Four Seasons. I might be on my way to Jackson Hole tonight if things go badly.

"Are you nervous?" Lucinda asks.

"I'm so annoyed with everyone right now."

"Why?" Lucinda asks.

"Because this wasn't supposed to happen."

"So why agree to it? You were under no legal obligation. I don't think either of them would've forced you."

"Because it's better to know," I say. She smiles at me, so I know she agrees and I just said something that makes her proud. I take a deep breath and let it out slowly, the way she taught me years ago. "I need them to know, I guess."

She nods her head at me and opens her mouth to speak, but a buzzer on her desk interrupts. "There they are. One second while I go let them in."

Lucinda has a private office. You can't come in the waiting room unless you have an appointment. She gets up and lets herself out of the inner office. But a few seconds later Bric walks in.

He looks... very nervous.

"Where's Quin?" he says.

"I thought he'd come with you," I say.

"He's not talking to me. But he's gonna show up, right? He's the one who wanted this."

I look at the clock. It's now quarter after three. He's a full fifteen minutes late. "He's not coming," I say. "He wouldn't be late if he was coming."

Bric takes the seat on my right, running both hands through his hair, like the stress is about to kill him. I can't help but feel the emptiness of the chair on my left.

"Well," Lucinda says. "What should we do?"

"Just open it," I say. "I can't take it anymore. I'm gonna rip it open myself if you don't do it right now."

"Yeah," Bric agrees. He frowns at me, then takes my hand and squeezes. "Just do it."

"OK," Lucinda says, picking the envelope up off her desk. I watch her fingers as they unseal the flap, and then she pulls out a thin stack of papers and shuffles through each one.

She looks at me and pauses. I want to reach out and choke her right now. *Tell me, tell me, tell me!* "I'm sorry," she says. Then she looks at Bric. "You're not the father, Elias. Quin is."

Quin is.

I say it over and over in my head. I squeeze Adley so hard, she starts to fuss loudly. Tears are spilling down my cheeks. "I don't know why I'm crying," I say. "I'm sorry." I wipe at my cheeks, doing my best to calm down.

But when I look over at Bric, his long frown and glassy eyes are enough to make me start all over again.

CHAPTER THIRTY-TWO

BRIC

"Would you two like a minute alone?" Lucinda asks.

I nod, unable to speak. There's a hard rock in my throat. So hard, when I try to swallow, I can't. I'm not even sure what that means, but inside I feel like... dying.

"Take your time," she says, leaving me alone with Rochelle and Adley.

"Elias," Rochelle finally says.

But I shake my head. "Don't, OK? Just give me a second."

Adley is staring at me. These past few weeks have been so much fun. I want to pick her up. Hold her. I imagined doing that so many times this week. I pictured it in my head. The moment when I got proof that I was her real father.

But now there is nothing to do but sit here and feel... loss. Adley was never mine. She was always theirs. I knew this. Even if the DNA test had come back the other way, and I was her biological father, there is no way we'd ever make it.

I'm not capable of normal. I know this. I have always known this. I am everything Quin said I was. And worse. He has no idea how much worse.

If I was Adley's biological father it would break us apart. But even worse, it would break *them* apart. And they are the ones in love, right? I was never in love with her. Was I?

I look at Rochelle. Her eyes are red from crying. "I was never in love with you the way he was, you know that, right?"

She shakes her head at me. "Don't do that, Bric. You're not going to do that this time. We had something real. You know we did."

"No," I say. Because I feel the need to make a clean break. This is probably how Rochelle felt last year when she left. Rip the Band-Aid off and face the facts. "The cat is out of the box," I say.

I get up, force myself to walk across the room. I pull the door open. And walk out.

I know she's sad. I know we had something real. And I want nothing more than to hold her. Hold them both and tell her how I feel. But I can't. It's not fair.

She's not mine. She's his.

CHAPTER THIRTY-THREE

QUIN

The door buzzes.

I don't get up.

It opens and closes.

I stay right where I am. Sitting in a chair, looking out the window in the second bedroom. It's dark out now. I didn't watch the clock today. I forced myself to stay in here where there is no chance of glancing up above the fireplace and seeing what time it is.

Three o'clock came and went hours ago.

I can see Rochelle's reflection in the window when she finds me. There's just enough light seeping through from the main room so I can see her clearly. She leans her hip against the door and waits.

I do not move.

"I see you made some changes to the living room," she finally says. "It looks nice," she says. "Very homey now."

"I did," I say. "And homey was what I was going for." But we can talk all about my new décor later. "

Where's Adley?"

She holds up the key to my apartment. "With Chella. She gave me Smith's key to your condo. Did anyone call you?" she asks.

"No," I reply.

"Why didn't you show up?"

I take a deep breath and exhale. "Because I wouldn't be able to take it."

"You're her father, Quin."

I turn around, so angry that she's so clueless. "I don't need a fucking DNA test to tell me that, Rochelle. I have been telling you she's mine for weeks. I *know* she's mine. There was never any question in my mind that she was mine. And for the record, I never thought you cheated on me. Give me a fucking break, OK? I know you better than that."

Her face scrunches up. Like she's not sure what to make of that outburst. "Then why did you ask for a test? Why walk out angry? Why, Quin?"

"I didn't need the DNA test, Bric did. And the reason I didn't show up wasn't because I can't handle the truth. I stayed home because I couldn't..." I sigh. This is harder than I thought it would be.

"Couldn't what?" she asks.

"I didn't want to see Bric's face when he found out she was mine, OK? I couldn't do it. I don't want to hurt him, but he forced me. He was fucking everything up, Rochelle. Can't you see that? He never loved you."

"So you say," she says.

"No, I *know*. Bric likes to pretend he's invested, Rochelle. And this time his little fantasy got out of hand. Those lies?" I shake my head. "I wasn't mad at you for that. I knew you'd never do that if he didn't fill your mind up with his stupid bullshit. He manipulated you. Just like he manipulates everyone. It was all him. And I know I'm the easy-going one here, I get it. But I have to draw a line somewhere. So I did. Those lies were it for me as far as Bric is concerned. I asked for that test to bring him back to reality. He walked out, didn't he?"

"Yes," she says softly. "He did."

"I knew he would. And even though I feel bad because I know somewhere, deep inside him, he feels bad tonight too, I also know it won't last. He will be right back to the way he was by tomorrow. He's gonna go to the Club, fuck a girl, get drunk, and pretend all this never happened. You just watch."

"So you hate him now?" she asks.

"Hate him?" I laugh. "I didn't go through all that bullshit because I hate him. I love him, for fuck's sake. But he's got to learn that people are real. They're not objects. They're not things to manipulate. I didn't do this to hurt him. I did it to help him."

We think about this for a little bit. She comes over to me and sits in my lap. "Well, I guess we've got him all taken care of. What about us? Where are we now?"

I shrug. "I dunno."

"You don't know?" She scoffs at me. "Either we patch it up, Quin, or we go our separate ways. And I'm not talking about leaving town with Adley, so don't say 'Let's patch it up' because you're afraid I'll take her away. I won't."

I don't think she'd do that. Not now that she knows I'm Adley's father.

"I'm just afraid, Rochelle."

"Of what?"

"Not being enough for you."

"You're kidding, right?" She laughs and squeezes me. Puts her face in my neck and inhales. Like she's missed my scent this past week.

I let my arms fall around her. It feels so right. But is it really?

343

"I don't even know why you'd say that," she whispers. "You're the only one I've ever wanted."

It takes me almost a minute to articulate the doubts inside my head. All the fear and uncertainty. "My mom is crazy, right?" I say. It's as good a place to start as any, I guess.

"I love your mother. She's called me every day since that tea party fiasco."

"She's so cool. She's fun, and happy, and just... she loves everyone, you know?"

"Totally. And I think everyone loves her too."

"But my dad never made her happy, Rochelle. He never could. When I was a kid she was so much crazier, but in the very best way. She likes costumes. She decked our house out for Halloween. Dressed up like a witch." I laugh, just picturing it. "She was Mrs. Claus on Christmas Eve. At Easter, she wore bunny ears. It was just... part of her. But my dad used to tell her she looked ridiculous. Shame her, almost. So she stopped. I was about six, maybe. And she just stopped. And then I forgot all about that crazy stuff until he died and she started doing it again.

"I realized then he never made her happy. He worked too much. That's why I took our days off work when we were together last year. He put the family first, and that's great. He went to work every day. He mowed the lawn every weekend in the summer. He coached baseball. But while he was busy putting the family first, somewhere along the way he decided to put her last. Everything came before my mother. The house, the job, the lawn, the neighbors, the kid. Some people might say"—I laugh— "some people *did* say that my mother was the selfish one. That she never appreciated him. It could be true, I guess.

But I lived in that house. I saw how it went down. He ruined *her*, not the other way around.

"And yeah, she was sad when he was gone, but she was much happier as time went on. Now, she's almost like she used to be. And I think my dad just never had it in him to be what she needed."

"Are you afraid you're too much like your dad and I'm too much like your mom?"

I nod. "Yeah. I'm just me. Just boring Quin."

"Boring?" She leans back and looks me in the face. "Are you kidding me? Mr. Eagle-Scout. Mr. I-Help-Old-Ladies. Mr. I-Take-Casseroles-As-Payment. I don't think you understand how much I want a family like yours. How much I want and all your so-called boringness."

"I don't know how that could be. I really don't," I say. "I like sharing women with Bric and Smith because there was never any pressure to be perfect at everything. Smith compensated for me in ways... well, I'm not sure how. But he did. I know he did."

Rochelle laughs, shaking her head at me.

"And Bric was the same way. He was good at things I wasn't. He was someone you could enjoy who was totally different than me. I liked the *us*, Rochelle, because I thought it was the only way I'd ever keep a woman like you satisfied. I come from a perfect family and even my dad couldn't do it right. And when you stayed, I mean, good fucking God, when I realized you were staying— that things were working, you know?—I just couldn't picture me being enough for you. I couldn't picture you being satisfied with just me.

"How can I compete with weird Smith? How can I compete with Bric's dominance? Isn't it better to let them do what they do best? And me do what I do best? It worked for a while. I just finally gave in and decided you'd never want me all by myself. You'd say you did, but you'd be wrong. Just like my mom. And one day I'd wake up and tell you to stop wearing those ridiculous clothes. One day I'd wake up and realize I'd ruined you."

"No," she says, pressing her face into my beating heart.

"It could happen," I say. "It might take you a lifetime to realize it. Like my mom. You could wake up one day and realize you're happier with me dead than you ever were with me alive."

CHAPTER THIRTY-FOUR

ROCHELLE

"Well, I was not expecting that." I am stunned by his admission. This whole time he wanted to share me to make sure I stayed. And I wanted to share myself to make sure he stayed. "We are so stupid," I say.

He laughs. His body rumbles from beneath me. "If I had known that Smith bowed out of the game, I'd have said something. I would've told you I loved you. I would've figured all this out much sooner. But he didn't tell us. I didn't know, Rochelle. I had no idea he stopped playing."

"He stopped playing because he figured me out, Quin."

"What do you mean?" Quin asks.

I take a deep breath and try to gather my thoughts. I've thought about this so much over the past several years, but thinking about it and putting it into words are two very different things. I told Lucinda, but it was messy and emotional. It took weeks for her to work out what my problem was. Why I was doing the things that made me hate myself.

I don't have weeks to set this right with Quin. I have this one chance to make him see me the way I want to be seen. One chance to explain myself and not have him see me the way that Helen woman does.

"When I was six my mother picked me up from school one day. She never usually picked me up. I rode the bus to a babysitter's house after school. My parents both worked. And then one of them would pick me up at dinner time and take me home. We never ate dinner together. It was me and my mom and my brother, who was several years older, so he didn't need a babysitter. Or it was me and my brother and my dad. But we were almost never together as a family.

"So this day she picked me up and she said, 'We're going to my friend's house for dinner. He's got a little girl your age too. You can play with her.' I was like, 'OK. Cool. I like playing.' But she took me to her boyfriend's house."

"What?" Quin says.

"Yeah," I say, a little lost in thought as I remember that day. "They disappeared into the bedroom. Told us girls to play dolls. I can even remember those dolls. Though I don't remember the girl's name. I never saw her again. The next time my mother announced she was taking me to another friend's house, there was no other child to play with while they had sex."

"What the fuck?" Quin asks. "Your mother was... like a prostitute?"

"No." I sigh. "I think if she was doing it for money it might make it better. She did it... well, she did it because she felt she had to."

"What did your father say?"

"As you know, my father has mistresses too. Helen, apparently, was one of them. I don't remember her coming over, but he brought so many women over to our house when my mom wasn't there. That was before my mother started taking me to meet her boyfriends. She did it out of revenge, I think. She knew he took me and my brother places with his mistresses. And I think she was jealous of that. She had every right to be, of course. But she didn't have every right to use me a pawn in her game of marriage."

"That's fucked up. I'm sorry that happened to you, Rochelle."

"Do you know what the really fucked-up part about it is?" I ask. But it's rhetorical, and Quin makes no move to answer. He's just listening. "Did you know that children who know their parents are cheaters are twice as likely to cheat in their relationships too?"

"I know you didn't cheat, Rochelle."

"Well, you're more certain of me than I am. I didn't cheat," I say, looking down at him. "I never cheated on you guys. And do you know why that is?"

Quin nods. "Because you had all three of us. That's why you played the game, isn't it? Because you thought you'd never be faithful."

I nod. "I have cheated on many boyfriends. All of them, in fact. Every single time I'd find a guy I liked, we'd date and I'd fuck it all up by finding a new one. And all it would take to make that switch legitimate was one conversation. Two words. *It's over.* That's it. But I never did that. I just kept hurting them. Over and over and over. And I never understood it until Lucinda explained it to me. That the children of cheaters are twice as likely to cheat too. They see it as... normal. Something people do."

I look down at Quin. I love him so much. I never wanted him to know this about me.

"It's not normal," I tell him. "I don't want to be that person. I don't want my children to grow up seeing me in that way. So I left home. I left them all behind and on that

349

last day, I told them why. I left my brother too. He was already repeating their mistakes. Girls used to come to our house crying. Begging him to come back to them. It was drama, Quin. My whole life was drama. My brother learned to cheat from my father. Those girlfriends who came over to cry and beg him to take them back were just like the girlfriends who came to our house as kids. Some of my father's mistresses got pregnant and had babies. They all sued for child support. So the whole town got to hear about my cheating father. He even divorced my mother to marry one just so he wouldn't have more support taken out of his paycheck. That's when I left home. I couldn't take it anymore. I hated it. So I left them all behind. But my brother and I were close growing up. And one day he found me, even though I never wanted to be found."

"That was the man you were fighting with the day before you left?" he asks.

"Yes. Smith saw me fighting with my brother. He told me my parents had changed. They were back together and would I like to come home for Christmas. I think he was truly surprised when I said no. I was pregnant and emotional. And Chella and I had been planning on her taking my place in the game for months. So I just called her up, met her at Lucinda's, and we set it up last minute. I'm sorry I left. It was a cowardly move. But life overwhelmed me at that point. I didn't want to be reminded of who I was. What I was. And I didn't know if the baby was a boy or a girl, but either way, if I let my brother take me back to that life, it would become a cycle. Something that couldn't be broken."

"So you left."

I nod. "I'm very sorry I hurt you. I loved you, I just thought you weren't interested in me that way and it was better to make a clean break. Start all over again. Stop playing those childish games. Stop pretending that you and Bric were my cure and face up to the reality that if I wanted to change who I was, I had to leave you behind."

He's silent.

"Please don't hate me," I say.

He doesn't say anything for a long time. I'm pretty sure that this is over now. He will decide I'm not worth the risk.

But then he says, "You are way too interesting, Rochelle Bastille."

I don't know if that's good or bad. So I say nothing.

"We make our own future. If you've taught me anything, that's it. I don't have to be like my father. I don't have to disappoint you. In fact I've tried very hard this past week to think of ways to be different. I'm not sure I'm so good at it yet. You might need to teach me the art of intrigue. I am way too boring for a girl like you, but I'm not gonna let you go out of fear. Fuck that. You're not getting away that easy because I think I just fell in love with you all over again."

"Are you serious? You're not gonna throw me out? Take me to court and tell a judge I'm a horrible example of a mother?"

"No," he says, tilting my head up with a finger on my chin. "No way. You are the best thing that ever happened to me. I'm taking notes, Bastille. Pages and pages of notes. Ever since you walked into my life and agreed to be one-third mine, I've been thinking up ways to be worthy. And yeah, it took me a while, so I'm sorry for that. But I think I got the hang of it now."

"What are you talking about?"

Quin stands up, taking me with him. He carries me across the room and stops in front of the door. "I'm talking about this."

He flicks the lights on and the spare bedroom transforms into a baby's nursery.

"What?" I say, stunned. "This is... This is..."

"All your stuff from the secret room up in the attic apartment. Our stuff, right? Your Christmas tree. Your record player. Your stupid vintage suitcases. I want Adley to know how fucking great you are. How original and perfect you are. I want her to be able to appreciate you. My father never gave me that. He never let me appreciate my mother for who she is. But I appreciate her now. I'm not gonna make that mistake with you and Adley."

I hug him hard for a few moments. He is perfect. Way too perfect for me, but just the right amount of perfect for Adley.

"I have a lot to live up to," I tell Quin.

"No," he says, taking my hand. "You be you. That's all I need."

I kiss him. I place both hands on his strong shoulders and kiss him. "And you be you," I whisper into his mouth. "We'll be us."

"I like the sound of that," he whispers back. "Now tell me what you think of this room. I need feedback."

I laugh and then turn around to take it all in.

The crib is something I would've picked it out. White. With a giant mobile hanging over it. Little bees and butterflies bob and dip their way around an off-kilter circle. The bedding is yellow and white. And one whole wall is painted with chalk paint. There are giant hand-drawn dandelions on that wall. There's even those little fluff things blowing in a make-believe breeze.

"Look up," he says.

I know what's there before I look, but seeing my drawings on the ceiling—my handwritten *I'll Fly Away* song—it stuns me. "What have you done?" I whisper, barely daring to breathe as I slide down his body and stand there, hand on my heart in disbelief.

"I really hated that nursery for Adley Bric decorated. I was only pretending to like it so you'd be happy. So I made a new one at my house. I went to every antique store in Denver. And I pried the sheetrock off the secret-room ceiling and took it to a local artist to replicate. He drew the flowers too. I was gonna lie and say that was me, but I'm way too boring for that. You'd never buy it."

Boring. I laugh. "No, Quin Foster. You're the farthest thing from boring that ever existed. You might be way too exciting for me."

"I knew Adley would live here eventually. I didn't know how long that would take, so I'm glad it came sooner rather than later." He shrugs. Like this is just what boring, normal men do for their crazy girlfriends.

He turns me so he can see my face. "I love you, Rochelle Bastille. I'm done sharing you with the world. You're mine and you're gonna marry me. You're gonna have to settle for boring, so I'm really sorry about that. But I'll try my best to make you happy."

I kiss him, whispering, "I love boring. Your brand of boring is exactly what I need."

CHAPTER THIRTY-FIVE

Once upon a time, I was unhappy.

I just didn't realize it.

I had no idea how much I was missing out on until Rochelle and Adley came back.

But they're not why I'm happy now. Other people can't make us happy. Only we can make ourselves happy. Rochelle and I faced our fears, just like Smith and Chella did last year, and our lives are so much better because of it.

The door buzzes.

Rochelle and I ignore it. We know who it is. I'm setting the table. This is the first time I've ever used this table and I can't think of a better time to break it in than for Christmas dinner with the people I love. Rochelle is busy with the food. Chella is bringing dessert, so she didn't have to bake.

We went and got our Christmas tree last weekend. All the way up to the National Forest. Chella and Smith came too. Watching Smith use an ax was almost the highlight of my day.

Almost.

My highlight was realizing this is the fourth time Rochelle and I have done this little trip and the second time Chella and I have done it. Adding in Adley and Smith created something new, and we don't miss the past. In this small way, we're happy to share.

It's an old tradition done a new way.

Of course, Chella and Smith's tree is filled with sophisticated ornaments and looks like it belongs in a department store.

Our tree looks like it came out of my grandma's attic. But hey, that's just how we roll here at the Foster house.

Adley went to the allergist. Turns out she's allergic to latex and Rochelle would've found this out sooner if she had bought cheap bottles with latex nipples. But she's a genius and knew better. Latex has some cross-reactivity with certain fruits—mango is one of them. It scares me a little. To think that fear of knowing the truth almost made me doubt what I always believed to be true.

Adley is ours.

We're petitioning the court to add me to Adley's birth certificate. And tonight, when everyone goes home and Adley is fast asleep in her crib, I've got a little sparkly something for my future wife. We'll be changing her name too. Sometime next summer, to be more specific.

Adley is sliding around the condo in the little walker Bric bought her. We invited him tonight too, but he's busy, I guess. Whatever. He needs to learn his lessons in his own time or not at all. But I'm done. I did what I could for the guy and I'm done.

He lives in a world I don't understand anymore. He lives in denial. Denial of the truth inside him that's dying to get out and denial of all the good things Smith and I have found now that we've stopped playing his game.

The door beeps and a second later chaos erupts. Three puppies—yes, three now—burst into the room barking and racing around like, well, puppies. Adley squeals with delight and tries to maneuver her walker to chase them.

Rochelle warned me about Smith's new addition. But I have to fuck with the guy. I can't help it. "What the hell is this, Baldwin?" The little husky puppy was Chella's gift to him for Christmas this year. Turns out she knew he was just going along with those rat dogs to make her happy. So she went back to the shelter and got him the dog he really wanted.

"Triplets." Smith beams.

I can only shake my head.

"Am I a lucky guy or what? I can't believe it," he says, looking down at the completely crazy husky pup as it runs circles around Ads. She's gonna get dizzy trying to follow him with her eyes. I'm expecting that little shit to eat all the couch pillows, pee on the floor, and probably steal food off the table tonight. But whatever.

The things we put up with for love.

Smith and Rochelle talked for hours that night we set things straight. She told him everything. He listened. They forgave each other for... well, whatever it was that kept them from seeing eye to eye. I think Smith was just looking out for me. I can appreciate that. And now I think we're all on the same page. We've moved on. Left the past behind.

That's all you can do, right?

There's no such thing as turning back.

All you can do is move forward.

Once upon a time I had no idea what it meant to be happy.

I know what it means now.

It's love—in twos and threes and fours.

Does the number of people really matter?

Yes. The more the better.

I'm happy with our new foursome. It's not what it used to be, that's for sure. We're just... normal, I guess. And that's not a bad thing anymore. It would be a lot nicer if Bric was here. But like I said, I did what I could.

He can turn back all he wants. He can live in the past forever, for all I care. But one day his turn will come.

And then he'll know what we know.

Game over.

Christmas Day at Turning Point was pretty much how it always has been. If you don't mind the fact that all my friends are absent.

I take a drink of my brandy and exhale. I'm sitting in Smith's bar, looking down at the Black Room. There's only about a dozen people left now. They've all got rooms upstairs and will stay the night.

Me? I'm just gonna sit here for as long as I can. No one is in the basement tonight. They are all with their families and friends.

Fuck them.

The revolving doors make that swooshing sound they do when someone is coming in. I can't usually hear it from up here, but it's so quiet down there, it makes me look.

A woman comes in. She's wearing a black fur cape and a long black dress. She doesn't stop, but keeps walking. Across the front lobby and right up to the stairs. Her head is perfectly straight, her spine too. Her long dark hair falls down her back, but jiggles a little with each upward step.

Who the hell?

But just when I recognize her, my phone buzzes on the table.

I check the text.

Jordan: *You wanted her trained? She's trained. Merry Christmas.*

It's that ballerina chick. She's been slapping him around for weeks. The wannabe dom, I chuckle to myself.

When she gets to the second-floor landing she pivots right and walks towards the second, shorter set of stairs that lead up to Smith's bar.

She stops at the threshold of the bar and waits.

"What?" I ask her.

She doesn't even look at me. Just stares straight ahead.

That's when I notice she's got a tag attached to her right wrist.

"What the fuck is Jordan up to?" I mutter, getting up from my chair. I walk over to her and try to make her meet my gaze. She looks straight ahead and then lifts her hand up. The one with the tag.

I take her hand and read the tag.

I will not speak, but the answer to all your questions tonight is yes.

Jesus.

I text Jordan. What's going on?

Jordan: *You're pathetic and sad. So I got you a present. Like I said, Merry Christmas. It's your turn, Bricman. Have fun.*

I look her body up and down as I circle her.

Mine?

I smile. That devious, deviant, I'm-gonna-make-you-sorry-you-ever-started-playing-this-game-with-me smile.

And then I take her hand.

I lead her to the elevator.

We go up to my apartment.

I tie her wrists together with rope.

Raise her arms above her head.

And chain her to the ceiling.

It is my turn.

EOBS

Welcome to the End of Book Shit, bitches. The part in the book where I get to say anything I want. When I came to the end of this book I wasn't sure I had anything to say. It's kinda weird. Usually there's controversial element in the book that might need explaining, but I'm telling you, this is just a love story. People find love in so many different ways. I think there's something to say for a traditional romance story. Most people are traditional when it comes to love, so they can relate to it and it sells really well in the book world. If I was smart, I'd write that stuff. Over and over and over and over and over. I'd certainly have to think less when I'm plotting a book. And I'd probably make a good living.

But I'm just kind of a non-traditional person. I'm not sure when I decided this, but I was young. Teens, probably. Because I was a wild teenager and I took a lot of risks. But at the same time, I was annoyingly smart. But I didn't want to waste what came naturally to me, and luckily my little group of friends at this formative time in my life were also annoyingly smart and non-traditional. None of us felt pressure to be one thing or the other. We could wear flannel shirts and leather jackets and still ace a science test. So my days started out with smoking pot before school, progressed into trying real hard in biology (because biology, right? So fucking cool.) And then at night I took it one step further. Because at night I had this whole secret life going on at a show stable jumping horses.

361

Most of my friends never even knew I was in the horse show world until I dragged them out to the barn to watch me compete. I like the contradiction I was creating as a teenager. I liked that I had a whole group of very close friends who spent every day with me down in a basement smoking pot and listening to Pink Floyd and Led Zeppelin, but they didn't really *know* me. They didn't know any of my secrets. I don't know why I found that satisfying, but I did.

I actually have a degree in horses now. It's called equine science and I was going to be an equine veterinarian, but then I decided to go to grad school and that totally derailed my life in another direction. I was a non-traditional college student, by the way. I was a thirty-year-old single-mom with two kids when I finally went back to finish my undergraduate degree. I always liked that label. Non-traditional student. After I completed my general ed requirements at a community college near Denver, I wanted to transfer up to Colorado State in Fort Collins and major in horses.

In order to help fund my education I applied for, and won, a free ride scholarship to Colorado State by writing a kick-ass essay on why I felt I deserved this opportunity. And when I went to that scholarship breakfast to celebrate my achievement, I realized I was the only person there who was not eighteen years old. Also, I was the only person who wasn't born and raised in Colorado. I was born and raised in Ohio, moved to Southern California when I was sixteen, and then out to Colorado when I was twenty-seven. It was a weird feeling to realize how untraditional I was. I have always felt normal. I have always felt that I was taking the road most traveled because that was all I knew. It was just my life. But I realized that morning at the scholarship breakfast that I didn't take the well-traveled road. I took the dirt path leading up into the unknown. I got lost and didn't even know it. But holy shit, it was a lot of fun.

When I was up at CSU I took riding classes as my electives. So I started jumping horses again. And it was very weird to realize that jumping horses now scared the shit out of me. I had done all this crazy stuff so fearlessly as a teenager. You're so stupid when you're that young, right? In my senior year at CSU I was in an advanced jumping class and got thrown off because my crazy horse refused a jump. I fell flat on my back and tore my rotator cuff doing that. But there was no way I was gonna let that fucking horse win. No way. I got back on him and made him finish that course. I didn't know how badly I was injured at the time, but I felt it the next day. And that's when I realized I'm just too fucking old for this shit. I took a couple weeks off to let my shoulder rest (no surgery for me, I was a broke single-mom-college-student) and then finished the class.

But there was a moment during the final exam when I thought my bastard horse was gonna throw me again. But I did not want to fall. That last fall really fucked me up in the head—if I thought I was afraid of jumping when I started the class, well, by this time I was terrified. And my shoulder was still pretty fucked up, of course. So I stuck to him like glue and made him do it. Everyone cheered for me. It was pretty amazing. All those twenty-something kids cheering me over that last triple jump. Which we did flawlessly and that was not an easy way to end the course. It felt really good to be a non-traditional person in a class filled with traditional people I would've never met if I had taken a different path in life. It was a mixture of relief, and pride, and the glow of achievement.

When I look back on my life I always tell myself – *Thank fuck I didn't know any better.* I said this senior year at CSU many times. I was so broke, a day out for me and my kids was a trip to the dollar store to spend $5 on crap toys and then dinner from the Wendy's drive-through to order off the 99¢ menu. Plus I was injured and I had to pass a physics class to graduate. I am not good at math. I have taken a lot of it as a science major, but I struggled pretty hard to finish them with a grade I could use for a grad school application. So physics was not my thing. Even though I love physics, I cannot actually *do physics.* I was so stressed out that year, just thinking about it now makes me want hide those memories away forever. And if I had known when I left Denver for Fort Collins that things were gonna be so hard, I *never* would've done it.

Three cheers for being clueless, stupid, and fearless.

I have written about contradictions before in other End of Book Shits but I think it fits perfectly with the theme of this story, which is about a very non-traditional way to find love. I love writing characters that aren't what they appear to be, and even though I knew Quin's back story before I started this book, I cannot even tell you how much I enjoyed writing the chapter where Rochelle figures out he's *normal.* He's the opposite of me, right? Quin starts out in a very nuclear family doing all these very nuclear family things growing up. And he ends up in a very serious plural relationship as he tries to figure out if he's capable of loving someone in a "normal" way. The only guy in the whole series who had a good example of "normal" as a kid, can't decide if he's normal. Such a great contradiction. And such a great lesson too. That you can do everything perfect and still fuck it up. I'm sure his father thought he was doing a great job. But there was a cost. To Kitty Foster, for sure. But also to Quin. Because all he saw in the end was his mother's unhappiness with his father's perfection. Maybe perfect isn't all it's cracked up to be? But the part of Quin I like best is that what he has with Smith and Bric *feels normal* to him. So it is. It's not weird. It just how it is.

The other day I got a card in the mail. It was a thank you card from a woman named Kathy who lives not too far from me and runs a sanctuary dedicated to donkeys. Now, if you hang out with me on Facebook you know I have two donkeys. (Paris and Nicole). People kinda think this is cool and unusual. Is it? I'm not sure. I guess I could've just gotten horses when we moved out to this farm ten years ago, but I didn't. I wanted donkeys. And there was Kathy's donkey sanctuary on the internet (Longhopes, it's called), proclaiming her love for all things donkey. And she wasn't far away, so we decided to go down there and get us some donkeys. Paris and Nicole were only two years old when they were rescued from an auction meant to send them down to Mexico to be in a rodeo show. I don't know what they do with donkeys in a Mexican rodeo, but Kathy was against it. So she goes to these auctions, buys these donkeys, and brings them back to her farm to get treatment and be cared for until she finds other people like her (and me too, I guess) who want to take them home. When we were there she had about thirty rescue donkeys.

She was the nicest person ever. You know how when you go to a shelter and try and adopt and the people make you feel bad because you have a job and can't give that cat or dog one hundred percent of your time? Or they tell you no deal on a pit bull because you have kids. (I grew up with pit bulls, their sweetness potential is through the roof). Or they say your fence isn't high enough or your yard isn't big enough. Well, Kathy didn't do any of this stuff. She said, "OK, It's a $650 donation for the pair. If you ever want to get rid of them you have to tell me and I'll come take them back and refund your money." *Refund your money, bitches.* She did come out to our farm to look over our barn, our fence, our pastures, and our dogs. She delivered the donkeys at the same time. So just super helpful.

You're probably wondering why I'm telling you about my donkeys. I'm getting there.

I got that thank you card in the mail from the shelter because they had sent out an email a few weeks before, asking for help. One of her donkeys, Bam Bam, had some really infected teeth that were causing him a lot of pain. He couldn't eat, he was losing weight, and he needed to see a specialist. So she took him up to the vet hospital at Colorado State University (the same university I went to and studied equine science) and they told her it was going to be about $3000 to fix Bam Bam. She doesn't really have an extra $3000 to spare for one donkey, so she sent that email asking for help. If she couldn't get him the help he needed, he'd have to be put down.

I send her money, not regularly, but I've done it a few times. And even though there are a lot of other things to spend money on that do a world of good (much more good than one lady with a donkey sanctuary) I decided

Bam Bam needed saving and sent her money for this too. It wasn't the whole amount, but it was a good amount. They met their goal that same day she sent the email. There are more people than me who believe in her and what she does. So I got that card in the mail from Bam Bam (seriously, from Bam Bam – it's got his picture on it and everything) thanking me for my help. He was scheduled for his surgery on April 4th, and he's gonna update me when he gets home to let me know how he's doing. So fucking cute, right?

But I had a little guilt about this. I'm thinking – I should be sending money to Doctors Without Borders or people who make it their life's mission to make sure underdeveloped countries have clean water. I want to help those people too, but I think Kathy and her mission in life—a very non-traditional mission—is worth supporting. She had a dream of helping donkeys. And yeah, there's a lot of bad things in the world that need fixing, but this was *her* dream. I liked it. I like that she turned her farm into a place for donkeys and then dedicated her whole life to it. It's a big commitment to dedicate one's entire life to something. Especially donkeys.

And so even though I don't have to justify who I give my money to, I did justify it by acknowledging her non-traditional life. I decided I'm helping her make her dream come true. I'm just a little flicker of light in her dream. Barely anything because she's doing all the hard work. Donkeys, man. Not he easiest animal to deal with.

I like the non-traditional path through life. I've made a lot of non-traditional decisions and even though some of them were stupid, I learned new things about myself, and the world, from taking those risks.

Whenever I get stuck writing a book I ask myself — what would be the most unexpected thing for this character to do? And then I do that. I started this plot process in my very first book, Clutch. I got to a point in the story near the end and I had no idea what this Junco character should do. Then I thought up something unexpected and unusual. Crazy, really. And made her do it. It changed everything. I knew how the book ended, but there are a million ways to get to that end. I have done this several times since then. I don't do it for every scene, only when I get stuck.

So when it came time to plot out the characters tor Taking Turns I did this with Quin. It would've been very easy to just make him have some sexual fetish that would shock readers. But that's doing things the traditional way. The expected way. I'm nothing if not non-traditional. I'm nothing if not unexpected. I was in love with the idea that Quin and Chella would be more friends than lovers. That Quin was sick over the fact that Rochelle walked out on him. And that he needed to reevaluate his choices and decisions. I loved the scene in Taking Turns when Chella brings him up to the attic and shows him all Rochelle's secret stuff. It was my favorite scene in the whole book because that's when it hits him. He thought he knew Rochelle, but he didn't. He only saw what she showed him and he was satisfied with that. The attic scene is Quin's first hint that he's not satisfied just knowing her that old way. Not at all. And his complacency might've fucked up his chances for being with his one-true love for good.

The theme of Turning Back is turning back. Reevaluating all those past decisions. Did you do it right? Did you fuck it up? Can it be changed? Are you willing to change? What will it take to change? Can Quin really give up the comfort he gets from being in a relationship with Bric as a buffer, and do it on his own? And I know Rochelle is the one who physically turns back, but this story is really about Quin.

I know you guys all like the sex, and I'm not gonna deny that writing ménage sex is kinda fun. But I don't write these stories for the sex scenes. I think this series would've been just as good without the sex. It wouldn't have sold as many books, but it would still have been great.

When I look back on 2012 and 2013 when I was struggling to make it as a fiction writer I get that same feeling I had when I was about to graduate from CSU. This shit is hard. And thank fuck I didn't know how hard it was gonna be when I started because I never would've done it.

Grad school was the same way for me. Grad school was so fucking hard for me. I got accepted into a pretty elite PhD biomedical science program after I graduated from CSU, but I quit a year and a half into it and got my master's degree from another school instead. I was done. I knew how hard it was and I was done.

But that failure is how I started writing. I decided to use all my science education to write science textbooks and made more than two hundred online courses for homeschool kids. (Yes, I homeschooled my kids – that was yet another clue that my fate was firmly rooted in the non-traditional). And after I got tired of writing non-fiction I started writing fiction.

I took a lot of risks to become a fiction writer because it's so different from writing non-fiction. You are not judged by the knowledge you possess in fiction like you are in non-fiction. You are judged by your creativity.

Which is scary because creativity is a very personal thing. I took this risk because I was clueless and fearless at the same time. And what a great ride it has been. Even better than finishing that final exam in show jumping class.

No, I'm not jumping horses anymore. I'm writing books that push your limits now. I'm writing books that make you uncomfortable but keep you reading anyway. I'm writing Julie books because... well, I'm Julie. And I don't see myself writing those traditional love stories any time soon. As far as traditional goes in love stories, this is pretty much as close as you're gonna get from me. lol.

I think my books, and especially this series, are all about celebrating the road less traveled. It's nothing against the traditional. I'm very traditional in a lot of ways too. But writing books about the non-traditional gives people a new perspective on things. Maybe the game of Taking Turns isn't the *best* way to find love, but it is *one* way. And isn't that what makes life interesting? All the different ways to get to the same end?

I told my Shrike Bikes fan group that the subtitle of this EOBS is Fun Facts About Julie. And even though I went about it in a very non-traditional way, that's still what I'm calling it.

I hope you enjoyed this story about Quin's non-traditional normal life (and this EOBS) and if want to keep going and get Bric's take on things, the next book is called His Turn.

Thank you for reading, thank you for reviewing, and I'll see you in the next book.

Julie
JA Huss

ABOUT THE AUTHOR

JA Huss is the New York Times and USA Today bestselling author of more than twenty romances. She likes stories about family, loyalty, and extraordinary characters who struggle with basic human emotions while dealing with bigger than life problems. JA loves writing heroes who make you swoon, heroines who makes you jealous, and the perfect Happily Ever After ending.

You can chat with her on Facebook, Twitter, and her kick-ass romance blog, New Adult Addiction. If you're interested in getting your hands on an advanced release copy of her upcoming books, sneak peek teasers, or information on her upcoming personal appearances, you can join her newsletter list and get those details delivered right to your inbox.

JA Huss lives on a dirt road in Colorado thirty minutes from the nearest post office. So if she owes you a package from a giveaway, expect it to take forever. She has a small farm with two donkeys named Paris & Nicole, a ringneck parakeet named Bird, and a pack of dogs. She also has two grown children who have never read any of her books and do not plan on ever doing so. They do, however, plan on using her credit cards forever.

JA collects guns and likes to read science fiction and books that make her think. JA Huss used to write homeschool science textbooks under the name Simple Schooling and after publishing more than 200 of those, she ran out of shit to say. She started writing the I Am Just Junco science fiction series in 2012, but has since found the meaning of life writing erotic stories about antihero men that readers love to love.

JA has an undergraduate degree in equine science and fully planned on becoming a veterinarian until she heard what kind of hours they keep, so she decided to go to grad school and got a master's degree in Forensic Toxicology. Before she was a full-time writer she was smelling hog farms for the state of Colorado.

Even though JA is known to be testy and somewhat of a bitch, she loves her #fans dearly and if you want to talk to her, join her Facebook fan group where she posts daily bullshit about bullshit.

If you think she's kidding about this crazy autobiography, you don't know her very well.

You can find all her books on Amazon, Barnes & Noble, iTunes, and KOBO.